I was a mate o

I was a mate of Ronnie Laing

ANNE McMANUS

CANONGATE

First published in Great Britain
in 1998 by Canongate Books Ltd,
14 High Street, Edinburgh EH1 1TE

10 9 8 7 6 5 4 3 2 1

Copyright © Anne McManus 1998

The moral rights of the author have been asserted

The publishers gratefully acknowledge subsidy from the Scottish Arts
Council towards the publication of this volume

British Library Cataloguing-in-Publication Data
A catalogue record for this book is available on
request from the British Library

ISBN 0 86241 813 5

Phototypeset by Intype London Ltd
Printed and bound in Finland by WSOY

for Nicola

Book One

1

I'd been off my head for years that December day when the fear lifted a bit and subtly shifted its emphasis towards survival. A rushing revival of life and courage flooding and flushing through hopeless dope and dereliction. A pin prick of light piercing painfully, brightening and tightening all the loose screws of this affliction. Till all this blinding finding of hope spooked me as a concept, hooked on Reason as I was – as lethal an addiction as all the others, that season of swamping pain.

Where's the reason in that? Good women should trust their emotions, lethal potions. Well I know that now, but was even then still struggling to be an intellectual, disembodied head, well-read, all that matters clever chatter in salons, pithy pardons, and epistemology for tea. That was me – a wrecked head without a bed any more, let alone a pillow. Just wallow with me a while, in a style you'll get accustomed to. Let it grow, flow over you. As I was trying to do that December day, my frazzled nerves all dazzled and dripping with a fine cold dew at 3 a.m.

Not that you'd notice I was having orgasmic revelations. Though maybe my bundle of rags twitched a mite more ferociously. Atrociously attired you'd say. All stitched up round the middle with string. Keep the warmth in grandma used to say, far far away grandma. And my plimsolls have no soles. They're school pumps, not trainers, like young arseholes all wear these days. I swear it's baffling how rich folk appropriate everything, even the sartorial habits of the gutter. Not all of them though. You wouldn't catch a yuppie having a wee behind a tree at half past three in the morning. A *female* yuppie that is. Keep yer pants up duckie you'll get all mucky. Oh blurt your squirt this way any day says an ox-eyed daisy, crazy as me for some nourishment.

My hair I declare is dank and elusive. Elusive? Well it falls out in lumps and clumps. But there's a fetching fringe left all round. And not a sound when I take my scarf off to display my tonsure to any sponsor I cadge vitamin B money from, with my silky story of the glories of vitamin therapy. Those middle class eyes flash guiltily, and cash rolls around to the sound of me clicking away my cider calculations – allowing for inflations and sundry debts to the girls.

There are four of us reluctant ladies of leisure, who found each other and stuck like glue. Yoohoo yoohoo, another sister. We couldn't believe our luck. No fucks, just friends. Godsends we've been to each other, like mothers on a rainy day. We stick together usually, but a prick in leather took Natty away for a blow job round the back of Sainsbury's. And anybody who does it there is daring indeed. The greed of scavengers in the trash cans is enough to unman any wanker. It's their hankerings for food, and you're in their way with that cock display. They'll laugh at a staff so bare and wobbly, your knees so knobbly. And your panting will have them chanting here we go here we go. You'll slow to a peter and stutter and flop, and Natty will stop – feeling a failure even at this. So low is a piss artist's glow of self-esteem.

I don't do services myself any more. A whore has to have hair on her head as well, bloody hell. A fringe won't do. In that last camera crew from the BBC, there was an old fat slug who wanted me right there on the rug, with the fleas and disease and perversity of adversity my dear. The fear and frisson of sexual slumming. So he's slamming away with me thinking he'd pay, but my scarf came askew, and I suddenly knew real rejection. Ugh he said. Ugh ugh ugh you're bald and ugly and he was coming and didn't want me to have any. So he pulled it out and it soared, while he roared through his cascading spray of spittle and sperm you're ugly you're ugly you're ugly and bald. Well you too sir I protested, a bit miffed and testy, and he biffed me one. Well male violence it's nonsense we don't take that. So I spat in his face, and he sat in disgrace, stunned and lonely in a puddle of his own making. Your own making my boy, now where's my booze money?

You floozy I don't pay bald women. Why there's no extra charge. Some loonies at large in the BBC I must say, but that day was the end of my frolicking. My feelings were hurt. So I keep my scarf on and my tattered dignity all intact. It sure is a fact that we all have a vestige of pride left you know. Even down here you never finally destroy human dignity. Except by death, and that happens a lot round here, and back to fear . . .

Yet this day the fear isn't as bad, as gripping and mad. I almost gladly greet the dawn with a skip in my shuffle. Somehow something has changed, rearranged itself in my head. The terrors are lurking but tranquil. Dread's at bay. That sickening deadening deafening dread is hovering, but not bothering me enough to consider the window at Victoria wines with a brick. You could swallow half a bottle before the cops arrived, sometimes a whole one. Though frisky old whisky was too much these days. Besides the alarm made my head ache for days. And sunrays are filtering down on the Moor floor, this sour dour northern stronghold of Sheffield. Pure gold to green fields nearby, and mountains too. Here a fountain all thwarted and clogged up with tins and cans from the market stall vans. But it has warmth this Sheffield, this North. Even at this hour, you're not terrified to sit and stand and stare. To dare to lurk and linger and hesitate and be vulnerable, in this city where disgust and distrust are the worst you get on the streets. Not the cold vicious kicks to the meek and the weak, as in London, New York, and Berlin, where the winners will kill the ill and sinners who litter their way with their truth of a day turned different.

So four of us usually sticking together, and it feels lonely and suddenly cold and shuddery without them. I feel raw and exposed. Just an overblown rose in ridiculous clothes. Tattered and shattered and silly and pathetic. But with them it's all a lark, that spark of humanity and confirmation that makes life still better than t'other. Though brother I'm fettered and focused on death usually and last breaths seem sweeter the weaker you are. Oh wandering star winking and blinking its offer of calm and seductive soothing balm of oblivion. Must hurry away from that one, beckoning ever stronger as it does. A daily reckoning I do – whether to give in to living defeat. To beat a retreat through death's door. It's ajar, and not far from down here on the floor. When you're as low as me, you don't have much to lose. Except somehow a breath or two gasping and rasping. Mine would never be graceful sinking as it should be, but raucous raw melody. I'm going I'm going please stop me please help me please see me I'm here I'm a person I'm frightened small and so full of terrors. DON'T LET ME DIE. Don't sigh and ignore me, my pain just remains as a litmus of your throttled bottled and pickled society.

Oh well. In view of these morbid preoccupations, indecent dwelling on hell and suchlike, I'll spike the gloom with living room scenes from childhood. "You never know what's in the post" a hopeful ghost of mother says. Don't do it, don't screw it. Death's so final. Leave the door open. No bespoken epitaphs. That's daft and dumb don't do it. Suicide's hiding and cowardly I'M ASHAMED OF YOU . . . you never know what's in the post, so always give it a ghost of a chance, to be different tomorrow, no matter what your sorrow today . . .

It only gets as spooky as this anyway when I'm alone. And though we're all alone in the end, I'd rather pretend in the womb of my friends, where solace seems safe. At least it saves me from myself, and anything is better than being all alone in my Black Hole. When we bring our four Black Holes together, the tortured souls sitting in them can cope a bit with the shit. It's still there, but shared somehow. And there we are, a multitude of solitudes, huddling and cuddling and stronger the longer we're together. We usually arrange and rearrange and shuffle our days so the haze doesn't lift, and the daze doesn't drift too low, so that one of us should find herself alone with her horrors. Yet here I am, grandslam in the middle of a hovering panic, and they're all absent my god-sent sisters.

Hurry up Natty. Big black blossom dearie Natalie. With her warm bosom beckoning, and reckoning always with two or three bedraggled orphans of the storm, lurking and suckling and puking and puling and feeding and needing her vitality. While her real extended family haunted her terrors "all dem uncles and perverts I seh no way to de family". Jamaican sunshine radiating from a smile so randy *dandy* man, she made the grey cold sterile pimply racists rot and wither and die as they wondered why her fire burned and consumed them and their creed. "Come on de day's long an gets better soon." She meant wetter in sperm and booze since one meant the other and "brother it's a hoot recoverin' dem Rasta roots mixed up wid Yorkshire". Confused and abused and false as a waltz, she even made the punters feel desirable. "I seh I'm thirsty for dem juices flowing for de glowing complexion man" and she'd stoop and she'd kneel and never reveal her pain and disdain . . . not yet . . .

Now Natty's licking juices from sluices so open and reeking she'll be there for a week, with him leaking and lunging and plunging it into her lovely luscious lips. And for tips she'll crush all her identity as Big Black She and be servile, while he masturbates away his own pain, and like rain it comes pouring into her mouth. Oh uncouth lady, such pleasure you bring. I want you to sing while you swallow it all, and I can stand tall and see you bent supplicant . . . humiliated . . . Don't get carried away mate. Natty's defiant and full of hate of the white man and she may just bite it off. These black bitches are cannibals too, a racist taboo you should know about, before you flout decent behaviour in all directions. She'll explode one day in an awesome way, raped repeatedly from the age of three, mouth taped up to stop her pleas. She uses that mouth now, she declares, to work it through, but who the hell can work through violation and outrage like that? She'll go on the rampage one day, and may you all pay, you misters who blister our sisters in hay.

The other two members of our gallant gang are banging their soft fragile heads against unforgiving walls. Drying out in their respective halls of Cure, enduring agonies unspeakable. A bleak way to spend Saturday night, in flight and purgatory. But they do it regularly as penance, both with crucifying guilt about their gross inadequacy as women. Deformed unnatural hags we alcoholic women. No roguish sinnin' and adventure for us. We're slags, old bags, pathetic,

7

poor. Just grimy old whores, a lush in a bush, a slut in a rut, what's the difference. The inference is we're weak and immoral and unfeminine too. Who heard of a roué female? No sale, no deal or appeal. Whereas male drunks, full of spunk, reveal masculinity, divinity. They're heroes with afterglows and sunshine and women and wine and song. Well boys will be boys and they're bound to make noise and it's allright when they scream and they fight. Slap slap take that I'm happy clap clap my testosterone makes me zap you baby.

Supposing self-loathing of women were externalised and brutalised like men. Imagine just hitting someone when you're feeling inadequate and small. Growing taller and taller as they squall and squawk and cringe away and you play Punch against Judy crunch crunch her bones a stoned lullaby of thump your rump you bitch you'll pay today for me feeling this way . . . Of course we don't want to be like them. But it's still not fair that men drunks are raffish romantics. I defy a man to look slutty in the gutter. It only applies to me and my torn, forlorn friends in our little female family. Slag hagbags see?

2

Loonies tell you a lot about yourselves. They're simply the ones with the courage to act it out. No no no you shout. Denial, denial. You WON'T be on trial and lumped together with any nutcases as basis for comparison. Your sanity is not in doubt NOT IN DOUBT. It's deafening, life threatening, your repression. What are you afraid of confessing? That you sometimes feel hurt and vulnerable and bewildered and crazy and loopy too? You'd like to see it through like a loony? See it through to the bitter end like those three friends of mine and me?

Here comes the holiest of the trinity, Bridie, fey and frigid as you would be too with her history. She sidles up, wary, huge translucent eyes just staring straight through me, desperately.

"Charlie you're there. Thank God and Holy Mary"

There's a lot of feverish clutching of the crucifix dangling twixt her boobs. And this from a former Art Student. It spooks me. But Ireland is different. No secular revolution for them.

"They dried me out Charlie. I'm clean and I can't bear it. That shrink said I had to be sober to talk and remember. But Charlie, as soon as I remember, I have to obliterate, I have to . . . I can't bear it . . ."

The mumbling and fumbling with her frontage continues apace, and I'm feeling testy sharing my space with this tortured face that grasps at God all the time when there's work to do.

"Well we'll have to wet you in again won't we?" I'm trying to be helpful but she starts quivering and gabbling in tongues like a baboon. They all sit round like this jibbering and jabbering for hours at the Charismatics Church up Broomhill, then they go off skippering in a holy herd, or flock I suppose. Except Bridie who comes back to us. I know superstition and gobshite are in things in the Nineties but

9

Holy Mary mother of God, does she talk to the shrink like this?

"If *he* had to relive a father like ours, and . . . oh holy Mary mother of God"

I try to nod wisely. When in doubt bloody well humour them. But she's on to me, slippery as a sardine.

"Charlie, you don't know what I'm talking about"

"Then let me guess" I snap huffily. "Around here it's a bit congested with folk on the run from daddios who won't take No for an answer you know . . ." It was tactless and crude but she was getting on my nerves with all this piety. Still I wasn't prepared for the eruption.

"You are the pits. The pits. You with your mocking of deep pain. You speak so glibly about something so horrible, so unspeakably dreadful, so immoral, so wrong, so *evil*, you speak as though it's like using the loo, you, you . . ." She was shrieking and wailing and wafting the cross back and forth and crossing herself and me with it, and God she looked so *ravishing* all the while that I was floored and overawed by the saint incarnate aspect of it all. Also its absurdity.

"Come *on* woman, cut the hysterics and mystical crap and we can have a conversation. I'm just observing the realities around here, to relativise you, to help you see . . ."

I sound like Humphrey Bogart, brisk and macho and insensitive. It was a risk with one so fragile. She trembled on and I waded on, determined she would bloody well look at least.

"We're Nuts 'n Sluts, and sooner or later there's an abusive man lurking in our pasts or presents to account for it. So there. You're not on your own with your demons. Don't be mean. Share them" I hazard a grin but it twists into a grimace as the tears fill her eyes and she shies away from me.

I wonder who the hell asked her to spend this morning with me anyway. I was weary of her fears and frightenings. It was always like this when she spent a night or two with the shrinks who sounded to me to get off on making her recall the saga of father endlessly repeatedly. Bloody wankers, exploiting a girl's tendernesses. Laing would have sorted them out. Voyeurs and vampires one and all.

Mind you Bridie, it's your hidden depths that win the wankers every time. They want to plumb you but get struck dumb by your pale wan numbness, and have to make do with a hand job, slobbering over your image but not daring to defile it. Virgin-Whore, oh please please more, I'm coming at the naughtiness. I once saw a man stand and wank next to you, never touching you, just staring at your distant dreamy face, and the place where you'd opened your blouse and shown him your nipples. He came at the sight of you, and all for a tipple of cheap crappy cider. You let him stare. I never saw him again. But I know he comes regularly, just staring at you, who show him another secret place every week, never speaking or touching. Just that pale expressionless face, its inordinate grace, and a sexy bit of your body. Would be shoddy and cheap, even funny, if anyone else tried it. But you, beautiful, remote, dreamy, can bring it off, making them masturbate, and keeping you on your snowy plateau. Just shows what snooty beauty can do.

"We're all nuts and sluts with cuts . . ." I smile shyly at her. C'mon kid, don't sulk. "You know, scars on the soul, that stuff, forever wounded, wandering into the darkness . . ."

She brightens. Reluctantly. Melancholia is addictive too. Especially when being In Decline is part of the spiritual self-image. The righteous magnificently wronged. Haunted artist. Gothic poet. Ah me. I profer a paw which she grips in a vice. They're so steely really these frail ones.

"C'mon that's better. We have bottles to battle with, and a public to scorn"

"Oh Charlie, you always manage it"

"?"

"You always manage to cheer me up in the end"

I just wish it was mutual. Still she looks radiant and floats away so who am I to say your song is wrong and ignorant and stupid as all religions and cut it out sister and grow up. Well you don't do you when someone is carried away and your example in life isn't exactly *uplifting*. I scowl my militant atheist glower-for-the-gullible nevertheless, but she's gone hey hey with such a display of inspiration, maybe we will get somewhere today. Anyway I'm alone again to concentrate on the tasks ahead.

So busy am I sorting out my dread leadbelly obsessions, I even forget to tell you that the day had dawned brightly, coldly, and definitely without sufficient warning. Maybe I mentioned it before, because the door's ajar to heaven, and the birds must have all flown away this day. There were usually a few cheerful sparrows about to shout good morning, so I could work out wisely with their encouragement how to negotiate the day's supplies. This day the enormity of the task defies my considerable initiative and experience. So I sit back again on the kerb, leaning against the little brick wall they'd put around an exotic evergreen tree, planted recently. A municipal mystery – why expensive trees can be afforded, lauded, as pretty scenery, but they can't afford shelter for the likes of me. Some priority. But I must get off this bloody tree thing. In my state things easily get obsessive, and branches will be sprouting everywhere unless I concentrate.

I'm peering intently at Victoria Wines for inspiration, but then start blatantly leering for here comes a real head banger, and the sight always cheers me. I see this sublime free spirit dancing towards me and it warms my cockles and tickles my fancy in one hot flush. We could form a sub-versity here between us if we weren't so far gone. Heather used to lecture in Literature, till his crisis sliced him straight in two Jekyll and Hyde when he decided his life's work as an academic parasite on writers was a sham and a fraud, and he sat and applauded when they axed and taxed his department out of existence, and collapsed it into Linguistic Studies, which abolished any reference to reality beyond language altogether. He always has heather somewhere – in a sock or button hole or fastened wound round string around his neck. Such a gent, they say here. Such a sweet and innocent soul rotting away in some private torment that he never shares, never dares to open up in case he can't close again and the wind would whistle right through him and expose his lack of substance.

An instance, this one, of caring psychiatry gone berserk. They jerked him with ECT twenty times *twenty times*, and now his Jekyll and Hyde is Jekyll and Hide, since his alter ego just resides in the darkest cover he can find. Under hedges he sits, muttering Italian revolutionary songs till the mood's passed, and he swings again into jolly Dr Jekyll feckless and free and everybody's fun son, full of polite gallantry.

He darts off when he sees me, scurrying hurrying, and I will *not* I will *not* be miffed by this new assault biff biff splat splat take that, to my dignity. We are organically linked whatever he thinks. Or maybe I just smell. Well so does he usually. Ah me. I feel as though I'm undulating gently in the breeze and not freezing over with rigid despair because of rejection. No. No. No. Cast around for distraction. Do not be so affected by these turds. You must learn to be cold and hard and brutalised and vandalised and defended and drawbridged but where's your castle first, oh feeble maiden? No good defending what ain't there. I'll hide in insolent nonchalance instead. Biding my time until my castle comes.

Somebody'd tied a hopeful bit of tinsel round this tree next to me. So it must be Xmas in a few weeks, though I tried not to reflect on that bleak prospect. Xmas and public holidays and even Sundays are the worst the worst the most hurtful hateful, when compulsive celebrations and families make the loners the outsiders the down and out and beside themselves grieve inwardly outwardly anywhere, spilling their misery, vomiting woe woe no no no. I'm alone without a phone without a home without a wife or life or child or parent just a lonely wailing lament, a torment of vile rejection, you happy holiday people make me feel – reeling rocking in agony away from your panoply of plenty.

But lonely as a cloud I ain't meant to be today for here comes Jean weaving her way along, head swung low and diabolical, its blonde fronds spiky and abrasive as the Pennine wind.

"God, Charlie, it's thee. Thank God"

"Well Lady Luck. What's up?"

13

"Charlie, they dried me out again. Then filled me full o' dope. I feel zonked and peculiar. Do I look funny?"

"Of course not honey, just cold. Let's get some lovely money, then it will be funny, we'll all be laughing and wet again"

She really did look far away, dazed glazed fazed ferociously chemically coshed.

"I told them I didn't want any tablets. I told 'em I wanted to talk. Tha knows, about Dick. But they never talk to thi in t'Sycamore, they think tha thick. Not like t'Beechwood where Bridie goes"

"You can talk to me Jean"

"Oh Charlie, tha knows how it is. He's a prick and a shit and I'm scared of him, scared to death he'll find me, and really finish me off this time. It gives me this constant lump in t'belly. I feel frayed and me legs are like jelly. He will gerrus in t'end. I'll just fall apart and he'll gerrus"

"No he won't Jean. We won't let him get you. We'll get him first. Grab his goolies and twist till they burst. Yippee. Leave it all to me in fact"

My castration complex surges fiercely at moments like this, but it's all frenzied fantasy I'm ashamed to say because I can't raise a finger, even in self-defence.

"No, perhaps all of us is better. We'll wait for him one night, and Natty can give him the Come On and Bridie'll jump on his back and choke him from behind and I'll whip in low and dangerous with a knife if you like, and you can just watch and gloat . . . and threaten him while Bridie tightens her grip on his throat and . . ."

"Charlie, Charlie. Bless yer 'art. He'd kill us all, t'great thug. But bless yer 'art, tharragrandlass, thy are"

She shouldn't doubt my intent though. I'd give it a go, ho ho. I'm up for any avenging angels number. It's just that I might fail them all at the last minute with my gut wrenching horror of violence. Just can't bloody well do it. Disgusting. No wonder she doesn't trust my promises. Dispatching your average wife battering socialist Hero ought to be a cinch.

Striker for miners and men, and striker of woman amen, gets struck. Oh it appeals mightily. Grrrr.

"I would still have t'kids tha knows, but I was scared to death he would hit them and kill us all in t'end" She shook her head and her eyes rolled and she began to heave and sob inside. Primally. I suppress an urge to giggle. Hide it hide it. It's just this victim stuff is so heaped and hyped and swipes you so *relentlessly* round here that I often emit a high pitched squeal of subversion. Which reveals my vocation as tragedy queen leaves something to be desired.

"I only live for my kids, Charlie, and now they're gone, banged up in that place, and I've got nothing. Nothing. I might as well be dead"

"Bugger that" I clutch her hand "Repeat after me. Bugger that. Everybody feels like dying when they're dry. Come with me and we'll get saturated. Beats me why you two always toddle off like masochists to dry out at weekends. Shows you're not dedicated, like me. Shows you're stronger. More defiant, tougher, more characterful, more . . ."

"Oh stop it Charlie. We're just guiltier than you. Tha free, thee. Tha dun't 'ave kids. And tha's not got God on thi back. So why should tha be guilty and get dry? I go as well because it's warm in there and something to look forward to every week, like an 'otel"

Bloody hotels of living well our nuthouses Beechwood Hall and Sycamore Hospital. For those of education and those without, respectively. And back to trees . . .

"Bridie's been here. She's the same. It all points to one solution. A mean obscene bottle, full throttle, what say you?"

"Oh Charlie, just do it. I can't concentrate on anything. Does tha know Bridie's gorra twin brother who ran off to join t'IRA?"

"Yes"

"Well I was thinking. Won't they let her join as well? She'd be better off than here . . ."

Jean has touching faith in political organisations, even after her shredding by a Militant.

"I don't think that's the solution"

15

"But it's better than going mad and starving, isn't it?"

"I'll pass on that. We'll raise a glass instead and everything will improve"

"Well I'm going back to t'Sycamore to tell 'em I feel more scared than ever wi t'new pills. I'll see thi later"

She swayed away with a hovering swooping movement waving her arms to balance. I watch her beadily for signs of collapse, but she navigates like a sinking sailor in her own private storm. So I can notice myself again after all these interruptions. You have to monitor yourself in this situation to stop something horrible happening. Before you can GETITOGETHERTOGETSOMEMORE . . .

3

I'd learned by now to trust the signals from my hands. They weren't wringing feverishly, and it was getting on in the day and I hadn't had a drink yet, and though wet with sweat and twitching a lot and my heart beating fit to break, yet my hands were *not* clawing and clutching and I wasn't panting. Though the trembling was coming on rapidly in fits and starts, so I knew action couldn't be postponed much longer. Time to hobble off out of the glares and stares or they could arrest me for loitering and a drink would recede to a dream cloud. I shouted out loud at that thought, and overwrought suddenly had to get some money sweet honey for nectar.

And then I spied her. Always a type I relied on, harassed yet rich. A pathetic old bitch. She knew what was coming, tried running and skipping away, but I was niftier, and within seconds had her by the throat, choking on her liberal conscience. I gloated shamelessly at her predicament. Exposing hypocrisy is a fantasy I always nourished as an academic, in those Departmental Meetings. It's all there, those years of frustration I spent, in my greeting to her. Bent, obsequious, shuffling, smelling, I advance. She backs away cornered, falling over the wall into the tree, blushing, embarrassed, trying to ignore me, beseeching the sky.

"Please rescue me God from this clod, this lump, this obscenity. Oh My God it's female Oh My God My God"

"Madam . . ." me mild.

"Oh NO no no no" flailing around her, but failing to make me vanish. A banishing hide-me-from-reality type railing, wailing "Not me. Please don't let it mean me . . ." swiping the air in my direction.

"Madam . . ." I shuffle close. A heavy dose she's getting. She's sweating too, and wetting her soft satin knickers I bet, poor pampered pet.

"Leave me alone"

That's testy that's true you're honest that's new. I nearly let her escape for that, but then realise her wisdom is woefully limited:

"You scum how dare you come near me"

Dear me she swats me with her handbag, Thatcher slag hag style, and all the while I fastened a pleading eye, wondering why I was bothering with her, stirring her middle class dignity beyond endurance simply by my putrid, paltry, paralysing presence.

"No offence, 50 pence and I'll be on my way, tripping off, sloth and slime right out of sight"

She takes fright at the hint of intellectual mischief, as in disbelief she recognises that maybe I'm not as rabid as I appeared. So I leer menacingly, not to confuse her too much. Such malevolence on my part for 50 pence. No heart at all when I'm cadging, back to the wall survival, revival of basic beast I must be at bottom. Rotten rotten in core and creed, boozy floozy wracked by greed, wayward wispy full of need, who will heed my desperation . . .

It's a desolate prospect all this hate I engender, as a harmless smelly bundle of rags just toddling along. I really need so little. Just 50p every so often for a bottle of cider. About every two hours. In fact a few 50 pees are necessary these days. It's always going up, and the fags the fags are so dear. But I'm happy with any old rolled up dog end. Dear friend, there's no need to sneer and revile. Do I frighten you? Heighten your fear and knowledge that there are people so degraded by circumstance, that their merry dance of life is constant pain and so in vain, that you daren't go near their precipice in case you fall fall fall yourself? Do you hear a call of failure from me that's familiar in your closed safe world of mortgages and rose hedges and garbage pails, where failures and rejects are collected out of sight, not hanging around to frighten you? The door's open wide for you to pass through too this way any day, should your tubby rich hubby choose to trade you in for a younger model, and throw you in some hovel. Not what you've grown accustomed to. You might up the gins to a sinful level, and become a nuisance to yourself and society too. And I, with my wise witch wires tuned to loons in low places am on to you, so watch it when I'm near you'll get peeled naked if you hurt my feelings by sneering too much.

"Madam"

"Go away or I'll get the police"

Such vice and venom and vermin and sin in the streets. You need policemen everywhere, in every lair you inhabit, and sure enough here comes my favourite slobby bobby to liberate the lady from my attentions.

"Now come along here Charlie, don't bother the lady. And you have to get out of here anyway there's a demonstration soon down there, and we want this section for police reinforcements. Is she bothering you Madam?"

"Oh dear. Oh thankyou so much Officer. Thankyou. Thankyou. Thankyou' Exposure. But composure resumed "Did you say you KNOW her . . ."

Looking at me, both of them. A blob of phlegm on the floor couldn't invite more contempt from four eyes. And me thinking for a mad moment she was getting wise wisdom at eyeballing me.

"Oh Lord of the free where'er you be come and rescue me . . ." I mutter, obliging them with a stereotype of tame loony lame wounded, but harmless and gormless as they come.

"The booze got her brain" the happy policeman confides sagaciously to Madam Outrage, and doesn't even bother to lower his voice. Oh brother, you've lost the last shred of respect for the former Lecturer, who taught your evening class sociology, occasionally thinking I could GET THROUGH, yet blinking anew I am now at your instant link with Madam Outrage. In '68, I used to secretly sympathise with you and your mates, having to beat up students, and hating us with justified jealousy of privilege. Yet you were the sons of the bloody working class and the ones we were supposed to be fighting for. A senseless war like they all are, with the oppressed destroying each other. Oh brother, be a brother. It's just a job like any other. You don't have to *enjoy* being a hero, though that's the way it goes I suppose . . .

"It's Charlie. Charlotte McCloud. Still living on one, looks as though . . ." awkward now as he divulged past affection for imperfection displayed here. "She used to lecture up at the University can you beat it Madam?"

"She *what?*" staggered and furious but now curious watch it Madam you'll get *involved*.

"Sure thing" pompous and glowing with knowing. Yet no, I don't hate you slobby bobby like I should, with my hungover left wing emotions that said you hate the fuzz in '68. Now I just feel timid towards anything tall in case it leans on me and I fall even lower in my estimation. Actually, I'm preening right now at the slow blistering of my sister here now she knows I've been a middle class citizen at some time like her. Like her, too close, too close. Like a dose of intoxicating medicine listening to me would be at your fireside, on your safety ride, now open wide to the elements.

"Perhaps 50 pee then" she says nervously.

"Well that's really decent of you Madam, isn't it Charlie, though I'm turning a blind eye while you do it. It's not allowed, this is gross vagrancy you know. A public nuisance. Come on then, public nuisance, take your 50 pence and be off"

"Be off be off I'm a sloth a sloth a pubic nuisance a pubic nuisance" I mimic with this mad poetry jumping around all the time, no reason, just rhyme. And I'm skipping off gladly at ripping off Madame Outrage, clutching my coin as first thirsty hope of a brand new day, tussling away, bowing and scraping, ingratiating and cringing. That's how they like their beggars to be. But above all grateful, hatefully grateful you have to be.

Now he's telling her the story of me being arrested for Barking at cars while still lecturing at the University . . . There I was crawling up West Street in front of a fleet of taxis taking home the topers, woof woofing. It seemed better than hoofing, easier on all fours, when you can't see doors and windows very well. Bloody hell the fuss the University made about that one when it made the "Star" front page. Vice Chancellor's rage and apoplexy proper vexed the whole Department too, though I ruefully apologised for the embarrassment to my Professor. Why the hell should that boring old fart be embarrassed? I was harassed and hounded for months, except by the students who thought it funny but a little *weird* you know for a woman. That was in '88 and things had straightened up significantly since '68, when everyone was more than a little weird, you could hardly hear me amid the babble and brokerage of average folk trying to be free. Flying flailing and wailing the wisdom of hisdom that was '68.

In that year of years, I was doing my first degree, a PPE at Poxford, and thought we'd all be free by the time I'd finished it. Instead of which, we were all stitched up again by old Establishments of Right and Left, and the real free spirits of '68 couldn't conform to norms at all again, and self destructed just like me. And I'll tell you summat else for nowt, there's a new generation of academic dropouts now fighting my lot for the territory. Oh woe, what's come to pass, this underclass has ineffectual intellectuals grovelling in its grime and slime. Time to watch it Boy, with hustlers and rustlers and revolutionaries of the Millennium GETTINGTO-GETHER bloody hell. You know very well what happens historically when disaffected intellectuals and the feckless reckless rest GETOGETHER and collaborate . . . hate gets tasted, folk get wasted, why your hour is coming Boy, and Ours, and it's danger danger all the way. From raw refusal to fond perusal of what's yours Boy, in one short overhauling journey. See we are far from illiterate tossers and self-pitying wankers like you bank on as you step over us and on us well thankyou thankyou Sir.

If only the intellectual dossers down here weren't so busy fearing their own shadows, fretting, bed wetting, bleary. And me, I was just as bad, too sad and defeated and beaten and used by booze and addiction. Yet that day as I say it was different . . . since I mentioned my glimmering shimmering dawn, the day hasn't tailed off, tragically derailing itself, about 10 a.m. as it usually does. I've been waiting for the dreaded hated moment when the first cider wears off, and it's time TOGETOGETHERTOGET some more to keep the horror display at bay. The terrors, the crawlies, that must be avoided.

I'd do anything, anything, to avoid the crawlies. And if you disapprove, you don't know what delirium tremens can pull on a sensitive soul. Own goals, these fantastic self-induced terrors. Just tell me how to stop them. So you yell, just give up the sauce. Of course of course. Don't you think I've tried, she lied. Gime another, you can't see what I'm seeing in my inside. I can't bear it I literally can't bear what it feels like without a drink and a pill and a smoke how the hell do you know what it feels like to be me? The solution's worse than the problem. It *is* the problem you say, and I hear you, I do I do but I can't get out of the solution or the problem's still there glaring waiting to snare me snap me up into jaws of terror it's all terror and horror and no way out.

Why should I recover when all that shit, every bit of it, pristine pure and putrefying, is waiting to hit me right in the eye, if I ever try to defy the bottle and face my reality soberly? Who the hell are you to moralise, wise stable smug guy? I tell you why I drink and take the pills. It's not for thrills any more, but just that they fill my hole my great Black Hole of despair just waiting always ready out there to consume me. So what do I do? If I were you, I'd shut up and not answer. You can't project into my situation. You don't want to be me. You flee from that kind of insight . . . only Laing would know . . .

Though it's not fashionable to have them, Laing is my *hero*. In his writings and books and his insightful looks, I'm hooked on every sentence he spoke to us. We poor mad insecure misfits, we loonies, came of age, understanding our rage and our pain, it wasn't in vain, when he spoke to us in our language, not bondage called *sanity*, which excluded our experience. The family it was. The family as homily from hell. The family had fucked me up and you up and everybody up and Laing said it long before Larkin was barking and growling and howling and sounding surprised about it. I wasn't born in a bad storm or something genetic making me click clock out of step with you, but my family'd been mad, it

22

couldn't help it, they all are, the structure ruptures and destroys everybody in them.

When it really feels like it's slipping away again my grip on things I long for Laing and the Longing alone validates my pain, makes me real again. Laing made me understand it wasn't my fault, I could climb theoretically out of the vault of self blame, self hate, and build a new self esteem overnight. Redeeming this plight as a gutter slut in my doomed old rut crying dying . . .

But theoretically's a long way from real emotional healing, and I'm not feeling cured by any means. Seems I've still got the horrors lurking to spook me. Hope new ray of hope isn't a fluke about to vanish along with the cold December day. Anyway GOTOGETOGETHERTOGET some more and Ah, mirabile dictu, I spy me a demonstration, students marching, marching, they're marching agin the government which as I speak is in the 18th year I think of the freak show at least I think it's about 1996 and quick quick millennia are crunching together in my lifetime though that would be a presumptious assumption. I'm trying to make out what else they're shouting about, it's Tories Out a lot as they come weaving, heaving, shoving, down the Moor. Socialist Workers' Party banners are all the front row, chanting and looking mighty fearsome to me as they pass. I plea with my jamjar "50 pee sir?"

"Fuck off tramp" he spits and anger stirs in me.

"Oppressed people, isn't that what you're shouting about?" I mumble meekly.

He stops, actually shocked "WHAT did you say?"

I try to shuffle off, dismayed, frightened, they frighten me all that aggression "I confess I misunderstood. I thought you cared about the poor, you socialists"

He's red faced and red haired and panting and ranting. Oh masculine scenes, tight jeans and energy nearly knocking me over "Who are you then?" stopping, stooping, holding up his line of the demo, people looping around him, enraged, staring at me. I don't want all this attention, don't mention me at all in your battle summary. I'm a bystander, an observer, a dysfunctional element in this life, and certainly in your senseless sectarian strife

"I just need 50 pee to get by"

"Why?" an intellectual here you can tell the inquiring mind you find rarely at these events.

"Why not?" as senseless defenceless as you baby

"Because I don't give money to drop outs who won't pull themselves together and help to build socialism so nobody will be poor"

"Why not" a persistent piss artist me when I want to be

"Because" kinder "Because madam" peering closer he senses what once was a woman, and leering courtesy appears, pulled from the depths of his macho little soul bless him "Because you are reactionary forces, no use to the class at all, you should be at home looking after your kids not here on the streets begging for . . ."

"For?"

"For whatever it is you'll buy with 50 pee."

"A loaf?"

"Hrrrrmph. You'll buy booze madam. Booze. Liquor. You smell of it. That's the downfall of the working class"

"That their women drink?"

He blinks poor sod, thinking hard. He was God to himself, this lump of lard. All red and hairy and raring to make a revolution five minutes ago, and now he's stuck having to patronise a loony. Because you can't miss a single chance for conversion, no matter how unlikely, the chatter must flow. Still, it's a bit off being wise and benevolent and a revolutionary hero all at once, while the demo passes by chanting decanting its wit and wisdom without you "Tories OUT OUT OUT"

"I agree with that and I'll go away for 50 pee?"

"NO"

"Take over your life and own it then sonny"

"What!"

"Take over your life and own it. Before they do"

24

"Fucking anarchist crap. You're an old hippy!" accusing
"Yippee yippee happy hippy 50 pee then . . ."
"NO!"

Well you can't win 'em all, and a by-stander, tall and free and
disapproving of this Left in action, gives me 50 pee in sympathy. You can be sure this Left wouldn't give a pauper a
penny. And a piss pauper should be shovelled away out of
sight before the glorious day of revolution dawns, when state
power will transfer and flowers will flourish overnight, and
the plight of the poor will be abolished. And if you believe
these charging surging macho bullies about that, you'll
believe truly anything. Like the story that the Council is telling
that they're not selling the land of our Hostel for profit. That
there's no such capitalist plot at all. That the hostel's just
politically unpopular, and the new policy is everybody looked
after by the community. Including the nutters. So they shut
us out in the cold in December. Well merry Xmas to you too,
Labour Councillors one and all. So I think I'll skip along to
that little old fleeting meeting at City Hall, where they're
going to push through the decision, rushing precision guaranteed, with no pleading-against heard. Who listens to junkies
except their flunkies. Let's find me a junkie's flunky then
who's in the parade . . .

4

Factions, fractions, democracy in action. City Hall has it all tonight, plus the gall of these ghouls we elect to demand respect. At least *you* elect them. I stopped voting when I fell out with men's politics and their shouting fighting boys' games of pushing for fame and power and hours of glory. But nowhere in the world, not in Prague nor Pisa, is there such a steadfast symptom of male power as in a Yorkshire Council Chamber. Pomp and splendour of the peacock gender, all proudly displayed on gold inlaid architecture round these walls of the banqueting halls they annexed for strutting and striding. The dignitaries dignifying nothing . . .

Yes I'm biased and jaundiced and prejudiced and too pissed to climb these tall steps. And then tripping and slipping on the red wall to wall carpeting down the steps. They must have known I was coming with the red carpet. I'm humming a sorry little tune I made up about being a loon in maroon, to console myself, as I creep with stealth, guiltily, in all this wealth and municipal opulence.

"Where are *you* going then?" He's big and burly, a surly sod playing God, and looking official. *Patronising* isn't the word. He's heard about loonies being on the streets and not locked up any more, and knows you have to watch them or they'll set up cardboard boxes anywhere. They'll sleep in your back yard on the hard cold concrete if you give them half a chance. So whatever you do, watch those loonies "You're in the wrong place here ducky, now just go back out that door again like a good girl"

He knows I'm a girl cos I'm showing the curl in my fringe for the occasion, and I've put some lipstick on thick and caked. A half baked clown, one of the town's unfortunates, I hear him whispering loudly to a worried looking secretary, who looks as though her ecclesiastical embroidery class is too hectic for her these dark winter evenings. By the look of her shock at my stock of elegance, standing there scruffing up the red pile, while they scrutinise my cosmopolitan attire. Not Yorkshire at all. I'm draped in an old Peruvian poncho from my trendy mind-bending days in the Andes, to show I'm no mere local hobo. Well you have to make an effort. But it smells, bloody hell, you can tell. Disgraceful. She's plump all over except for her knobbly nose, which she wrinkles, not just at my clothes.

"I suppose we should get Security" she contributes in frigid tones, as rigid her back, as her voice is incapable of moaning with passion or groaning with pain. Oh woe, what remains of the laughter you must have had as somebody's baby daughter? Or did they stamp it out of you too? Oh dear your fear of me is terrifying, life denying. Stop trying to pretend I don't offend your whole credo. You know I do. You're bristling with fear as you engineer my departure. Yet I'm totally powerless against your callous contempt. It hurts to be stepped on like a piece of dirt. Have you ever thought of that, haughty fat bitch. I might be a witch, but God help you with your wobbling thighs. You'll get a surprise in a minute.

He puts a great paw on my poncho, pushing, pushing me backwards.

"Take your hands off me please" I'm teasing with my snottiness, but he pulls his hand back as though I'd bitten him.

"You can rest assured ducky I don't want to touch you at all but you can't come in here"

"No dear you must leave here or we'll get the police. Now GO ON" Icy secretarial secretions, stalactites, while his are mity, sticking up, pricking up, making me shiver in my bones. These tones could turn you to stone.

"A vaginal orgasm's best, don't you believe the feminists" I remark. But my bark's worse than my bite. In fact I haven't got any biting teeth left. You don't need to jump like that.

"Fancy that" sez Hercules, secretly pleased at her discomfort, which I regret. Compared with him, she's Boadicea, overseeing municipal property like a Princess.

"Shurrup Rupert Bear I've come to see the Council Meeting, which I have a right to attend as a citizen, a denizen of the streets I am. And if you try to prevent me *I'll* call the police" and they get a whiff of the niff of my bottle of Strongbow, held low under my poncho, and topless as a tart, needing art to negotiate its passage in flight. That cop took the top right outside the shop I'd just bought it from. I dropped it in front of him, and he said sadistically if you drop any more litter, I'll nick you for vagrancy. But I'm not begging. But you will be when I've finished with you lot, you'll beg for mercy the filthy lousy cadging scrounging lot of yer. So without the top, the booze goes slop slop all down my trousers. Yes I'm wasting a tasting, as I shuffle past the glazed amazement of these two uptight ones, using every bit of concentration to keep upright. And there's another bloody flight of stairs facing me "A lift a lift me queendom for a lift"

"Don't let her get in the lift for God's sake. She might ruin it"

How do you *ruin* a lift? Nevertheless, Boadicea can conceive it. So she rushes forward, flushed and panting, clutches my poncho tail, and wails all the time. So I compromise, wise old thing I am, and humour her. And we go together, her waddling and wading with her weight, and me toddling along obediently after her, like the smelly old hearthrug dog she's decided to look after. The day's getting dafter, she thinks, and I wink at her conspiratorially. And she does cheer up, yes she does she does, and the jowls wobble ferociously for a second. Then she laughs she *laughs*. You must never believe any human being's beyond hope, don't be deceived by their fronts as cunts and careerists. At least, not the women. The women can be saved by a giggle, though Thatcher would wriggle away from any redemption.

I should maybe mention at this point that coming to this joint and attending Labour Party conventions isn't usually my thing. These gigs are all rigged and fiddled to favour the few and the mighty. What would a slightly insane has-been, want to voluntarily spend time with them for? And it's not 'cos I'm lonely either. It's only to witness why we're on their hit list of services to be terminated because of cuts.

We want to know the arguments, and then we have something to go on in working out the real reasons, to see if we can do anything. Though ringing anybody, canvassing, doing anything in politics needs money and respectability, or else they don't listen. Labour don't like loonies either, detest and despise them. We're too weird to be working class respectable. The working class hate us. We're dirtier than them, and flirting too much with danger, disease. Ill-at-ease and uncomfortable we make them. They want to be safe and the same, but better than each other. And above all sane, and blaming us who don't work and just shirk our responsibilities. Especially the women among us. We're just evil and lazy and choose our fates in any case. So we get all we deserve.

And you'd think if the Left failed us on account of its puritanism, then the feminists would take us women on board, glad to hoard us as a miserable cause to uphold. But folded unto the sisterly bosom we can never be, because sobriety and sanity are prime requirements of proving the superiority of the sisterhood. Sober up sober up and then you can come in. It's like winning when you've won. But what if you haven't, don't know where to begin, and why get it in all the time about our drinking?

I don't blame you though. I reckon if I was a fighting righteous feminist, and saw a gang of slags and slappers beckoning at men, I'd feel mortally offended, distended with grief (or blasted relief?) at their blatant mischief, and lack of self-respect. That's a joke. I hope you know you're being funny, hilarious, referring to self-respect as a concept for us. Do you know what it's like to be eaten alive by a craving so dire that you rave on fire, you'll do *anything* to stop the nightmare. Riding bare and brazen down the High Street on a horse would be nothing. Godiver for a fiver any day.

Anyway, depression's at bay this day, hooray hooray happy holiday. May I take your arm fair lady? I've come over wobbly with vertigo at the prospect of being inspected in company. People tend to object to my presence you see. I see, she sez in a heavy attempt at humouring me, and guides me gladly to the bit of the place where visitors sit – in disgrace, by the sound of the tuts and throat clearings as I saunter past, trying to look jaunty and hanging on to Esmerelda the secretary for dear life. You see how relative it all is. A few minutes ago she was the biggest obstacle. But now there are many more amassed, and the speaker seems to have stopped in full flow to draw attention to my awful entrance. Woeful, wistful, and winsome, I try to look, as he's a handsome buck, this Labour politician. He has to be Labour with a beard and a jumper and an intellectual air in his glare at me:

"Well if everybody's ready I'll continue"

"Please" I wheeze and consider striptease his face is so stuffy and stern.

". . . As I was saying we have an emergency item on the agenda this evening which can't be postponed since it has been proposed by our distinguished member of parliament who is here with us tonight and is prepared to speak to us about it"

It's not their night for pomp and ceremony, these dignitaries. The tone's not right. It's interrupted as Jean appears, and leers at the speaker too. Yoo hoo yoo hoo Jean, I hiss, in a loud obscene whisper, and blow a kiss. Gizz a swig, gizz a swig, she answers, relieved, heaving her bum onto the seat. No small feat, I can tell you, as he's glaring at her now, vexed as hell, and daring another one of our gender to materialise and jeopardise his splendour again "Well as I was saying"

"Hic who hic who he hic" comments Jean "He's allright 'im oh yes I fancy 'im"

I nudge her but she's not there where she was suddenly. She's down on the floor slugging away at my Strongbow, making slopping gurgling noises.

"We'll be chucked out" prim reprimand from me makes her giggle and hic even more.

"*Jean* we've got to hear this shurrup"

She sits contentedly as a cat swilling cream, licking her chops for the slops, don't miss any "You listen and tell me"

30

"Yes ahem yes" and now it's the blessed MP peering at me over his glasses "when the ah hum ladies are ready" Now steady on mate. There are titters all round from all those assembled men, behaving like hunters who've cornered a couple of foxes, as we huddle in the visitors' box, harmless as fleas, but spelling disease for these uptight upright gentlemen of the Left.

They wait expectantly. They've baited us and want a response of fear. Or else it's no fun, they can't jeer. We have to run and hide and try to conceal ourselves. They can't cope with revealed naked vulnerability exposing itself, defiant, staring back, as I'm trying to. Though my hands are trembling more than usual. BULLIES I want to scream. BLATANT BOORISH BULLIES. But I manage a fragile smile instead.

He even manages a wan one back. Surprise surprise, a gent in disguise. No he isn't. I know exactly who he is under that smarmy MP appearance. He's a working class lad from the town who donned gown and mortar board like the rest of us baby boomers, running, escaping. Yet he wasn't escaping at all. He was a prudent student of civil engineering here at his local university, without imagination to want bigger wider worlds beyond the parish. Too risky and full of foreigners out there. But here, near home, without roaming, he could still be rover, a top dog. A hard slog up the Labour Party ranks then, in their think tank, the way to get promoted, voted for. Would be better than building bridges and leaving Sheffield to do it. Nay lad. He could stay and be a politician, with trips to London if he became MP. But still live with the family in Sheffield. Never strayed far from home, our lad. Why he even stayed living at home as a student in '68, courting Jenny, and couldn't understand what all the fuss was about. He'd kept his head down then and worked like mad for his finals. A pint or two with his dad in the local was still his social life, with his future wife watching his darts matches. And other students were hatching revolution. While your solution was determination not to be changed in any way by middle class education. Cloth cap crap. That summarises your enlightened attitude to the world. Keep it closed, narrow, parochial, and local, and shut out bad influences.

Frowning you are at us, now now Sir. How do I know all this about you? Because it wasn't such bliss for your docile Jenny at home, who wanted to roam after a few kids, wanted to see and to learn and to open up, wanted to live in London, when you became MP. But that could never be – the idea was for hearth and home to stay put and shut up. But you were away, and she enrolled one day in my evening class on Alienation. The same evening class as the policeman. And that's how I know about you, Brian Cheetham. She used to collar me after the lectures with weepy stories of her frustration, and I gave her feminist stuff to read, her pleading to come to parties at the university. Did you know about your wife's sallies? Been on rallies at Greenham too. What did you do about that? I never found out what happened after she came squashed and defeated, resigning from the Course. You'd had words and heated arguments about the duties of an MP's spouse being trapped in the lousy house. Though I expect you didn't put it like that.

I never saw poor wounded Jenny again. But if ever a hen was ripe for running off and learning to fly, it was that one, clutching those feminist tomes to her chest so tightly that the knuckles were red as her bright puckered mouth. Tight and tense and terrified, she lied, It's taking up too much time you see I can't stop reading – pleading with me to do something to set her free. Me *me*, sinking into my own prison so fast I could hardly see any more, how could I liberate anybody? By then the sauce had got me. Divorce divorce I whispered hurriedly, hurrying to the pub, her worried look haunting me guiltily for days afterwards. *I let her down* there's no way out of it, and left her to you. You fat pompous pig, wriggling and squirming for your audience, just like them. That's why they love you, these other self-important boastful self-made men.

Yet believe it believe it I can't conceive it a woman opens the door and stalks in, and what a woman. They start talking and nudging each other and Brian Cheetham changes his tune, this one's worth waiting for "Good evening Madam. And welcome"

"Hi" waving a nonchalant hand, sighing, sardonic glance around, hesitating on me with faint amusement "Just the press"

"Well we're honoured I'm sure. It must be the national press. I know the local hacks"

"Just carry on and ignore me"

"Well it's difficult Madam. But nevertheless" he's preening, his overweening pomposity attributes her presence to himself, appropriates it as a compliment, all in a matter of seconds, and he waves a hand for the chatter to stop and continues more suavely in her direction. His every inflection a sexual sibilant coded symphony. Though I didn't know at the time he was doing it entirely tactically to win favour. It wasn't the rush and blush to the balls it seemed at all.

5

The newcomer drapes herself across a chair near us, non-chalant about being instantly pivotal to the proceedings, bored already. Dreadful way to be, though I could see her attractions. All black hair and black clothes and mincing convincing stilettoes, and the kind of black tights that frighten all but the bold. And the men in the room duly become lions lurking to put irons in the fires of this one. From London – you could tell by her arrogance, insulting flouncing dance of contempt for the provincial Northern hicks, whose dicks nevertheless were rising hopefully to the occasion. They wanted her to enslave them, beat them. A masochist's fantasy woman she became, and who could blame the poor sods, with that amount of Fidji perfume floating about the room, shouting seduction . . .

She has them all swooning and licking the floor. Such adoration shows what's possible, with poise and pong. But the noise and the throng are interrupted again when the door flies open abruptly, and in marches another fine figure of fortune, flashing his rings and opulent things. You could see from here how pushiness was his middle name, with ruthlessness a close second. The way he reckons up the femme fatale as just the gal for him, and sits down next to her in the gallery, making three of us so far. A bit squashed, with Jean on the floor sloshed, and the posh couple leaning hard away from us to avoid the booze smell and contamination. Though I'm subject to examination by her, sort of sideways, assessing. No messing with instant dismissal of us, like most folk do. No. There's a curiosity, and interest perhaps. To do with being a Jew. She feels some solidarity with outsiders, in this room of gloom and glory of the Inside Left of Northern worthies, whose intimacy in Brotherhood made my flesh crawl.

Jean isn't having a ball either. In fact her eyes are suddenly wide open, on stalks, and she's pulling my bottom fringe furiously. The woman peers curiously, and stops looking bored, straining to overhear, leaning towards us. Careful dear, we're weird weird weird.

"Charlie that's Gavin Knutton wazzee doing 'ere?" Jean's pointing at the pushy one with the rings. The only one she can see down there. Getting frantic about him, her antics will get us thrown out.

"Shhh quieter who's he?"

"Ee's a millionaire, a millionaire! I mean it. A rotten bugger an' all. Grew up in Peashill Street, you can't get much lower. Just goes to show. Made all his money from nightclubs. All over, ee's got nightclubs everywhere. Bet ee's upta summat. Wazz ee doing 'ere?"

"Don't know Jean. Ask him. And for some of his millions. Could save the hostel..And get us a drink"

"NEVER. NEVER. He wouldn't give you the snot from t'end of his nose he wouldn't. He's evil. EVIL. Used to hit smaller kids all the time and torture animals you know the type"

"Charming" says Salome listening

"Whoshee?"

"I don't know anybody Jean except this awful unctuous prick Brian Cheetham"

"Fancy Gavin Knutton. Summat dirty's up if ee's 'ere. Wazzee doing 'ere?" She was so agitated, I resented him upsetting my friend. Her nerves weren't in the best state for a hated foe to appear so near, so suddenly.

"You're Dr Charlotte McLoud, now known as Charlie. Hannah" says Salome, thrusting a perfect paw at me, all flashing red talons. I can't respond with dirty hands and nails, all blackened and torn, so nod vigorously and keep them under my poncho. It's no go for social occasions living on the streets. You have to have some warning when you're going to shake hands. I mean, who could have imagined that for once I really resent my niff, and wallow in her perfume, hoping it bathes both of us and overcomes my disadvantage. Speaking of which, I wonder "I'm afraid you have me at a disadvantage"

Aeons of polite education come flooding out, no matter how you've degenerated. I feel feebly chuffed at that, and occupied with the implications. So I don't hear her reply at first, and am getting very thirsty by now, and there's no plugging Jean, who's glugging my Strongbow like no tomorrow. Which of course in this predicament there might not be. So you can see her carefree point.

"I said I'm a friend of Toby. Toby's your friend too isn't he?" She's speaking slowly and carefully, as though she's the one trying not to be drunk. But of course that's for our benefit. She's humouring us, I realise, with a fast twinge of despising her for it.

"In a manner of speaking. Pleased to meet you Hannah"

"'Specially if there's a drink in it" says Jean without blinking or batting an eyelid.

"Oh surely yes. We'll go for one. Oh, can you go into a pub? Oh, we'll get something anyway afterwards if you like, whatever you like" The lady is bathed in golden hues suddenly. Not black at all. Good old Toby.

"But wazz she doing here?" It's all getting too perplexing for Jean.

"Ladies and gentlemen observers, if we could continue" says Brian Cheetham in his poshest voice. "We're here to discuss the proposed closure of the building at the Moor Foot, currently used by dropouts and gypsies and sundry women of the streets, as a kind of hostel. Its official use as a Social Services Advice Centre has long lapsed, and the place has a very bad name among local residents, because of the kind of drunken disgusting women who hang around there"

"Booooo" bawls Jean from the floor behind the wooden panelling. They can't see her, assume it was me. All eyes swivel disgustedly.

"Quite. We seem to have a representative of that ilk with us this evening"

Well. I didn't think I looked that bad with my fringe in place and my face made up, well a lot of lipstick. But some pricks, there's no pleasing. Even with my poncho teased back over one shoulder, like they do these days in fast plays about

New York I've seen advertised in Village Voice, which gets dumped in an American academic's trash can I visit regularly in Harcourt Road, on my way to the hippy house. Though I don't go there much now. A very bland brand of violent anarchist there these days. No "Peace, brother" any more. Though they never bothered with sisters much. Shouldn't have touched them with a barge pole for that. But in the old days before I was bald, I called there regularly, and you could always get a smoke of dope and a spark of hope politically that things weren't written in granite, and you could plan it would be different . . .

But even then you had to lay the man in charge of the dope supply, who was usually a large dirty hairy hunk in denim that had seen better days of revolution, before his permanent haze descended. Nevertheless, he was sexy as hell, and particularly well adjusted to slow dopey fornication on the floor in the dogends. He used to send me crazy with his lazy tickling and licking, when his prick wouldn't function properly owing to the pills he'd overdosed on. It was really thrilling lying there being undressed for two hours. I confess by the end he was driving me so wild I could have eaten him alive in that dive, all littered with loot and booty from a life of hustling beyond the margins, in dens most folk never dream existed. Except for sliving into secretly in a raving wet fantasy, when tucked up in your soft clean sheets, fantasising a fuck with a lean lump of meat like he was. Like a bitch on heat, like we all are capable of being in private. Even you lot would be, with practice at getting in touch with your sexuality.

Bob was his name. Bob the slob, who looked like Che Guevara. But his only commitment now was how to hold his addictions in control, so his role as pusher was safe. But god is he sexy, and the thought of his tickling and licking even now makes me prickle all over with desire. Which is unfortunate, pinned here in between Jean's head and the brain dead municipal men in suits. No, there's another woolly pully here tonight, looking liberal, besides the handsome Marks and Spencers. But he's a New Man and knitted it himself, all kitted out for a feminist meeting, you bet. A wet old wimp with a limp and listless one to match. Either that or premature ejaculation – that flattering invitation to kill a man. I would truly kill a man who comes quickly and overwhelms you with sticky and sickly apologies and finger poking, to compensate, when you're choking with anger and grief and disbelief. I've often cried go steady go steady not ready, but he's died on me dead as a dodo, no go, just deep contentment and saturation, with me all resentment and frustration.

You see I don't trust these New Men. I think it's a ploy by the sexual failures to enamour themselves to feminists. It's a line to undermine women's resistance to macho rough stuff. Love me love me, you can even like me and trust me. I'm a nice man and I respect you. I would never boss you around or toss you on the bed and jump on you, god forbid no. My style is to sidle up to you and see if you're interested. But who the hell's interested in a woolly cap and a fuzzy face sidling about, when we all know that Mills and Boon's heroes have to stride and fling to make you sing and scream with desire. The best lovers I tell you are the old heroes tamed a bit. They still have the arrogance and the sexual flounce. They're not maimed and fumbling at feminists. They say I'm here and I'll give you an orgasm lady if I've been doing it wrong. But I'm strong and I'm twice as virile as the nice ones.

What's sexy about being nice? And you have to agree unfortunately, that the call of the wild is howling and haunting, every time one of these prowlers comes flaunting and taunting you. When you thought you were all safe and secure, wrapped up with your New Man and ideologically right-on and tucked in, be careful. You're ripe for a swipe of the primeval paw, seducing you away. Reminding you of juices you'd put away and dried up, ready for the long grey winter of middle age. You're at that dangerous stage of despair with affairs of passion. You're over it, you're too old. Don't believe, don't ever get sold on that, or safety. Since sex at its best has nothing to do with safety, but being on the edge of an abyss of bliss and blazing crazing devastating highs. Not those placid old sighs you're allowing yourself when your New Man's fanned a flaccid response, though you know inside it's not enough not enough not tough assertive not powerful enough.

I tell you, the worst hell is wondering whether a New Man wants you or not. He's so hesitant and considerate. He's read all the manuals and hardy annuals about clits and tits and what to do, and he's so far from being carried away and transported by passion that you hang about having to make all the moves. I want to shove their faces and tepid embraces away, and say call it a day, so far are they from turning me on with this display of empty erudition and knowledge. Dull porridge without practice and passion and power. It's an assertiveness of manishness that's missing, that's massacred in a million feminist manuals, mistaking trust for lust and leaving the latter behind . . .

Oh God the lack of colour of the scene before me, oh for a black or a brown or a Jewish face, anything but the eternal greys of the undiluted English displayed in front of me, on dignity, by the look of him:

"I must say, it's a recent phenomenon, drunken women. It must be a sign of the times, a harridan for Prime Minister and drunken women on the streets. But I'll be damned if we should support their drinking on our taxes, and many people think this too. This place is an electoral liability. I've come here tonight to speak to the motion before the meeting, to close the vermin-infested place down as soon as possible. We must not be seen to be giving a haven to women of this kind, beggars and tramps and what have you, frightening decent people and making them wonder about Labour Party policy, I can tell you."

"Hear hear"

"Absolutely"

"Yes yes"

"Hear hear"

"Boo" says Jean belatedly.

"There there" I sigh, comforting her a bit. Her tears are looming large and glossy in distracted eyes, brassy bleached hair and fat thighs merging into a big white beached whale, sailing on her back down the aisle. I want to scream at them, but know it would prove his point, and I'm sweating again, wetting the seat through my trousers. I can feel the sweat trickling down my face, and feel full of distaste and disgust at myself, next to this Paris model. Perhaps I could toddle out without them noticing, and slink off for a drink alone somewhere. If I dare ask someone for some money now the trembling has started. I should never have let it get this bad, and wouldn't have, but Jean pinched my emergency supply. I want to die, sitting there, waiting for the wave of panic to subside. Safety ride all the way home though, if I could stick it out, this vision would buy us a drink, and we'd be floating free again. But I can't hang on, I can't I can't. Don't make me. Whatever am I going to do I can't stand it in here with this heat, no relief. But disbelief disbelief. I stare at the hand in front of me holding a leather bound flask, a flask a hip flask just there. I daren't ask questions, but pray it's not an hallucination. It must be. I shut my eyes to clear my head. That's worse, with crawlies waiting to climb all over me. I open them quickly and it's still there and this time I grab it gratefully and glug glug as fast as I can. Whisky it's whisky, but not rough and cheap. This is vintage and smooth and soothing. Wasted on an alcoholic, I can't help thinking. But never blinking once, I empty it in one long slug, giving it all my attention in case it should disappear as summarily as it came.

Such is the real sophistication of the lady, that she murmurs only Thanks when I push it back at her, quick to withdraw my paw should she inspect my battered hands. You see my hands and elegant long nails used to be my mark of distinction. I'd been a model for nail varnish in the impoverished student days of the Sixties. I know it's not much, such a small bit of your body. But those nails were perfect then, and the ugliest things about me now, apart from being bald, are these worn, torn, blistered, and bruised things, without rings or adornment, at the end of my arms. I suppose it's because I can't see the rest of me usually that they loom so large and important. Mirrors aren't something you carry about round here. So I feel mortally ashamed of hands with this woman, and blame her bitterly for hitting me right where it hurts, making me expose them, my wilting roses beyond repair. I dare say she never noticed, and knowing her now it would all be fascinating anyway. But you never realise that at the time, do you, when you're ashamed of something, that it could possibly be an *advantage* in someone else's eyes. Mind you, I know now the trick of always turning disadvantages into their opposite and making them part of your success. But I didn't know this key survival trick then, or things would never have got so bad.

She cocks an indolent eye at me, and I could tell she would never allude to the neat half a bottle of Scotch I'd just disposed of, or ask me if I felt better. Such a rude intrusion is not part of the perfect poised get-up of this one. Thank God for some insight. I suppose that was her way of introduction, and now we have a confidence to share. I wouldn't dare rebuff her and go away, crudely conscious of my lower needs and their demands. She's got me now like a remand prisoner. I owe her, but can't for the life of me imagine what she wants from a wreck like me . . .

6

As it turned out she got the works and a brilliant career. But I wasn't a seer, and didn't know the afterglow of my antics would turn into a romantic reverie one day. We'll see about that, if I can ever get on with telling you the tale without these digressions and confessions taking up too much time. Though they're very relevant and you won't understand the all without the bits, and certainly not how it turns out.

Well, wit wasn't exactly flowing in the Council Chamber either, so I showed a bit of initiative and stuck up my hand – which didn't look half so bad now I was canned as pickled fruit – and waved it to and fro in a distracting way at Honourable Member Cheetham.

"Er, I'll take questions and discussion at the end. Oh yes, that *is* the end. That's all I've got to say, and I don't think we're having an open discussion with the public is that it gentlemen? Or?"

I suddenly thought of Hanna Schygulla in a Fassbinder movie, finishing every sentence with ". . . oder?" to convey deep existential doubt, and giggled at the thought, pleased that my memory definitely *was* still working in fits and starts. The witless worthies look uncomfortable and want a way to be able to exclude Jean and me from the meeting, but keeping the other visitors there, and they don't know how without calling their own bluff of democracy.

"I think it's observers only today. Best way to get through the business, sorry Madam" says a bright young thing shooting up and down in his seat faster than lightning, and such a frightening clipped correct tone. Another one incapable of sexy moaning, whatever you did to him.

"Yes Bernard" the Leader, if it is he. Must be. Looks in charge, and distinguished, in a burnt-out, disillusioned-steel-worker sort of way.

Bernard stood up, blustering and bragging and bristling, from trade union constituencies 20 miles deep. The sweep of his rhetoric accordingly enlightened: "They're slags. Shut it down immediately. It's a brothel. Nothing more. It's got to be full of whoooers the way they hang around outside begging."

"That's a contradiction"

I jump as the vision next to me erupts. I discover in amazement she is furious, and all her glazed blase phase has vanished. And now *I'm* curious. Maybe she has something, this clotheshorse. A divorce or two, making her angry. Now I can relate to anger. It cheers me up immediately, this tense taut metamorphosis next to me.

"Pardon Madam?" Bernard is dropped on, slopped on by dirty dishwater from a dizzy height way above his head.

"No interruptions" the prim clerk barks, up and down like a jack-in-a-box.

"Oh well, I think we can make an exception" You old lecher Brian Cheetham, I think smugly at the time. Tut tut, that'll cure me of glib judgements. Things are often what they seem unfortunately, but when they're not, oh boy and girl, what a tale comes tumbling out.

"Do carry on dear"

"They can't be whores if they need to beg, that's all I was pointing out"

"True true my dear. True true"

"Perhaps they're unsuccessful. But whores, nevertheless"

They all join in a chorus, defining whores like a philosophy seminar "When is a whore not a whore"

"When she's a bore" "Tee hee" "Hee hee" "Ho ho ho"

I cough in disgust, but distrust my own ability to intervene gracefully, with my skinful of peat washing round with the cider very precariously. If I get angry I could just throw up, and that would waste it all. Let alone poor Jean, snoring gently under my chair just now.

"Slags they're all slags"

"Yes Bernard?"

"They're all slags. An insult to decent working class folk"

"You mean decent working class *men*" The angelic

Hannah is sprouting wings for me. I *wish* I could intervene and support her.

"No" shouts Bernard, ruffled. A belligerent hyper-tensive man, with hanging jowls and braces dangling over his big belly, and a nice wife at home, never left it. Sure enough:

"NO. I mean *all* people. My wife hates them too"

"Your wife may end up there" She drops it like a perfectly timed bomb on their festering campaign. They regroup, shifting in their seats, shuffling, muttering in vain against this rare bird. A female peacock who turns out grander than the males.

"How DARE you" screams Bernard.

"I dare. I dare." Aware too of her effect. She must be. She has 'em by their willies so they can't ignore her. Silly sods. Torn between anger and a sore need to be manly Gods for a Queen. Yet sympathetic too. How could you woo a feminist for the first time? These intrepid Tetley bitter men had displayed their feathers for a lady, and she isn't behaving herself. Turning into a bitch. Mocking them. But looking devastating, and mating instincts are still making them twitch.

"Now now gentlemen, *and* ladies please let's keep calm" Unctuous slime Brian Cheetham slides around in his seat, enjoying himself, his power, his authority. In this piddling pond he feels safe and smug and supreme. Swimming around slowly like a pike, and oozing holy self-righteousness from his dead eyes. Suspicious in itself. I should have got wise to him sooner.

"I resent this woman's insinuations." Only fearless Bernard doesn't fancy her, or can't dream of aspiring. So sour grapes and glowers ". . . about my wife. What's my wife got to do with it? Any decent respectable person knows what goes on in that place, and wants an end to it. Any *respectable* person that is . . ."

She gazes back at Bernard, unfazed, flicking a fleck of dirt off her sleeve symbolically. And he's losing, and oozing cholesterol, looking like an imminent coronary with too much salt of the earth flatulence. Such nonsense in the mid Nineties of Care Blair New Labour in Islington they say, yet these men still talk like this in Yorkshire. Dour defensive and dull. But Woolly Pully is intervening: "I dare say there's a compromise possible somewhere"

"How so Peter?"

"Well we could turn it officially into a Women's Centre run by Social Workers, with facilities for women's activities, and Rape defence, and legal advice, and so on. And these other women would be their responsibility. Get someone responsible down there, with financial control. And answerable to us. Statutory responsibility we need. Give it some clout. Take these issues out of the voluntary sector. Give them some money and . . ."

"NO" cries Bernard

"NO" echoes Brian Masters

"NO NO NO" chants the chorus

"Why not?"

A tight-lipped prune raps out the rules: "The policy of this Council for years has been *not* to support and finance separate women's organisations or women's committees or separate women's centres. They're divisive and reactionary and completely against class solidarity, as well the comrades know"

"Hear hear HEAR"

"No. I'm not convinced" says Peter "What do the women say?"

"The women" the prune says with distaste "The women in the Party we consulted, agree entirely"

"Well where are the women tonight?"

"Oh come *on*" says Cheetham testily "They've had their chance. They like vice dens as little as the rest of us"

"It's supposed to be a Refuge. You can't close it because you disapprove of the morals of the refugees. That's ridiculous. We should call a special meeting for women councillors and let them vote on it"

"Absolutely not" says an anaemic weasel next to him, full of diesel oil of vitriol it turns out, as his nasal shout turns on me "Look at *her!* Look at her! have you ever in your life! Who wants something like her near decent women? They're all diseased and mad, and if we give them half a chance they'll grow . . ."

"*Grow?*" says Peter.

Even Bernard's mystified "How'd yer mean *grow* like?"

Brian Cheetham's worried "Do you mean they'll expand their activities if we give them room?"

The weasel nods "And she and her ilk will get everywhere, these militant wimmin do"

"Militant?" says Peter "They're hardly *militant*. If they were *militant* we could mobilise their energy. No, they're very sad. Er, excuse me Madam. I wasn't being personal, and I don't think anyone else should be. Is that clear?"

The weasel purses his prim mouth "I was only making the point, and it's still true they'll somehow expand, and influence our children behind our backs"

Growing without them knowing. Like triffids. I rather like the idea. Taking root in Victoria Wines. Climbing up Sainsbury's Christmas Party Selections. Fair flowering at Moorfoot Winebar.

Gavin Knutton is clapping. I want to slap his wrists. Clap clap you moron. But I can't do anything since I'm wobbly and wounded after the weasel's onslaught. I just look fraught and frightened with my fringe askew. I know it is, always is when I get flustered, and I'm getting sweaty again and wishing we could go home. Very funny. This is why we're here. They're taking our *home*. These neanderthals are actually legislating our very lives here, and there's nothing I can do. Rendered impotent by my heinous condition and trembling hands, which have stopped being divine wands of intervention, but look ugly and desperate again as I finger my poncho. I must have been very hurt by that remark for it to have sparked such a response and overcome the whisky. But it did it did, and disconsolate, I hid in my seat, all low in defeat, and desperation rising from my gut.

"Sluts and slags. We'll shut it, and that's an end to it" Bernard announces, and Gavin Knutton claps. Unaccountably, Brian Cheetham delivers him a furtive look of intense concentrated warning, which I can't twig at all. What call is there to shut him up? The gleeful applauder of our home's marauders, he's on their side so much, it makes me slink deliberately down down in my seat to avoid thinking too hard about kicking him right across my lady's delicately crossed ankles. But she wouldn't thank me exactly, and I owe her. And anyway, the impact of one shaky foot, shod only in a pump and fishing sock, would be very feeble. But I'm willing allright, in my rage ready to fight, on stage too, with this imbecile clapping and tapping his patent shoe towards Hannah. Footsy footsy he wanted to play, then lay her later and leave her sated and begging for more. Such is his store of fantasy and self-acclaim, by the looks of him. But who can blame him wanting to fuck a Jewish delight like this one. It makes me wonder how shiksas plunder the store of Jewish men, like I do, or did before my Fall, – when their women look like this. Must listen, she's hissing at me: "Say something for God's sake. Tell them. You've nowhere to go"

"They know they know"

"But you've got to fight"

"I know I know"

"You can't let them do this"

Gavin Knutton is listening and withdraws his footsie hurriedly. He stamps it instead and clamps his jaw round a cigar which he clearly can't light in here, but dearly wants to break the rules. I love to see his discomfort, dying for a smoke. It almost makes up for the clapping.

"Charlie pull yourself together and *argue* with them"

"Screw them. They'll do it anyway, whatever I say. In fact they'll do the opposite if I say it"

"Try it at least"

"OK"

I lean forward and clear my throat "I want to say that I want to be heard as a person who wants somewhere to go and I have nowhere to go at all left any more. And I want to say I'm not a practising whore either. Nor am I wanting to grow anywhere, just rest at night. God bless you merry gentlemen" I think that sounds the right mix of loopiness and earnestness and deference, but Hannah looks outraged hissing hissing.

"You're taking the piss. That's not the way"

No it isn't it isn't. They're staring at me and my rude interruption in contempt and mockery, and trying to flick their glances into seductive ones on the left side of their faces for Hannah to see. Hee hee the machinations of men in hot pants, all cant and hypocrisy.

Hannah turns to them ". . . you can see this woman is mentally disturbed and needs a place to recover and feel secure. The community must take responsibility for such people, the hospitals won't." She is beating her great black velvety angel wings for us. I must cooperate and stop sulking and skulking. If *only* I could GETITOGETHER and look deranged in an appropriate way. I'm all awry as a loon, not goony enough, or gullible perhaps. That's what I seem to lack, gullibility and grovelling: "I only need a hovel to call a home. Don't take it away or I'll only have streets to roam and you'll be finding bits of me everywhere, splattered about in your gardens. Think of me in your gardens in fact" I perk up "If you close our hostel down we *will* come and camp in all your posh gardens so there"

I swear I was winning the argument until the bit about their gardens, and they all visibly hardened. Even Peter, who petered and puttered to a halt, now somersaults right round to their position. And it was all my fault. I can see my Angel anguishing next to me and them wanting to flee post haste, not waste their time with rhythms and rhyme and interruptions. I can see it was all counterproductive, my little shove. But I've tried, and now shied away from any further efforts, looking fey as I could. But Brian Cheetham's wooden and steely in front of me. I reel backwards at the sheer naked loathing on his face. It's not the place for such emotions, the Council Chamber. Though I can see you *would* despise everything about me, premising your life on respectability and dignity and pomposity, like you have done. *And* won your place in history too, as a battling man of the working class. And it's come to pass, that such battering rams want to evict women

48

trespassers from premises. And won't concede that their own lasses bleed from the same gender as we vermin, left to fend for ourselves, on discarded shelves of municipal madness you hail as good glad policy for the voters. Find the underdog. Isolate, and appeal to everyone to join you in hounding them, wounding them, crucifying them, as examples of what happens to the unworthy immoral undeserving.

"I propose we visit the place tomorrow. It's getting late. We'll take a delegation down and inspect it and then decide" says Brian Cheetham, and they all agree relieved, and rush for the door, past the whores and the Angel and Gavin Knutton, who stands up suddenly and stares at Brian Cheetham, who stares back and nods imperceptibly. I thought it was imperceptible and subtle anyway, but Jean appears above the parapet and leers at them:

"Did yer see that? Fick as fieves. Whazz going on? Whazz *ee* doing 'ere?"

"Jean this is Hannah"

"Hello Hannah. Is there any chance of . . ."

"Hannah's taking us for a drink" I say, firmly. A lot firmer than I feel, trying to stand up and look purposeful, as if I have somewhere to go. Oh slow, go slowly, oh show me the way to go home, if I had one. Left all bereft at homelessness. It's a concept I've avoided lately. Like being an intellectual. Too much too much. Such vistas and blisters therein. Such welters of sin, running sores, no doors to close either. No space, no trace of privacy. What violation of a human being on earth it is to say no place is yours. You're just a whore. No space no floor no doors. It's the doors. Most important of all, I'll miss not being able to shut things out. Not being able to go some-where safe and settle and sit and have a shit in peace, secure. They'll follow and penetrate and move you on when they've done. I want to run away, but stagger and slip and trip instead and lean on Jean, who suddenly seems full of energy and vibrant glee, while my head is spinning spinning . . .

"You winning?" says Hannah, finding my other arm under my poncho and guiding me, floating floating, dizzy as a voter, no choice, no voice, but still that flickering faltering feeling of

pe, as I sway along with them, saying yes yes yes to any-
ing, praying it's not closing time. For where do we go from
here?

7

There's a lot of vacant staring into space involved in being a drunk. An enormous wasting of time, and sense of energy betrayed, reflected in everything we don't do. We sit around dreaming and scheming of escape from the scrapheap. Yet contented as sheep as soon as a bottle appears, we'll sit and peer into the future, philosophical. A silent army of impotent seers in trances and tragic romances with death.

It's a shame, you'd say, if you saw Natty here, drunk as a skunk on the floor, rolling around and gasping between the groans. She's having a bad day and wants to be far away, with her rasping breathing and heaving breasts. She says she can hear the Reaper a-calling. She's tired of stalling him and can't hold out much longer, this liquor is stronger than any of us. She sez It's killing me, I can feel it in my insides, something down there just aches and aches, and my heart's breaking to see her splayed displayed like an animal, legs apart, farting freely, and really rollicking out of her mind. She's finding the hard way out of the DTs this morning. You have to pay so dearly, they come without warning and take you in tremors. My frolicking's done, she says, so tired, I'm afraid old maid yu can't get laid any more, the whorin's begun to get your liver lady, yu can't give dem it all fe a fiver. For to do it again to any more men will tek too much out of me. What will happen to us without my earnings, yu three parasites? Then she laughs with glee at our three horrified mouths wide open, instead of hers working hard for a living and giving and sharing the proceeds with us, and so far not resenting it. But every worm turns eventually and her big black ass has lolled long enough down the Moor for us. We'll have to keep her somehow, though I can't think of anything at all right now.

You can tell this scene offends Jean. In spite of her love of Natalie, she's prissy about bodily functions like belching and farting. Her dear departed husband did nothing else except hitting her and talking about shitting and excreta. To an extent that she leant over and smacked Natalie's rump firmly with a loud thwacking thump, and Natty fled from the attack without looking round, curling up into a ball, rocking, and her bright red shawl and woolly turban falling off, making her suddenly helpless. Her red clothes were her acts of defiance, and without them she looks gross, obscene, just dross on the dirt pile like the rest of us.

"I just can't stand that she's so vulgar" says Jean.

"Come on come on let's have a song" I say, worried at the blow. I know she hurt Natty, who would die rather than harm a fly. But if I complain, Jean will say What do you expect of a mean working class lass? She's hyper-sensitive to criticism, like all bullies, and oh dear I see a bit of a bully coming out here. But Jean catches my look and gets worried too about herself.

"I shouldn't have hit her. I'm sorry Natty. Natty talk to me"

"Love ya ladies, love ya" says Natty, muffled, tired, but always wired up to being mummy, consoling, comforting even her persecutors. Women's own goal of time eternal, what a role, bloody hell.

"She's drunk. Couldn't feel it" says Jean.

"You don't hit drunks nevertheless" I point out primly, reflecting grimly on the times I've reeled before blows that echoed the flow "You're drunk you're drunk" take that thwack thwack, you don't shack up with an eminent academic and imagine he *meant* it about being civilised do you damned fool? Nor that he would never ever hit you. Nor flick you away afterwards like a flea. I'll never be infatuated by creeps again though, no more weeping over Professors speaking nobly from pulpits, no more Gauls with Gauloises ... no more boring story of him making me gory. Do not *do not* wallow morbidly. It gets sordid and sad and sour if you do, and I will not will *not* be sour.

"Mebbe I swallowed a bit too much of dat stuff last

night" says Natty, coming round a lot, and sounding hot for some more already.

"Dirty bitch. I don't know how you can *do* that to a man"

Oh woe, oh woe, such prejudice shows you really are a narrow working class woman Jean, who's seen nothing, and assumes therefore it must be bad.

"Dem racist pricks won't touch me from de front de real way fe laying a woman. Has yu thought about dat? Least ways, lots of dem won't. Dem seh, Go down, go down, dirty black bitch. But it's good fe de knees"

Just born to please, our Natty.

"An I ain't seen *yu* come wid any ideas fe dat drinking doh, Lady Muck!"

Doesn't fuck at all does she Natty? Shall we call the bluff on tough working class Jean, with her proletarian snobbery and self-righteousness and No jobbery like that for me. Virtue is a big handicap in your situation, same as ours entirely. We're desperate women, and you sit there spinning your homespun morality tales about what's right and wrong behaviour for a woman, and what you wouldn't stoop to at any price.

Ding dong ding dong bells of morality ringing everywhere for Jeannie. And it's not fair to fling your follies after ECT at you, as you claim you were not yourself, doing all that with those kerb crawlers who you thought were giving you lifts. On a permanent night shift you were one time, doing it in cars, and drinking in bars afterwards with the proceeds. Never bringing any home to us and sharing like we did, but keeping it to yourself on the sly, and then dying with mortification when you came round from the drugs and remembered with relish. Natty said you enjoyed it secretly, embellishing the rancid bits with distaste on your face. In fact Natty says she got off on your stern disapproval of how they took advantage of a poor working class girl released from treatment. It was the minute attention to detail that turned her on, the way you started breathing heavily when you got to the undressing bit. When it's about tits, Natty always gets overexcited, since nobody ever bothers with hers on her jobs, and the only slobs who do are wimps and blimps, who cling to her for sustenance not romance at all.

"I wish he'd done dat to mine for an hour" she'd moaned, feeling her own big mounds and soundlessly coming in a corner, with her back turned. While Jean spurned her, in icy contempt, and started to tell me about a rapist she'd encountered in a comfy mixed hostel for alcoholics in Nether Edge – who'd taken the pledge. Her tones of total disgust I'd begun to mistrust by now. A kind of Victorian salaciousness in the telling – how she'd been yelling her head off for hours during the ordeal, but nobody came, and they'd generally been so kind and caring even letting the kids stay there. But the kids had gone that day. So she hid away, shy in her very own room. And he found her, dared her to have a drink, and then soon it started, the slow undressing and forcing her face down and then having her backwards frontwards sideways always, except that dreadful way reserved only for Natty.

Jean's attitude to good behaviour and fantasies about herself as decent and above our ploys, reminds me of middle class socialist attitudes to deprived folk as suffering and noble. But we're real and steal and reveal that poverty brutalises down here in the slime. It's no nursery rhyme. You try it some time through need, and not patronising fraternising with the natives. Your anthropology will end bitterly if you don't get wise to the basics pretty quick down here, and speaking of slumming – our Social Worker arrives. We have a Social Worker no less. A nerd named Toby, who did my Alienation option for his M.A. Of all things, a former student now studying me in my new incarnation, with even more fascination. There's no repelling a sociologist. They dwell in a privileged world of causes and connections, and if you're not careful you become a statistic for them. But I seem to be an independent variable for nice New Man Toby. Irreducible, till he discovers what really makes me tick. Then he'll nick my life as data for a Ph.D later, and vicariously follow my vagaries like a stoat, riveted, since he missed the boat of experience himself. One of these secondary livers of life, leeches on others. Like Lit.Crits. and all the sundry academic vampires lurking up there in the Arts Tower, shirking their duty as human beings to be real people. They're paper people instead, dreading a real intrusion of reality to steal upon them in the night. Though fantasising it might, ripping them to shreds, and stripping in bed their lofty softy liberal pretensions.

Toby thinks working class people are wonderful, and working class life vicarious escapism from stifling petit bourgeois pretensions he'd grown up in. He wallows in the coarseness, crudeness, and vulgarity, swallowing every piece of shit they throw at him, getting secret thrills every time he hears swearing – not the affectations of students, but real teeming expletives as part of normal conversation. Tell me tell me give me hell. He's George Orwell, exposing middle class socialist remoteness from working class life, *but still he gets them wrong.* The throng the sweaty song of the common man are not nice little slices you can have for tea with equanimity. If you really get in there, the nastiness stares you in the face. So Toby turns away. He doesn't want any trace of cynicism to poison his celebration of real people, and I sympathise that academia is stuffy and shallow. But these down here will tell you lies, and have you for a callow youth. Doesn't do to romanticise their absolute and perfect truth.

Toby's confused now as to how to handle the visit by the dignitaries:

"We need a strategy ladies"

"We need Hannah to put her spanner in like she did at the meeting where is she?" Benevolently I smile at him trying to look innocent.

"Do you *like* her then?"

"Of course"

"That journalist. Yes she's got money fetch her" says Jean

"Dat de spirit Jean suck 'em dry suck suck suck" Natty makes lascivious sucking noises at her and Jean looks ominous, threatening.

"It's sickening this situation I need a drink so badly when are they coming" I say feeling panicky and prickly.

"Hannah's coming. I'll fetch you some fags at least. You

know NO drink I'd lose my job if they see me bringing it in especially today"

"PLEASE" I wail

to no avail.

"No Charlie. NO. NO. NO"

I look round at them. Not a sound. They're bewildered by Toby – he's authority, or should be. But here he is, buying us fags and even booze sometimes, and on our side. They're looking at me expectantly, and I look back, wondering whatever we'll do when they kick us finally out on the streets. This room is dark and bare and there's a bleak Pennine nip in the air, as it whines through the broken panes and whips round and round the bits of paper and rubbish we've accumulated on the floor, and whirls round our store of dog ends, which Bridie tries to rescue. But the effort's too much. She's such a frail little thing, even Jean doesn't disapprove. Whatever she does, Bridie is insubstantial somehow, hardly with us. What a trio they make, sitting there in the debris and dusk, awaiting their fate meekly, exhausted at the thought. Only Natty radiates a bit of energy, which Jean hates her for, saddled with her overweight and lethargy, she waddles not walks lately, maybe that's why she resents Natty's spark of something dark and dangerous. No matter how heavy her body and that bum and boobs must weigh plenty, Natty always looks balanced as she strolls along and rolls among the hustlers, head high.

As for myself, I've always been on the skinny rag and bone side, sloppy floppy limbs too long as a child, not very strong either, but very wild. So always breaking and fracturing and shinnying like a colt caught out and ready to bolt away if anybody tried to get near me, even then. A toss of the mane and I'd be off, finding my own blind insane way. Everyone else thought I was crazy anyway, then lazy, as I always stayed in bed to hide when there was nowhere to go that day. Nowhere they would let me go that is. Nowhere safe for little girls with curls and cuteness in a world full of men, waiting, rapacious, or so I was told, and that's how they knock the boldness out of little girls – with pretty frocks and restrictions.

Was quite a shock to discover later that men didn't hate you on sight. You didn't have to fight them, and run in flight. In fact they were very pleasant. *That*, my mother said firmly, was the point. So I squirmed around, uncomfortable, rearranging my bony limbs, and waiting. And now my bones are sticking out more than ever. I suppose though I never think about it really . . .

There are bigger things to fear around here than not being an English Rose, I can tell you. Though it's a sin to watch Bridie going so thin lately, with bruises where her breasts should be. You could see them so often exposed as her old satin blouse frays and tears away. There's no playing at being desirable with her any more. I can tell she's more than drunkenly unwell, as if she's given up hope, swallowing dope and pills like Smarties. Yet she can't get enough to shake off whatever it is keeps her awake night after night. She had a haunted look, fair spooky and frightening the sight today, sucking her cheeks in and chewing them. I want to cuddle her and say it will all be allright. But she has a certain supercilious delivery if you say rubbish like that, which freezes you chilled to the bone. Never moaning, complaining, just silently mocking you sometimes, with your comforting platitudes. Not meaning to be rude, but rocking to and fro, all closed up in her private frames, reliving, unforgiving, fading away from us I feel today.

"Don't go Bridie don't go"

She jumped. How dare I invade. Well I dare. I'm scared for her.

"Where? Don't go where? What are you talking about?"

"Wherever it is that's on the end of that stare you have into space" Disgraceful intrusion, I can't help it, can't stop it, she's going away.

"Do you ever taste meat in your mouth? Like a strong taste of . . ." and the blood flows all at once and shows I was right to be worried a flood a flood of raw red blood pouring out of her mouth as she sits there hunched over in a broken chair, choking, and I just stare in horror and can't take it in for a few seconds.

"BRIDIE'S BLEEDING" I manage to scream and fall back fainting dizzy, inadequate tizzy I'll never forgive myself for, and of course Natty takes over, crawling along the floor to the door, grabbing it, and throwing it open, with her head back, hollering HELP HELP HELP.

It's all screaming and shouting for ten minutes of bedlam. In a way, what the delegation had come for, standing there open mouthed at Natty, and then Bridie behind her, spluttering and splattering them with her life blood, and Jean ineffectually waving her arms and bawling like a baby, and me hammering on Brian Cheetham's chest for an ambulance, and everyone frozen in a pose of such incredulity, I'll never forget their incompetence, their terror, their mesmerised horror, as they stand transfixed in the doorway, with Natty at their feet. My usual fucking position, she'd have said, except for beloved beautiful Bridie draining away before us.

"Oh God an ambulance" says Toby's voice from behind their heads, and after a hundred years of horror when it all blurs together and I'm hurtling into hell with all bells ringing no they're sirens screaming, I hand over my sodden bundle of Bridie's head.

"Let her go. Don't hold her. She'll choke"

"She's choking already" I'm angry, but these medics are kind, so kind and gentle with her, I want to weep. A bit of that kindness before could have prevented all this.

"Looks like a portal haemorrhage. NO you can't come" as I try to climb in the ambulance.

"But she's my friend"

"She's my friend too, we've got to help" says Natty

"'Course we have" says Jean

"NO" he says "NO NO NO. You look after yourselves. We'll take care of her. Does she have a family?"

"That's us. We've *got* to come"

"NO"

"I'll go Charlie. You stay with them" Toby sounds in control, but his brillo pad hair is sticking out wilder than ever and I know he's struggling "Please Charlie. No arguments"

Torment in hell and damnation. They're taking our baby away amputating a limb and we can't go with her.

"She'd want us there"

"NO Charlie. She wouldn't. She won't. She's out for the moment. I'll get back soon" and he was off with our lady our love our life.

"That's what comes of it" says Brian Cheetham, and Jean takes a flying leap at his chest, hammering like I'd been doing.

"Take her *away*" he says, and weasel obliges, taking her arms like a policeman, while Cheetham shakes himself, smooths his hair, stares at me, "God the *smell*"

I hit him, I can't help it. Something comes up from my stomach. I want to knock his smugness for six. I leave a bloody handprint on his cheek, and fall back weakly, fainting, fearful, tearful at last.

"BRIDIEEEEE!"

"God what a mess" He wipes his cheek with a spotless handkerchief and I can see Jenny washing it as I close my eyes

"I think this answers any questions gentlemen" says weasel somewhere miles away above my head.

"Yes I'm afraid it's an open and shut case after what we've seen"

"Oh dear that poor woman who *was* she" says Peter's voice hoarse with emotion.

I try to focus on him but he keeps swaying and I shut my eyes. Not wise really, since the scene when I do is as bad, blood rushing and gushing in my head.

"Please God" says Natty. But he's out to lunch it seems, this moment of nightmare daymare, when the chaos in your head collides with the madness out there, and it all merges horror everywhere.

"I think we've seen enough"

"Yes"

"Yes"

"Oh yes"

"Our minds made up"

"Oh yes"

"This is a disgusting hovel. Like I said" says Bernard's voice from a cloud he seems to be singing.

"It needs demolishing"

"Yes"

"Absolutely"

"The fact that this is a prime bit of Real Estate wouldn't have anything to do with it – ?" and there she is our Guardian Angel.

"You can see for yourself Madam"

"Yes Madam"

"Come on"

"Yes"

"These are futile obliterated wasted lives. You can't just walk off" she says.

"Hear hear dat's de truth" I can hear Natty in control control.

"Well they're not our responsibility. We've made our decision. Come on."

"I thought you were a socialist council"

"We are Madam we are and that means looking after our own working class people who've had enough of these trollops"

"Some socialism"

"What's *ever* been in socialism for women" says Jean

"We look after our own – decent women who behave themselves"

"Come on"

"Aye lads off we go"

"Bastards" says Angel

"Madam" says Brian Cheetham "Goodbye"

I open an eye and see the gruff bluff ghouls of the Northern Labour Movement retreating in disgust from pain, and Hannah staring at the blood. Coldly venomously "Bastards" she spits "Bastards bastards bastards. Ladies it's time for a drink"

8

A bumptious bruiser from the Council arrives next day, with us in total disarray and misery over Bridie, who they stopped us seeing. So we'd formed a miserable little queue outside the Northern General Hospital, where she lay with blood transfusing into her, and we wouldn't leave till they told us she would live this time. But next time would be the end, and any more booze would do it. We were shoved away, too worried and weary and numb and weak to speak to each other at all, and when we'd hurried the long way home, this git is standing in the hall with boards he proceeds to nail over the windows.

"But we'll have no light" Jean pleaded with him "There's no electricity you know"

"Not my business missus. I've been telled to seal 'em up keep out tramps are you in or out?"

"We *live* here" defiant.

"Oh yeah. You squatters like"

"No. It's our home" poor Jean had to try to be respectable whatever.

"Squattin' "

"No. It's a ladies' lodging house"

"Yeah. Word is I'll be puttin a metal door on next week with metal bolts and you be in or out for good"

"It's ours"

"What gave you that idea?"

"It's a social service for ladies to stay till they find their feet"

"Yeah. Ladies is a good one"

"Piss off"

"Yeah. Seewarramean?"

"Turd" says Natty.

"Now look here I don't have to take owt from the likes of you Bongo"

"Man yu really sumpin wid dat hammer fe a dick. I am outta here and find me a real big cock to suck. A black cock. Big black cock" She socks it to him slowly, as if sex were dripping down her chin at that moment, and slid out past him licking her lips.

"Bloody cow. Bloody black cow. I never did. She should be locked up. And sent home where she came from"

"This is her home" I say flatly.

"Yeah. Well I never"

And I never have either. Homeless courtesy of a Labour Council, the whole lot of those assembled patriarchs acting like a Mafia against a group of wretched women. Acting in fact as the *enemy* of oppressed women. Where are women supposed to go then politically? Not to the misogynist family men and its working class party with working class prejudices ruling the roost, and of course socialist men are the most conservative of all in personal life, which is why feminists with any sense have left them to it.

I think these thoughts grumpily as I trudge up West Street. There's no hole for a sensitive soul in need of hope and critical reflection. We now live in a Britain of greed that despises education unless it's a straight way of making money. Honey filled days of speculation and critical thinking seem to have gone for ever. I'll never know how these Tories got away with the transformation, abolishing philosophy departments all over the place to nip thought in the bud. As if they could and can. Or can they?

This philosophy department is my old abode of employment, eight floors up in the Arts Tower, and if I weren't so sour about the situation, I would find it funny what I'm up to today. Getting a kick out of rebelling still at my age, the more outrageous the better. But this is pretty mild really. I'm only stealing their booze from the cocktail cabinet in a little room at the end of the departmental corridor, to which I still have the keys. But not the presence for a philosophy seance, so I'm in my cleaner's gear and steering clear of questions of identity, which get very heavy on this particular corridor. If I go in the back door on the ground floor and down the steps, I can get the lift up from the basement, without harassment from officious security guards on the desk at the entrance. I could tell them a thing or two about security. I used to sleep zonked out many a time in my office, and they never knew. It's not allowed, but I've had crowds sleeping on the floor drunk as puggies and they never found out. Or maybe they did know all along, and that's why the letter suggesting I resign was so strong and moralistic in tone. Perhaps they did hear the moans of passion after all. But it was quite the fashion in those days to lock your door and lay a student. Though not prudent if you were a woman academic making noise with toy boys. "Randy old bag" doesn't sound half as gallant as "He's a devil for the women" now does it? So partially this is my revenge.

I pass the room of another bit of revenge. Old Etonian Mark Shepherd D.Phil poncey pants, was propping up the bar in the "Old Bell" in the bus station in the summer, when I was wearing Natty's red wig and Bridie's satin frock and stilettos and sunglasses, and I asked him if he fancied a fuck, casually, after leaning heavily against him and feeling his response. He started panting like a dog and nodded and produced whisky after whisky, thinking I was a tart in my party frock. When it got to closing time, I said languidly that I'd always thought his book on Althusserian Marxism was the most pretentious piece of polysyllabic wanking I'd ever read, and in view of the fact that I had to respect the men I bedded for future wedding bells, I couldn't sell myself short and sleep with him after all. So Nightie Nightie Dr Sheppard, this leopard has changed her spots.

He'd been so dropped on, his false teeth had rattled into his glass. I've never made a pass so successfully as in that drippy drag outfit that night, looking a real old hippy tart and playing the part and turning on a fusty old fart like Shepherd, who'd been so tight-lipped and prunish a pillar of prudery when I taught there. He used to stare at the legs in mini-skirts going up in the pater noster lift, and say with distaste they invite dirty minds, and his was grubbiest of all. Still, I saw him fall flat on his face that night. Disgrace escaped him by the skin of his false ones, as I rattled off, skin and bones sticking out where the curves should be. But still capable of raising a fly or two or three, and he'd no idea that his temptress was his old foe from long ago, criticising criticising, always wanting to know why they had to mystify and shroud everything in this impenetrable language, a bondage of esoteric nonsense, I used to say at his seminars, too dense to deliver any meaning. Which seems to be the intention, I cried, fraud fraud you're all frauds, you Althusserians. But he was Lord of Linguistics, they applauded every word. I heard he'd become Professor and rejected Althusser and joined the Liberal Party. But he's still got a lot to answer for.

The door to the Seminar Room is open, and I shuffle past with my fag arranged, drooping out of the corner of my mouth like a louche uncouth cleaner should, and brandish my brushes I've collected from the broom cupboard. They even gave me a key to the broom cupboard when I taught there "Never know what you might need in an emergency Dr. McCloud" and this is a rare emergency allright, the week between the Social Security fortnightly payments, when we all ran flat out of funds together, and no prospect for another week. It concentrates the mind woefully that second week, a vista so threatening and bleak if you don't mobilise wisely the first day in advance. So I'm doing my bit, and prancing past the intellectual ferment in the corner room, where I used to sock it to 'em on David Hume on Fridays. Did I tell you I taught all sorts of philosophy, not just Hegel and Marx. Though I specialised on Alienation, a purpose built philosophy for me, and a few others besides.

Even in the Eighties you still had to know a bit about Alienation for any kind of cultural cred, and I was tolerated as Sixties relic to teach it, but now they never mention it at all I gather. They'd rather it was over, that palaver is essentialist, and smoothy post-structuralist wisdom is wedded to the Now. In this constipated syntax like a foreign language. But foreign languages live and give clues to the real world, whereas this stuff seems to be an endless ritual of self-referential bluff, I think an elaborate well-paid con. They really won, these philistines like Shepherd. Then I hear them say Foucault, and think I know about him and madness, and try to plug into the discussion from down the corridor. But this is even worse, about discourse and signs, not real live whines and whimpers of mad people, which had been the scene with Reich and Foucault and Laing, before such slang and substance was passed over as naivety by these new jugglers of jargon.

Of course it could be brain damage, the reason post structuralist post modernist discourse theory always sounds garbage to me, as I lean on my broom and try to glean a bit of room, a space for my kind of contemplation in their discussion. But I can't even speak the language or negotiate the signs. So I give up convinced they're only wanking. I deeply suspect it is all circular, and criticism has been abolished methodologically – there's just no way in help help you can't win if the universe is self fucking referential and closed to outsiders, but there, so is everything these days.

Maybe my brain cells really are too scrambled and scorched by the booze. It does happen eventually. But No I don't think it's brain damage. They're onto something definitely different to what we were doing, and they *look* different, all neat and sweet and tidy. Can these be the same corridors that once vibrated with hatred of bourgeois ideology? When you got turned into mincemeat by long haired loonies who'd read more than you, who you screwed afterwards for the sheer hell of proving who was teacher, and because they were wild, and you still a child of the revolution too, wanting to woo them back to radical texts, but they had slipped away, and by '90 when I left, it was transformed utterly into a corpse eating its own entrails. If this shit is what the Left is in love with and nobody can understand them because they are deliberately esoteric to preserve their status, then who the hell is left to offer a progressive critique of anything?

Though that's not why I left, I had no choice. They asked me to resign, which means I was sacked without warning. Though the storm clouds had been gathering since I set foot in the place in '80, fleeing the embraces and violence of the French fascist who was actually a Professor of Serious Shit. I was in denial about his violence and his intellectual nonsense and often confused the two for the next ten years, as I flee and fly away to be an academic of my own with my Ph.D and teach in the Northern England of my childhood. Instead I drew blood in a hurry, just nerves and worry worry worry and sinking into drinking when the pain came, the fear the anxiety the panic, that blind manic panic that beset me like a vice before a lecture, that heart stopping fear of exposure before a lecture hall, that terrible impulse to strip and to shout and to flout every rule in the place. Couldn't face myself or them must drink amen.

With an Oxford First, I could have drained my thirst for a few years, and then got on with it, and been a Professor by now. Like other bright young things of the working class, who grew wings and flew to Oxbridge. But I rebelled all the way, even against achievement, and it wasn't drinking for fun it was drinking to run. Like it always is anyway when you overdo it, and I always overdid everything. Even now I can't be content with one or two bottles, I have to empty the cupboard, and stagger off clinking and clanking and drinking too much before I get out of here to the safety of the streets. Thank god there's nobody in the lift as I go, clankety clank down, with my bottles rolling around in my mop bowl, and hoping they don't find my thankyou note of Merry Xmas in the cupboard before I'm out of the place. I hurtle yes hurtle across the bridge to the back door. It's locked. I'm so shocked, I stand and shiver for a minute, ready to deliver the goods and confess all to anyone who asks. I never imagined the task would demand further initiative after getting the booze. But I can't lose it now. Yet how the hell to open this door? It's always been open before, bloody thing. I kick it, and lo! it was sticking only, and flies open, and I stagger out arms flailing and sailing, straight into the lonely hunched figure of Heather, standing behind it, staring forlornly into the building.

"Heather! For Chrissake, get out of the way. Come on,

I've got some goodies, come ON" and he runs without question after me across the road to the "Star and Garter" pub.

"Gotoget some fags Heather. You got any money"

He nods slowly, lugubrious again, and plods inside with eyes wide and suddenly blank and vacant. I hope he's not having a turn, they can be nasty. But no, he's back, smiling suddenly, and piling the packets, dozens of them, into my mop can, and planning a safe route home.

"I stole some money" he says proudly.

"Good grief Heather, that's brave"

"Yes"

"Come on then"

"I thought I'd ask you to fuck me next time I saw you. And I see you"

"Ah"

"Will you then?"

"When?"

"Now"

"How? Where?"

"Anywhere"

"Well OK. For a friend"

"Good"

"Oh"

"Thought you would"

This is the *end*.

9

Now don't get me wrong. I don't have any strong feelings one way or the other about fucking or mucking around with fellas for fun. It's just that I'm in such a mess, that any caress with feeling behind it would send me reeling rocking into space, into a place I couldn't cope with at all, and the dope wouldn't stop me being small and naked and vulnerable if I fell for someone in this state. I tell you it would be fatal, me being so dedicated to the bottle and fragile and frail. That's why I stay with the girls, and the trouble is Heather is trouble is trouble is trouble. He's such a brilliant mind, and I find it so warming and nourishing to talk to him about anything, but never bring myself to physically contact him. He's made overtures and avalanches before, and ever more so recently. But he's so ethereal somehow, it would be like violating a saint, to taint him with touch, it would all be too much, and break him in two. Especially him being prone to bifurcation in any case. So I can only face it really as a favour to a friend. If I put it like that, it will just be like shitting, and no way will any hitting of emotional chords be possible, I pray I pray. I can't say No you see. That would be agony. I've always wanted to make love with Heather. That's how I dream of it, make love with him, you see it's that kind of level, which is why I've avoided it. Oh shit, there's something so powerful about brilliant men. I could never compromise these days with a toy boy. I need destroying utterly in argument to respect a man, mind fucks get me really entwined, and Heather can do it, in the gentle way he tentatively says "that's silly" and proves it. I love it I love it. The earth moves when a man can rise to the occasion intellectually as well, bloody hell. Though I'm scared of what might happen when he says

"I'm afraid of you Charlie"

"Oh dear"

"But that's exciting"

"Oh *dear*"

"I want you to hurt me"

"Oh NO"

"I have to find out"

"What?"

"The depths of the soul"

"With me?"

"And the body"

"Oh dear"

"I want you to humiliate me utterly"

"Oh NO"

"You will you will"

"Will I?"

"You must"

"Must I?"

"You have to"

"Why?"

"Oh yes yes yes. Please"

You can see why I feel a bit wobbly about the prospect, with him wanting me to beat him and defeat him utterly like this, and me wasting my time with elevated love thoughts, and he just wants a bit of good old kinky S & M. Oh men, you can't win, and it's sin sin sin to try. However I'm determined to defy gravity with these bottles weighing me down and him dancing along next to me, never offering to carry one, and dreaming about being hit or worse. Daft git, I curse you intellectuals, all the way down West Street.

"You need dominating then" I say conversationally.

"Yes yes"

"Why is it?"

"You can't analyse sex. It destroys it"

"You want punishing"

"Controlling. Punishing. Utterly"

"Have you always been like this?"

"Yes yes. Underneath. But I always got admirers and worshippers who wanted me to be dominant just because I had a brain. But there's no connection"

"Yes there is"

"Between brain and sex?"

"Well your intellectual power lets you lose control in bed. If you hadn't got the real power you couldn't do it"

"Whatever. Don't philosophise. Just hurt me"

"I don't think I can"

"You can. You have to"

"No. I like you too much"

"That's got nothing whatever to do with it, you poor confused woman. I like it and want it you'd be giving me pleasure"

"You sure?"

"Oh yes yes"

He strokes my arm affectionately, sending alarm signals all through my body. A thoroughly shoddy affair it seems to me, and it seems he can't wait, and opens a little gate in the wall next to the "New Bengal" Indian Restaurant, pulling me through it, my bottles clanking to his wanking, which is what it turns out to be, so quickly done and no fun for me at all. He wants hitting hard. Of all the exciting performances, that back yard smelling of vindaloo was the coup of boredom in whoredom at first, him saying bite my balls, and me thirsty for a loving encounter. I know you can't win 'em all, and there's my baldness to consider, but that day I just wanted to get rid of him in a hurry after that. But it's not so easy, it never is with intellectuals. As I try to depart in a friendly way, he starts squeezing my breast with me protesting, but there was more in store obviously. What does he want now? He stops suddenly and mops his brow which is sweating profusely, and I'm finding it distinctly confusing. I don't mind him using me for relief but what was he playing at touching me up like this when he's come so much? Because the trouble is it's working in a dangerous way.

"Give me a love bite, hurt me" he's pleading, offering his neck, and kneading away at my breasts. Well playing vampires isn't exactly what I've got in mind either, but I do it, and start sucking his neck like mad, and he pushes me against the wall and I feel a cold bottle between my legs, and hear myself begging "inside inside" and I'm ashamed to remember opening my legs as wide as I can so he can shove the bottle of Johnnie Walker up up with me all the while eating away at his neck in sheer sexual starvation, and he's no stranger to this practice of turning a woman on so entirely that I lose my mind for a few minutes, as he massages me with one hand and moves that bottle in and out with the other, so I'm shouting and spluttering and chewing all at once and start to come in great heaving gasps, as I see his eyes mocking me, as they'd always done in discussions, shocking and supercilious, and I know in that sickening bilious flash, who is in control after all, and feel a fool such a fool drooling spittle like this, like a randy fish wife desperate for him, and reduced to a whimpering wreck by the one who should be victim.

I simper "By heck thankyou"

"Now we drink it" and he opens the bottle and puts the neck of it all covered in my white slime in his mouth glug glug glug glug "tastes better for the additives"

I look away, shamefaced "How did you know?"

"How did I know you were longing for poetic catharsis? It's obvious. The ultimate trip for an alcoholic is to be screwed by a bottle. Now you do it to me"

I hadn't meant that at all. I'd meant how did you know I was falling for you and would do anything anything for you and would respond like magic whatever you did and now as I slid this bottle into his bum and squeezed his balls hard as he told me and hear him coming coming I know I have to escape. He's danger, this man, more dangerous than many I've known, maybe any I've known. He has the trick, whatever it is, he has it, and now his prick is spurting again, and he's looking at me coldly, devouring every moment as a power trip, even as he flips and comes. It's the same calculating look of loathing and power. Oh the hour of misogyny is here and I feel fear and frisson, and an imminent prison of passion if I don't escape.

"Rape me between the dustbins. Rape me" he says, even now as he bleeds from the bum, I can see it dripping drip drop in my mop bowl, and everything told me to run. It's no fun any more, it's nasty, he's playing nasty games, but I have no choice and this precious inner voice is ignored. It seems there's nothing I won't do for him and he has me climbing on him biting him eating him and finally forcing him inside me as I straddle across him, glimpsing somewhere in my head a vision of a raddled old has-been pumping up and down on a tortured aesthete, thumping his chest and feeling myself coming again and again and again and him in pain beneath me, pain and power, the witching hour again.

"Well I think it's luvly" says Jean, looking like a Yorkshire fairy queen with the tinsel she'd put in her hair "Dare say he'll be back for more, they can't leave it alone the kinky stuff once they start"

"Naw dem types no good Charlie. Leave dem be"

"I love him. I love him" Silly fool I am, I know it. Play it cool or else you'll blow it, I keep telling myself the usual mantra when I go crazed over someone like this. But it's true I've fallen for him, all tall angular blond schizophrenic lot of him, and you should never fall for psychotics fool fool woman, but we're all schizophrenic aren't we, whatever it means. It's just a way of distancing him, isn't it, to call him that, my golden rule: never categorise, empathise instead. But dread dread I feel it in my thinning bones, no good can come of it at all. It'll end up in a crying do, I remember grandad used to say every time anyone laughed, and I'm definitely not laughing but chaffing away. He's revealed himself as controlled and controlling in sex as he was in seminars. A star of the literary establishment, who'd rejected the lot of 'em, and hangs around writing his wistful poems in eight languages and several of his own gibberish, confiding his genius to very few. Well I knew all that, and how to run a mile from self-proclaimed genius, but all the while I'm drawn irresistibly, and worn out with the effort of resisting the inevitable.

"Nothing inevitable *about* it" snaps Bridie with unusual alacrity, as I perch on her bed telling it all.

". . . it's just your awful self-hatred's been activated by somebody else. I know what it's like. When they hate you it's reassuring because they confirm what you feel about yourself. It's like that perverse pleasure in fucking the ugliest freak you can find. This repulsion is after all what you deserve. It's curiously consoling. Totally destructive though" Her nose tube wobbles and the drip starts bubbling. She lays back exhausted but looking rosy and flushed, very cosy lying there, and blushing as though some secret lover were stashed away under the covers, giving her that faint smirk at the corners of her mouth. Oh Bridie, hide me here safe too with you, and warm, and your fine intelligence nourishing me back to sense. It feels so secure here, luring, even a sterile hospital bed. Instead of the dreaded cold and slippery streets.

"It's pissing down outside. You're in the best place, all snugged up, I'm almost glad for you Bridie" I say, producing a tear, which she doesn't see, thank god. I must go before they flow, fool fool, can't visit a hospital without wanting to stay, be taken care of, some respite, some let up, some safety from the predatory world of scrounging and being scrounged upon.

They come to chuck me out, no doubt in the mind of the stern nursing Sister I'm vermin first water, and deserve everything I get out there. Except laughter. She'd deny me laughter. They all would, right back to my grandad, and so would life. But they can't take it away, and it erupts even today, when I turn the corner in Havelock Street, and in the gathering gloom, see Heather lurking by the wall with a woman, his bony back to me, unmistakable, and her arms wrapped round him and sucking sucking at his neck. After the first lurch of my stomach and a kind of white rage, I start to grin with relief. I'm released from my passion as suddenly as it came, and laugh out loud at the idiocy of having finer feelings in my position, when every feeling you have reveals only the awful state of mind you're reduced to.

Or maybe I'm rationalising. It's easy to be wise when facing a fait accompli. I see him steering her towards an alleyway between boarded up terraced houses, and feel strangely aroused, my pulse rate soaring, about what's in store for her. Not bottles, that's for sure, this one's a demure student with her black and mauve Arts scarf flying, as she disappears with him, a leer on his face I catch sight of, and the cold cold contempt. I know he'd be furious, but I'm so curious, and this is anyway a derelict alleyway I often shelter in. It's always deserted and hidden away. He must have sussed them all out for his little clouting sessions. I see her standing over him, hitting him with her umbrella as he lays face down in the wet, his bum in the air all bare and exposed, and this sweet English rose type beating hell out of him for all she's worth. It may of course be academic revenge for all those failed essays. But maybe there are more women turned on by this performance than I dreamt about till it happened to me.

I should flee and hide, but I stand there, no pride, wide-eyed, and getting off on the sight of it, and my own dis-approval thrilling me, and filling me with a terrible chilling envy of any women who're allowed to hurt him. I rave there in the rain, I'll get him and keep him close, and give him a dose daily of any pain he wants, as long as *I'm* the one inflicting it. Oh oh he's yelling oh oh OH and he's kneeling up and guzzling her crotch now, her skirt pulled up around her waist and him tasting and teasing her this time, which pleases me in a way, in spite of the jealousy, knowing he believes in equality of pleasure at least. Such a feast of the senses before me and I want it want it want it.

"What I don't get" says Jean later "is why *you* an intellec-tual should be so pie-eyed about *his* brains. I'd have thought you'd see through it all and know he's not God at all"

"Just a poor kinky sod by de sound"

"Yes. That's it. He's bent and loopy and you've fallen for it just because of his brains when you've got just as many. Beats me."

"Yep. Me too. I can understand me and Jean falling fe dem big brainy bums but not yu Charlie yu too cute fe dat *servile* stuff"

"You an intellectual with all them brains it beats me why you ever drank so much in the first place. If I'd had your chances I'd never go near a man. What can a man give you if you've got a career?"

"You're luvly Jean," I say, "but it's not like that. There's no relationship between brains as you put it and feelings."

"Well dem gotta be den."

"Yes there must be it's silly. Otherwise, what's it all for?"

And Jean, you've got a point. What was it all for if there is no relation between reason and fear, which is beyond reason, at least this kind is. Why did an intellectual woman turn out such a disaster as a person, running running from traditional roles and tight little holes of convention and marriage, only to end up like this on the garbage heap, no career no love no babies no nothing. Just keep on running and running and blotting out hormones that scream babies, and never be bold enough until recently to admit there might be something in it after all. Giving birth might be worth all they say it is. Because being a disembodied head might be allright for a man, and that I doubt. But for a woman, it's a nightmare eventually, because these emotions bodily come from the depths, and who am I to argue with feelings that keep saying You're denying me my right to be a woman. But why can't I be an intellectual *and* a woman? Because being an intellectual requires that coldness I saw in Heather's eyes, that detachment, that remote objectivity as the highest value. Even though it's always pseudo-objectivity in practice, it excludes everything warm and wonderful that women are capable of, as negative irrelevancies. Not that women can't be as cold as men. We learned that from the dreaded Thatch, and look at the hatchet-faced cost she's casting in her long black shadow. It's as if it's life-denying, to pretend a woman has no other needs than reading, that she doesn't bleed every month for any purpose.

Or maybe it's the contradictions that are too big for a working class girl, running running, nobody ever to talk to who feels the same, tearing apart with constantly starting again somewhere new. Too few roots to rely on. To get on must sever them. A clever girl doesn't need such sentimental ties. It's lies all lies of course. We do. We need all those despised bits of home like everybody else. But we can't afford them. If you want to get out of the sticks and away from the hicks, you've got to say a firm goodbye and fly off ruthlessly, wings flapping and brutally slapping down anything pulling you back and down into its warm and milky cowlike embrace. I'm saying you have to hate your background enough to get out of it, and if education's your tool to climb, you cling on to it, fanatically ringing out of it a value that's ultimately not there, and your spare frustrated emotions are wasted along the way. You've tasted success, you'll pay dear, you're blessed with knowledge, but no knowing, no glowing after life.

Whereas men can have it all, since they don't need so much. An intellectual man does his span at the university and lays the beautiful women on the side. The women don't have to be intellectuals too, god forbid, we know how fucked up *they* are. Whereas I need a mate who's an intellectual too, and they're all off chasing the dopey ones. So there's no wonder I freak out and speak crazily of love when I find an intellectual who's sexy and unconventional too, no matter how he screws. I'm delighted he exists at all, a man I can respect, well I'm trying, but he's making it difficult, disappearing all the time up passages with a different student every day. It's funny how he still hangs around his students, having left the place. Whereas I couldn't face them and fled, and hide in disguise, which is me now. But he still looks the desolate aesthete, uncommon, unusual, aloft, a toff – as Jean says deferentially "and they're always the worst".

10

It's a couple of weeks before the unspeakable Council puts up a notice saying "This building is due for closure on December 20th". Just in time for Xmas exposure to the elements. Can't wait can't wait for Xmas Eve and "last minute reprieve due to inmates' militancy". A fantasy for sure, but not without allure, since there's very little else to hope for as we mope around outside, watching the man with the hammer at it again. The pain in my tum reminds me that the worst feature of the future will be the monthly Curse, and the problem of finding hot water for my hot water bottle. I expect you'd think it would be the least of my problems, but this monthly business gives me more aggravation than any other aspect of the general feeble prospect around here. I fear it's the menopause approaching, encroaching on my hormones, and personally I've never called it a curse like many women do, but rather regarded it as a mixed blessing. The mess and ache are awful, but you do feel such a raw emotional bundle at that time, and not all of them are negative. I usually feel very creative about this time. Though it's been confined to creative and nifty shoplifting of booze in recent years, the potential is there in all of us at this time, for strange and wonderful things . . .

Mind you, I admit it's all very subjective. Natty gets possessed by demons all of her own, and yells incessantly at foes invisible to us, but so real right there to her. Then she says afterwards she's just a batty old bag lady who talks to herself and not to take any notice. But you can't help noticing when you're next to her trying to kip, and she's hectoring some baby-mother who's just a fucker like dem all are, dem pimps and baby-mothers, who conned her out of her birth-right. Jean fights everybody who is there, which is worse, shouting curse curse, when will it be over? She's longing for her menopause, imagining sexuality will be over too and she'll be safe. While Bridie wanders around at that time like the sensitive waif she always is, pensive but almost totally silent, and holding her belly as if she were pregnant.

So it's only me who feels positive at this time and in touch with the larger lunar forces, and very very sexy and special. Though it's hell if I don't get my hot water bottle. I could throttle everyone in sight. But today I've got one tucked down my long school knickers from the Salvation Army handout, and if you're wondering about personal hygiene – they're clean as a new pin, and so is the fanny that's in 'em. I bet you thought we never washed under these rags, old slags sloshed and slovenly. But all four of us are most particular about regular washdowns, even though the water's freezing, and you have to put the dirty clothes back on – unless it's laundrette time. Like now, I've still got a supply of clean drawers from the last visit. Oh we try our best. But best is not good enough for the working class, all dressed in *their* best, tarted up like mad at the moment, and poncing past us, wanting to piss on us, rather than give us anything, as we three sit huddled together in the Car Park of Greenwood Progressive Working Men's Club – wonderfully named without a tree or a progressive working man in sight. This lot are raving fascists by the sound of their reception to us:

"50 pence for a bite to eat?"

"Gerroff yer black bitch. Gerrooerm black slag"

"Filthy scumbag scroungers"

"Gerrout yer scum"

"Yer loadashit"

And that's only the wimmin. Ah me, feminism missed this lot of ladies.

"50 pence sir?"

"Gerremoff yer fucking ooooer"

"Come on then darlin' give us a feel"

"Coo they've gorra nignog fancy a bit of 'ot chocolate 'arry?"

"Eeers 10p. Crawl for it darlin' and sit up and beg"

"Open yer gob, I've got summat betteran money for yer"

We'll try the couples, surely the gent wants to impress her with his generosity.

"50 pee for the children sir?"

"Gerroutamyway scum"

"Tell 'er Roy"

"Give it 'er Roy"

"And as for that black slag she should go 'ome"

"Ooooo don't go near you'll catch summat Roy" and Roy tries to kick me, impressing his lady friend like mad "Give it 'er give it 'er they want shootin' "

A dignitary comes rushing out of the Club, waving his arms, "You can't be here you lot. The members are complaining. Now move along. This is a decent place for decent folks to have a night out"

"50 pee?"

"I work for my money and so do these in here. Not like you. Go away"

"We only want to listen to the music. We won't ask anybody else. It's Xmas." I smile at him but he's scared and backs away.

"Any more complaints and it's the police"

A big burly bloke dawdles deliberately. He stops dead in front of us, staring at Natty. She says softly "You want business den big boy" and he nods "How much?"

"It's twenty to yu an a drink an a bottle an a smoke fe my frens"

"NO NO we don't need it" says Jean, embarrassed in front of her own folk of long ago.

"Who don't? Back soon babies" and she saunters off with him, blowing us a kiss, smiling, taking his hand. They disappear round the corner, for all the world like a courting couple on a summer day, not a whore he'll have to pay with the kids' Xmas present money for hanky with a bit of darkness he couldn't resist. Not many can resist sister Natty when she's in her four inch heels and red slit skirt and old fur jacket like tonight. She brought back a huge pile of goodies today from the Rag and Tag, Sheffield's clothes market, and we're all decked out in finery. It's a shame these tasteless morons don't appreciate us. But who can blame them with their tight little lives and nasty wives egging them on to earn enough to bring them out to celebrate. Saving up all week for this, and they're just stepping out after sauna and shampoo and set, and then they get us in their path, wanting their precious pinched pennies. No, it's not good enough at all.

But I begin to notice that happy couples aren't much in evidence. It's mainly gangs of men shouting abuse at us, and separate women gangs echoing them. But they're not together, not yet. What's going on? Jean explains:

"It's Grab-a-Granny Night. Dance Night. They come to get off. It's a knocking shop"

"Only more refined than us"

"Oh yes. The women dance and the fellas stand around deciding. Then they'll get 'em a drink just before closing. And that's it. They're away"

"S'cheap"

"Yeah"

"Cheaper than Natty"

"Yes" she snaps

"Why did he then?"

"'Cos she's black"

"And?"

"Well there's no black stuff in 'ere you can be sure of that. And he'll think she's different"

"Exotic"

"Yeah. You know the stories"

"No"

"Well they have a reputation"

"What?"

"Hot"

"Hotter than us?"

"Oh yeah"

"Do you think it's true?"

"Oh yeah. Bound to be. All that sun"

"But she grew up in Sheffield"

"No but it's in their blood in it?"

"Jean that's silly"

She looks huffy and offended, but I bet it wouldn't stop her taking advantage of Natty's heat if the black bounty's extended towards her tonight. It's not right to do that but denigrate her all the time, and lo as if she knows it too she says "Praps I'm jealous" with a wan little smile, which makes it all worth while being together again, and fun and friends, in spite of the bastards and blowing freezing Pennine wind with snow flakes dancing in the gusts.

"Trust her to bugger off with a fella to get us out of it. Makes you feel stupid, but ever so grateful as well. But still stupid that we're sitting here like stuffed dolls while she does the dirty work"

"You're so right Jean. I know. We'll sing carols door to door how about that"

She laughs and her face glows at last. All that grief and anguish showing in lines round her mouth vanishes, and I can see a thirty year old woman shine through. Sublime moment of truth, when I could rant and rave at our sad depravity, but can't do anything. Just sit glued to my beer crate, hating the world for a minute, and wishing to god I could ask the sods in this establishment to fill my hot water bottle.

"Why Grab a *Granny*?"

"All t'women are divorced or married to somebody else. In any case they're over t'hill. Past thirty-five."

"How do you know?"

"I've heard of this place even from home. It's an institution. They come for miles every week to grab a granny"

"And then?"

"Then what?"

"What do they do with them?"

"What do you *think*?"

"No – afterwards"

"Well that's it. It's only for t'night. Next week they 'ave a go wi summat fresh"

"One night stands"

"Yeah. Or in cars mostly"

"And it's free"

"Except for that last drink"

"Grab-a-Granny Night. Well well"

"You don't know owt Charlie. You and your education. You think students invented sex in Sixty-summat but this lot 'ave been at it a lot longer"

"I know. I'm only a working class lass myself you know"

"Yeah. With letters after your name to prove it"

"My family was real working class"

"And you left it a long time ago"

"And look at me now"

"Yes but you're er having a problem. You're not one of us any more though. No matter how poor. You've got class Charlie"

"Middle class"

"No. Class. Classy. Posh talk. Oxford accent. You *know*"

"But poorer than them"

"You're richeran any of 'em. And you know it. God if I'd had your education you wouldn't see me for dust . . ."

"Yes I know"

"You want your bottom smacking my girl throwing way all them chances"

"I know"

"And then there's 'im. That 'eather. Ee's the same."

"No. He's public school and privileged background"

"Well that's even worse"

"No it's not"

"Yes. Ee's thrown even more away"

"But the working class gave me my education. I should use it to help them"

"'Elp 'em!" she yelps horrified "'Elp *them*. Look at 'em. Bloody rubbish. You should 'elp *yourself* my girl. And t'working class gave you *nowt* – they'd have taken it away if they could – you a girl and all"

She's right of course. Nothing I've ever done has gained working class approval. Which is why I revel a bit in their disapproval of me, the devil incarnate, returning to Yorkshire, in an awful frozen replay of girl-made-good-went-bad. Not sad though, it's her own fault the bitch, stamp on her, blot out her struggle to be different. Cot death would have been better and not so expensive. All that education.

"All that education" Jean's saying "It beats me. And your bloody politics is summat else. Still on talk about socialism. Don't these Council bastards teach you duckie – *there's nowt in socialism for women*. Nowt at all. It's men. First last and alluss. Alluss 'as bin. Lass *wake* up!"

"All that education" she repeats fascinated.

And here comes Natty, leading her trick by the dick. He's looking pleased with himself, and she looks sanguine and languid and lazy, a bit dazed, and dangling a bottle of Scotch from her hand, still holding his with the other one, unusual.

"I enjoyed dat" she says "Man dat was sumpin"

"Yeah" he says

"Man *dat* was sumpin"

"Yeah" he says, smiling slightly, but no improvement. He's horrid horrid. A heaving hulk of hero I spent my teenage running from.

"Yo yo yo"

"Yeah. Well. I'll be off. Will you be 'ere next week?"

"Mebbe mebbe 'bye baby 'bye baby" and she looks reluctant to let him leave, this neanderthal from the football terraces, gazing after him.

"You look stupid" says Jean, mean bitch. It's true though.

"Shut yer gob"

Natty shuts it, licking her lips "Wow man I came I came. I liked him I liked him"

"Liked licking him, ugh" says Jean in disgust.

"Not dat yu fool. No dis was different. Wow man. Wow man" and she showers Jean with cigarettes. Be pleased and leave her alone, it's her business. "Ah Charlie, I *felt* sumpin wid him. Dat's bad ain't it Charlie?"

"Lucky lucky girl" I say, while sour old Jean just glowers obscenely.

"Dat whisky fe sweetening yu up sugar pie" she shoves it at Jean.

"It's a pity though all the same" says Jean glugging grateful girl.

"Who's to blame all the same. We are greedy and cold and desperate and willing to do anything within our powers"

"Not all our powers" Jean glowers.

"Well whatever we can"

Except a man for you, Jean. We know we know it hurts too much to contemplate it. But leave out the moralism, the pursed up martyred disapproval of Natty, our glowing gorgeous benefactress. And such a temptress – another slob is approaching. He's been nudge nudging with the first one in the dance hall. There's more exotic stuff outside, a bit of rough, a black cocksucking slapper, make you dapper and dizzy with delight, a bit of allright altogether. 'Urry up, 'urry up though. She might get cold. He's hurrying, scurrying towards her.

"You looking for business baby?"

"Yes. How much?"

"It's cold tonight. £30? And a bottle of Scotch"

"OK" and they're off again, she sauntering, him trying to rush her, push her along. He's big and strong too, like an ape, ambling shambling shivering with cold and the prospect of Natty's black skin, and putting it in her glorious mouth, or some new practice she's devised, ever wise to improvement. As long as it doesn't get personal, which she finds disgusting.

"She's disgusting. A real tramp. Fancy *enjoying* it"

"Come on Jean"

"*Enjoying* it. It's disgusting. I can understand doing it for the money I suppose but *enjoying* it is disgusting"

"Perhaps she's making the best of it"

"She *enjoyed* it. Dirty bitch"

Oh fate. It's not fair. Natty dare enjoy herself, which you prim mother of three resent her for. Enjoying anything, that's the thing that you hate. That Natty has her fling in spite of it

84

all. You prefer Bridie, isolated up there in hospital. She never enjoys a minute, and you can relate to that. But this lusty lady, who keeps you in fags, whose gutsy get-up-and-go keeps your drink flowing, – you despise her trusty appetite for living, a leftover which doesn't show much these days, but when it does raise it's spirit, you will it to go away. Hey hey, now you're turning on me:

" . . . and I don't know why you're so nasty about them feminists. I explained to them about 'Women Against Pit Closures' and they were allright. Said they understood why I didn't join back then in the Strike. Said there'd have been no point. Said they could see there was another point of view besides them drippy soup makers who supported their men regardless. So there"

I stare at her for a long while, dumbfounded. What can I say? Except you'd never understand why the feminists treat you differently, reverently, Jean. Especially when you've no booze and you lose your way. The darlings only want earnestly poor decent prole women like you when you're sober, wailing about your kids. It's the sweet inverted snobbery of feminists and socialists alike, who think that middle class neurotics like I've become should pull themselves together. Oh where do we go when the middle class won't have you and the working class don't want to know, and déclassé intellectual sounds so hollow.

"Now I'm saving myself fe Father Xmas" says Natty, jaunty, flaunting a new bottle in Jean's face, which contorts painfully.

"Dem Grannies can't be no good at all tonight, dem grandfathers would rather be wid Natalie. Hey hey, Misery, lighten up" She pokes Jean, whose face does brighten at the new bottle pushed at her. Enough for tomorrow morning. What sorrow's possible with two bottles of whisky to share? It's dawning on me gradually that Jean's a pain in the bum, but I didn't know then that pains in the bum were precisely terrorising her. Me and my wise advice to Jolly up in our family of three at Xmas, and her mess a mighty untold hellhole she was sitting in, cloistered, claustrophobic with her fears, and all by herself for years and years, with no-one to summon or phone. Just absolutely alone, as a mother always is, with *that* suspicion, the big one, the Unmentionable.

11

We weren't about to find out about the bomb Jean was sitting
on that night. She clenched her teeth, grinding them around.
An awful sound, that makes me shift away, stumbling over
my plastic bags as she grumbles and grinds away behind me
in the gloom. I stare through the window into the nightmare
of Grab-a-Granny Night festivities, but can't see much. It's a
dark alcove for fumbling in, but the couple in front of me are
locked in heated conversation instead. Well that's all allowed
to two men in this place, I can tell what they'd do to a "queer"
in here and it wouldn't be gay and civilised either, or nice at
all. Then in a trice I recognise the creep MP Brian Cheetham
looking furtive and flapping his hands a lot, and the man with
his back to me is trying to reassure him, but failing singularly,
as Cheetham starts wailing. I can see from here he's
thoroughly agitated and hating every minute.

"Hey hey, come here, look at this" I call, and they come
struggling over with the bags and bottles and debris, too drunk
to see, by the look of Jean. But no, I'm wrong again about
her.

"Bloody hell it's Gavin Knutton again wazzee doing 'ere?"

"An dem not frens at all"

"You sure it's Knutton?"

"I'd know them measly shoulders anywhere. Wazzee
doing 'ere?"

"Careful don't be seen"

"Whazzee doing 'ere with 'im?"

"Yes dem doing no good Charlie"

"Wish we could hear" But the valeta was rolling, dah
dah-dah dah-dah dah-dah, and reaching its crescendo.

"I suppose it could just be social"

"Shit social" says Jean "They're not socialising in this
dump. They're *hiding*."

"Hardly"

"Yes they are then. Away from his posh friends Knutton is. Well away. He wouldn't come slumming here any more in a million years. Only to meet Cheetham"

"Why's Brian Cheetham MP here either?"

"Canvassing?"

"Already?"

"Dem's plottin' yu can tell why don't I see if dem want business when dem come out"

"He wouldn't" says Jean "not with a whore"

"My my my my" Natty smiles but it hurts I know it

"Wouldn't need to" added Jean leaning on me

"But why are either of them in this place. It's very odd"

"I know I know" Jean says excitedly "It's to do with his Nightclubbing. He's always buying up working men's clubs and doing 'em up into posh nightclubs so different people go and they serve meals and it's all flashy *you* know"

"But they wouldn't sell this it's an institution you said"

"They're dying out though" says Jean with authority "Not like a few years ago. The new thing is nightclubs up town with scampi and chips and an all-night disco music and dancing costing five times as much"

"But this is packed out"

"Yeah but they're on t'road out. And Gavin Knutton's the one who's doing it. He's made millions out of it. If he can't shut these place up at first he builds a nightclub next door so they start by going afterwards and then stop coming in here altogether and it's gorra close"

"But they'd never shut places like this"

"Yes yes. All them Tories who've bought their Council Houses want a better class of entertainment" putting on her posh voice she mimicks these the traitors. Yet who were the true ones – she says there's nothing in socialism for women.

". . . and they *should* be shut down. No women members, it's disgusting"

"Surely they'll have to keep a few open as dumping grounds for the unemployed. They can't afford scampi and nightclub prices"

"Not if 'ee 'as 'is way. 'Oo the hell bothers about t'unem-ployed anyway"

"What about all these women if there are no women members?"

"They're Lady-Guest members only. Not full ones. They can't vote or go to meetings or owt"

"Dem night clubs nobody would vote at all"

"I'd rather nobody did than only the bleedin' men. That way at least nobody has power over anybody else"

"Nobody has power in a posh night club except the owners"

"Better than this bloody men's mafia"

I'm inclined to agree with her, seeing this lot arrayed round the dance floor, prancing proud peacocks displayed to best advantage, now the women were full of vintage Pils lager to save their waistlines and get at least one kick of the evening.

"The prick's got something in a packet"

"Dirty photos" I'm joking. But there's no poking fun with Jean

"Yes I bet"

"I'm a getting freezing girls" says Natty, shivering and quivering with cold.

"But whazzee *doing* here?"

Whatever it is, Brian Cheetham is clearly dismayed by his outing. Not going well at all. He starts shouting "No way, no way" We can hear it from here, and Gavin Knutton patting him on the arm and going to the bar, leaving him staring wildly, far out into the black night, yonder past us, nose pressed. He's away in some terrible land of his own despair. I have a rare moment of satisfaction that evening on behalf of Jenny. Whatever this shit is up to these days, he's not enjoying it, nor benefiting good public relations. Though Knutton wouldn't be a supporter of a Labour baron in a million years. A self-made man with a cannibal's instinct for the kill, he's chewing up Cheetham into grizzly pieces and spitting them out well aimed all over the club – whose hubbub is dying. It's closing time, we can hear bells clanging and slanging matches breaking out all along the long bar.

"Time gentlemen *please*" and they slam down the steel grating on many a furious finger. Oh England England. You eternal land of the closing pub and the dosing drug addicts who don't realise you've shut them down till you shout time time in every town from here to Basingstoke. I'd stick to coke if I was starting again and planning to live in England.

But we're insured inured against the dark encroaching cold chilling us and filling us with the same unspoken fear. Next week nowhere to go at closing time. We all need a bit of security, Jack Kerouac had his mum to run to, and every little bird has a favourite branch, and our little ranch, our homestead instead of a home, is that mouldy old hostel with its cold water and darkness and damp and mildew and a few hungry mice who think we're nice but skinny with the food. We don't go in for food much. So it's a draughty old hutch at the best of times, but it's all we've got, it's our sanctuary, and we fall silent in face of the enormity of them taking it away.

"We'll be naked"

"Stripped bare in public" Jean shudders.

"Well yu ladies mebbe but dem bastards ain't taking no clothes off dis one. No Sir."

"What'll we do with our stuff?"

"Bag ladies"

"Bag ladies! I'd rather die"

"Jean youse a bag lady wivout a bag right now. Dem's gonna jus mek yu carry dem bags dat's de only difference"

"Yes Jean it's the moment of truth"

"An dem time for Jean's moment of truth"

"Natty. Not now. We're in this together" me primly. God knows why I'm trying to protect her. She looks so bovine there in the dark, hapless and hopeless suddenly, with drink trickling down her chin and matting her bleached messy tresses. But at least she has hair to mess up.

"If I was black and beautiful I'd earn money too" she says, sulky.

"Liar liar dem's lies yu'd never yu can't touch men yu

know yu know. Mebbe yu try wimmin rich dykes up Ecclesall Road I'll introduce yu hey hey hey yes man"

"You bloody disgusting black slut we know you'd do owt but don't mention lesbians in my company"

"Dem's some fine ladies"

"Ugh"

"A big black dyke's what you need Jean. You could get over racism and manism in one go and be a liberated lady of the streets. Think of it! Dem's fine ladies round Brunswick Street, if mebbe the rich ones ain't such a good idea"

"Ugh" Jean really looks sick. I wink at Natty.

"Well shut de fuck up den about black sluts and I'll be peace an' Karma sister. Yu think nobody got no right to no misery only yu. Every white person thinks a black one is gonna be jolly every day a dat life, de swinging bluesey mama, singing to de stardust. But I tell yu, dere's no room fo melancholy in dat story, an we black folk get plenty dat, but we denied our right to be fucking miserable by yo poxy stereotypes, and dat's why so many of us end up in de loony bins, just to be fucking miserable . . . so yu don't call me no slut any more and I won't call yu no vag whacker, tee hee hee, cunt licking Jeannie hee hee hee"

Jean moves to swipe her but topples over and lays still on the carpark floor. It's getting late and the cars are going around, hooting and tooting and taunting from anonymous forms behind headlights, blinding. They're winding down the windows.

"Come and look at this darlin' "

"Gerroutofit slags"

"Let's go let's go" shrieks Natty, pulling at Jean. We pull her, haul her, upright, blinking in the flashing lights, rubbing her eyes:

"Gonna be thick"

"No Jean NOT NOW" orders Natty, and Jean obeys, shutting her mouth. We carry her, staggering stumbling along ourselves, so sloshed we sing her favourite song to cheer her up. "*Show me the way to go home.*"

"I'm tired and I wanna" sings Jean "Booooooohooooohooo. Go to bed. No bed NO bed"

"Yes yes it's still there tonight Jean" I reassure her and we sway along quite merrily, until she stops us dead.

"It's him it's him. Look that Jag! IT'S HIM. No them. It's both of them. They're up to summat I tell yer" She's shouting and Knutton looks back in anger at what he thought were three strange women. He shows no symptom of recognition "Whazzee doing 'ere"

She keeps up the refrain all the way home down the Moor, stopping again outside a posh nightclub "That's a Knutton's yer see what 'ee does tarts up buildings and gets the smoothies in"

Smoothies going in stare at her, and the bouncer decides we need encouragement not to loiter:

"Move along ladies" he recommends pleasantly enough. But Jean kicks him viciously.

"Whoa" he gasps, surprised at her strength. We clutch her arms, dragging her away.

"She's sorry mister" says Natty.

"Yes yes" I say, trying to shield her silly fool. She's bigger than me and far fitter to defend herself, but he grabs her hair from the back and yanks her right out of our grip. Oh god oh god it's all slipping away from me. It's whisky, I can't cope with it. I help out considerably by fainting, and leaving Natty to it all by herself. Just coming round to see his face an inch away, pressing my chest, with all his weight on top of me.

"Steady on, help help" I gasp, realising he's trying to revive me, while Natty seems to be sitting on his shoulders, screaming, pulling him off.

"Natty I'm OK" I yell, as he lets me breathe again, standing up and tossing Natty off like a fly.

"You ladies better go home I mean it"

"Yes yes yes yes" I say, sicking up all over his feet. Better beat a retreat, but Jean's pulling his arm now, poor sod. No chance to play god with the customers, who're filing past delightedly, he's too preoccupied to vet them for unsuitables, He's found enough to last him a lifetime, standing here with a sore leg and sick on his feet, and Jean scheming something else.

"Tell me, does Gavin Knutton own this? He does eh?"

"Yes ma'am. Now move along. Do"

"Any more he owns in town?"

"The Cat's Whiskers" He was so polite, considering. I wonder why? They aren't usually like this. "There's talk of another next year at Moorfoot"

"Where?"

"You know. YOU know. That hostel place"

"Ah"

"Ah"

"Ah"

"Goodnight and *thank* you." And waving to our saviour we trip off with the tip off of a life time.

12

It's wonderful waking up the next day and taking a swig of whisky and orange straightaway, first thing. Good old Toby – bringing orange juice supplies, in a wise noble effort to get vitamin C into us somehow. Especially now, since whisky neat makes me vomit, and you feel you're eating something with orange juice. Haven't eaten since Tuesday, and it's Thursday. Except some beans in a tin we shared, and don't feel hungry at all. Though I think that's a bad sign, our bodies are designed to give us messages, and mine are all awry. But I try now and again to stuff something in, though it seems a sin to spend money when we get it on anything other than essentials of booze and cigs, and the other item we use is tranquillisers. But they're still free so far to the likes of me and the other three loons, though Bridie can't be accounted for at the moment . . .

It's always a dormant fear with me that the doctor will cut off my supply, and I'd rather die, truly, than face that situation. It was bad enough when he tried to ration me, and cut them down. His frown of disapproval deepening darkening, as he's not one of these antediluvians who never question anything, but a bright young thing who tries to wean women off them. Well he'll never get anywhere with most of them, and I swear most women round here are on them. But he's particularly concerned, as he puts it in his expensively modulated tones, about a woman like me with all these qualifications, who refuses therapy and clings to her tranx, and thanks very much Doc for your concern. But these are my life's thread, and any talk of taking them away fills me with such dread and anguish you might as well brandish a knife at me and finish it completely. You see the withdrawal from this dope is like a quadruple dose of the crawlies that doesn't let up or leave you alone. I spent days lying on the floor writhing

and moaning and groaning and in constant terror, till somebody told Jean about me and she came round and found me
gurgling and trembling fit to bust. I was having convulsions of
panic, not just waves, so she shoved some Librium in me and I
held her hand more gratefully than anybody's within memory.
That's how we gotogether, and later Bridie joined us and then
Natty, 'cos they knew Jean as a faithful provider of tranx. If
you ran out, she knew the scene on the Housing Estates
around Pitsmoor where they swap them and hoard them and
sell them sometimes, and you can always find some spare in
an emergency. Though how the hell anybody could get rid of
theirs, I can't imagine.

It's a feeling like being eaten alive you're dealing with,
and nothing the DTs can pull can equal it, because it doesn't
stop. It never stops. It goes on and on and on. You've screamed
and panicked and trembled and sweated and fretted to utter
exhaustion, and you collapse, and even then can't switch it
off. It pursues you, like demons in your own head, hammering
eating clawing away. You can't close your eyes, in case they
get you, your eyes I mean. Seem to be drilling your head
away. And Jean's seen it all so she relishes her role as supplier,
since there's no direr fate than to be suddenly savagely with-
drawn from good old benzodiazepines. The thought alone
makes me wince in pain; the memory makes me tremble.
Better have another whisky, and take deep breaths of that
biting Pennine gale that's whistling through the window
boards. And whoopee, a snow flake takes me completely by
surprise – sneaked through the holes it has, to wild applause
from us little assembled welcoming committee for snow to
the city. So sensitive are we to the usual grey dirty aspect of
its streets and alleyways, and snow *snow* will make it fairyland
and us all Xmas glittering fairies, covered in a white layer,
concealing and healing. So even the hairless can be abroad,
and not care less. Yes, the snow is a great Leveller. Like the
booze.

Abuse them both, and they'll take over. As we discover,
setting foot outside and sliding flat on our bums. All three of
us, giggling and wriggling around in our new found friendly

foe, making such slow progress up the Moor, wrapped in spotty white overalls before too long, and playing snowballs, shuffling along, singing "God rest ye merry gentlewimmin! May nothing stop you sinnin . . ." and making up lines as we go. So overwhelmed by our hilarity that we forget to look forlorn for a while. The torn mien of tramps has disappeared under a vampish visage as snow-queens in heaven-sent finery of flimsy flakes. So whimsy it takes us over, slipping along one two three arm in arm, full of charm and cheer. I wish these fearful twinges in the back of my neck would stop, and then it would be perfect.

"Nerve pains" says Jean "they must be nerve pains" She's holding my head, and Natty's massaging my neck. They give me a Librium, and the last swig of whisky and orange mix. Though they've added something else to that too. Fixed it, so my head blows off when I swallow it. I buzz all over, and float float, fairyland floating, and bells tinkling, and snow glistening. And oh oh, it's ecstasy, this feeling. All the tension in my neck peeling away, and my shoulders drop a good six inches. My two friends have me locked in a new kind of clinch between them, their hands together, and me coddled in between. Divine arrangement: as we toddle and tussle towards the Medical Centre, which is where our venture is headed. Not without dread – of a hassle for all of us, as there's always the possibility of failure to get a repeat prescription automatically, and having to see the doctor. Which tactically would be disastrous. All wrong, and ponging of booze as we do. Those three different indifferent doctors would unanimously cut off our supplies. Imagine none between us, no Libbies nor jellies nor sleepers, no Dalmane, and the raw pain ensues without patience or pity, and our shabby old comfy city becomes a terrible place full of demons and grotesque faces in the dark, chasing us around. Its parks full of menace and meanness and anger lurking everywhere. Jumpy isn't the word. The lamp posts all fell on my head every time I ventured out last time, and I seemed to be climbing hills slowly all the time, yet never moving. Except to fall down flat on my face, ill and sick and shaking, and never wanting to wake up, or get up, when a solicitous passer-by tried to help me. They *do* help you in Sheffield, if you collapse completely. Don't like it, don't want to, don't relish it. But they *will* help in the end, embarrassed and muttering and resentful, but *there*. And caring that tiny bit. Which you'd never get in London where they don't give a shit for anybody.

Like my two friends here, helping me carefully, weaving round the puddles, so I don't slither through any on my wobbly legs. I feel so much stronger for this cuddling together. Can face anything. Just wish it could go on longer. For ever. But I know that it never lasts. Bliss like this is only given to be taken away. So grab it while you can, and don't ask fundamental questions about your entitlement. It's not the place. And anyway, there's no trace of justice about it. Some get godly-given every advantage. And some get none, not one. I know a woman who's so ugly, of a really repellent ugliness so you can't look at her without grimacing to yourself. I've tried every way to see some human beauty and character in her, and there isn't any. She's just ugly, with a personality to match. And vicious. But that must be due to her ugliness, maybe. Now Toby would say, What disgusting crap – Everyone has some positive point and potential for development. And theoretically, I agree. But I can't see much starting point with vicious Vera at the "Collier's Arms", a landlady of such vast charmlessness and nastiness you'd think the brewery would pay her to go away.

"Still. We can't all be the beautiful people" I say happily to my friends, to convince them I'm OK. They can now concentrate on worrying about themselves again.

Natty chuckles. "Yu've come round Man. I see you fainting clean away den"

And Jean grunts almost affectionately: "Yes, pull yerself together luv. We're here now"

Indeed we are. In the carpark. Feeling frightened, and fear fear fear is no help at all. You have to be healthy to get anywhere at this place. And it's awful as we go in. They all stare, and nudge each other. Those rows of hostile eyes. Even the children stare with open mouths. It's terrifying when children reject you, they're usually so trusting poor lambs. Which is why they get into such messes. Or maybe this lot are brutalised by messes already, and that's why they all seem to be fixing us with steady malevolent glares. As if planning a pogrom – and we're the Jews. A few wretched innocents, without a cat-in-hell's chance.

"Well dat's all 'appening here ain't it. What a party" says Natty. We all giggle nervously, sending waves of whisky over the receptionist. She really is such a dried up prune, you could squash her flat and wouldn't get a drop of juice.

"Yes" she snaps, and spits at the same time, taking a step back, as the fumes hit her,

"Yes Yes" rap rap.

"We've got prescriptions"

"Names. Your's first"

I tell her my name, in a low apologetic voice, and she writes it down.

"Address" The bitch.

"I. No fixed, I'm afraid". Head up. Dignity does it. Think of daisies in a green field, with a Jersey cow mincing over daintily on her high heeled hooves, and lowering those eyelashes and pouting like Bardot, and her lovely orange hips swaying.

"Moooo" I say, carried away.

She looks from one to the other of us, carefully, and takes off her glasses. Putting them down so she can't see us any more, and looking myopically over our heads.

"You have to have an address to be registered here"

"Yu know we don't. Yu know dat's not de truth. Yu just showing us up – making dis fuss"

"You have to have an . . ."

She's capable of playing the tape all day, without modification. I decide my best Oxford brogue is required:

"Listen, Snot Bitch. We're all registered patients. We all have a doctor, and you know that. And we have three repeat prescriptions waiting for us here, which we collect every month on the same day, because we're friends, and because it happened like that. And you can't deny us access to a doctor.

You can have the address of a Social Services Hostel where we stay, but there's no way you can refuse us. So *please*, can we have our prescriptions?"

"NO"

"Pardon?"

"NO. We've stopped repeat prescriptions. You'll have to see the doctor"

"Oh Christ." Jean clutches by arm.

I try again: "That's nonsense we never did before"

"Well you do now." She'd changed her tack, and forgotten addresses.

"And there's a queue for all four doctors, as you can see. So who do you all see? And I'll find your records."

"Oh *NO*"

"What'll we do Charlie?"

I feel sick, and wish I wasn't the one always expected to cope with officialdom. But there's no way out of this one:

"We'll have to see 'em"

"Oh Christ"

"Come on Jean. It'll be OK"

We give her our full names, and she says "Where's the other one? The Irish one"

"In hospital"

"Well, well. What about *that*." She looks vindicated, triumphant. Jean looks dangerous.

"Let's sit down"

I hurry them away, to the only seats left at the side facing the hateful audience. Natty sticks her tongue out. Three lager loutesses, facing the foe – the pious pursed-up public. Unfortunately, not so pursed up. A fat juvenile turd starts shouting at Natty:

"Nig nog nig nog wogs go home"

"What a sweetheart" I say, enraged, and feeling desperation rising in my throat, choking me, checking Natty's expression. Which is blank.

"Go fuck your mother" she says, under her breath. But not low enough. There's a deathly hush. They heard they heard. And then three fat women rush to the front:

"That nigger swore at my boy" pointing back at Natty unnecessarily. They're all grey English stews in that room otherwise.

"Mind your language you over there, or you'll be out" says the receptionist.

"Shut the fuck up" says Natty, calmly, casually.

"Listen! Listen!" shrieks the fat Mother.

"Out. Out. You're out"

"Do it den. Put me out" Natty picks up a magazine. There's a lynching mob of fat Yorkshire matriarchs, focusing all that anxiety and poverty and dread of coming to the doctor's on their timeless victim. And not just matriarchs:

"Gerremout!" yells a fat father, with tattoos on his fists he's shaking at us.

"Eyup. I know 'er. It's that Sykes slag. 'Er kids are in care. They took 'em away"

Jean's face is livid. She lunges at the woman, who's come close to check her identity. But I deflect it, and hold her hand instead:

"Jean Jean. We need the stuff. Jean, please ignore them" Jean starts blubbering, big dirty tears washing down, and grinding her teeth. She's drowning in grief and guilt, and I try to see the funny side of all these sickly persecutors savaging the sickest, the smallest. Because there usually is a funny side. In any situation. And this is what saves me when I'm desperate. But here there isn't one. There just isn't. If I work on it a million years, there's no humour rescuable from this: bold brassy brash faces, leering, accusing, menacing, hating. It's the working class in all its pristine glory and claustrophobic conformity, sensing outsiders a mile away, to despise, disparage, destroy. To puff themselves up better, bigger, for the cosy hate experience, congratulating each other afterwards. An ugly, ululating mob:

"We showed 'em"

A doctor appears, looking harassed and thin next to these big fat demented creatures, calming them with his white coat and authority of the stethoscope bulging in his pocket:

"You lot will have to leave. You're causing trouble" he

says to us. And Natty stands up over him, tall and regal, making him ridiculous. And them and them, these puny people, waiting for us to be punished for existing. Eager, excited, baying for a fight. But prepared to wait, if he'll take over the hate campaign.

"Dem's racists. Yu too?"

"It's nothing to do with racism. You're causing trouble in here, and you've been drinking. You'll have to leave"

"Balls" says Jean. "And bounce 'em"

"NOW. You'll have to leave NOW ladies. We don't treat people who've been drinking"

"What if I was dying of drink?" I ask.

"Then you'd be hospitalised. Which might be a good idea, looking at you. What's your name?"

I tell him our names, and stare at him long and hard. He's my doctor, and he knows my name too well, and he's delivered many happy homilies on my personal tragedy. But I don't want to be special. I'm with them. It's the herd instinct. They're my friends under threat. But I'm sweating like mad, and on the point of collapse again, and he can see it. As large as the lady from reception, who's looming in front of me. But it's swimming around, a sea of sound and fury signifying so much. But I can't focus. I'm fading fading. He touches my arm, and I feel the alarm. It's instant electric, and old as the hills, a doctor's concern, you've got to be ill. Oh God I don't want to let them down, and he's frowning and guiding me away from my friends.

"She's our fren. We go wid her"

"No you don't. You're out. I'll just see her a minute" he says to the receptionist. "Get the nurse"

"Look. I'm only pissed. Let me go with them"

"Bloody queue jumper" the fat mother shouts.

"I've found their prescription forms Doctor. Shall I give them to them while they're drunk?" says the receptionist, deferential, coquettish, yuk.

"You cow. You said they'd stopped it" says Jean.

"You see Doctor, how drunk and aggressive they are.

I didn't dare give them prescriptions like that. It could be dangerous"

"Yes Miss Tonks. Quite right"

"Miss Tonks Miss Tonks de bonking Miss Tonks" screams out Natty.

" . . . who honks" say I, feeling so wonky it's excusable. Because finally there's humour to rescue me, and I can focus again. I start laughing, a bit hysterically, but laughing. And there's the faintest glimmer of humour at the corners of his mouth, this doctor. Suddenly I trust him. I even lust after him madly in that moment. I'm so glad he's responding humanly, not the wooden effigy I'd painted him. But I'm fainting again, slipping, sinking into his warm embrace. It's warm, it's warm, his arm's so warm and calm and comforting. I want him so much . . .

And next thing, I'm blinking at a harsh bright glare above me, and feeling bilious with this ghastly grating in my throat, and a big black face, it's beaming at me, but I don't know it. It's not Natty. What the hell's going on? Or is this heaven?

"You'll be allright now just relax dearie"

"What?" I try to say, but my throat hurts so much, I cough and splutter, and that's worse, much worse.

"You just lay back and rest and don't worry 'bout a thing." It sounds like a ring-a-ding dong song of childhood, flooding over me. All maudlin memory I become at once. But it didn't have these Jamaican accents then, like a reggae beat. Yet it was the same taking away of pain by that refrain "don't worry 'bout a thing", she says it again, and I want to hold her hand. But she's standing too far away, so I wave my hand and she leans over and takes it, and I feel such unbelievable peace and joy and infinite release for at least three seconds, till my brain my bloody bloody brain starts working overtime.

"Where am I?" rasping gasping choking.

"In hospital my love. Yu be fine now. All dat stuff's gone away"

"Stuff?"

"All dem spirits inside yu making yu bad yu'll be better now"

"What happened?" don't tell me.

"Yu'm sick in de doctor's so dem bunged yu here and yu had yu insides cleaned out an yu outsides too an everything's juss fine. I cleaned yu outsides an yu clothes is in de laundry I not s'posed to but I see'd to it myself"

"Clothes? You've taken my clothes?"

"Only fe tonight" she looks hurt.

"No I'm pleased thank you very much. My throat. WHAT HAVE THEY DONE TO MY THROAT?"

"Dat's de stomach-pump. Yu be fine now"

"You mean they put a pipe down . . ." the vision is too awful. I feel utterly betrayed by my doctor. I'd been on the point of laying him right there in the waiting room. So much for sudden rushes of affection or passion when you're weak.

"Yu a lucky lady" she confides.

"Tell me, tell me"

"Dem didn't put yu in Ward 56"

"Oh" Lord be praised. She even raises a wan smile in me. I've heard of the House of Horror for drying out – the dreaded psychiatric Ward 56 of the Northern General. This *is* the Northern General? Yes, it says so on the sheet red spider stitching, like blood, like veins should look. I'm spooked at my proximity to the nightmare house.

"Dem get you in dere yu never be free. No yu be lucky lady"

"You don't think they'll transfer me?" nervously.

"Not if yu behaves. Yu got a visitor"

"Can I see them? *Please*"

"Only one" Oh God what happened to the other?

"He's right here do yu feel well enough?"

"*HE?*" Ah yes, it must be Toby. Go to hell Toby, with your Meaning Well looks. I want to be alone. "No I don't feel so well. Not just now" But she's already smiling at somebody else behind my head, beyond the curtain.

"That's nice. Flowers. Now you be a good gentleman and only stay two minutes" and she's off. Oh God don't leave me,

I only just found you. It's all happening so *fast*, I can't take it in, and feel so so sick.

"A gentleman caller" says the man in a soft Tennessee Williams drawl, and it's Heather, standing there with a big bunch of it, fresh from the Moors. He's tall and gentle, and I wave my hand again, which is a trick I must cultivate. It's magic. He's holding it and kissing it, *kissing* my filthy mit. I can't have it, but lo, the hand's clean, I see I'm scrubbed pristine. But that means . . . oh God, Good God!

"WHERE'S MY HAT?" I screech in terror, clutching my head, but with the other hand – I'm not about to release him.

"Who needs hats with a head like yours? Charlie you're beautiful" he murmurs "but you're fading away from us"

"NO I'm NOT" I say, and sit up sharply. My throat hurts so much, but not half so much as my pride – a raw gaping wide wide wound that my secret love has seen my baldness. Bottomless perdition. "I've no dignity if I can't cover my head *please* Heather *do* something" and he reaches into his carrier bag and brings out a bottle of whisky "This will take care of everything"

Which has a familiar ring of truth about it. A sweet seductive ting-a-ling, and I want to drink it but it won't go down. It burns, and I retch, and it's all over the covers, and he's looking at me, disapproving, disappointed, and gets out a joint instead, lighting it with one hand, I won't let him go.

"Oh NO yu don't, young man. Ah me, she's sick. NO smoking in here. Yu can smell dat spirit in what she's sicked up. Now off yu go. She's not well enough. Put dat out!" and he drifts off in a cloud of dope, with a bitter backward glance, my hope my chance my solace my last battered shattered romance.

13

Anyway, the day doesn't have to end up as badly as it started, I always say, and indeed this one improves by the minute, as Bridie suddenly appears round the curtain, and cheers me up so fantastically I want to weep, and sweep her into my arms, and dance away off down the aisle, waving farewell to hospitals in style, and all hells on wheels like this one feels, tucked firmly in as I am, and forbidden visitors. Except this vision, who's run all the way down two flights of stairs when they told her I was here.

"They said the Professoress is in Emergency. I had to see you, now they've moved you in here. So near but so far. Oh Charlie, you look so *ill*"

"Rubbish. How are *you* fair maid. You look wonderful" and she did she *did* – all wild hair, though frail pallid and pale in a way it's valid to be if you're Irish.

"I feel a lot better. But Charlie I'm *dying* for a drink and a smoke. I'd just *die* for them"

"Yes. Yes" Oh dear "Yes"

"They say it will kill me if I do. But it surely will if I don't. You won't try to stop me, will you Charlie?" anxious, urgent, pleading.

"Not on your nelly"

"I was so afraid you'd all say I couldn't, and would exclude me from our little group for my own good

"Nothing so virtuous"

"Oh Charlie it's so good to see you. I'm still the same, but I had so many transfusions – it's a wonder. I'm full as a tic of other people's blood, perfect strangers and all. A bloody vampire I be. Oh Charlie, it's so *good* to see you". She hugs me, and I feel full of tears and terrible fears for that little body. I can feel her bones sticking into mine, *mine*, I remember a sign to remind me of my own bloody plight. Not much better really, though I hadn't spilled my life blood yet. Oh the memory of it flooding out of her mouth makes me squeeze her so hard.

"It's just no sodding good being locked up as a sinner. We must get out and off and about our business" I declare womanfully, and with more energy than I feel "When can you go?"

"When I want"

"And you want?"

"Oh yes Charlie"

"Come on then" I'm out of bed and in a dressing gown and off down the corridor, pit-patter with bare feet cold so cold on the stone floor.

"Where's the laundry?"

"A fine time to be washing" she smiles. Luvly luvly smile.

"They've pinched my clothes to wash. Where are yours?"

"Upstairs. I'll go and get dressed and meet you here"

I'm rounding the corner, looking for the laundry, which my nurse had said was down here, and straight into my doctor, and feel like Jean with my question: Whazzee doing here?

"Ah. Dr. McCloud" he says weighing me up "You're shivering"

"Yes, and some blithering idiot has taken my clothes"

"You should be in bed"

"How so?"

"For observation and tests. I want them to test your liver. I came to see how you were" and he delivers this, plop, into the space between us, as I realise he's doing me a big favour. In spite of myself, I savour the moment, still fancying him slightly, in his tight-lipped sternness, with the mirth lines at the mouth corners that give him away.

"Hooray, hooray, pleased to see you, but I must be on my way. I have a life to lead" and I'm not pleading either for my freedom. I try a salacious grin, but then remember my head's bare, and overwhelmed with shame, I start to blame him for everything "There was no need to push me in here"

"You were in an alcoholic coma"

"It happens"

"Often"

"It happens" I feel uncomfortable and so bloody cold standing there, bald and revealed, as if he's peeling off layers of protection just staring at me congealing in my own mess. I must have a drink, my head's spinning, but the cold's winning and I let him escort me back to bed, where he sits on it, trapping me, flight aborted. What about Bridie waiting?

"You'll hate me for saying this but . . ."

"Then don't. I prefer to like you"

". . . but you'll be dead in a few months if you don't stop it. You're vomiting and fainting and malnutrition is written all over your face. Are you still menstruating?"

Well I don't want to talk about periods with a hunky medico, no matter how modern and bristling. "I'll just go if you give me my Librium, and get out of your hair"

"Dr. McCloud, I can't let you throw away your life like this"

"S'mine"

"Yes"

"All I've got left"

"Yes. Why why why"

"No point without a joint?"

He sighs miserably.

"Cheer up. I really will go away. Change my doctor. You won't have to worry"

"I will worry whatever you do"

Oh my, and I was trying to be flippant and free, and he was *serious* about my life. It makes me panic, that and withdrawals. I start shaking, and put my hands under the covers to conceal it. He knows.

"You're lucky it's not serious DTs, but I expect the tranquillisers are still in your system"

"Listen. I have got serious DTs coming on. Why don't you bugger off and leave me. I only want my tablets"

He sighs again miserably. "OK" and pulls his pad out scribbling.

" – and a sick note. I need a sick note for the DSS"

"OK" he's finished. Defeated. It makes me frantic. But I can't rekindle his interest, not now. The only way would be by saying Help me, and that I would never ever ever say, because the buggers would, and then God help me, drink and drugless and facing it all over again, when I know I couldn't. It's always lurking, waiting to take me over – the panic the fear the crawlies. How could a smug pig like this one ever understand about the crawlies eating you away.

"And here are some multivitamins. You need B complex by the look of your scalp"

Oh mortification

"Thankyou Doctor"

"Good luck Doctor" he says with sarcasm now, and he's off and I'm free, and there's Bridie clutching my clothes, looking scared of the doctor.

"They'd even washed your pumps"

Yes they had, and nearly disintegrated them finally, and my four pairs of fishing socks were dangling over her arm.

"I came to look for you in the laundry and found them all laid out and folded, like a Dry Cleaners. Oh Charlie, it was comical, even your scarf's been washed. They're kind people, surely they are"

"GOTOGETOGETHERTOGET some booze" I state the obvious with such relish that Bridie cheers up, and we stagger off away away from the place, and not a bit grateful. They'd saved our lives. It meant taking responsibility again, and there'd been something so secure about being tucked up tightly, not fighting every minute for drinks. But here we are, wondering where to start, and I'm determined not to think about Bridie's bleeding. She's heeding no warnings. She can't, she says. She can't stop taking it, she's out of control, the booze the fags and the tranquillisers have her soul, and there's no role for reason in this scenario. You just go with the flow with the vibes eating away at your insides, not turned on, but off off off, you want it to be switched off, the panic the pain the fear.

We get our prescriptions, after ages trying to sign the forms on the back. My hands are shaking so much I can't hold the pen, and then I fake Bridie's signature too, she's worse than me. How can that be, two weeks in pure clean hospital conditions? But she's been brutally starved of her goodies, and is now just a dumb pining wino who's got to have a fix. Yet the ghouls at the post office won't give us two envelopes for our sick notes to send, so we wend our weary teary ways towards the hostelry and hope our sisterhood can come up with something good. Doubtful doubtful, Jean's in a mess, I can see as soon as I open the door, something is alarming her. But it doesn't stop her warm welcome.

"I would have come to fetch you silly girls with some booze, but I've got some here here here" so it's all OK for the moment.

"What's wrong Jean"

"It's my kids"

Her kids in care are such taboo, you never dare mention them, but here she is volunteering her sorrow, like no tomorrow. It all comes tumbling out "I'm worried I'm so worried. It's horrid up there, and all the kids are scared of something. There's summat going on. Summat *evil*. I know it"

"How evil, Jean" asks Bridie, who's convinced it exists.

"Just evil. I feel it. The kids won't talk to me properly, but little Melanie's terrified, and they're, you know, *embarrassed* with me"

"With you? Their mum?"

"Some mum" shamefaced "but yes, with me"

Jean tell us what you mean, spell it out, say it, this hell is killing you. She screws up her courage:

"I think they're being messed about with"

"You mean sex abuse"

109

"Oh God Oh God"

"Come on Jean, calm down" I take her hands as she's standing, shaking from head to foot "Come on tell us Jean. It's OK"

"Oh God I can't bear it"

Then share it, you can you can Jean. What a bloody time for a cathartic therapy session, when we haven't a fag between us. But there, you can't arrange these things.

"I can't talk in front of *her*" and she grimaces to the corner. I look for the first time, seeing another bundle of rags, huddled up, head down on the floor "she's a *real* loony" Jean even now clinging to status and exclusion of the Other, who mutters mildly "ten tins of baked beans four sardines Mr Kipling's cakes yer fucking piece a shit ten tins of baked beans four sardines and Mr Kipling's cakes yer fucking fucking piece a shit" and starts over again.

"That's all she's said all day" says Jean, imploring us to do something.

"Come on, she's not listening at all to you" Bridie says "tell us about your kids"

"Well" and the door flies open, banging, and we all jump. Even the lump in the corner lightens her load an octave or two: "ten beans sardines Mr Kipling . . ."

"Dem bastards dem. Charlie, Bridie, wonders wonders" and we are four again, and no fifth column allowed. A closed cliqued crowd. It disgusts me. I never trust in-groups. Always been the outsider myself. Don't want this stealthy, smug, sealing of boundaries, with folk outside. Like a bloody family, my God.

"So tell us" I say, and Jean looks around her, dismayed, nervous, about to betray the worst secret of her life. Let go, let go, we'll help you, let go.

"They joke about sore bums. Like it's an infection going round at that place Brampton Lodge. And I've heard stories. Stories about the dirty raincoat brigade up there"

"What?"

"Men going up there when it's dark. I've seen 'em myself"

"What sort of men?"

"I told you dirty raincoats"

"Real wankers" says Natty "In a kids home! Bloody funny dat's weird man"

"Couldn't they work there?"

"NO" she's contemptuous "Bridie whazz wrong"

Bridie's staring in horror at Jean, eyes wide, blazing.

"I *hate* them. I *hate* them"

"Who?"

"These men. Let's find out. Let's destroy them"

"Are you sure Jean?"

How dare I question a mother? Me, whose dried up womb is a tomb of insensitivity on the fact of children.

"Silly bleedin' bitch – would I say?"

"No. Let's go and see them your kids and talk to them. Could we do that?"

"Well . . ." she looks nervously from one to the other, fixing on Natty.

"Nope. I won't go, big black bongos, frightening de natives won't do, will it Jean, don't worry" She's offended, I can tell, and flounces out the door. But Jean looks relieved, and apologetic at me. She knows I hate it hate it, this vile pile at the bottom of her, at the root of the culture she comes from, rotten stinking racist cancer.

"Will you help me Charlie?"

"We'll help you" says Bridie, giving me a look at once ethereal and regal and regimental, meaning *it's not the time*, and she's right, stop fighting on all fronts, let it go, the poor woman's suffering enough without prim moralism from me. But how is Natty feeling?

Nevertheless "Yes come on" I say "let's go and getem"

Brampton Lodge is a big grey grim splodge on the horizon in Crookesmoor, a dollop of concrete with a few struggling trees, and a discreet sign saying its name. But no matter how demure and pure and sterile, its fame is that of a rowdy place of untamed delinquent kids, which should be closed down, like us, as an offence to decent citizens, as the inmates spend their lives contemplating thieving violence and all kinds of predations on the public at large, criminals too young to be charged with anything.

"You see, the Social Worker won't listen to me 'cos I'm mental. Well she thinks I'm mental, and imagining things"

"But a mother knows her kids" says Natty, sagacious and graciously charming to Jean by now. She's agreed to go to the home with us, to look after us convalescents and lurk about outside, in case she's needed later.

"Yes. A mother knows" says Bridie, and where comes all this worldly wisdom into motherhood, written in the runes stuff, from these two, who as far as I know haven't had any either. But both are confident, nay arrogant, about it. I can only cower away and count my prune stones.

"Doesn't she Charlie?" they nudge me, struggling along between them, and I feel wings are beating on both sides to prise me into the plot. But

"I'm the first to shut up when I don't know"

"'Course you *know*" Natty digs me harder this time.

"Well it seems to me kids can be conniving sickening little brats, and their mothers are often the last to *know* and recognise what's going on . . ." I don't know why I suddenly had this inane passion for my version of the truth at that moment, trudging up West Street again. It must have been the hospital swill out, but there's no doubt whatsoever it was a huge mistake, as it always is – getting philosophical and fundamental on social occasions, or anywhere really in England, speaking the truth as you see it, instead of gluey social noises of rank hypocrisy. So dark and dire this mire of treachery, I was glad to live in France, for a while at least. I know it can be different, but here even Natty, our good straight Yorkshire Natty, is on the side of solace and comfort, and anyway it's myth about blunt Northerners, that's just euphemism for rudeness. They tell you to your face you're a cunt to please you almost, where they detect a posh accent. I'm on their tails, no matter how Yorkshire they wail their wily ways in a dim haze. But you do find it warmer and

superficially friendlier in the North, which is why I'm
breaking the rules here with my cool attempt at logic, not
needed, not required. Women must give each other confidence, not say cold cruel things that bring them down, in the
name of truth. Stop playing the male game. You were educated like a man, bad luck all those spurious universal values.
Now pass the buck, and shut the fuck up, which is just what
Natty is saying:

"Shut the fuck up what do you know about it"

"Well quite. I admit it. Listen we don't always have to
have a consensus. You don't need to feel threatened 'cos I
don't necessarily agree"

"Aw Charlie"

"Yes dat don't go down Charlie"

"Yes Charlie it's not right when I'm worried"

And here it is again, that old old feeling, that timeless
reeling away from emotions that I've had all my life, since
schooling started, telling me you don't have to be a prisoner
of your emotions, and I had carefully cultivated my mind to
stop being a blind useless bough, bending with every wind. I
wanted to think and control my life, and look at me, look at
me. They're right. I must fight my training and join in
harmony, fitting in togetherness they all admire, and I need
so bloody much myself. I want my freedom, just like a fella,
to bellow my reason and bully the world with it. Yet flee to
the warmth of the womb when it hurts. All that big bold
brave belligerence. In fact I need a wife, as all intellectuals
do, a warm bundle of emotions by the hearth and home to
wait for me – wanderer in realms of the rational, the real, the
outside world. Not that the real is the rational at all, would
that it were. But in trying to make it so, we incubated from
emotions, by that desperate sublimation game which made
us intellectuals in the first place. Oh, by the grace of some
divine freak, I was doomed to speak in twisted tongue
of the emotionally blind, and when it does finally unwind,
this repression job, we blow completely, defeating any
rationality whatsoever, and harmony the ideal is thrown over
for this revealing chaos. I'm in the sin and loony bin of

educated wimmin, so I draw back and forth towards and away from these warm wonderful women. Neither woman nor man I am, just intellectual spam for the world's androgynous sandwich.

I'm sitting on a window sill, making a snowball by myself, rejected by group disgust, thinking how you can't trust appearances because the place looks bright and homely today with its face snow covered and the dourness not showing at all, when a little bundle of fury comes comes hurtling out the door, sluthering and slipping in the sludge, and landing on the floor near me in a pile. It's Melanie, the daughter, screaming her head off, and I'm no expert, but she looks very distressed, and if that's how visits from the blessed mother make you feel, well really I'm glad I abstained on the judgment.

"Aunty Charlie Aunty Charlie don't let them make me don't let them." She spied me from inside the building, and now clings to my bottom layer of skirts, covered in dirt herself from her fall, and telling her all now to the infidel "It's my bum they want to know about, my bum sore, and I can't say. They won't play with me any more if I do, so don't make me say, Aunty Charlie." I'm listening, fascinated firstly by the way her speech rhythms emulate the way my brain functions, always this chiming rhyming. It must be that the booze has arrested my development and frozen it at about the age of six like this.

"Aunty Charlie don't let them get me"

"Who Melanie?"

"My mum and Aunty Bridie. You hide me away" and she tries to get under my billowing hippy skirts again. It's getting nippy when she lifts them. God it's *cold*.

"Listen, little one. You have to say what's wrong with your bum for it to get better"

"NO" she screams.

"Is somebody hurting it?"

"NO NO"

I don't believe her, to put it mildly, and now Robin and

114

Mark gallop up and start cursing at their little sister "You better not a teld"

"I dint I dint"

"You betta not"

"I dint I dint"

"I'll smack yer one if yer did. Wallop wallop"

"Hello" I say intervening starkly with dark threatening looks of warning, but their hooks are too deep into this little girl. She closes up completely.

"Won't *ever* say"

"What won't she say Robin?" I appeal to his seniority as boss man, but he's poker faced as her, and the three of them run off together – a boy on each side of a little girl's truth, crushing it out of her. But I know for certain now that she's somebody else's toy too, a blonde little pawn, pulled and drawn into black holes of hell, where only horrors dwell, and it's time I helped her out . . .

"No need to shout bloody hell" I yell back at Natty, who's screaming in my ear about her fears for the kids:

"Dem been BUGGERED"

"Yes"

"BUGGERED Charlie. Dem's just kids"

"Yes"

"What yu gonna do"

"I'm thinking"

"My God dem's BUGGERING kids an she *thinking*"

"How do you know Natty?"

"I only heard 'em talking to yu, but I KNOW AN YU SHOULD"

"Where were you?"

"Round dat corner having a drink and yu have one here now an a fag an we decide calmly WHAT DE HELL WE GONNA DO"

"Where's Jean?"

"She fell apart wid Bridie helping her"

"Useful"

"Aw Charlie yu saw dem kids is bad fe her"

"I know I know"

"Yu do sumpin Charlie. Yu do it. I'm telling ya. It's gotta be done"

"Yes"

and next morning in my cleaner's gear and scarf low over my face and full of cider, I set off again for the place, to do what a girl's gotta do . . .

14

Getting into buildings where you don't belong is a pantomime
of bluff, and it's easiest for me in my cleaner's stuff than the
other way, which would be pompous bluster as a Ministry of
Health Official, or sartorial Professor visiting from Albania,
with my thick Russian accent, which is ever so fluent and
flashy, and got me into academic bashes and banquets at the
top table several times. But they're pastimes requiring clothes
for the pose to be effective, and I can't be selective in my
present discomposure. So it's Beryl the Cleaner, lured from
her last job by the higher salary here, which endears them to
you no end, so friendly you can't get on with your work, and
a woman's work is never done. I tell 'em Must get on, Don't
stop me, and they're ever so pleased not to, easing your way
by cups of tea and sandwiches free, as long as you never see
a real cleaner. It would be a hatchet job invading their patches
for a bob or two they'd think, never dreaming you were
scheming something different and not blacklegging at all.

The snow is melting slush slush slurp under my pumps
and down I go sluthering slithering on my bum bump bump
thump, and it hurts more than usual this floor contact 'cos
my cleaner's kit has thin trousers under my overall, and not
the flowing padding of my hippy outfit with it's seven skirts
swirling and whirling and willing and free. Still mustn't
grumble. I've got a bottle of cider inside me, and £2 in the
till from this morning outside Victoria Wines where they're
all buying their Xmas stock, and I've got enough real fags to
last me, without rolling. You can't be rolling when you're on
a mission. It gives me a self-importance I haven't had for
years, though there's always that residue of fear lurking to
knock me sideways if I get a phase of panic. But I can get me
some more cider if it happens, can't I? can't I?

Nothing to fear at all in this entrance hall of slime green

walls and bright lemon lights, enhancing and heightening the bilious effect. As I stand there, entranced, and dreaming about colour schemes that would liven things up, my tummy tightens as I hear voices, and scoot down the first corridor, not seeing a soul. Wo sind die Kinder denn? A bloody kids' home of silent ghosts so far. Where are mine hosts then, and all those bare kiddy bums I've come about? Though I'm not likely to interrupt a happening. They must take place behind locked doors, which they all are along this corridor. I pause to reconnoitre. Without a strategy it seems the only thing to do. What *do* you do? Holler Yoohoo, will any pest sex-molesting children please come out and be counted. It's all a bit hammy my detection, so I shuffle further on, mopping away, swish swosh sloppetty slop, with my fag hanging out like Bogey from the mouth corner, and thinking of mouth corners, I get very horny reflecting on the good doctor and his worthy concern for me, which would be such earnest stuff were it not for that touch of hilarity round his gills, which he's doing all he can to cool and overrule and chill to the bone. But I know it's there, and I'm on to him, and he knows I know, but he wouldn't dare would he, and there's my baldness to consider after all . . .

"Put that cigarette out!"

I jump a mile.

"NOW, I say." He's a greasy little weasel, just 2 ft 6 in square, but a smug little thug nevertheless. They're always the worst, the little fat ones, compensating.

"You should clean the top floor first, particularly staff quarters and dormitories"

"Yessir" I stub out the fag with my fingers and he screws up his face in disgust looking hard, so hard, at my neat little feet hanging out of my plimsolls. So off I gallop slop slopping to the stairs and heave ho up them as fast and nimble as a lamb, and at the top of three flights get a sighting: "Staffrooms." I trip through there very rapidly, there's nothing happening or likely to. Cold white and gleaming places with brown blankets and chairs, without a photograph or hairbrush on show. The real cleaner must be a go-go girl, it was spotless and obviously not where they live. Or do the staff live here anyway? But a man comes in and says Good Afternoon. So I shuffle out and on to the next corridor, which is full of bedrooms as well, but telling tales of children this time, with clothes strewn about everywhere on the beds behind neat little curtains of blue and the next room pink, and no prizes for guessing what those colour schemes mean. But not a child in sight.

Then I see why, through the window on the playing field behind. They're all out there, shouting and waving and running after a ball, boys and girls together having fun after all, and the streaming sun of a frosty afternoon making it a magic winter wonderland of happy family harmony. Except we know there's no such thing don't we, or they wouldn't be here, the little dears, the walking talking disasters in the wrong hands. And what male hands are right hands I think nastily. But not meaning it a bit, since I love nothing better than a strong pair on me if the mood takes me, and it keeps coming back today that I feel that way. But I always do with my period. Randy as anything. Great bursting breasts, and wanting a thirsty old male to suck and suck and suck. By old, I mean over fifty you understand. I don't go for toy boys at all, and prefer them on the old side, mature looking at least. Though we know it's only appearance, having a feast with my breasts like a greedy infant suckling suckling, before they take me and fuck me right back into the womb they're coming coming hello mum I've arrived. But it's a million miles away from being a child just feeling and acting like one and the idea, THE IDEA of sexuality around kids appals me so deeply that I'm almost weeping at what I might find evidence of here. And where do I look for it anyway? At kids at play so innocently on a suddenly dark December day?

And dark December gets darker by the minute as I explore that top floor east wing, following a trail of Xmas decorations to where they end abruptly at a locked door. But the next one's ajar, so I push it wide and slosh inside, nodding at the occupant – a sleepy giant with a beard, and I'm sloshing round him. So he puts his feet on the desk, and I glance craftily at his long long legs. Just my type long ago, when I chose the masculine hairy strong ones. And he'd do fine now if it wasn't for my fringe, and the fact that I'm supposed to be his char. Though the latter doesn't matter. I've known many a gentleman lay his charlady literally, and many more fantasise about such delicious slumming. You'd be surprised how screwing the real wretched of the workers turns on the bosses, especially the ones with expensive coiffured perfumed wives. They do it to them dreaming of the cleaner's grey bloomers wrapped round her ankles as they push past her overall and have her hard and mean like a sex machine, they say afterwards to themselves, gloating with glee at the kinkiness of it.

How do I know? Well I do, and it's true I've been at this pretend cleaning lark for a few years now, and I've had many a leer and lunge round the bathroom with them plunging their hot little mits up my knee length bloomers and grabbing my tits in the study. It's studies that really get them going. The trick is to carefully dust their books, climbing up on ladders with your own laddered tights showing as well, like Nora Batty, and even a smell of Flash doesn't do any harm. I turned round one day and there was the Senior Lecturer busy with himself saying "Funny word that *Flash*" and he asked me to finish him off in my mouth. So I pretended I hadn't heard him and carried on dusting the bottom shelf, and he came all over my head instead from behind. I said Thankyou very much indeed, such speed and delivery, and he said come tomorrow with red ones. I said red what? He said knickers, long knickers. She used to wear long red knickers. And he gave me fifty quid the next day to parade in long red bloomers I got from a jumble sale, and then let him come inside them. Just inside the elastic near my knee, and then he said witheringly "You despicable trollop", and I haven't mentioned that he'd asked me to do a dollop for him to watch as well. But I'd refused that ultimate indignity. We have our pride and piles to consider. See there's not much I didn't learn about yearning on my rounds in the houses of the wealthy. Not to mention the booze you could down. Which is why I went –

to drown in it. But I got caught so many times in the end, that I only do it now in emergencies or for a friend like today.

And here I am, like a stray dog stranded in an alien land, the ground under my feet turning to quicksand as this beard scrutinises me, suddenly interested. Though he's definitely not the usual type of bottom wiper.

"My mum's a cleaner" he says in this husky voice, and there's a tusk or a tooth or a catch in his throat and I try to gloat with pride in my profession, though I don't know how to look gloating and end up shuffling quickly to the window, with a remote glassy distant expression at the kids below. Do not show any reaction. You will betray yourself. He's a Social Worker and they suss out booze a mile away. So I keep my mouth shut stern and firm. Who cares about your mum?

"She's not my real mum. I was fostered. Then adopted by them. That's why I do this now. She was the kindest mum in the world, but we were very poor . . ."

I start to polish a chair vigorously.

". . . so poor, she took in washing as well when dad left her"

I nod gravely, thinking Poor exploited bitch, slaving away so you can sit here all day on your degrees. Like I did for years, but always felt guilty when I had a cleaner fussing round me. I must fuss more to look authentic. I now dust his ashtray, longing to pocket those long dog ends, but throw them away with a sigh.

"Why are you sighing?" he says.

I was dreading a question.

"Xmas" I growl, and he nods. That will do. He knows about Xmas phobia from his poor deprived past, which he's going to treat me to if I don't scarper quick.

"Come back after, when you've done" I glide out, forgetting to shuffle for once. I have to hide myself better than this. I'm fucking dizzy and need a drink, so light a cig which makes me keel over, reel over with vertigo. But what he doesn't know, the languid Son in there, is that I pocketed his handful of keys on the way out, and with the speed of light I try them all in the next door, and the last one fits, and I'm in quick as a flash. It's all splashes of Xmas colour everywhere. Trimmings of streamers and mistletoe in a great big bunch hung from the ceiling over the chair, and ashtrays brimming over, and bottles and glasses. My God it's a real den of vice. I sit down on the chair under the mistletoe, see the filing cabinet sticking out of the cotton wool snow covering everything, and I pull the top drawer and peep inside with the widest eyes you ever saw. There's video equipment and cameras I take in with one horrified peep, and go down the drawers. It's full of photographic paper and flash bulbs, but nothing actually incriminating. Except video cameras always arouse my suspicions, and I'm so nervous and twitchy that when the door flies open I fall over my mop can with a clatter in the clutter, all clanging and banging and raucous row. What now? Who's this? What fate? I bet you'd never guess Charlie. It's Knutton, marching in mightily miffed about something, and searching searching and picking up boxes and papers and shooing me out. Then wondering about me for a minute. Then rushing out himself. The wealthy whiz kid in a frantic tizz of panic, I'd say. Does me good to see it. But why? Well he didn't explain or say goodbye, and I beadily watch him speed down the corridor, dropping something I greedily snatch up, and whisk it away into the toilet and lock the door. All this happened within three minutes, so I was sweating and dizzy and trembling and my heart pounded fit to bust.

But I'd got something that I couldn't open for my shaking, and finally tearing it open with my teeth. Photos. Oh God. Oh Grief. Oh Santa Claus, with his great dirty paws up the dress of a little girl, who was smiling beguiling and cute for the camera. Then she's there with no clothes on Santa's knee kissing Santa, and then her little brother on his knee and Santa's hand is holding his penis, and then pocket Venus on the next one a girl of about thirteen wrapped around Santa with her legs apart laughing. All naked children on his knee and he's touching them and they're nonchalant, smiling, eating chocolates, kissing him. These kids look practised camera fodder, professional little models, all coy and one little boy's got his hand on Santa's penis which is showing, and another one's giving it a blow job, and you can only see his bare arse bending beckoning to the camera. It's farcical in a way, dare I say it, and my reaction after incredulity is to grin at the caricature of dirty daddy Xmas and flirty little tempters with their winning ways. Such a clever production of casual seduction and playing incest sublimation so savagely that it could be happening in anybody's front room on Xmas morning. Till the full extent and horror starts dawning that these are kids with that great fat penis looming over them, and this is a promotion for paedophiles at its most blatant, telling you how to do it, you buy them prezzies and while they're playing with them you're playing amen amen to innocence.

And here was Melanie with a pose like Marilyn Monroe, coquettish, aware, transformed. Where was that wistful little creature who'd come to me yesterday? This was the sultry, almost sullen look of a tramp and a vamp. The look that says I know what you like and I've got it. Where had she learned to look like that before? Who'd bought her favours like a whore and taught her to stare, ask for more, with a mouth that parted like a full-fledged sex siren that men would die for? I try to control my rising panic. I will have to show Jean this scene, but can't. I won't. How can I? Who could show this to a mother who thinks her little girl, her joy, her pearl, and the boys too, are her babies, her pride. Whose side would I be on, destroying her for ever. Yet had she never suspected? Could she *know*? Oh no. Oh NO. And suddenly Jean's wooden withdrawals and manic bouts of drink made sense, made me think she knows, she does, and the memory comes back in flashes through the drugs, and she's thrashing about frantically failing to forget, and how I'd not understood. But now I would. I'd make good and clean those wounds of Jean after all after all these appalling scenes I'd make it roses all the way.

Little bitch, I hear myself say. She was clearly Santa's favourite, featuring in many of them, wrapped round him like any loving living daughter. Except this one's naked and ready for the slaughter and willing so willing. I feel myself filling with rage at her. Now steady, hold on, steady. She's the victim.

But what a victim. She's asking him to do it. Luring him with eyes too wise for a girl of six. An atrocious precocious sexuality sitting on her face, and insolence in this disgrace and violation. She's defiant, self-reliant, almost liberated looking. No wonder they mate her and fuck her, have they fucked her yet? Has Santa dared here in his lair of fantasy come true has he screwed her too? Has he ravished and raped a minor? And as soon as I think of it like that, my finer feelings break through distrust and disgust of little girls inviting, inciting, what nonsense I'm fighting. Of course they don't deliberately entice anybody in the beginning. They're taught to act this way as it gets rewarded, and the boys the boys the buggered little boys, just as savaged, somehow even more pathetic than the girls, since it's custom sale for girls to succumb, but a different tale for boys and their bums are sort of sacrosanct, until they decide to probe themselves. Except for the fags at public schools, where the rules are different, or are they?

Anyway this day my mind is so thoroughly blown, I must unwind fast with a bottle. This is all past a joke on a fragile structure like I am. So fragile and shivering now and shaking again. It's taking every ounce of strength to look at these lengthy languid frozen images of lust and titillation to the last one. I must though, must know, and on and on we go, on and on till I'm sobbing hysterically and throbbing with such terrible anger, I just focus one question at this orgy of hocus pocus paedophilia: Who the hell is Santa? But I can't make him out, except, except, his flat nose and eyebrows a bit like the devil. I can't swear, but I've seen those eyes that stare before, and it looks like Cheetham to me, it does. It *is* Cheetham. I know it suddenly with certainty. Oh God. Oh God. And all I can think of is Jenny, and those many many hours in the pub explaining feminist theory, and she'd shivered, and said men are beasts with such feeling, it didn't match her marriage to the MP and happy family and all. Did she know? Had she known? Oh God oh God the evil sod, the awful ghastly twisted mind who finds sexual pleasure in children. These are surely the vilest of men, I think solemnly, as I walk soberly, head held high, dignified, out of the building, elevated suddenly above everyone in there. Except the darling brutalised babies, who I would save from men and themselves. An avenging Angel with rabies, ready to bite, I was that night, fearless and fighting and somehow freer.

15

That uplifting feeling of freedom wasn't just because I forgot my mop can either. I was lighter and liberated from this wretched fated drifting lack of purpose. I had a goal. I was going to expose the poseurs, the corruption, the filth and the slime of the nursery rhyme tale of repectabilia rotting at the core, and I was going to shout it from the hilltops of Sheffield. I knew the score about Knutton and Brampton Lodge and what stuffy old stodgy old Brian Cheetham does up there, and I was going to make them listen from the rooftops. But meanwhile how could I tell Jean?

I was so excited I bought two cans of Pils lager to celebrate. They're so strong that before long I would have worked it all out without waiting for a consultation with the others. I felt I should be mistressful and in control and present them with a plan. Otherwise chaos would ensue when they knew about Melanie and Mark and Robin and the man in the Santa Suit, an old fruity corrupt lecher of an honourable member, at least he was old compared to his prey, though actually he was my age, the naughty stage for men they say. But they say anything to justify the sins of the fathers. This would finish him, if they would listen to me that is. They'll have to, have to, this time. There'll be no more wafting me away – Go say it to the ducks, Sunshine, they said last time I protested that Council dustmen were stealing our blankets to sell. They were as well, though I couldn't prove it then. But this time I had evidence, didn't I? A nice little set of kiddie porn photos tucked in my drawers right here, weren't they? No they weren't. Where were they? I'd had them when I'd gone for the booze and had a wee in the public loo first, where I got my money out of my bottom skirt, and I'd taken them from my poacher's pocket in my jacket and put them in a packet I'd found, and then in my knickers. But I couldn't feel them now. Where were they? I must strip, this trip is getting too difficult to manage without a drink. So why don't I concentrate on drinking, instead of sipping the stuff. Right. I'll sit down here in front of the Cathedral, and collect myself on this seat, and frighten the shoppers away with such a display of anti-social Xmas drinking, they'll all think how superior they are and how far the city has sunk with women drunks littering their streets and loitering, defeated, derelict, deserted as the men.

Can't light my fag in this wind. It's making everything wild anarchic and out of control and usually I would love it. But I'm trying to concentrate mightily and the elements are interfering, and there's an awful fat slob in a bowler leering and lurking and invading my space, which I always reckon is a two feet circle around me into which they must not tread.

"Ay say, are you absolutely down?"

"Down?"

"On your luck"

"Could say so"

"Well I'd like to help. Don't be offended." He's extended a paw and I take it absently, shaking it to and fro. I'm worried about my evidence, which I can't feel any more.

"No"

"Ay say I'm so glad you're not offended. How much do you need?"

"What for?"

"To *equip* you"

"Equip?"

"For life's big adventure. Haw haw"

I peered at him then, this leerer, but couldn't detect any lechery. He was just leering and lapping over with good cheer and benevolence. No surely that must be a cover for something devious. I wait, looking at him blankly but curious. Whazzizzgame?

"Do you need clothes? And shoes and underclothes I should think"

Here it comes and black suspenders and will you render

me a little swan song wearing them and black stockings and these high heels and nothing else and squelch squelch I want you to walk over me in them.

"I don't want to pry"

Well try moving on then old Son, and stop lying so much. You're longing to touch and invade, like they all are, and I thought you looked different for a minute but I wasn't looking properly. I'm really worried about my envelope. There's all our hope of justice in there and I don't dare to feel carefully in my pants in case this turd gets the wrong idea. Though I fear he has that anyway so let him pay for the privilege. I've got my cleaner's outfit in a bag again, and it's back to layers. I lift one provocatively. He stares bewitched.

"Not here, not here. We could *go* somewhere. My car's parked in West Street. Let me give you a lift. I'd be glad to escort you somewhere"

"OK, I'll follow you to save you embarrassment"

"Oh it's not embarrassing at all. Let me help you. Let me take your arm"

Oh I can't explain how it is with some men, but they must have the dregs, the dreadful, the unspeakable, because they have everything else, and it bores them. So give them a dirty old time with a raggedy whore and they're panting fit to bust. I'd never trust a good bourgeois husband again to walk past the gutter without temptation to have the scruffiest slut in sight for the hell of getting dirty, preferably bloody too. Bleeding's an advantage they never rampage with fire and need during wifey's dire week. But down here it makes them weak with desire. It must be the contact with the forbidden, and this one's now looking so smitten, I don't think he'd mind my baldness even. But I pull my scarf down firmly in case. I must be feeling a bit wonky to go with him at all. My strategy is avoid cars and lonely places. But this one has a Rover and a mini-bar in the back, where he puts me as if it's a taxi. But I'm not questioning. I just get in and sit there, wondering about my evidence, and while he's driving out on the Ecclesall Road, I thoroughly search my knickers. But it's gone. I've dropped it. Probably near the booze shop when I got confused about the money, and a profound depression sets in, giving way to self-hate. I can't prove anything now. Oh how could I lose it? So when he gets in the back on a dark lonely track some time later, I can't refuse him anything. I'm such a failure and a freak, I can't even speak when he asks me what I'd like to drink, and he's opening champagne suddenly, with me sitting wooden catatonic dazed, and that's just how they like you some of them, and after two glasses of bubbles I'm hearing his troubles with his mother. He's talking about living with his ninety year old mother, who doesn't understand him and his needs.

"Which are?" I manage, mumbling and drinking quickly. I'm vaguely nervous about what he might get round to "I need to be admired and appreciated and thanked for my troubles and nourished a little"

"Thanks" I bark "Thanks thanks" and nourishment means tits. As soon as they mention the word nourishing, I know it's a Show me your tits. So I do, slowly lifting my layers and put my head back against the seat, and roll my eyes starwards, thinking of envelopes and murdered hopes, and there he goes sucking sucking till I'm sore and still he wants more. "Say: 'You've had enough Son' and try to stop me" he says and still in a daze I do it and try to shove him away and he gets more and more greedy, so needy you mummy's boy, and I stare at the stars, wishing I were far far away. But mysterious as these things are, I feel very worked up too, and start squirming around under my skirts, and he's saying "Say NO." So I say NO, meaning yes, and he's still sucking, and I want him to fuck me now. But how the hell can I ask him to? I've never had to ask for it before. I've no store of readily available experience. No repertoire of Come hither Come unto me into me at all. But I writhe a bit obviously, and he draws back and snaps "Say NO say NO NO NO." But I want to say yes and my nipples feel raw, and it's time to draw a conclusion. But I say "NO" obediently, and the confusion compounds as he utters a sound half way between ecstasy and scream, and that seems to be that, as he draws himself up and tries to regain his dignity, pulling my top down as if he can't bear bosoms, and wearing such a deep frown I think he's hurt himself. But no. I know this scene so well. It's shame, and when mighty men are ashamed, who to blame but the woman? I sit there in mid air, suspended, and gradually my passion subsides all by itself trickle trickle away . . .

"Here" he says roughly, pushing two notes at me "Go away. Get out"

"It's dark and I'm miles from anywhere. Couldn't you give me a lift."

"GET OUT"

"No need to shout" I sniff nervously, noticing his rapid transformation into a demon, which often happens, and fumble with the door. But not before he's pushing me sideways savagely "GET GET OUT GET OUT OF MY SIGHT OH GOD OH GOD" and he wrenches the door and pushes me flying on my face, and some things after me – landing on my head on a bed of heather. Well at least I'm not dead, and could have been, could have been, in a situation like that. Silly girl stupid girl. It must have been the Pils lager, an old saga of cheap thrills and unexpected horrors. Still I'm here in one piece, and though the envelope's gone, I'm here all alone and feeling quite strong again now the men have departed, and my heart warms up to even them when I look at his missiles and see a bottle of Black Label Johnny Walker nestling on my cleaner's bag, and the notes he gave me were two Fifties and I'm a hundred pounds rich for two sore tits. I reckon that's not bad going. An orgasm would have been icing on this fairy cake. But it will still take a long time to get home.

And then I hear the most normal thing in the world. A bus, a *bus* is coming, rumbling grumbling towards me, a double decker, lights flickering fleckering, now beaming and streaming up the hill. The good old Castleton bus going back to Sheffield. I'm just above the "Fox House" pub, all lit up like a fairy palace and twinkling winking beckoning. But not to me, not tonight. I start running, flying towards the bus and wave it down just by the stop.

"Yer nearly missed it lass" the driver lets my appearance pass without a word. They're used to hikers and strange sights out here, such relief, such absence of fear and loathing from the passengers, who just nod pleasantly as I sit down with my bottle and bag, so glad I'd found change, fumbling in my folds with everyone watching when I got on. What warmth it gives me to be accepted at last for a fast fleeting minute on a dirty old bus rumbling towards Sheffield across lonely moors with the doors closed and the windows steamed up cosy cosy rosy and I fall asleep and dream of weeping children and old old women with withered breasts who scream at their sons yes please yes please yes please.

The next day I wake up near the bus station in a store room they don't lock up sometimes in the old Polytechnic. It's now called Hallam University this place I know that at least, though I'm disgracefully ignorant otherwise about these recent elevations in education. It was my lucky night curled up in a box they'd thoughtfully provided, and I'd brought my own refreshment and sat there staring into the blackness and watching the glow of my ciggie and making plans and swigging whisky. It all seemed much better then. I thought I'd send a letter to everybody I could think of with power: Radio Sheffield, *The Star*, the Ministry of Health, the Social Services, the Labour Party, spreading the story, without them seeing me. If they see me, I'm finished. They'll dismiss it as drunken fantasy, and without the envelope there was no hope at all. Bloody fool I am to lose it. Yet how can I GETOGETHERTO write a letter? I'm so spaced out and racing heart and hands trembling so much I can't sign my prescriptions. So how to write a whole letter? No that was hopeless. I know, I know. I'd tell Toby. He'd believe me. He would, he would, and his friend, our friend, she'd raise a banner for us. She'd help us. They'd help us. They would, they would, and so I felt happy a bit and that hovering panic stays hovering not bothering or invading, till I get to the hostel, like Borstal it is by now with bars and bolts across the windows. Though the door's still open.

"Breakfast ladies" I call, and the bundles twitch, and eyes

peer out of hair all matted. They should wear scarves too, some of these hairstyles.

"Fuck off fuck off yer bleedin' fuck pig" says the one in the corner. She's the newcomer, not accustomed to us yet. So I offer her my whisky bottle and she stares petrified in huge disbelief. I don't blame her. Black Label Johnny Walker in a dosshouse is a mirage too large for a lady to absorb.

"Fuck pig fuck pig fuck pig" she insists, but glugging down nevertheless.

"Charlie yu a vision from dem clouds" and Natty hugs me and glugs away with no problem at the smoothness going down for a change, and I give her a long cigarette and wave the fifty pound notes in her face.

"Look what we've got girls it's Xmas"

"Father Xmas been Father Xmas been" Natty dances round, poking the other two bundles "Father Xmas been Jean." God, I think, dear God, how do I tell her *how* he's been?

"Where you bin Charlie?" rubbing her eyes.

"I went to the Home yesterday"

"AND"

"And it's bad"

"Yu prove sumpin Charlie?"

Bridie was awake too and they all huddled round the bottle and me, even Edith "I'm Edith Piaf", wanting to know. So I told them everything, keeping my face firmly on Jean, till I got to the Santa scene and then I looked away, and she grabbed my shoulders and shook me

"Charlie Charlie tell me tell me you're hiding it from me. Were my kids on them?"

Well she had to know I think, even though the photos were lost. But I realised too late when I nodded that the cost was too great, the horror would break her. So I tried to shake her off and change my tack:

"All the kids were on them"

"Were *my* kids on them? Look at me. Again. You just said they were. You just said my kids were in blue pictures. You lying bitch you lying lying bitch" and she starts pummelling me on the chest and my tenderest parts are taking the brunt again.

"Leave it out stop it stop it" shrieks Natty, grabbing one arm, and Bridie the other.

"God help us, that's no way to talk to Charlie. She's trying to help you, Jean. Come on now" says Bridie, hiding her face. She's terrified of violence and is now so white and clenched, I know she's fighting so hard for control. I roll over and away and out of Jean's range.

"You shut up Jean. I know you feel terrible, and I didn't want to tell you, but have a drink and we'll think what to do"

She's moaning and rocking between the other two, rocking rocking, a desperate mockery of motherhood betrayed.

"Mangle mangle fuck and mangle" says Edith.

"I don't *believe* it you lost dem. Man dat's jus too bad to think 'bout"

"I know I know"

"Come on, it's not Charlie's fault. We'll tell Toby. He's the one to know"

"Yes. Toby"

"Fucking cunt fucking cunt a mangle a day"

"And Hannah"

and her spanner in the whole rotten works we want. But who will believe us? It's my word against the world, but I'm pleased so pleased these three believe me without hesitation. I need to feel their unconditional support. I know it's not the unconditional love I feel I really need to get over things, but it will do. It's the most you'll get when folk are falling apart and fretting about themselves on a full time basis. There seems to be no place in the world for unconditional love, and heavens above, a space for it would be a haven that could save our lives.

"The trouble with wives" says Jean sniffing "is that we keep too silent too long out of loyalty, as if admitting summat's wrong in t'family means it's our fault"

Silent about what Jean? Assault and abuse? Does it mean

133

you're used to the idea of your kids being violated, and though you hated it there was nothing you could do you thought, being true to your man and marriage. Until with a last bit of courage, when he hit them, you ran and took them away. He swore he'd make you pay, and look at you, consumed by guilt, and you lost your kids anyway. Whatever can we say to such a patchwork quilt of happy family dialectics? Not that she's admitting much. We're all listening intently, but trying to look casual about it so she doesn't scare off with intensity. Getting heavy is something she's scared of. Don't get under my eyelids, she says often, when we try to soften all that pain by bringing it out. But you can't rush it. The subconscious only lets things out when it's ready, when you can face it, steady enough to place it, integrate it into your life. Don't push it, don't go too far. We know it for ourselves, you blow it if you dust those shelves too vigorously. So we wait, and stare at the pitiless rain through the open door. Or is it pitiless or is just that witless convention says so? It's actually very consoling pitter patter doesn't matter . . .

"It's pissing down buckets" Jean notices at last.

"I'm missing my mop can, speaking of buckets" I try to make neutral conversation, but it's not my forte. I've never been a sporty hockey sticks who could charm and disarm folk with my witty platitudes about the weather, though I reflect on it a lot. And here comes hot shot Toby straight from the kids' home. He was under orders to act dramatically, but the facts as he said need proving, though he believes me too without a murmur. Just looked moved, then worried to death when I told him.

"Well it's all very difficult" he says, as he gives us a sandwich each and empties cigarettes from both pockets "Oh. I only brought enough for four. I didn't know"

"Fucking bastard fucking bastard fucking cunt fuck fuck fuck pig" says Edith.

"Quite" he answers apologetically.

"Come on, share mine" says Bridie to Edith, who snatches her sandwich and cigs and scuttles off to the corner, cursing us all. But we grin. It's no sin, this off-the-wall behaviour when you're down and out. It's a healthy sign in a way. She's shouting Have a good day, in her own weird way. She's acknowledging our existence at last, which is better than trapped and fettered in her own past imperfect like she has been.

"Well it's really very difficult, but I got Margo Thompson to agree to come down to talk to you"

"The bitch"

"Who's she?" says Bridie, beautiful today. She's washed her hair and it shines and shines, wish it were all mine SNOT FAIR SNOT FAIR.

"She's the Social Worker in charge of Jean's children, and the only woman Social Worker there, I've discovered. She'll be here at 12. Can you be here?"

"I'll ask my diary" says Jean, and we all fall about laughing. It's such a big thing hearing humour from her.

"Yeah, I'd better ring dat secretary to check"

"And I'll have to cancel the hairdresser" I say, showing my sensitivities are under control too, in solidarity.

"She's a lousy piece of baggage" says Jean "a real snotty cow I bet she won't believe it"

"The best is if Charlie just tells her story straight I think" says Toby, looking at me a bit too long for comfort, like he does when he's worried. But he hurries on, realising. "And Jean if you try to keep your temper. And Natty if you could get dressed a bit. Otherwise . . ." he tries to smile "she'll find it easy to discredit everyone"

So I tell my story in all my glory, standing in the middle of our sad little nest, with the rain pouring outside, and the door open wide to let light in, and the sight of this woman already appals me. She's six feet tall and intimidating, with big horn rimmed glasses which hide her eyes so you can't assess her, while Jean stands too, with her head bowed, bless her. She's vowed to behave, and I keep getting waves of nausea. I haven't had a drink yet, in order not to smell for the occasion, and it's playing havoc with my alcohol system. I think blood might be getting in it oh dear . . .

"You don't expect me to believe any of this" The horn rims flash as she snaps it out "it's preposterous"

"Oh NO" moans Bridie, and Jean and me swap swift tight glances of shock. Natty, who's sprawled on the floor in total sloth, belches belligerently.

"You doubt my credibility?" I try to sound Poxford and posh and plummy, but my tummy starts rolling at that precise moment. This is *awful*.

"More than that, whoever *you* are. I question your very right to be in the Home, as you claim, in the first place. Our Security is quite effective, and we certainly don't allow random vagrants to wander about"

"I wasn't random. I was deliberate. Very definitely with a purpose. The mother of those children, Jean here, had told me of her suspicions and I was verifying them. We wanted proof"

"Exactly. You fabricated a story between you and dreamed up a crazed way of doing without evidence"

"NO. NO. NO. You have to listen"

"Yes you must"

"Yes Margo. Dr. McCloud really was a highly respected and brilliant University teacher. She deserves your attention" says Toby warmly.

"*Was* being the operative word. She's a dropped out drunk who's so far gone I'm surprised you listen for a minute. Do you actually believe her?"

"Yes"

"Well I seriously doubt your professional judgment then. And I shall be making recommendations accordingly . . . this is wasting . . ."

"Shut up and listen" says Toby so fiercely she's taken aback, an attack by a pet lamb and he's slamming into her viciously "You're grossly insensitive Margo, charging in here with your crassness and your categories. Alcoholics can *feel* you know"

"I doubt it"

"What's more to the point they can see and hear and

there's nothing wrong with Dr McCloud's faculties at all. Nor her integrity"

"Hallucinations"

"Oh God"

"I maintain that if she really believes this nonsense and it's not just an elaborate hoax for attention, or some personal vendetta against the MP – who by the way could bring libel and slander and defamation of character charges against her – if she really believes it then she must be having delusions"

"Why?"

"Because it's preposterous"

"And that's a tautology" I observe grimly, with growing gnawing wrath.

"Oh really" she says to Toby, not addressing us directly the whole time "this is wasting my precious time listening to the ravings of a mad woman, *five* mad women drunks, and a besotted Social Worker who has lost his objectivity on the way." And that's all she had to say, stomping out the door, our frail hopes clomping away, sailing into the sunset, like those with the last word and the power always do. It's the witching hour again the bitch the bitch and it's not sunset at all but rain endless rain relentless refrain soothing soothing. I suddenly cheer up.

"We'll think of something Jean"

"Yeah Jean dat's not finished wid"

"Yes Jean we need some thought" says Toby "Why don't I tell Hannah the whole thing and see what she thinks. Would you mind?"

Jean looks at me. She's meek and bewildered. I hate to see her like this, all the stuffing gone, weak and wobbly. I nod.

"OK" she agrees and flops on the floor near the open door which is sopping and slippery and needs mopping I think and wink at them all so sad at the ball four ladies of leisure must give them some pleasure so I hop off to Victoria Wines and get out my delicious £50 note before he hustles me out.

"We're having a party" I tell him "Fill up a box" and it seems a good idea a parting party from our home, just girls together, but here comes Heather, and who likes parties anyway? Let's go away and make love in a dark hole and I'll play any role you want me to, spanking to your wanking you'll end up thanking me and begging me for more, and he did. That night Heather asked me to marry him.

16

He'd seen my fringe too, and not a cringe or whine. He said it's fine, I don't care about hair, I just want a daring woman, who'll do wild things to me, who's not afraid of her sensuality. In fact he quite got off on being whipped by a bald woman, he could pretend I was a nun and we'd really have fun, him being reared as he was in a Jesuit school in Liverpool, not a public school at all like I thought, and he bought every bit of my eager performance. I tell you I had him dancing and drooling and frothing to a frenzy as soon as I got over my hangups that beating a man was somehow wrong, and he should be strong, he should be the one with the mighty mouse stuff. Yes I played it rough in our little house down there in the Polytechnic basement, when his self-abasement sunk low enough for him to come through it, and transcend it somehow, and taking me in ordinary missionary glee in the end.

By the morning I felt a new dawning, though not without warning myself it might all be due to the booze supply, which never died or dried up with fifty quid's worth. We slid into stupor quite gracefully. He spoke to me so gently, and Bacardi and coke in a plastic cup made up for all the rest of the discomfort and cold. It's a test a test of our feelings, I thought, inspired. If we're fired with passion in these conditions, it will live forever. Well you must forgive my stupidity, but I'd had a thing about Heather for ages and not wanted to listen when the sages of the street hinted at dark forces. Well of course we can always get divorced. I want him to be mine mine oh desperate time and the hangover comes and says it's the wine after all.

Nevertheless I was standing tall and proud in the afternoon, waiting for my date with Hannah, which they'd told me about when I rolled back home to give them some sustenance from the second £50, as my new romance had swallowed the other and Heather had disappeared with the leftovers. I noticed when he recovered from waking up that marriage plans didn't take up too much of his conversation. He kisses me briefly and says It was a good celebration. Then steals off like a thief with the rest of the booze while I was washing freezing in the loo and looking forward to a drink when I'd finished. Girl you've been used, and he'd no idea I had more money either. He just left me to it, but I still felt happier than usual. That intimate human contact when you thrill to flesh and skin and a body that you fancy, though his brain remains the key attraction, and his dissipation frightens me. I feel our debauch could lurch out of control into some demented fantasy land, which is the attraction of course – the search for danger dangling from deranged hands all over you and those eyes so wise and mocking and knowing and shocking at the moment of truth in their ruthlessness, but calculating constantly. It frightens me and excites me so much, and his touch and tone are often so tender as well, that it's heaven and hell in a package, racked ravaged and ready for eating as soon as you meet him. There are no preliminaries any more. No foreplay. No What's in store. Just straight to the core of what he wants, and he gives you your pleasure in ways you never dreamt belonged to you, responding to a song you never knew before, unsung chanting wrung from you, decanted from your dregs as you lie panting begging for more.

Natty was cynical, raising her eyes to the sky. I asked her why she was so distrustful of Heather, a mild academic who'd gone off his head, but still mild surely until you knew him. Or could she detect wildness and lust underneath the scholarly mode and upper class looks?

"He's a fucker I knows it I juss knows it Charlie – the type that'd do yu in one night an yu juss don't come back Man"

"No you've got him wrong"

"I *never* gets dem wrong Charlie. Never"

"No Natty. NO"

"Well yu was warned"

140

"Yes"

"I like him" says Bridie, and my suspicions flare, she sees this "NO NO not like *that* Charlie. He just seems a gent and God knows they're rare"

"Yes a gent" says Jean.

"Yu all stupid Man" says Natty "I got a bad feeling fe dat man"

"Fuck pig fuck pig fuck pig fuck pig" says Edith.

"Well well are we all going?" says a voice behind me, and there's Hannah, looking so seductive I feel the futility next to her of pretending to be a woman, and having a girlie conversation about a man. How can I ever compete again with women like this for the male? I can't I can't so forgeddit girl fast *why compete admit defeat and sisterhood will flood you shit shit shit to that too.*

"Where we going?" asks Bridie.

"We're trailing Cheetham tonight – Charlie and me – I've tracked down his favourite pub in Derbyshire, in Castleton. He goes there to play darts every Tuesday and I thought we'd ask him a few questions. Do you want to come?"

"No I'll stay here with Charlie's parcel"

"Me too" says Jean.

"Yeah. Dem bottles too good to go 'way from Man"

"So it's us, Charlie" she looks me up and down and I cringe and crumble into fifty pieces, and plaster myself in crevices bit by bit, effacing myself so entirely I must disappear any minute.

"Well come on, the car's over there"

It's a Volvo, smooth as her, rolling along, floating. I hope I don't smell. Sitting next to her makes me sensitive to being gruesome. An intimate twosome like this in the front seat not very hygienic for her and the heat is terrific. I haven't been so hot since, well only last night I suppose, my clothes rinsed in Heather's sweat, and sperm sticking to my breasts even now, since I'd only washed the vital bit today and everywhere else stayed high. Oh dear, I sigh ruefully.

"What's the matter Charlie? Are you cold do you want more heat?"

"NO it's an oven in here"

"Oh no, you must have a temperature"

No, but I was drunk and so was she.

"Maybe"

It's dull, this driving. Full of pregnant silence. I know she's dying to query me about existence and truth and other profundities. Every journalist is intrigued by my apparent acquiescence to devastation. But she can't summon courage. It's the closeness together. And then she drops the bombshell.

"I was with Heather today. A fascinating character wouldn't you say?"

"You WERE . . . WITH . . . HEATHER?"

"Yes. Why not?"

"Where?"

"Where? What does it matter where?"

"Where? I need to know where" I growl losing control and grip the seat-belt.

"In my hotel room, if you must know"

"Why?"

"*Why?*"

"Yes why? Why the hell should an alcoholic dropout be in your hotel room?"

"For the same reason one is in my car I suppose" she says staring at the road "They are fascinating people and I want to help them"

"Only some are fascinating. Story fodder. Academic failures. I bet you're not interested in Edith"

"OK"

"What was he doing in your room?"

"Why?"

"Did you fuck him?"

"It's not your . . ."

"It bloody well is. Because I fucked him all night. And he's got fucking phenomenal fucking energy to hop into you straight after me and take my drinks along too. Did you *enjoy* my drinks? I worked hard for those drinks in a car out here the night before. Just about here on the Moors, I earned my

142

drinks money so he could bring the drink over to you. Fucking
BASTARD"

"Oh"

"*Oh* you say"

"Oh. I didn't know you were having a scene"

"You shocked?"

"Er no. Just surprised"

"That he could?"

"That he would be so hypocritical. He reeks of such
integrity. He told me he loved me. He's been living at my
hotel for two weeks"

"Except for last night" I say with grim satisfaction.

"Yes" she says sadly. "He said he got lost"

"LOST?"

"I believed him"

"Lost. I like it. Lost. Little boy lost. Tell me do you beat
him?"

She looked perturbed, just slightly. A bit white round the
gills. But determined sophistication won.

"Yes"

"He makes you hit him"

"Well he couldn't *make* me do anything"

"Don't you believe it"

"Well I do it voluntarily"

"Do you enjoy it?"

"Yes"

"Is this the first time?"

"What"

"That you've beaten men"

"Good God NO"

I was riveted. It was clearly her thing.

"Tell me"

"What?"

"Tell me about beating men. He was my first"

"Tell you?"

"Yes. I need to learn from experience. Does it turn
you on?"

"Obviously"

"More than anything?"

"Nothing else does"

"Except beating men"

"And women"

"You beat women?"

"Oh yes"

"You're bisexual?"

"Of course. Aren't you? Isn't everybody?"

"NO"

"Rubbish." She put her hand on my knee and squeezed it. We were racing through Derbyshire villages raping and pillaging it seemed to me, with one eye closed trying to focus in front of me, and wishing the hand on my knee would go away. Don't want to play games with Hannah hurting me. Got enough on my plate. She should masturbate soundlessly by herself and not charge around hitting folk who want a quiet life and a drink in a corner. She took a bend too fast. I gasped, she grabbed the wheel back with both hands, and I felt easier. That scene was too complicated to contemplate. But somehow her fleeting interest in me had relativised my trauma at my man's infidelity. Infidelity? To her or to me?

"I can't see how you could want to hit women"

"Oh oh oh lady you've never tried it"

"It's no better than male behaviour"

"You're confusing violence in a general sense with sex"

"Rape is both"

"I don't rape anybody"

"You mean the women want you to beat them?"

"'Course they do"

"NO. I don't believe it"

"Believe it"

"NO"

"Come on Charlie don't be *naive*. Every woman's constructed to want pain"

"NO NO NO"

"Oh come on"

"NO. Do *you* want beating?"

"Sometimes. Depends"

"On what for Chrissake"

"On who's doing it. What she looks like how big her tits are, *you* know"

"NO. NO I don't"

"Oh grow up"

"No. Honest. I don't know"

"I'd like you to beat me for instance Charlie"

"Oh my God"

"Oh yes"

"Why?"

"I think it would be the worm turning. The underdog finally leaps up and takes power by the throat. The dirty tramp dominating the perfumed fashion plate. And you're also very sexy Charlie"

"Oh *NO*"

"Oh yes. And beautiful too. It's hidden. You hide it very well. You look worn out and haggard, which is beautiful too. And Toby has told me tales of your conquests. A woman with a past like you is fascinating Charlie. And you take risks. Your risks are written in every line on your face. Oh yes I'd love you to beat me Charlie. With a whip"

"Oh NO. I don't believe it"

"Believe it"

"Does Heather know?"

"What?"

"That you're bisexual"

"Oh come on. I told you. Everybody is"

"NO"

"Yes. Just give them the right time and place and person"

"Not beating though. You're not suggesting that's universal?"

"Yes. Inflicting and receiving pain are very deep in all of us"

"Hannah, this is unmitigated pernicious bollocks I'm hearing and I can't listen any more"

"Is it turning you on? You'd like to beat me"

"Not in the least"

"You would"

"No Hannah"

"You will. One day you will"

"No Hannah"

"Never say never"

"Let's change the subject"

She gave me a look, meaning Coward, which I resented. What had this spoilt Jewish Princess ever dared in her life except a few sexual shenanigans? But we did change this subject. It got worse actually. A feminist discourse and scolding me for not towing political lines. They were old so old these familiar arguments with faded yellow pages, though not for ages had I had them reeled off at me. So why couldn't I ever relax and sit back and be driven? The fact was I needed a drink and couldn't think of a way to get one. I should have brought a supply, why didn't I? And I needed money again. I'd twice spent £50 at Victoria Wines. A fine way to carry on, but it's Xmas, and I bet they're enjoying themselves back at the ranch a lot more than I am, listening to this piss.

"I really don't understand why you won't mobilise the feminists round this issue. Come to a meeting and tell them the whole thing. Child abuse is a feminist issue, and you're behaving as if it's your own private crusade"

"I've tried too often to mobilise the sisters" I say, tired and defenceless. I know what sense she's talking, but she doesn't understand how they treat me "You don't understand"

"NO and I never will understand such silly individualism over a political issue"

"*You* mobilise the feminists. I really would welcome their involvement"

"What's wrong with *you* doing it. It's *your* story"

"I thought you preferred other people's stories" That was pure heresy, but I couldn't stop it. Thinking of Heather and her stirred up such jealousy, I was spitting venom all over the place. I glanced at her face. She was silent, impassive. What a bitch witch I became in my inflamed state, all filled with hate and hurt, and that was unforgivable dirt Toby had confided in me strictly privately. That she'd lost her journalist job in London for plagiarising a story from a colleague. Which is why she was here looking for scoops to rescue her credibility and reputation, and I'd rubbed her nose in it for fucking my fella. Though I suppose she was entitled to be jealous of me.

The silence surrounding her sounded shocked and I felt uncomfortable, prickly, locked in next to her, wanting to climb out get out escape run have some fun on the highways and byways, not sit here with this glum festering feminist getting on my nerves which were jangling enough already.

"I expect you need a drink" she says, civilised.

"You betcha"

"There's one in front of you. Open it"

I could have kissed her or even whipped her. What bliss. The fucking glove compartment was full of cans of Pils. She must have done her research on me, for surely *she* didn't drink this stuff.

"It's very kind of you" a cringy creepy Uriah Heep

"Don't grovel Charlie"

"I have to these days"

"You don't. Ever"

"Well, high principles are for better days. I wish you were right though, but it's preachy irrelevance in my situation. Don't you see that?"

"I see a self-perpetuating situation you don't break out of. The feminists would help you"

"They won't though. They sneer and tell me to come back when I'm sober"

"Isn't that fair enough, they're serious political workers and you dance around drunk hindering them don't you?"

"Listen Hannah" I say, warming to the Pils. "Feminists scare me. Political certainty of all kinds scares me. Prim clipped certainties rapping at you from tight-lipped dogmatists"

"But some things *are* certain, like male violence, what's *wrong* with you, you're terrified of commitment"

"No. Just terrified of them and their methods. Exclusive. And closed. And moralistic. They disapprove of me completely. 'Cos I can't getitogether. They make me feel worse. Much much worse. Small and hopeless. Smaller and more hopeless than ever"

"Feminist groups just aren't like that. They're warm and welcoming"

"Oh yeah"

"Yes. Definitely. You just *want* to be an Outsider"

"NO. Not at all. I just don't, do not, fit in. They're puritans"

"No"

"Oh yes. Yes. Can't *stand* conformists. They're so *straight*. A whole New Orthodoxy. Political correctitude gone berserk. Cold clipped certain. Callous to dissent. No concept of contradiction"

She looked annoyed and bit her lip a lot, then grabbed my Pils can and swallowed it with such speed, I could only gape at boozy greed in such a cool collected one. Or was it all a front?

"You've been a Marxist intellectual. You're here in Sheffield in the Socialist Republic of South Yorkshire. Yet you're stuck in the most stupid kind of individualistic negativity I've ever heard. Just won't be political at all. I can't get over it"

"It's the politics on offer, not me" I plea, but in vain. She remains stony faced and angry looking all the way. I don't know what to say any more, except "we have to make a space to take care of our mad and our sad and our thoroughly bad in an alternative movement or it ends up as authoritarian as before, – *exclusive*." My dream of a new politics is elusive I know, but it's a feeling I get living in the underclass. That they reveal so much misdirected energy that it's here we start, and not with parties or preachings or teachings of anybody from outside. The new radical militancy is right here inside these networks of survival and self-defence we try to set up in our nests of cardboard fragile futile refusal against the bitterly cold, but showing that old old dream of a special place of our own on earth and an ability to build it in the most terrible adversity, is ticking over, flickering, chilled to the bone, bewildered, forlorn and torn to shreds, but alive, and fed and nourished so little it's pitiful tragic, but strategically there.

I'm aware suddenly of her voice bossily telling me to Get

out. She's glaring at me viciously. I wish I'd never come for tea to your house missus, but I try to look dignified. Two can play at that game, though the odds are stacked for those with hair. We climb a stone stairway at the side of the pub and into the hub and happiness of Xmas jollity. Oh fun frivolity with a crackling fire and silver streamers, no place for dreamers in here. But I'm hustled through to a side room where Cheetham is indeed ensconced with a whole gallery of young fans poncing around him, waving darts. I start to shake, and have to hold a chair for support. But Hannah sits me down quickly, her manner getting frostier than the air outside. What am I doing here in this cosy intimate tap room, very upmarket classy tap room with a carpet and horse brasses?

I look around, savouring the atmosphere of beer and smoke, taking deep lungfuls of its warmth in the pokey overstuffed room, when he says in a gruff Northern voice.

"The press come in all shapes and sizes these days then" He's trying to be pleasant I realise, but it doesn't stop the hurt. I know I look weird and dirty with my skirts and my poncho, but he's got a beard without wanting one and enough Vaseline on his hair to slide home. Come on Hannah, hurry up at the bar. You're the star of this occasion. Don't leave me with the social niceties. I've forgotten them and was a failure anyway. A failed Faculty wannabe, that's me, and something else as well . . . I test him, bloody hell I can't resist it

"I knew your wife"

He looks shocked at my voice, expecting slum not plum.

"I doubt it very much"

"Oh yes"

"Well never mind"

"Charlotte McCloud. Used to teach the students at Sheffield University a bit of emancipation theory. Your wife for instance. Jenny."

"Who?" he knew allright and peered closer "McCloud. I remember that mad McCloud woman. Jenny was never the same. But McCloud was very different. Oh very different. Don't be daft. You're nothing like her . . ."

"Oh yes"

"Except the voice. You sound a bit, familiar. Did you know her? She used to break marriages up just for the hell of it. An evil evil woman"

"S'mee, honest"

He looked appalled, incredulous. I always have this effect on family patriarchs.

"Really really?"

"Yes"

"I remember thinking they should sack her long before they did. She was disgusting. Used her position to stir it up. Try to make women discontented with their lot . . . That was YOU?"

"Yes" head bowed.

"But whatever *'appened*?" he's shaking his head, looking at me, wrinkling his nose "whatever on t'bloody 'ell earth *'appened*?"

"Life" I mutter portentously.

"God if you ask me it's your just deserts for all them loopy ideas. Well well. There's some justice after all. Just fancy, how the mighty fall. Well Well"

"It wasn't my ideas that failed me. It was the, er, reality, that got in the way a bit . . ." I was trying to be post-modern and self-deprecating but he was devoid of irony.

"Serves you bloody right. Trying to fill women up with ideas they can't fulfil. You should be put away, you career women who mess up real women's lives"

"Career women are real too"

"Yeah, and just look at where it gets 'em. Look at you. What a waste of all that money on education. Well I never. You should be ashamed to exist"

"I am"

"That's something"

"But not because fellas like you disapprove of me. In fact that makes it all worthwhile" I smile at him sweetly and think of Santa sweating and panting in his Santa Suit, but with his hand on cute little kids, posing and preening. You obscene arrogant overweening thug. I want to hit him, me who hates violence. But Hannah is tugging my poncho and struggling

with drinks on the full table. I never saw so many drinks all
lined up. They must buy him one each as they come in, wages
of sin called corruption where I come from. Can tell *you're*
no son of a prim Victorian.

"What have you said to him?" she hisses.

"Only reminiscing about my pretty past"

She looks perplexed, then resumes her snotty expression
"Well I'm going to confront him so you keep quiet"

I actually had no choice in the matter, as a voice stops
our chatter, bellowing across the room, no hello either.

"Hey you. YOU there, you YOU out, OUT, I said. Didn't
see you before. NO hiking boots or tramps. Out. This minute.
Out. Out. Out"

It was like a demo chant, a howl of rage. He advances,
waving a towel. A type who prowls round football fields
beating people up, but trying to be a yuppie landlord with a
nice word with the MP – who I bet he's protecting from me.
I get up gracefully as can be, with my usual line, "Been banned
from better places" and leave, weaving between disgusted
onlookers, and flopping down on the steps outside. It's better
now, the big wide world unfurled at my feet. I watch the
flurrying scurrying snow and know things are changing. I can
feel the shift again slowly slowly, a rearrangement realignment
of tectonic plates grinding away inside my layers. My subconscious is doing battle very near the surface, something's about
to break through. It's there just out of focus off-vision, out of
the corner of my eye, a film of dust round the edges of the
screen, focusing focusing . . .

"Curse curse shit and derision bloody hell he's escaped"

Cheetham had done a bunk, saying he was off to the loo,
and the amazing thing is he must have done it right past
me and I never noticed, head down preoccupied. Hannah's
hopping mad though, a not unpleasant sight – Hey, who's side
are you on? I ask myself.

"I told him I had information I intended to divulge about
his involvement with a paedophile ring. Just testing, you
know"

"Very subtle approach"

She flashed a look of temper at me. Remember your place Charlie, it's a long walk home.

"Well I guess you can't be tactful about it" I say.

"No. And the bugger's jumped. He was up and off in a flash"

"Oh yeah" contempt "Sorry"

"We'll never get him now without proof"

"He'll have gone home. Get him later"

"Yes OK. Let's go get him later"

It turns out though, after several days searching for the honourable member, that he's vanished disappeared done a bunk. I even speak to Jenny herself personally, in my ex-Lecturer capacity, and she verifies "I don't know what happened. He came and packed and vanished without a word. And no-one's seen him in London either. What can I do?"

You can thank Heaven, that's what you can do, and certainly not for little girls and boys. Oh dear, I fear I'm a hypocrite sometimes telling her it would all be allright, and good night Jenny there's nothing to worry about. I go back to watching the flurries of snow, only this time it's a slurred sensibility. I stare with a blurred bleary vision fearing the worst, and not wanting to go in and tell Jean we've failed. So I sit sopping wet and solitary outside on the wall, wishing I could call up Heather for a cuddle, my mind in a muddle. Of course he's cuddling *her*, and the world's full of omens suddenly, women huddling together caring for each other until treachery takes over when men appear. Oh yes, I fear the worst. It's bursting out all over me, my skin's itching with dread. That ray of hope of the other day has fled again, and left a dull thudding leaden layer sticking to me, flattening me out, deafening, deadening. I need a drink to make me think it through all this. A Jewish witch has taken my play-mate away, whisked him off to a posh hotel with booze and joints and whips and high pointed heels slicing into his flesh as she strips and steps all over him. I envy them both, but it's not worth pneumonia and moping out here. I've been away for days, so I lean on the door to go in and face Jean. But instead my dread tightens like a vice and I stand there trembling in shock at the big bolted padlock.

"No admittance. By order. Sheffield City Council."

the Socialist Republic of South Yorkshire had shit its potful for me.

17

"We've been looking everywhere for you" says Toby crossly and Natty gathers me up from the floor where I'm sunk in stupor, not entirely due to the booze. She's bossy and busy and brisk, I wonder where her energy's come from, when I'm steeped in the deepest kind of despair at this ultimate socialist betrayal. I'm festering and licking old sores and settling scores in my mind. One day I'll come back and find you Councillors all and haunt you with your socialist spectres of fellowship comradeship fraternal greetings brothers all and no seating for women. I take a cig from Natty and a swig from her cider bottle.

"Pigs and bastards I hate them hate them HATE them"

"Yeah dat don't matter now. We four going away fe de weekend"

"Away?"

"Yes. Charlie you wanted to go to the Conference. We'll go"

Goody goody, a Conference on Deviance and a Workshop on "How to deal with Alcoholic Clients". We were going as object–subjects, but mainly I was going to a workshop about Laing, which was going to demolish the concept of deviance I hoped. So I tried to hide my usual intense annoyance at Toby calling me Charlie like everyone else, as though my new identity had submerged the old entirely. He ought to be more sensitive. Since noble sensitivity was his thing, he could bring a bit more to his relationship with me, which was ambivalent enough anyway. Your former teacher collapsed at your feet would give anyone else an ego trip. It certainly chuffed students no end if you fucked them and reversed the power roles, though there shouldn't be any power in sex I hear you saying, leering and laughing at the illusion of fragile ideals I cling to about equality. Yet I'm very aware of darker forces within us, conditioned cantankerous, denying us respect and orgasm in the same sentence, though that wasn't relevant to Toby. I couldn't fuck Toby on the darkest night and desperate. Though that's a wild claim and I know it, but I've rarely been so turned off by anybody as this archetypal New Man with brillo pad hair on his head and his face and his woolly caps and his clinging cloying embrace when he helps me to walk as now. But he's stalking me always somehow, waiting, biding his sharing social working time till I turn on to caring. But how is kindness ever sexy?

Such sacrilege I'd be shot for, but I find him repulsive the nicer he gets, as wet and soggy as an overripe banana hanging there, staring at me, always under those hooded lids. A droopy reptilian look lurking waiting. Yuk I hate him, though fucking him would put him out of his misery and stop that enigmatic buttoned upness. It's so unhealthy. Yes, I must do it and soon. It's really a job for a friend to relieve him, liberate him. I have a mission. I'll do it. Especially since he's taking us to London now. I'll take him aside as soon as possible and help him on his way. Every good Social Worker should have his day in the sun at last, but not so fast, he's got his arm round Bridie now, helping her. Perhaps he's getting kicks out of this – his four drunken mistresses of the streets in his van. Any man would explode at the possibilities, but not so tight, tense Toby as he ushers us all inside, pushing me finally in next to him in the front. I give him an ambivalently withering Come Hither look, meaning Fuck you later, and a glimmer of excitement lights up his eyes. Yuk I think. Yuk yuk yuk. But I must do it, I've decided it's my mission. Even bald, I'm bold after my affair with Heather. I never knew whether he fancied me. Now I know I could still arouse passion in a man, so this little fan should be no problem. He should be so grateful and none of that hateful infidelity as with Heather.

No, Toby would be loyal unto the grave, and death-like preoccupations start haunting me at the thought of this assignation already. It will be like poking a corpse into life. I can't imagine he's ever had a night of passion. Perhaps I should provoke him into one in London, oh magic metropolis I'm coming I'm coming. It seems like freedom train all again, like the first time I ran away from the frozen solid stolid North aged seventeen full of dreams and schemes of escape. A rape of these hopes these present days of dope and drink. You'd think I'd always avoid the North, no matter how low I sunk, if you'd known me then – burning up with such a powerful rage against parochialism, provincialism, localism, Northerners, and finally the only job I could get in University brought me to this city, this pretty snow covered city perched on the edge of the Peaks, with a bleak Pennine wind whipping it again today. I'm weak and shitty to stay around here, betraying all my cosmopolitan principles. But I haven't the strength to leave and give this endless gloomy Yorkshire fog, its bogs and slime, the shove the heave ho I should, loathing it like I do. But truth is, I don't have strong emotions about anything any more, feeling flattened and deadened, which gives way to dread and terror. But that's not feeling, that's flinching. A basic elemental gut level cringing of indescribable panic, where nothing of human refinement remains. I wince away from the memory of terror which often brings it on. Must have a fling, sing a song, anything for distraction, convince him I fancy him. I lean over a bit.

"You lived in Paris with a Frenchman for years Charlie" he speculates, fiddling with the gear stick. I put my hand over his and smile. The silly prick whistles slowly through his teeth. I blow him a kiss. My friends in the back must be mystified by now, but they're slurping away happily at cider, enjoying their ride, and Bridie burping gently in my ear as I leer shamelessly at my driver

"Yes yes yes. An absurd and brutalised turd. The fixation of my feeble life. He nearly took away my life in the end as well, revolutionary fucking Professor. An arrogant vain Lacanian man. Met him first in '68 on the barricades at the Sorbonne when we were tearing up the paving stones to find the beach underneath. He was a leading enragé then and took his megaphone to bed. The sun shone out of his bum. Then he joined the bastards and became A Deconstructor from inside the Sorbonne. I was trying to be cosmopolitan see. I thought he would imbue me. A suave Frog from the Academy. To civilise me. How wrong can you fucking be"

He looked disgusted "What's that supposed to mean?"

"The dominant conquering macho heroes of '68 were worse when they were Frogs. Or Krauts for that matter. They swept a winsome woman fair off her feet. Do you realise I'm celebrating the 30 year anniversary of '68 next year all by myself, none of you lot knew or cared a damn about it. England nearly scuppered radicalism again, but there were a few of us, but too few for the brave new world . . . Oh give me a Kraut and a Frog for supper. At least *they* must be celebrating this anniversary . . ."

"What disgusting racial stereotypes you indulge in"

"Aw shit, Toby"

"It's true. You're outrageous. Krauts and Frogs. You wouldn't say wogs. Why Frogs then?"

"Dunno. It fits"

"Charlie you're not serious"

"You noticed"

"But racialism's so serious and deadly. How can you play around with its stereotypes"

"Like Yids on the Skids, you mean"

He looked hurt, deeply deeply cosmically offended, distended with outrage, growing by the minute. "You disgust me", and I knew I did, but couldn't help it. I wasn't going to explain again that it's to do with fun being allowed with dominant nations, but not never ever with oppressed people, isn't it? Because my principles are to do with oppression and not protecting sensitivities of overbearing bullies and boorish imperialist nations. I take the piss out of the bloody British all the time in the name of the Irish, and anybody else they happen to be sitting on and shitting on at the time, and Israel has to stop its genocide against the Palestinians before I start hallowing the sacred name of oppressed Jews. There are too few of them around and history can't be on your side for ever. What about the never never lands of the Arabs there where they've lived for centuries? But I'm not mentioning all this now. I know how irrational he is about it. Perhaps I'd be irrational if someone slammed my sensitivities, ramming home healthy lustrous hair. If they dared, I'd kill 'em. No I wouldn't. I'd want to go away and hide for ever. What a mess these delicate feelings nevertheless.

"Listen Toby I refuse to conform to this heavy lefty politically correct censorship where you can't call a spade a spade"

"Cooooooeeeee" whoops Natty in the back "Dis Spade needs a loo soon"

"You're disgusting Charlie. You do it to shock"

"No way. I just avoid the censorship that's all. I refuse to censor my vocabulary for the thought-police. I'm not a racist. I co-habited carnally with a Frog. I've loved lots of Yids. Big black men turn me on completely. What's racist about that?"

"It's the racism that's the turn-on" says Bridie quietly, startling me out of my skin. Now certainty's a sin in my book, but it took Bridie to make me start questioning my inflexible line on this one. She had me squirming, confirming my own deep suspicions about myself.

"Absolutely" says Toby, turning round to beam at her in the back and giving her a long lingering look, making the van swerve, jangling my nerves all up. I felt ridiculous in light of that look. Imagining he wanted to fuck me! That *I*, Lady Muck, would be doing him a favour graciously, when he was eating here out of Bridie's palm, with her calm depths of wisdom, unplumbed before. I'd treated her like some Mother-Earth Irish virgin-whore before, hadn't I? Well hadn't I? A sad-eyed Lady of the Dole Queue who knew a thing or two about art and folk music, but was just a hairy fairy really. And here she was, with steely insight, fixing me rigid in my seat, and defeating all ambitions and missions of me as Conquering Heroine, making Toby crawl. Why did I want to anyway? It must be to avenge this role reversal, an undress rehearsal for some future intended re-emergence from this shell. Even then I understood it was temporary, this fate, a date with my demons that would soon be over. And here I was, recovering from sermon-like admonitions from the two of them, with Natty joining in as injured party, with hearty good laughs at the lot of us, earnest earnest. Getting our categories right, to deal with her *lived* reality.

"Bloody intellectuals have no business getting this emotional about language" I grumbled, knowing it was rubbish, but lamely defending myself against this unholy alliance. They were staring at each other again. Oh brother. At least I assumed she was returning his gaze from behind. I felt dazed and bewildered and jittery about his sudden abandon with driving, and tried to unwind the window. I needed air, becoming aware of jealousy. He was *my* fan, and she'd pinched him, this lazy Irish colleen. I wonder what Toby would make of her prick-teasing for money for booze? how she uses her sexuality for monetary gain? I grinned at the idea of his solemn response to that vision. My mission might be rescued after all. I thought of a way to tell him tactfully. I've told you pretension-busting was my thing, and Bridie preening herself primly in her new intellectual status, and him trusting it and lusting after it, made me hate them both, though I'm loath to admit it.

"We stoppin' soon?" says Natty

"Yes we will. At the next Services stop" he says, giving me a vicious look meanwhile. In the dog house am I, you lousy uptight pompous little prick. We'll see if you stay so sanctimonious, or it sticks in your throat, when I gloat over your maiden's mishaps with her tits – pap happy for anyone under Wicker Arches. My malice goes marching on so megalo-manically, I don't realise this is simply Hell Having No Fury. And the jury's still out on my racism. They haven't decided between them whether I'm fit to speak to, and hanging Judge Jeffreys here in the front is going to make me swing and dangle for a long time for the sins of every waspish racist he's ever encountered, while saintly Bridie will polish her halo and glow ghoulish green light in my direction, eliminating my imperfection and ignominy, while she carefully selects bits of herself to show him. And not the bits on display at Wicker Arches on a Saturday evening I'll be bound. I chuckle at my new found anger. At least it shows a sign of life. I sound hollow and fish-wifey, cackling, and don't care.

They carry on staring at each other all the time over a cup of tea TEA. Well he drinks tea, and she sips cider carefully poured into a plastic cup, not to disrupt the proceedings in the caff. And it is a caff, a Greasy Spoon for a honeymoon in clover. Old Rover's brought us into the drivers' eating room, a rough saloon where they look you over like lumps of meat. But we take some seats in a corner. Jean looks squeamish at the dishes piled high on the table, and even I lift my skirts daintily to step over the newspapers and cartons flying about as I make for a loo, pursued by Natty, who's very chatty and full of herself.

"I could make money fast in a place like dis. Yu just delay 'em a bit Charlie. I'll go get us some pocket money" and she sailed off out of a back door, plumage all backcombed. At least I think that's what she does to straighten her curls. I love this girl, she's so beautiful and brave and fun. No slave to misfortune, she would dance with glee at the faintest fortune, a black shiny queen with her sequined scarf trailing for Xmas. You could envy any slob seeking bliss in her gob, as she puts it.

"I'm off for a gob stopper Charlie" she says, and winks. How could they say I'm a racist when my love for this one knows no bounds? Heavens above, I mustn't let them get to me, these thought-police with a new found identity as racist – me ME of all people! I'll show the smug little slug where to put his slurs on my character, though my mirage in the mirror is so blurred and bleary I feel very weary all of a sudden and sick of defending myself. They could think what they wanted, these ridiculous slanted right-on Lefties, with such hefty doses of moralism for everyone else.

"You're not a racist Charlie, just anti-Semitic like most people in this country" he says, as I join the happy tea party.

"Don't start again" I warn. I'm really not up to it.

"You must see the point Charlie. For such an enlightened person, this attitude is criminal. You libertarians would fight every battle for Blacks and Asians and any other Ethnic, except the Jews, who you think overdo it and moan too much, don't you? don't you?"

"Shit Toby. I'm not well"

He's selling me short and I can't help it today.

"You think Jews are powerful oppressors who're full of self-pity and persecution and paranoia, don't you?"

"If you say so"

"Charlie!" says Bridie "You don't think any of that"

"She does, she does" he's getting agitated thumping his fist on the table. Agitated, petulant, pathetic.

"Oh leave her alone" says Jean, who's been silent all the way today so far. We're all respecting her reverie of misery and contemplation of her kids, but wish she'd join us again. I take her hand gratefully and raise it to my lips, planting a kiss, wishing Toby would shut up, but knowing he won't. He's like a Scottie dog, worrying worrying, shaking tossing chewing worrying a bone, and never giving up till he'd destroyed it utterly. I need a drink I'm thinking, wondering if I dare drink Bridie's cider. She seems mollified and on my side even. I pluck up courage and take a long swallow, and buck up a little immediately, feasting on visions of Natty's mixing of fucking and sperm and spittle on the premises nearby, and twisting it all round with a lascivious sigh, to make a wonderful erotic fantasy all of my own to replace his solemn face in front of me.

"Charlie, look at me"

God knows I'm reluctant to at the best of times, but I try to focus. He's taking us to London after all, locus of power and underprivilege, calling calling, where the rose hedges disappear for ever behind long straight walls and marble halls, a metropolis to get lost in, be anonymous, rootless, without the curse of the families and ties that bind, freedom, anomie, what they all deride as problems of contemporary living, but giving me freedom to be me me me, away from the confines the grapevines of local vocal parochial hellholes. No community, they wail, these sociologists, but I hail it as total liberation, a queendom all mine. These humans can cluster, but I must wander alone, drink wine and be free, be me, if only I could see a way to do it, be alone, when my desperate dread at the moment is that state precisely. I'm frightened to death of the self-confrontation involved in privacy. People who can't stand their own company are always right. So I compromise with mediocrity all the time, fighting down my contempt rather than free myself, I think spitefully, looking at him in the face now, concentrating on every blobby pore in his sore overworking face muscles. Mediocrity. Bores like you I have to endure rather than my own pure company because I'm afraid of being alone with my demons.

Aren't you honoured to have me around? I think loftily, but he's definitely not sold on that idea, sounding thoroughly disturbed and determined to nail me as baddie baddie Jew baiter, when all I hate and ever have done is Zionism and triumphalism of the kind sitting on his face as he decrees my disgrace is absolute.

"Your kind of liberal hypocrisy is the most pernicious of all. You sling around words like Yid and Frog and Kraut and when people are justifiably deeply offended you call them humourless bores"

"Do I?"

"Yes. I've heard you. Witless Worthies is your favourite expression"

"Witless Worthies. I see" It fit him so perfectly, I must have been inspired.

Jean giggled, actually *giggled*. It was getting truly farcical then, anyone could see. Though a shadow flitted fast across my mind: in this conversation I don't want Jean and me on the same side. She really is open wide to racist accusations.

"It's up to oppressed people to decide what is offensive, what their senses of humour can take, not the oppressors" he says, snottily.

Which makes me a bloody oppressing member of the master race, I suppose. His insults finally stung me into responsibility.

"My French slimeball used to call his fellows and sisters Frogs in English"

"And lots of Jews are anti-Semitic" he snapped "their self-hatred doesn't excuse it or justify you doing it"

Bridie was looking complacent, admiring her Hero almost. I drank a toast of her cider to that woeful thought, and glanced at the floor. She'd brought four more bottles in her carrier bag. I'd better revise my desire to stir the dirt and blurt it all out about her tricks with the prick in the lavender shirt. But I gave her a look. She wasn't getting off the hook entirely. She would have to share her cider to buy my silence if she wanted him and this unspeakable nonsense he kept on about.

"You can't have it all ways" I say icily, entering into the frigid spirit of the thing "you tell me I'm turned-on sexually by Blacks because I'm a racist and this perversely appeals presumably. Or at least Bridie does and you agree. Then you say I'm not a racist just anti-Semitic. Which is it racist or not?"

"Charlie you're not a racist in any way. I've heard your lectures against racism and imperialism and I know you're not. But your language is degrading to oppressed groups"

"Because you don't think they're oppressed, is that it?" says Bridie "Jews and the French being so powerful. What about the Irish, do you call us Paddies?"

"My grandad was Irish" I say huffily.

"That's irrelevant. I told you" says Toby.

"Are we Paddies, Charlie?" Bridie insists.

"NO" I say sulkily "No. Only in joking. You can't cut humour out of life or you're dead"

"So Irish jokes are OK"

"NO" I sulk. They've cornered me, and it's not a corner I want to see. I wriggle.

"Leave her alone" says Jean. Oh dear this is obscene.

"Charlie, you have to take responsibility for your language. It hurts. I feel hurt by the word Yid. I hate you for using it. And I know you know better"

He makes me cringe like a schoolgirl, winging and whining like that. I nearly spat it out yes you do moan too much it's true, but I bit my lip. A slip like that and I'd be joining the Nazis for him. His prim self-righteousness made my flesh crawl. I wanted to bawl out I'll use the names I choose for nationalities, but had an uncomfortable feeling there was an argument here needed rescuing for him from all that supercilious slime he surrounded it with. I suspected I agreed and must pay heed and mend my ways, but I looked at his smarmy face and decided he could fend for himself. It wasn't up to me to defend his arguments. He wasn't my student any more, and nearly so nearly, I'd been imprudent enough to seduce him. How he'd have reduced me to tears if I'd tried. I realise I got Toby all wrong. He hasn't been a wimpish fan burning up with lust for me these years at all, but a strong moral man with an axe to grind, whose trust in teacher was finding its natural limits. Oh umbilical chords were severing all over the place and spilling guts around on hallowed ground like me.

I want to flee rapidly from this nasty little nest, which is getting on my nerves and preserving a tight band of tension round my head. My hands are trembling too. This won't do on my trip to London, and here comes Natty from the loo looking lovelier that ever, licking her lips in mock derision, and swaying those hips, a vision in scarlet for lorry drivers, a big black harlot to wet their imaginations. Though it's more than fantasy that's won this bottle of Scotch she's brandishing and plonks down on the table.

"Now DEN boys and girls. How *dat* for de journey?"

Jean twists her mouth into a tight mean line and Bridie sighs *she should sigh sadly* like that. I discover my new malevolence towards Bridie, who should be glad and pleased for the booze, not using her new position as Consort to disapprove of us.

"Where did you get that Natty? I thought you were broke" says Toby.

"Dat Father Xmas, he poured forth and multiplied all over me, didn't he den?" she laughs, and I wonder what it has to do with him anyway.

"Natty I'm responsible for you all on this trip. You mustn't disappear. Did you steal that?"

He really didn't understand her did he?

"I thought they didn't sell liquor here on the Motorway. In fact they don't. Where did it come from?"

"Well a man wanted a bit of hot chocolate. Which is Me. So we swapped"

"Where?" he says stupidly.

"Where?" she mimics.

"Where did you go for this?"

"Over there behind the lorries" she waves her arm.

His eyes narrow under those lids "You mean you prostituted yourself for a bottle of whisky"

"Aw Man, don't mek dat so miserable-soundin' "

"Natty that's prostitution"

"Don't be so *dumb* Man"

"I can't allow it"

"Juss don't yu worry yu little sen 'bout me, let's go, let's go" she says, looking furtive suddenly, as a big blond man trundles in and over to his mates at the next table, smirking at her and telling the details. They all let out hollers and whistles and Toby looks mortified, Bridie about to cry, and Jean all pursed up. They make me sick as the pricks over there all staring with tongues hanging out at Natty's slit skirt. I actively seize the initiative, and herd everybody out past the nerds and the turds assembled now in a row round our table, wanting their turn. It's getting dangerous. I'm learning fast about transport caffs. You don't act daft and seduce the natives without bargaining for a football team.

"Don't go. We want some"

I suddenly think of Howling Wolf singing Let me have some and how different it sounds.

"Plenty more of us to go round" they leer "let's have some fun ladies" and we break into a run outside the door, scrambling in the van, and off we're off, as the blond man's friends tumble out, chasing us cursing and waving their arms.

"Merry Xmas" shouts Natty, in the front seat now, with the window down, leaning out and waving laughing loving the excitement and Toby's raving beside her.

"Listen you bloody stupid black bitch, you could have been killed and it would have been my fault"

"What did yu call me den Toby?"

"What?"

"Yu called me a black bitch. Now den Toby, what did yu call me? A black bitch black black black"

"You are black aren't you" says Jean.

"Yeah but Toby don't believe in callin' a spade a spade. Least dat what he say"

"You stupid stupid bitch" he says.

"No yu said *black* bitch"

"I didn't mean."

"No. Nor did Charlie"

"Oh heck let's forget it"

"Yeah Man"

"Oh Lord"

"Yeah yeah yeah"

"Oh shit"

"Going down slow"

"Oh God"

"Toby Man just shut the fuck up"

"Oh Christ yes yes yes"

18

He's miserable all the way to London down the M1, and we're turning onto the North Circular Road before anybody says a word. It's Jean, rousing herself next to me.

"I've never been to London before"

We've promised not to mention her kids during this trip, though it's tough not letting things slip when we're all outraged at developments, and the stuffed up inhibition makes us all feel constipated. I can tell, looking at the others, pofaced. Only Natty is laced with a bit of humour. But the rest steeped in gloom. No room for Xmas. Let's try to change the tune.

"London's luvly" I announce firmly "I love every brick of London"

"I'm thirty-three and never seen dat Queen"

"I've never been here either" says Bridie in a small voice.

It's incredible, they've never been, but I don't show the shock. There's nothing in Jean's narrow life as wife and mother would have brought her here, and dear Natty's too busy living wherever she is, to travel afar or follow false stars of dreaming. While Bridie's just never drifted this way. Well what can you say to such a lack of drive and demented greed for experience as I had, needing London when I was young like a limb, a lung. I depended on it being there to rescue me from everything awful, loathsome, petty, and primitive in life so far.

"You love London because you don't come from it. If you did, it would be dirty and tiresome" says Smiler, driving.

"Tired of London, tired of life" I say, clichés ready, and ready to run if the son of Sodom would let me out.

"Rubbish. It's a question of where you're coming from" he snaps.

"Yes I've heard of relativity too, but London is absolute and unique, even if you've lived there for ever"

"I don't agree" says Bridie, looking at me, carefully plucking up courage. It's daring stuff we're getting today "You always romanticise what you haven't got. Grass is always greener somewhere else. So many people love Dublin. It leaves me cold. I couldn't wait to leave. It all always seemed to be happening somewhere else far away"

He's gazing at her in rapture. She's captured herself a Social Worker for life.

"It's true Bridie" he nods, eyes on the road again. "Charlie hates the North as crude and brutalised, but I find it friendly and warm"

"Like a bowl of stew, a thick gooey glue of sentiment and bovine stupidity. Should appeal to you, I can see that"

"Charlie!" protests Jean.

"Wow dat's some temper, Charlie girlie-o"

"How can you generalise about people like that. You're doing it again. It's so crude" says Bridie.

"She does it deliberately" he says, summarising me like men like to.

"Oversimplify. Don't deny the truth though" I'm sticking to it "I detest and despise everything the North represents – working class communities cuddling together in bigoted prejudiced small closed ignorant superstitious claustrophobic HORROR, a welter of HORROR. A place of patriarchs and communities oppressive to women, that crucify sensitivity and individualism, and murder MURDER anyone wanting to be free, to be different, like me me me. Do you know what it was like learning Latin in the middle of a festering mob of football hooligans, fighting for my homework when other girls were curling their hair to go a-courting. No aborting either then, you were stuck married finished tied up trussed and cussed and cursed for life, a working class wife in Yorkshire. I don't know anything more hateful to be bashed and bruised and battered from every angle in a cultural spiritual DESERT that they actually LIKE. That's how oppressed they are. They love their oppression, those fat docile lumps humping kids from pillar to post to bingo hall and to pillow and back. I'm sorry Jean I didn't mean to . . ."

"It's true it's true" she nods vigorously "I'd do anything to get out, to have had your chances. But it's taken me till now to wake up"

"And you YOU YOU" I get a new wind and start prodding this pompous sod from behind "a cosmopolitan Jew *you* should be, instead of skulking up there in the sticks basking in its bloody *warmth*. A big fish in a small pond I suppose is your game, and of course the bloody family the families the holy working class families are everywhere there for you, one big happy Jewish family after the other, even though they're not Jews they have the same sodden stupid sentiment about nuclear family holocausts" I sink back exhausted, and swig the whisky they're passing round. I've gone too far with him, but my philosophy is you might as well be hung for a sheep as a lamb. His smugness has made me flip and *her*, sipping whisky on the other side of Jean. I stare at her as though it's all her fault, – the North, the Family, Everything.

"My brother lives here" she says indifferently, and they all fasten on to the fact in a solid act of ignoring me, the embarrassment in their midst. Oh God, to be an Outsider with these three is too much even for me.

"Where Bridie? Where exactly?" asks Toby, keenly, urgently "You never told me. What does he do here?"

"In Kilburn. He doesn't work, if that's what you mean. He's in a Squat"

"Oh" Toby is disappointed. It runs from his ears and trickles down his trousers, anointing his lousy overrated and underskilled prick. Though I've no experience, it's a safe bet with these wet woolly hat types that he'd be hopeless. Helping you not loving you. Plugging a hole not searing your soul, like they should.

"He's a good boy though, my brother"

A GOOD BOY the ancient Irish matriarchy floods over us powerful protective and blind.

"Hasn't he ever done anything?"

"He's sort of political" she says vaguely, and my ears fold

forward avid for details. A retail line in IRA shoddy goods is the basic body of Kilburn trade and parades aren't public and Bridie's hiding her knowledge clean away from us and our indiscreet drunken tongues. She's looking the sweet innocent colleen again but *I want to know.*

"Maybe we could meet him" I say and she looks startled but not opposed.

"Yes, we're going to Kilburn. A friend has a flat there, floor space at least" Toby says, intrigued again that the beloved's brother is at least not a hopeless dropout, anything but that, he wants her brother to work, be a worthy, like him.

And indeed we're upon it suddenly. Here's Staples Corner and Cricklewood Broadway and we're shooting down Shoot Up Hill to the Kilburn High Road, that long Roman Road to Marble Arch, jammed solid, tooting at traffic. It hoots all the way and the dirt smells different, exciting, inviting, alive, though the dives and the dreariness are every bit as bad as the North. Worse even out here. But it's this feeling that anything's possible, it's London and I'm Doris Whittington. That fabulous feeling of hitting town for the first time. Adventure, don't mention the cost.

We're all behaving very well, I reflect. Sitting here sedate and respectable almost, in the van, while he negotiates floor space for us inside this big mansion block off Willesden Lane. And we clamber inside, up and up, to a top flat, sparse and bare, just a chair and a table, and it's freezing cold. But we're told This is it, so we all sit down on Toby's sleeping bags and finish the whisky in cups. I'm feeling old and sad. It's a bad scene returning in failure to a place. So I make a mad face at Natty, who laughs and wheezes through her smoke. She's pleased, I can see, by all these new experiences, and her pleasure reflects back to me. I cheer up "Come on, let's find your brother Bridie"

and we do, a few hours later, climbing up the stone steps

on Maygrove Road. He looks about thirty, but her twin must be younger, tall and fair, with long blond hair in a pony tail, but pale and a bit frail I reckon for the IRA. But his face transforms as light dawns and he recognises sister Bridie. Kissing her, it's bliss he's feeling. Sends me reeling off to deal with my own resentment about her. Could be simple jealousy, I admit, though shit, I never felt it before. I loved her till the moment Toby looked tenderly at her. I will not will not be jealous, I say to myself. It's something irrelevant to our friendship. But you know, it's not. It's just too hot to handle for me, who fancies myself above that sort of thing, and here I am ringing my hands with envy at the way all the men in the room greet her, so pleased to meet his beloved sister they've heard about. I hear myself shouting above the din to Toby "It's all very homely here isn't it?" My sarcasm sounds bitter and twisted and he looks away.

"Yes it *is*" says Natty "finding a brother in London is better than a sister in Sheffield, which is all I've got"

Bridie introduces us all to Gerry and his eyes flicker with interest at Natty, who flashes back so many signals that Bridie seems shy between them, and hero Toby rescues her. So the couples pair off into corners, after a long time when we all sit listening to tales of squatting and cousins in Ireland and Bridie's haemorrhage and her thinness, which worries him, and ways to screw the Social Security. "There's a pub down the High Road cashes cheques" says Gerry.

"A cheque would be a fine thing" says Bridie.

"I work the Lump now and again, building, and they pay straight cheques, no messing. So you can get your dole OK"

"Gerry be careful"

"That's OK Bridie, not to worry at all"

"I mean be *really* careful"

"I am I am"

"No but"

"Bridie baby *you* take care. Don't worry about me. Not at all. *At all*"

He seems in a hurry suddenly that we should go.

Including Natty, who sulks furiously, but comes along after a cuddle and huddle in her corner with him.

"He's NEAT" she tells Bridie outside "Woweeeee he's *really* neat"

"Yes. But don't get carried away Natty. He's a devil with the ladies that one"

"No kidding" says Natty, eyes narrowing. I don't believe it and want to tell her so, that Bridie is warning her off for another reason. But the other reason would be even more difficult to accept and anyway I can't tell for sure if that's a real IRA cell. Was it all pure bluff in there the easy camaraderie and those other three making tea and the silent punk in the corner and conversation like good kissing cousins from across the sea. No sinister plotting or balaclavas and not a whiff of gelly or Semmy in the dank flat, but then the Ceasefire would have stalled everything anyway. Her brother had a haunted look at the end, and the big question which struck me hovering bothering me all the time Does he know about her drinking? What was he thinking when she described her bleeding? She nearly bled to death Man. Back in the van I pondered on this a lot, his lack of action about her, in spite of his love. Must mean preoccupation with something else more important to him, and only a mission could rate higher than his sister. I could see that through my film of jealousy.

We get to the Conference next day at the Central Poly in Marylebone Road, though now it's called the University of Westminster. I have a terrible slanging match with the Security Man through the hatch in his glass box. He won't let us in to attend the workshop. I wax long and loud in all kinds of strong epithets about the kind of authoritarian that rules the place, but the Conference Committee has hastily convened and decides we're decidedly bad taste and not to be admitted at all, as object–subjects or anything else. So Toby trots off without us, and I'm left shouting impotently that Laing would have let us in, It's a Sin. But of course this was predictable, the rejection of the real raw data at the door. So eventually we stagger across the road and sit on the steps near Madame Tussauds and the tourists.

"50 pee Sir?"

"Move along move along. You can't sit here, and no begging or you're nicked sweetheart, geddit? NICKED"

He's big and strong this man from the Met, who flicks me aside so I fall over off my step, floundering in the slush and the wet, with my skirts all dirty. And worst of all, my scarf slips off, flip flop I'm a doley and a dosser in a London street, just tossed aside with a casual flip flop of the wrist, with the other flotsam of the Capital floating flitting across its bright gleaming surface, where dreams are made and madams like us flayed and laid bare on a dump to die, if we're not very clever and cunning at running away.

"Let's go back to Kilburn" I say.

"Hooray hooray. To see your brother?" says Natty to Bridie who shakes her head.

"No Natty. Let's explore" and we call for some booze and fags with the £20 from Gerry and sit sipping it on the Jubilee Line, feeling things are fine, improving by the minute. Though with pangs of regret that I missed talking about beloved Laing, damn it and blast it to hell.

"Well I reckon we've a better dressed street person in Sheffield. It must be the 'Rag and Tag' street market. This lot are *derelict* with no flair at all" I say, sitting on a seat in Kilburn Square, where it all seems to be happening that night for street people, folding themselves away in shop doorways, in pieces of cardboard. There are several groups, quite a crowd, where the Salvation Army van stops with soup and gives us a blanket each. I'm overwhelmed with relief at this gesture in this vast city, with my past striking such self pity in my mind when I remember it. I'm finding it very painful indeed coming here. Not at all what I expected. This is only a place for the hopeful, the positive, the bold, the successful. For the rest it's a perpetual test and harassment, with everything faster and colder than Sheffield, though the actual temperature's much warmer. I feel calmer altogether in the North. For what's the worth and the value of the land of opportunity in my state of immunity from self-improvement? I feel small and remote and cut off from an impossibly fast and efficient moving world here, striking fear all the time in my tum. Boom boom goes my heart too, over beating, arrhythmic. Oh dear, this is a dismal state to be in.

For my sins, I'm being lectured by a priest. At least, he's dressed up clerically, and the men skulking around with cider bottles keep calling him Father. What a wild way to go on the town in London, with a Holy Joe and Strongbow to drown my sorrow. For tomorrow we must return and burn my hulk of a metropolitan boat, and see my hopes floating away down a river of vomit and cheap cider. There's a wider context of course. Always is. And that's my complete divorce from any sense of reality induced by these pills. I know it is a lack of perspective on my life that is the price to pay for blotting out panic, in blotting out everything. Yet here in London, images are winging into my consciousness in the storm, as the wind rattles the windows nearby, and my meagre wrappings are flapping and flying, and God is trying to get through to me, apparently, says the priest, lying through his teeth. Mine are chattering. I pull the blanket over my head and cross myself so he'll go away convinced he's bled me dry of lust, though I wouldn't trust him an inch out of range of these fluorescent lights. He's too much hair for one thing, dark and curling onto his shoulders and down his nose and over his hands. Anyone so hirsute has got to be sensual too, though there's something repellent about him which I can't spell out. He comes too close to me, breathing my air, staring, sinister, wary of you mister. Go away and play with Bridie. She's hiding a crucifix under all those layers. Make contact and lick her soul clean. Mine's mean beyond redemption.

Altogether, this London's not been too happy an outing and these three sit in a row behind, doubting my judgment about the place, silently suffering as we hit the M1 next day. Xmas Eve, their faces long as fiddles as we race along weaving in and out of traffic that's thick and tight and irritable, as everyone's

174

rushing pushing to leave London. I wonder what it's like to be going somewhere purposefully where there's a welcome waiting, and you not hating yourself, but full of Xmas spirit. Not that we're empty by any means. We're drinking Jean's whisky today. She says she needed it to face going back and Toby gave her the money, I bet. Though he doesn't usually give money for booze, he could hardly refuse her. Depression is written so deep in her lines and furrows and expression of such abject misery, I could leap out and kill every motorist who overtakes us, making us brake and jolting the flow of liquor down her throat, glug glug glug glug, like plugging a bottomless pit of hopelessness helplessness powerlessness pain.

"I'm-going-to-get-that-bastard-by-the-throat" she spits after a while.

"Knutton?"

"Knutton and Cheetham. I'm-going-to-kill-them."

"Here we go, here we go" sings Natty.

"Here we go here we go here we go"

We all join in, even sour old dour old Toby who's kept very quiet about How To Treat Alcoholic Clients. But his workshop's cooled his passion for Bridie, his treatment must be unethical. He's rigid in regard to her, frigid and cool. The rules must be resurrected, you could tell, though this was playing hell with her nerves. He swerves round a bus and she screams her head off.

"Christ, Bridie shut up" yells Jean, but she's screaming and screaming a weird piercing sound that turns into a howling and then back again scream howl scream I can't bear it and Jean slaps her head hard but it's worse and reaching a higher pitch like some deathless witch being burnt alive.

"Shut her up for God's sake" shouts Toby, but she's still screaming raw terrible wracking screams from the bottom of her being it's unbearable I can't take it she's been attacked by the devil himself her heart is breaking and the van's braking and the tyres screech and it's all screaming and screaming beyond belief

175

and then everything goes black .

Book Two

19

Looking back, I can say that crash was the best thing that ever happened to me. But it didn't feel like that when I woke up one day, feeling so sick and panicky and painful and terrified, I thought I'd died or fried alive, so burning hot did I go, and prickly, and so slowly did I come to enough to suss things out, and then I didn't want to live anyway, when they told me Natty and Bridie and Jean had all been killed instantly in a crash that cut the van in two on Xmas Eve, and it was now Boxing Day, and I was the luckiest woman on earth to survive that. In the front seat with Toby I'd been, while the back was sawn clean away, with my beloved sisters burning as it turned over and over. A nurse had seen it on the telly. They'd been filming the Xmas traffic jam, and wham in the middle of the newsflash we go crashing across the screen in pieces, pursued by a huge jagged juggernaut which buried the back of the van and set it alight. This nursing sister told me with big frightened eyes as she felt my pulse, and monitored the shock she was causing. Then they shot my bum full of tranquillisers and pain killers and I went into a three day sort of coma, just coming round barely conscious to eat and drink. I remember thinking how starving I was, but aware of nothing else except the kindly sister of mercy, my substitute for deepest roots so tersely severed, cut in two, sliced apart, my dear departed sisters of sin where are you?

The worst thing about death is its finality, the idea that you will never NEVER see them again, they don't exist. No matter what you do, you will never go through it with them, and never say never is my motto. Yet now I'm stuck in this gruesome grotto with NEVER in big bold letters and blood running down the walls. The thought appals, but something else is coming through. Something new and true and so significant, I can hardly take it in at first, so unsuitable does it strike me for my mourning period. But I actually want to live. I have this extraordinary yet ordinary lebenslust, and from out of the blue a new confidence, and the trust it gives that it would all be allright, and a long fight ahead would get me on top of the world where I belonged by right, and the endless night of the last ten years was over. I wasn't dead. It was them instead. I'd been saved to live and rave again, and by God this time I would make it crack.

But mostly I was ashamed of this feeling, at first kept pushing it down as inappropriate. Like my ravening thirst for water of all things, *water*, and cleaning and purifying, which consumed me and compensated for the jitters and shakes, which were constant. Every waking minute I felt a fear of shadows, and the dark corners of the long narrow room in that hospital they'd put me seemed like a coffin with the lid about to shut. If I didn't shout and shove enough with every bit of effort to keep my head above ground, I'd vanish from view. Nobody knew me here. I could disappear without a trace. On the other hand, that place with its bilious green walls saved me entirely. I couldn't face telling them I was a hopeless derelict. They were so pleased to have me, a survivor. I provided them with endless tales for tea of how lucky and plucky is she getting over the death of her loved ones, her family I'd said, deepest irony coming from me. 'Course they knew we weren't a real family, they'd had to deal with the bodies. But I said the dear dead departed were family to me, we were so close. Yet I didn't, I couldn't, mention the ties that bound us compounded the lies that we sold ourselves. I told them instead we worked and lived together, which was true, and then came Heather, and they knew I had problems, but never seemed to deduce that his killer the booze had reduced me to my sorry state too.

I'd never noticed his ankles before. Well you don't do you, when spanking a person on his bare buttocks in a frenzy of passion yourself, practically coming the whole time with the rhythm and rhyme of his moans and cries and groans and whys why don't you beat me harder, grovelling down at your feet at that point where pain and pleasure meet in one climax. It would take a lot of tact and detachment to mention his ankles are swollen, but as I say I never noticed. It was my first transport into fantasy enacted and I was none too exacting about details like the state of someone's ankles. But now it's unmistakable as he stands there shaking and white at the foot of my bed with a bunch of battered irises. I HATE IRISES. Unfailing in a crisis these men, to make things worse. He's such a sight, and out of his head too. and reeking of booze.

"Well Charlie, you're a mess my girl"

Oh thanks very much for the joy you bring.

"Terrible accident" I sniff.

"It wasn't though"

He lurches towards me and a nurse stands worried at the door.

"Will you be allright?"

I say "Go away"

It's embarrassing. I don't want them to hear any of his rambling.

"For ever and ever Charlie" he grabs my hand "and that may be any time"

"What do you mean?"

I don't feel *that* bad.

"The cirrhosis finally got to me. It can't be long. Look at my legs." He peeled his shoes off and tattered socks and I squeezed his hand in shock. He appeared to be wearing wellies. Only it was his own body making the bulk, and the swelling extending half way up his leg like a massive padding of fluid round legs and feet. He'd cut the toes out of his shoes and wore the laces loose.

"You didn't tell me" I breathed, so wretchedly sad, but glad somewhere too that he was out of my life at last. His promiscuity still rankles. I swear I'd rather a man died than betrayed me any day, and here it seemed I was having my way. Though the real reason I was so unfeeling is the quantity of stuff they kept shooting into my bum for shock and delayed shock and all possible freak outs imminent after my crash. Though they'd no idea that this was comparative comfort here

183

after my life, and that I felt calmer and warmer inside than I had for years, though terrible fears were lurking, but they could lurk. I wasn't berserk with panic at all, and if it should come, let it do its damnedest. I was safe here from even my own fear for the moment.

"No accident?" I remembered.

"No. Toby's coming to tell you. The brakes were faulty, and they weren't when he left Sheffield. He'd had an MOT on the van. I feel dizzy, Charlie. Must go baby, goodbye goodbye" and he was gone. I know for good or ill, but gone, done, finished. Another epitaph over. How many people would I lose this week? I could hardly speak when Toby did arrive, looking haggard and awful, and crying all over me, inappropriately as ever. I was never cut out for a Jewish mother, though I often get shoved into this sorry role by bleeding hearts. A funny part for a shiksa, despised for amorality otherwise.

"I can't get over it" he sobs, gripping my wrist like a vice, as I stroke his beard. What price now your vicious racist? I hiss into his curls before I can stop myself, but he doesn't hear anyway. Full of himself and Bridie presumably, though he's incoherent and ill I suspect with grief like he's never known. But New Men like him can show it respectably, nay desirably. So he sobs on and on.

"Are they upsetting you these visitors?" says the worried nurse, frowning round the door, "Stella" her name displayed on her chest. A new informality pervades this best bit of the NHS.

"I'm OK" I smile weakly, wishing he'd shut up. It's embarrassing finally, men wailing. All these women who want men to emote should carefully watch them wailing, then reconsider. "And it will be OK Toby"

"No No NO. The brakes were tampered with. Do you understand? And the police are investigating. And the Social Workers at Brampton Lodge are saying you were a lot of loony feminist drunks who dreamt the whole thing up to get at the Council. And the Council say the same. And Brian Cheetham's still disappeared. And Hannah's coming to see you. How are you Charlie?"

"These things are connected" I say experimentally.

"Yes. Of course. Hannah says the Council is behaving like a Mafia and won't answer any questions about anything like who they're selling the hostel to. There's an elaborate conspiracy. Oh Charlie we need you. You do look well you know"

It was true. In a week I'd floated on a cushion of tranquillisers and pain killers for my multiple bruising, and eaten and drunk gallons of water, and felt better than I had for years. Except for the pangs and visions and visits from tits like this one who started sobbing again, all gushing like rain down my arms where I cradled his head on my breasts. They do love it, I kept thinking. He was actually holding my breast and stroking the nipple through my thick flannel hospital nightdress "Oh Charlie" he says, panting. But I let it pass as passion misplaced on the Motorway that ghastly day that saved my life, as it lost them theirs, and here he is wanting mother. Why do some have to die to save the others I ponder not for the first time in my life, and his hand wanders now to my other breast. This is no accidental rubbing in misery either. He's throbbing and thrashing around with his head between them, making the bed rock, and me liking it too much this so tender touch. I willingly let him undo the buttons and get his hands on them properly. It's such a shameful thing to be doing. We're crazy and mixed up. Madness mingles with pain, and he kisses and sucks, and the water jug comes crashing down on the floor, saturating us and the bed. He pulls back looking flustered, afraid, instantly guilty. I cover up quickly to smile at Stella, who's tutting and clucking around us in seconds.

"I must go" he says, visibly shaking himself, trying to waken from some trance he's in, making advances to an anti-Semite. Can't be right by anybody's standards for a good Jewish boy.

"You can't go all wet" says Stella, but his face is set and steely. Though it doesn't really come off him looking stern. He's too short and cuddly, like a squashy teddy covered in

185

brown fuzz, and sexless as hell. As I know damn well, I could get a buzz out of anyone touching me up at the moment. I'm flying high on a wave of optimism. *My life has been saved and I'm going to make the best of it*, and this moralistic shit wasn't going to bring me down by his look of evident rejection – now he's come round from sudden lust, and was remembering how disgusting I actually am.

"I'll come back very soon. How long is she likely to be in, Nurse?"

"Don't know. See the doctor on your way out. It's mainly delayed shock we're afraid of, and there's blood in the urine. Her kidneys got a knock, but she's the luckiest girl alive"

I twinkle at this and wink at him, but he flounces off as if it's my fault his assault and snuggling. Prim mug all re-arranged now.

"You can't win 'em all" I tell Stella, and struggle into the dry nightie while she makes the bed with fresh linen, and out of the corner of my eye I see a figure staring, watching it all. He's tall and dark and ugly as sin and wearing a dog collar.

"Come in, come in, Reverend. She could do with a bit of a blessing" says Stella.

"Actually . . ." I start to resist, but happy sister of mercy insists and draws him up a chair too close to the bed. I push it away hard before he can sit, but his fixed smile of benevolence doesn't flicker for a second. He's unctuous before he starts speaking and there's something familiar about him. I've seen a similar sickly grin somewhere out there lately, ugh he's hateful, leering, ugh ugh ugh.

"Go away I'm an atheist"

"Aw surely not"

"Why not?"

"Such a nice girl"

"Ugh"

"God loves you anyway. He saved you. His higher purpose needs you alive"

My ears prick up in spite of the sanctimonious tone.

"I must admit I'm lucky"

"It's God's will you live"

"But they died"

"You've been chosen"

"What for?"

"That will unfold"

Now I know you're thinking what piss and balls. And I know this is the flattering stuff that we all want to hear and I was ripe for conversion, lying there, lucky lucky girl. But where *had* my fear gone? It disappeared in that crash in a flash of fire and screaming tyres. My terrors had gone. Cured, and obviously I could be lured along to religion calling as an explanation for a vain woman who'd ditched her pain in a miracle show. I felt glowing all over at the thought of it. Me with a mission again at last. But not so fast, a lifetime of atheism takes a bit longer to expire.

"God needs you"

I'd no desire to be needed by anybody. It smacked too much of responsibility, and I've been avoiding that all my life. Never a wife because of the need for freedom and frolicking, fucking perhaps. But never mucking in with marriage vows and How was your day hubby and all the grubby grind and mind blowing boredom of chores and charity and conformity to wedded norms that stink as much as the sinks and loos you clean these mean obscene chattels and chains these lives in vain get rid of matrimony before we all go mad.

Though I am quite mad as mad as a hatter those shrinks all say in Sheffield. But here I'm playing an elaborate game of hide and seek. Don't seek out the freak and ye shall not find one. They've never asked me if I'm a nutcase and it's not the kind of thing you go around advertising. I'm simply responding to treatment, though I have a hunch a nasty old crunch will come fast when they start withdrawing the tranx, and I have to thank Toby for not claiming me as his Social Worker Client. I feel defiant about my past identity. Why should I be stigmatised? I'm telling lies in a way by not saying so, that I'm classified in a certain way, they ought to know I suppose. But meanwhile the tranx are flowing. I haven't felt the paralysing need for a drink or a cig. I just act normless and gormless and pleased to be here. Your average delighted-to-be-alive citizen.

Why should I shell them with Sheffield Skid stories? They've enough worries without me.

Now I see this slime is edging closer all the time. What is it with me in a hospital bed? They're all losing their heads and trousers to a lousy beat up heroine lying back on the pillows, and no scarf either, but a few hairs growing proudly. It's hilarious really, and the priest here's dying for a feel as well, I can tell by his heavy breathing and heaving chest. I put on my best bright halo and say:

"Thank God you came today to bless me. Now I must rest"

"Ah yes, you rest" and he puts his hand on my forehead and crosses me carefully down and across each breast, hesitating a bit longer each time.

"Is there anything on your mind, in your heart . . . ?" pointing ". . . before I go do you want to share any anger any pain anything you think is wrong that has happened . . . that might cause you to doubt God's wisdom . . ."

I think immediately of Melanie and Santa Claus, but pause for thought. I ought not to pour forth to a perfect stranger though I'm bursting with it. There could be danger if the car *had* been tampered with. Who knows what's going on when powerful sons of bitches know someone's on their tail? Even a few frail dropouts howling and wailing in the gales and the dark might light the spark that holocausts . . .

I lie back exhausted with the enormity of wanting to concentrate on myself and my mending, and why aren't I mentioning my friends very much? Such callous cold self absorption is a sign of disintegrated personality you might say, and in a way you'd be right. My days of fighting fear are over. The nightmare's suspended. Could be dreaming, but it seems obvious all of a sudden that my emotion for those women was an affair of collusion in decay, a bunch of headless corpses holding hands in the fray, go away go away reality we can't see you, and my sisters confirm. So no, it's not grief I feel, but vast unplumbed relief rapture. I'm off I'm free up up and away it's me it's me I'm rooting for and a way to be that's different, that doesn't involve the 1824 Vagrancy Act shoved up my bum every Saturday night by men men men. I want to be loved by them instead. Sleep in a bed again. I'm getting used to it in here, and the fear lifted at last, and the past receding. The pain the bleeding open wound in my psyche is healed somehow. I lie revealed and naked now, waiting for a new human to emerge on the ashes of the old, and it clashes with the image of those other three women victims. We were victims posing together as victims, and closed in a vicious circle. Shackled shackled trapped forever in the stasis of crisis of confidence in life. Victim powerless cackling victim for ever and ever and never recover revolving round and round a mutual support group misery-round our mutual soliloquies resounding ringing out over the Derbyshire hills as we swallow our pills and swill our potions a sense of motion of change is excluded TAKE OVER YOUR LIFE AND OWN IT.

We used to say in '68 now wait wait till we've had a drink and a think and *then* we'll do it. Well *then* we'd never do it and life waits for no woman, she spends her life waiting for *it*. Aw shit, he's stroking my head with its three hairs, and my breasts as well. It's hard to tell if he wants to though. It's as though he thinks I expect him to. He's got a faraway gaze, like a doctor listening with his stethoscope. But this grope has got to be better. It's the clergy interfering with the laity in the course of their conversions. I expect it's the Hand of God, so I might as well enjoy it. Enjoy Enjoy as Americans say, and here today I do. I shut my eyes and feel the massage of the priesthood doing me good, goodness flowing all over me, growing growing and whoops into orgasm before you know it, with his hand caressing me under the sheet and the other hand blessing me all the time on the top of my head. The bed shakes and rocks. I stare with shock straight into his cold mean eyes, as I come convinced he's the devil in disguise at that moment and don't care, don't turn one of my three hairs as he gets up and goes. All black flowing garments like a giant crow with gentle hands. Oh my they're claws I see. He turns at the door, beckoning greedily, grinning, feeding my full blown fantasy of possession. I tell you it was a hard sell, but I'm converted allright. A bright shining star hovers just out of sight to the right, flashing, and my dashing prince of darkness and light has flown.

I watch Hannah carefully the next day, as she sits on my bed. It's starting to cross my mind that visitors aren't taking my convalescence seriously. The idea of me fastened in bed chaste and charming, releases all kinds of alarming demons in them. I wait for her to pounce with not unpleasant anticipation, but she waves a bottle instead. She's not ready for me in my new incarnation, and pours a big one into the glass.

"I'll pass Hannah, really"

"Whaaaaaaaaaat" she steadies herself on my shoulder

"They're filling me with so much dope, it could finish me off"

"As you wish" she looks amazed, but swills it down herself and puts the bottle in her bag. I keep staring at it wistfully, closed and sealed, the end of an era.

"What are we going to do?" she demands

"Do?"

"Yes, DO. These bastards have closed ranks. Nobody will talk to me about anything. The Councillors deny everything – Gavin Knutton: they never *heard* of him you'd think, and he's built all their new clubs. Gavin Knutton won't speak to me at any price. There's a Security Guard outside Brampton Lodge and no-one can see Jean's kids since she died. Brian Cheetham's obviously panicked and run off. Charlie this is the biggest, messiest, most enormous scandal of the Century. The story of a lifetime. The Pulitzer Prize if we had one. And we don't have a bloody shred of proof. Not a bloody speck"

"Except the accident. If we could tie them to the accident. If we could make it murder . . ."

"Murder, Charlie. Murder! Do you really think? Murder?"

"Mass murder"

"My God Charlie, we've GOT to do something. Get up, get better, help me HELP ME, let's get them, the bastards. Oh. By the way. Heather's dead."

I had another visitor the next day. A great hulking hercules, who nevertheless I wouldn't touch with a bargepole in a million trillion years or lifetimes.

"Hope you don't mind me coming like. I've been in a bad way and they won't let me see the kids still and I don't know what to do"

"You're Dick" I knew he had to be handsome virile tough and weak and wobbly as a jelly.

"Yeah" gruff, bluff, ghoulish in my eyes, a terrible surprise seeing him here, hovering on the edge of my bed, holding red roses. They must have cost him his dole this week, poor bleak devastated bastard. Don't weaken. Melanie got those Come Hither eyes somewhere long ago, and not by saying no to daddy, was it WAS IT? Incest child molester, don't come near me.

"What do you want from me?"

"Just that you knew her, I never saw her since . . . . since . . . oh God I didn't mean to, I never meant to, I never did it, I never wanted . . . ." sobbing sobbing. But this one's not borrowing my tits for handkie. I'm getting wise to these guys and their grief.

"Believe me, believe me. You've GOT to believe me"

"Why should I?" I say crisply nastily irrelevantly.

"You're the only one left. Please, *please*. I never meant . . ."

Oh Lord, repentance is nigh. I wonder why they inflict it on me? and then I remembered I was this year's vessel for God's goodness and I listened hard, but couldn't hear His forgiveness flooding through me, at least not yet. Maybe he had a few years penance to do for cutting that van in two indirectly. He's as responsible as the brake breakers. I take a very dim view of paedophiles, so all the while he's crying I set my face severely, and stare at the wall, still noticing how tall and hulking his colossal bulk fills up my nativity stall.

"Go and holler somewhere else. I feel ill" I say eventually, and his crest falls so far I can't bear it. So I hold out my hand like a magic wand, and he charges over, grabbing it, kissing it, crying, kissing me on the mouth and cheeks, but at least my tits were free this time, and he rushes out "Thankyou thankyou. Thank God" which I think is pushing it a bit far.

and then the horrors hit me

20

A feeling as if my head's going to explode with tension implode with the tight band twisting tighter tighter with pincers squeezing every pore ringing wet with sweat pouring reeking leaking forever from an open wound that my body'd become alien possessed paralysed with fear and convulsions what is this fear a fear of death it must be so completely does it grip me a feeling of falling and vertigo when I lift my head from the pillow a swimming sea of things on wings revolving rolling round the room when I lie still with my eyes filled with vicious visions when I shut them nightmare flashes and something crawling and eating away behind my eyes I tell no lies when they reduced the tranquillisers by half next day saying time to go home soon my new security nearly jumped out of the window with me hanging on dangling desperate to escape from my own head never being able to switch it off and panic like I'd never known before racing booming heart and terror sheer white mortal terror as I stared at the wall calling calling for help trying to make sense of it all and Stella rushes in it's time to confess.

"Stella get the doctor, a shrink, get me a shrink. I must explain things"

"Now now dear not very well are we, it's only a slight come down from the tablets. You'll be fine in a while"

"NO-I-WON'T" I grab her collar and start shaking her with my face an inch away from her. Startled, flushed, frightened, she goes.

"GET-ME-A-DOCTOR"

She frees herself and scuttles off and returns with Matron, looking sombre.

"What's all this, you mustn't make a fuss, silly girl, we're all very busy you know. You're so lucky to have a room on your own, now stop being silly"

"I-WILL-KILL-MYSELF-IF-YOU-DON'T-GET-THE-DOCTOR"

"Nonsense. Silly girl" but she looks scared, ever so slightly, and disappears for ages. I hear them coming and going and talking outside the door but nothing happens and nobody comes. I start screaming and hyperventilating at the same time so they both come back and stick a bodkin in my bum, upon which I float float remote remote, but remembering as soon as I wake up, I'm never taking that again. I wait for the doctor's visit, full of hate for the running down of the Welfare State and the NHS, though I'm doing very well in my private wing near Leicester somewhere, haven't a clue, don't care. Just want to get better. I realise my optimism's freeze-dried only and hasn't disappeared. The change is fundamental. I must get well and get over it, but I couldn't put up with that, nobody could. Was that what I would be like without "medication"? That was too dire to contemplate. Life was over if that were so. Where could I go to escape from me?

"Severe withdrawals" she said "That's all. Don't worry. But you should have told us you were addicted to tranquillisers before we gave you any. We'll sort you out now. On a slowly reduced dosage over months and months. A month for every year you've been taking tranquillisers it will take. You'll have to be very patient and see it through no matter how bad it gets"

"But it's a nightmare" I can feel myself contorting up.

"I dare say. As bad as heroin I do believe. And much more protracted. But now we know we can do it properly with the correct dose. Now tell me exactly what you've been on"

"How do I know I should stop them?" I wail "What if this is the real me and not just a withdrawal state. I was like this before, that's why I take them. Why do you assume I should come off? How do I know I don't still need them"

"You don't know. But it's a risk worth taking. To see how you are under that blanket after all this time. Nothing is worse than addiction. You have to break it. These tablets are not a long run solution to life in my opinion. Now tell me how many have you been taking?"

"I don't know" I sighed how could I admit to handfuls of the things some days when it was bad to a woman doctor like this, so cool and calm and collected as she inspected me over her half moon glasses "I feel I may pass out any time but I don't . . ."

"You won't. It's only a feeling. Take deep breaths. Don't fight it. Try to relax"

And lying there, staring at the green ceiling when she'd gone, a miracle happened. I just knew I could do it. From somewhere deep inside my being came the absolute certainty that this was all a temporary horror, though a necessary horror, part of a prolonged story. It had not been in vain all the pain. I had been healing inside, under my cabbage exterior, these past years, and all my fears and terrors were being laid to rest, and this present mess was a blip of chemical withdrawal which I would beat, defeat utterly in fact. There was a positive side even to that. The worse the withdrawal, the stronger it meant my unpoisoned potential self was fighting back on the attack, with every prickling pore that persecuted me night, day, endlessly. I will win this thing this battle and be better than ever before, and I was glad I hadn't confessed to alcoholism too. I wouldn't at the time, so ashamed was I in front of this Power Doctor asking why why why destroy yourself? You have so much going for you . . .

Of course she knew that was the stupidest question of all, presupposing that rationality is immediately visible, arguable, and the same for everybody, and if I'd shared her uncomplicated approach I wouldn't be here in this leaking lurching boat. I'd be high afloat a liner with fine career, not a freak and a failure littering up everybody's streets and side wards, loitering without intent, lurking, lingering, oh so long. No. Somewhere along the way something inside me was saying a huge NO to the paths I'd chosen of Faculty Rose or perfect partner. When what I really needed was time to recover, withdraw, solve it, sort it, don't abort it, see it through. How new this perspective, suddenly flooding me. Instead of being an aberration, these past six years had been a scream of silence, a cocoon, a living room for me to dwell in, a tiny hell as home, protected from the big bustling world of contradictions I couldn't solve, I'd built a shell of tranx and booze to dwell a while, till the wounds healed, and the miracle is that I didn't kill myself in the process, caught up in the cure for my soul as killer. Own goal for my poor abused body and nervous system, whose rhythms awry was why I suffered so much right now.

And how I did it in the next crucial months is another story. But I never looked back from that day in the Leicester side ward, when I stopped shaking when taking my daily reduced dose of Librium. It was so sudden, I stared at my hands for ages in disbelief. Then relief rushed over me, washing away any reservations I might have about leaving. Run run out into the fresh air, clutching my plastic bag with my hospital knickers and reduced strength Librium and sleepers and £20 Hannah donated on her last visit.

I'm giving them all the slip as I set off on my brand new life. They expect me to go back to Sheffield, helping them uncover the plot. But Hannah was hot shot investigative reporter, she could manage without me. I had to run fast and far from the past and its livid scars that might suddenly vividly splutter up and rip me to shreds. So I went tripping to the station, flipped out, wonky and wobbly, huffing and puffing, but determined as an old steam train that the rain pissing down and the fates hissing all around were not going to get this girl down ever again. I'm on my way, hey hey baby. Off to decadence in crevices of the big city for me.

And then a curious thing happened. I cured myself by the opposite of decadence, and the furious rage disappeared *dissipated* itself in the course of my self treatment and rebuilding myself almost from scratch. When you're as low as I'd been, you do have an option to going up, no matter what they say. You can sink into death so easily, without anybody noticing. Hardly a ripple on anybody's surface when a hardened old tippler takes the rope finally and swings swings hanging in a pit of hopelessness. So coming from the mire takes inordinate effort. Don't ever let anyone tell you different. Especially when every pore in your body is yelling for more and more of the poison, and you know that the wobblies and the shakes and the ghoulies will all disappear after one little drink, and the lamp posts will stop falling on your head if you up the dose of the tranx again to cabbage level. But you don't do it. You do not take the first one. You turn your face away instead and take the first tentative trembling steps to a total new life, and the high the high comes from actually defying the old patterns, and then a permanent high takes over as you start to care for yourself in ways you never knew before, building up every day stores of self confidence and self esteem through your own effort which will never leave you again, bless you bless you bless you baby.

I want to stress too how difficult it all was at this point in the tale, before you wail or sneer it can't be done or any other endearments from wise ones, minimising my high rise. They say You can't have been at bottom to cure yourself, but I was, I was. I've told you where, right there on the heap. It makes me weep when you don't believe me, or simply haven't the imagination to realise the limits of your own experience. It defies common sense what I did, all alone, homeless jobless and penniless, and never happier in my life, and off to London in the opposite direction to Sheffield, towards healing and feeling and freedom. My queendom for St Pancras, where this lass from the frozen North arrived, convinced for the first time of her worth and her right to be, sufficiently, to rush past the street folk around Kings Cross, identifying like mad with them as usual, but needing to flee in case I get sucked into negativity, and that false solidarity of victims propping each other up in oppression, but never ever escaping. No, my destiny wasn't there, I felt sure. But where, where, wherever else?

Well. I expect you'll be sceptical, but it lay in the drama of a health routine, like nothing you've ever seen, and dedicated pursuit of a home, done roamin' you see. I presented myself with a loopy smile at Camden Council's Homeless Persons' Unit, complete with loony certificate from Beechwood Hall, saying I suffer from nervous debility, vague, yet comprehensive enough to make them try to pack me back to Sheffield. But the certificate is dated eight months ago. Since which time, I tell them I've been dossing hopelessly on London's streets, but am now desperate to straighten out and need a flat to do it, and to resume my career. Though I fear this last fell on deaf ears. They judge me by my derelict mien and say you've said amen to academe, and I say Things aren't what they seem always, and behave a bit manic, really starting to panic when they say you'll have to go to a hostel. I'd rather die, I say. I'm too sensitive for all those drunks and noise and dyke approaches.

"You anti-gay?" they accuse at that, and I spend a useless hour trying to fend off charges of homophobia, which remind me in absurdity of refusing to be a racist. I want to take the piss out of these earnest worthies, but know I have to be humble. So I apologise profusely and say I get confused so much, it's my mind – all blurry and furry round the edges, and within a week I have a flat in Kilburn, of all places, near to Gerry's Squat. *I have a flat* and the keys in my hand, and I'm standing there in the doorway, Queen of all I survey, and it's wonderful just bloody wonderful too wonderful for words. But I dare say I'll manage a few. It's all so new and shiny and incredibly tiny, a home in miniature with no furniture, all white like I like it, with orange tiles and a loo, *a loo* and a bath of my own again at last. The past long ago comes flowing back. I must buy a mirror a mirror a goal, and an Andrex toilet roll – the first luxury showing I'm right on track for success. Bless you baby you did it you did it.

Weeeeee I'm free in a flat in London weeeeee weeeeeeeee I'm finding me the me beneath the filth and slime and shit and prison it's time it's time to leave the slime and I sit on the floor against my front door as proud as a princess, defenceless no more. I've got my Motte and my Bailey and the drawbridge is going up slowly but surely against any intruders

198

and space invaders. I'll set my face against any interference
with my recovery, in or out of trousers, that tries to bugger it
up again. Insane the way men have dominated my fate up to
now. How could an emancipated woman allow it? From now
on I'd be a frousy frumpy sexless spinster, enjoying celibacy.
Yet even as I say it, I know I'm tasting the waste of such a
non-solution. But I'll work that out later.

Meanwhile I must mention my total cure for addictions.
My own invention entirely, which I'm so proud of, considering
where I'd been, with so many afflictions. I effected a miracle,
a bliss, all of my own making, and taking advice from nowhere.
The basic premise was filling the hole left by your chemicals. The goal a total change of life and values and pleasures.
It's a measure of how low you've sunk, how far you'll go to
define yourself against that past. At last at last I want to live
and give my body and mind and nervous system a complete
overhaul. I'd destroyed all three, but particularly the nervous
system. So I had to purify and purge, and the methods I used
gave me such a surge, a kick of health, that a whole new
world a wealth of sensation opened up and flowed into life. I
glowed for the first time ever, on my own I mean, without
champagne. I glowed with health. Well I know athletes are
used to this feeling, but it sent me reeling with wonder, this
was waiting all the time. It had been in my power from the
hour of birth to feel like this, so much self-worth, and I'd
been distorted and thwarted from realising this potential all
along. I was purged from the past and its pickling in chemicals.
So well I feel with my new regime of diet and exercise and
meditation, of rest and peace and contemplation, of swimming
a mile every day, and running in the sun that summer every
day it came out, where before I'd sulked, resenting the sun
mocking me in misery. I was now having fun from the sheer
joy of living all alone and loving it, and relaxing with yoga,
and getting in touch with my subconscious in meditating.
Instead of hating it, bashing it down, and smashing my soul
to pieces.

Now I was rolling around on rugs from the market.
Rolling and lolling and hollering, Hell, I've broken the associ-

ation of pleasure and leisure with booze. When you lose the connection, you discover the pleasure of simple things that are free, the air, the sea. It's easy to sneer when I'm all sincere but it was paradise I tell you to be naive a big reprieve from a life of blasé blunted stunted sensation. This was elation without losing it, without being off your head, without being out of your mind. Well I know you won't believe me unless you've saved yourself from chemical raves and ravages too, then you'd get burning light of a new true Puritan coming through, God forbid, I'm kidding again and I realise it's over the top and too much to take but I'm not faking the details, it's just the tone which is making me cringe a bit, all new born and carried away at the risk of turning you off completely.

Anyway, I went to Brighton a lot to stock up on my prahna and I don't blame you if you go Yuk Yuk New Age Gluk. I would say the same if I didn't need to feel the fear and breathe deeply instead of running for my life. I cried the first time in years, years of tears, what are you telling me? I listened in fearfully, and then the anger came back, attacking me unawares. It came from all sides, welling up and up boiling boiling spilling over and levelling out into sustained rage, and the shit I'd been blocking and holding inside exploded, blowing wide open as it splattered on the ceiling. I stared at it fascinated, a stoat gloating over entrails of her past before she sails off light airy liberated at last.

21

"She was murdered, Gerry" I find it actually very easy to say, facing him, bracing myself for tears. But I needn't have worried. He took his own unhurried time to assess my story. I feared he'd dismissed it out of hand, so long did he leave me standing there, feeling wan and overwhelmed by it all, as I told it, remembering the lurid setting of Santa Claus with his paws in the loot. I suddenly wanted nothing to do with any of it any more. Yet I know I was the only one who'd seen the proof. I couldn't play ostrich and pretend I hadn't seen, could I?

"What do you mean you lost the evidence?"

"The photos. I dropped them" crestfallen. How do you tell a hardnosed politico you *lost* the evidence. Wouldn't make sense at all. But he flashed me a brief look of empathy, which meant You're off the hook for me, to my relief. I felt so inadequate about it already. Now steady on girl. Your new philosophy is Forgive yourself. Don't get back into those old negative grooves. Just kick your hooves and off again, tossing your mane, doing your colt revolting number.

"I wonder where the bastard's gone" he says musing

"Never seen from that day when we told him our suspicions to this"

"He must appear at the Commons though for debates and business?"

"Hannah's tried all that. They just say he's away, ill"

"How many are involved in Sheffield?"

"Well, this Knutton for sure, though I've no proof. But he *has* to be involved. Hannah says he wants our hostel space for a new Club. I think he was blackmailing Cheetham. It's the only thing that makes sense. Does it make sense?"

"Very much so. Yes. Well Charlie, that's good work. My little sister would be proud of you. God rest her"

I look aghast at such a blast of religiosity from this modern street-wise lanky man, thanking me for devotion to his sister. Hey mister I hated her in the end. I betrayed her friendship, jealous she'd pinched a fan. A mere man broke up our love, and you're invoking heaven above for her memory. I'd better slip away, this fey stuff embarrasses me. No mystery why, I'm guilty as hell. I know damn well she was lovely. My envy so ugly is shameful. Still, I can't be blamed for the accident, the murder. I heard him saying softly.

"She loved you, you know, she told me about you that last time I saw her, she pointed to you and said *she* makes my life worth living. She's saved me from suicide so many times, I owe my life to her Gerry. I hear her now saying it. Oh God" he breaks down, and I take his hand, and make bland remarks about She's at peace. When all I feel is terrible terrible anger swelling in my chest. It's heaving, I'm breathing faster and faster. At last he mutters

"The fucking fucking bastards"

and I feel better. He's not so wet and sentimental after all. Somehow I need him tall and strong. The time for crying is over. She's lying dead, they all are, and somebody is responsible. It's horrible, and I don't know what to do.

"Was the funeral? . . ." I stop guilty again. I'd been lying in hospital when the bodies were claimed. I know he'd taken her back to Ireland, and Jean's husband had sent for her, and a sister of Natty had been found in Sheffield to take her. How lucky I didn't die, I'd thought. Nobody would have claimed me. Still, I wouldn't have been stuck with self-pity on that occasion. But I feel obscurely responsible for Bridie. I should have escorted her back to her hated Dublin. So why take her back? He hates it too. It must be a much deeper Place and Root thing than I can ever appreciate. Oh fate, why did you take them away?

"Leave it to me Charlie" he says quietly, a frightening sort of quiet. But I fight down the fear and release his hand, realising I don't want to hold it. Something told me to let go. There were messages flying between us, sparks igniting, as we stood there in the growing darkness. I was fighting an impulse to kiss him so tenderly, trying to mend all the fences defences strewn about in the path of anyone coming close to him. But the moment passed, and I fled away to my bed so wearily, saying to myself Near one, girl, be careful of the mean political men of violence. No sense in an emotional anarchist making herself miserable over the masochism of loving one of them again. Dangerous games they play with people personally, and there's no way you can tame them either. You tried revolutionary heroes. Full of woes. I'll salvage my reason this season and avoid them, whatever shape and size.

A wise middle age I plead as the withdrawals and fear recede and finally disappear after half a year just like the doctor said, and all the while the police had been conducting a desultory investigation into the brakes of the car and Brian Cheetham had resigned as MP and vanished on "extended sick leave and convalescence" and a by-election had installed another macho Brother who sneered and jeered at Hannah's suspicions "loony feminist nonsense", indeed threatened her with allegations of libel if she didn't shut up, and her disruption of a Social Services summit meeting to discuss her fuss about child abuse at Brampton Lodge was a farce with all the male Social Workers rounding on her in apparent horror. The only woman Social Worker had dismissed my story as hearsay of an alcoholic. Even Toby, so noble usually in underdog causes, was pausing for reflection that my marbles might be drastically rearranged by the chemical inflow. That I may have you know imagined the whole thing, and of course my three dead friends had vanished without a trace on the face of the social fabric, a bunch of derelicts, he shouldn't have taken them, they probably grabbed the wheel. And the evidence, the solid evidence, that the brakes were faulty, tampered with? Well one of the crazies could have done it thinking it's clever, you never can tell what they'll do next. So it's looking very bleak for justice in Sheffield as I speak to Hannah on the phone and she tells me the police are going to close their investigation. They haven't come up with anything at all, and Hannah, who's never doubted me, is shouting now how awful it all is and how it wouldn't have happened if I'd gone back to Sheffield in my new incarnation as saved old raver. But I think she's wrong. They'd never believe a loony over anything – would *you*? Well truthfully?

The only one who believed loonies died, and I'll never get over it. My guts still churn and I have a burning rage at those Obituaries in '89 sneering dismissing undermining patronising. They were always jealous of him other shrinks and when he died they had a field day. While the Left the *Left*, who should be bereft as me at the passing of a true revolutionary, ignored his death completely. With its last breath world socialism should have beaten a drum for the greatest radical thinker of a generation. But blinkered blind they can't afford the truth of Laing, it would unwind their vanities, inanities, and precious sanities and unman every damned last one of them tek mi forra nutter or summat?

I put the phone down, resenting her tone, hectoring harrying me – while seeing her point her desperation, it's becoming a futile operation, but something's got to give, I'll never live with memories of photographs and Melanie's smile. If I have to, I'll find Brian Cheetham myself. Well well though, that's when things take a different turn, for slowly slowly grind these mills of God, which makes him a sod for the impatient. I suddenly smell wood burning and see the smoke pouring under the door. Why didn't I notice it before it got this bad? Always the inevitable Why? Question before action, playing fucking intellectual while Rome and home burns. I grab the phone dialling Emergency, but flames appear, I have the sense to exit quickly out the window, yanking the window open first, astonished how consideration about damaging property can appear in a blazing building, petit bourgeois aspirations, must be. I remember glimpsing myself as in a slow motion dream, thanking God I'd spoken to the Council about the paint sealing the windows up only last month, appealing for help, a loony needs her fresh air, and it rushes at me as I climb out, cold crisp autumn air, and here comes the fire engine and police police everywhere. One charges over and picks me up.

I say I'm allright, but he carries me across the road lock stock and curlers I'd put in to train my struggling tendrils, and now stand shocked, taking them out hurriedly

"That's my flat on fire" worried worried "MY flat MY home" You don't know what that means you man from the Met, 'cos that's what he is. Why is a Met man here on a local fire anyway?

"No. It's the one next door to the one you came out of. Yours is just the hallway, we'll have it out in two ticks dear don't worry"

DON'T WORRY! "It's my home" I mutter teeth chattering. He slings a blanket over me and suddenly I realise everybody else is falling out of their houses in all manner of attire. I ask the nearest one "What the hell is going on?" Tall and handsome he's a big improvement on the Met. I've noticed him before, who wouldn't, a hunk like this, who I've heard is a psychiatrist, with silver curls and a beard black and grey, could have his way with any woman so I summon instant resistance. Hey hey I fancy you but will never admit it and turn the other way soon as I see it's him.

"It's a bomb scare. They think it's an old bomb factory that's exploded next door to you. I expect they don't know the rumour that *you're* the IRA Queen. Not next door at all is it?"

Humour too. He was going to be fatal, *and* a deep sexy voice husky and chain smoky, and come to bed Jewish dark eyes, what about my wise middle age though? I try to ignore him but the street's full of pushing people and he pulls me out of the way of a police car. I was stepping into anything to slink and slide away from him. I glide gracefully out of his grasp.

"Where are you going?" he asks and I melt again, silly bitch. He's all gravel and grizzle I'm practically slavering he makes me dizzy just being there beside me. I daren't look at him directly. I don't. He won't know what's going on inside me will he? Or does that kind of man always know women are willing a mile away don't have to say anything just casually save their lives and then look nonchalant and you have them for life fucking wife slave I won't I won't I will not

"Is this yours?" He's holding a curler fastidiously as though it's dog shit. That proves it, he's a middle class monster who deplores girls in curlers. Like many who rant and rave that they'd die saving the proletariat but wouldn't have one in the house. This one's another snob. WOT A SNOT I say to myself, turning away to smile.

"What did you say?" he demands.

"Nothing. No, s'not mine" I said

"You didn't. You said what a snot. And maybe you're right. But I wasn't disapproving. *Was* I?"

"Yes. Anyway s'not mine"

"It is. I saw you climb out of the window in them"

"You NEVER"

"Oh yes. Rather endearing I thought" haughty patronising git.

"Aw shit"

"Yes"

"A girl gets no privacy these days"

"Do you want it?"

"Oh yes"

"You sure?" He's grinning and any man who grins wins me instantly, especially if they look like a handsome Karl Marx. Though it's dark I can see his Mark of Cain, that arrogance, disdain for the world in general, modified only by his concentration on the immediate object hurled at his feet, a will to defeat then move on.

"You've got me wrong" he says.

"Never. I never get them wrong. Go away"

"OK"

Well there's no need to go with such speed and I watch my hero vanishing in the crowd and the loud music and uproar that's filling the air. My God it's a party developing and with reggae music blasting from a speaker behind me hung out of a window and couples grinding together slowly on the road behind the police cordon surrounding all my side of the street, and everybody greeting each other like long lost lovers, Irish and Black folk and ethnics in all their laid back loose limbed glory and only a few random boring whites all wan in the light. Except one that is. I noticed he was all sun tanned in spite of his feeble staying power. I wish he'd lingered an hour at least, but the beast in me says there'd be nothing least or less about that affair. It would be the best of a life time and therefore to be resisted. The blisters still burn from my last learning project with a bastard. You're bound to be a bastard, stay away.

As I'm saying this I'm surreptitiously peering through the gloom for him and soon meet a face peering back, and it's not handsome and grizzled either. It's flash bang an attack of instant panic racing round my stomach clutching my heart gripping me ripping me apart. I start to shake and take a deep breath. It's like looking death in the face somehow. The last place I saw that leer I was letting it embrace me, or anyway touch me up under the covers of my hospital quilt. The guilt the embarrassment chase the fear, and then something else I can do without. My memory of the orgasm he gave me, made me, mesmerised me into having, with those cold steel eyes of a real raving psychopath I recognise, as I stand shivering and dithery and dazed and trying to erase the sexiness the lust that's rising rising. What a bloody irrelevancy this sex can be and I'm petrified at the same time as I'm fantasising that he might take me down an alleyway and make me come again, just be feeling me where it matters. I'm shattered by this recognition of raw naked sexuality so strong in me, stronger much stronger the longer I'm off the tranquillisers. I'm para-lysed with fear by now and longing oh Lord a longing so strong to be taken and touched by such a sinister "priest" touched and pawed and played around with my layers of repression peeled off as I stand revealed taking my clothes off for the dirtiest the ugliest the roughest a tumble in the hay with the harvester as I lay helpless beneath him sowing his seeds savagely mowing my needs into pulp as he trammels and rams away with his own if only he'd do it without me meeting his gaze I go glazed at the thought of being fucked by a man with a frock on and look round but he's gone

207

vanished it's as well really the fuckings I was working up to do other women have such lusts for imperfect strangers and all the dangers involved I trust they do.

Yoohoo the silver-haired shrink from across the road seems positively meek after that dirty reverie. I *think* he's a shrink. Of all things for *me* to meet. The lady next door, who's 84, from Prague, says he's a good Jewish head doctor. Just what I need I must say, feeding on fantasies of priests disrobing. Could he cure me of that? I bet he could, and a lot more frustration I've endured lately. Giving up the low life and becoming respectable and healthy has lost me my stream of steamy encounters in sordid dives which nevertheless dealt with my wanton drives now and again. But now there was nothing, and I do need men now and again. A DIY job isn't the same, whatever they say, and I'm still into men, yes I am, no matter how feminists pray for a conversion for me. You see I love pricks and penetration, and that clits-only brigade make me think they've never had a proper fuck in their lives. It's bad luck but there's no need to generalise into a wise philosophy for all wives and wimmin everywhere – don't let them in it's a sin these men violating our bodily integrity. These sad sisters ought to sort themselves out with some humility instead of using their failures as bases and theses for the rest of us. Personally I'm up for a violation of the old boundaries any time, roll on the rollicking, lead me to it . . .

Yes yes yes, though men need showing where to pressurise, if you like, once they're inside. But get them in first by God, and then make the sods do it right. What other justification on earth can men pull if they're denied their hole role? It's their big advantage and there's not much left if you leave that out. If they can't wave their tools about, you don't have new rulers, you abolish the game entirely, which if played well can give you heaven and hell in a nutshell. I'd sell my body and soul for a happy hole having huge contractions round a thrusting pole. It's a satisfaction next to saintliness. I feel holy in a wholly floating ethereal way afterwards and it can last all day but as I say you have to teach 'em not put 'em on trial, while leaving 'em beached like whales in a heat-wave. You never get anywhere if you don't save somebody's self respect first. If you salvage that and move with tact you'll win the world and everything that's in it my daughter. A world of wonder at what's free and available for two humans to transcend any old shit that life can send. Just bend a little towards him, help him, show him, melt the foe instead.

And dread dread dread I suddenly know why that priest is there, and where I saw him before the hospital. It was that night in Kilburn Square before the crash, and my hair stands on end in terror. I must be slow and having withdrawals, but now it dawns on me all at once, this ponce is following me evilly for a purpose, and it's not sex. It's simple. He wants to kill me. He's *tried* to kill me. That's *my* flat that should be burning down. He's trying to kill me kill *me*. It fills me with such excruciating terror, and panic strikes fast, just bellow the belly. I'm going to pass out mustn't mustn't he'll get me. My God what can I do? Where can I go?

And so I do the obvious. I get very drunk. Well it happens with the best will in the world. You fall off the wagon in a heap, and within an hour I was back to being cheap a snivelling whore begging for more of everything that booze can bring, singing my head off then crying crying hysterically at the thought of that beast that beast a pretend priest who would defend me keep the beast from the door.

"Just the person" I snivel, talk drivel a while, then smile and cry at the same time, wishing I wasn't doing this with a silvery shrink who'd think he'd got a patient.

"Why are you crying?"

"I'm not"

"I see"

"Let's be jolly, life shouldn't be so melancholy"

"Why are you lying?"

"I'm trying to save you the story. I'm boring"

"NO I don't want your life. Not at all. Not now. Just why, specifically, at the moment, are you sobbing so much?

They put out the fire. There was no bomb factory. Your flat was hardly damaged, I just asked them. So why the crying?"

"They're dead"

"Who?"

"R.D.Laing's dead"

"They?"

"He's my saviour. My saviour is dead. All the best people die. Why why why do the best people die tell me tell me" I'm tugging his sleeve, knowing I'm being dreadful, can't stop it, take another swig from the Pils can. The party all around me is hectic. They're all shouting and drinking and I'd done the unthinkable, put my head down and shot like a bullet straight to the off-license with money from Beatrix, the Czech old lady, who'd rushed out from the fire with her savings box in the night attire of the Countess she claimed she was, silk frills and a mop cap, with a long white plait down her back. Now she'd lost her false teeth and was twinkling.

"It's such a relief not to wear them. Ah I see you've got the good Jewish doctor. Look after her, she's a good girl" tinkle tinkle went her voice, pealing. She'd been an actress long ago and it showed. She was even appealing to Hercules, bending low over her, smiling beguiling. But how could actresses be Countesses? Maybe in Prague they could. Oh bloody bloody hell and blast it, I'm past caring for anything. I start singing. No. Wailing. A funeral dirge.

"R.D.'s gone this is a song for R.D. boom boom boom don't leave me R.D. boom boom"

He glances at me casually, interestedly? No, casually. And suavely as well. Then drops the bombshell.

"I was a mate of Ronnie Laing"

and from then on I might as well have been jelly wobbling slobbering, a slutty serving wench, prostrate, putty in his hands melted, felt silly stupid standing there staring at him, my magical mystery man.

"You're a fan of his obviously"

I nod stupefied.

"Shut your mouth dear" says Beatrix.

"Yes, I was a mate of Ronnie. We shared a house for a while. Did you know him too?"

I stare at him numb struck dumb.

"Why are you getting drunk?"

"I've met the ghost of R.D.Laing here tonight to save me. You're going to save me"

"I don't know I want to"

"You're going to save me. R.D.Laing has sent you"

"He wouldn't bother. He'll be in enough trouble sorting Him out I should think"

"Who's this R.D. person?" Beatrix wants to know

"He's God"

"No dear, there's only one"

"Why are you so drunk?" he says.

"R.D.Laing" I shriek "R.D.Laing is dead"

"He's been dead 7 years and you've only just noticed?"

"It seems like yesterday" I look deviously up through my lashes, trying for a Princess Di effect. "I've been indisposed, er, a bit chemically inconvenienced, you know how it is . . ."

"For 7 years?"

"For 37 probably"

"Ah"

"An existential crisis of a lifetime" God I wish I could shut up " . . . and you bother about *drink?*"

"I think you've had enough"

"You're not like him"

"No. I'm not"

"He'd never have moralised"

"No. But I'm not"

"Laing was a drinker"

"Yes"

"Harry Hegel was a jughead too"

"I see"

"Beatrix, he's a moralistic bore and I'm a drunken whore and I love you and R.D.Laing"

"I don't know this person dear, do you?" she asks him, cupping her deaf ear.

"Oh yes. I knew him well. I was a mate of Ronnie Laing"

"I hate I hate the miserable mate I hate the mate of Ronnie Laing" I sing, with considerable sangfroid I imagine. But he looks frigid and cold and really quite old but oh how I do want to fuck him.

"Will you be my mate too?" I say coyly as I can muster.

"For tonight. I'll be your mate for tonight" he growls, and I'm off howling to the night.

"Allright. Allright. ALLRIGHHHHHHHT"

22

But I wasn't prepared for the sheer joy of that encounter. Even boozed and whoozed and fazed out, I'm reeling from the first moment he touches me, feeling dazed and dizzy and bloody silly really. As he takes my poncho off, I clutch at straws before I drown. Like: isn't it a coincidence you knowing R.D.Laing and me loving him all my life since I knew he existed? He just says You're pissed and we'll talk seriously later if you want to, and meanwhile he starts to strip off all my layers and defences together. I watch warily as my jumble sale tatters slip to the floor in all their glory. I'm feeling shattered overwhelmed, a sense of imminent awe that I'll never recover from. I've always been a sucker for understated erudition, and this one reeked of it from the gills. I felt quite ill with all that poison on a pure system, and say demurely

"I'm a drunk you see." Well you've got to start somewhere, and I wouldn't dare tell him sober. But he doesn't bat an eyelid from his concentrated attention on my tender parts. It's really an art, making love the first time, getting it right, and he was practised, oh was he practised, almost oiled I thought, and repressed it. I must have looked a sight, my few hairs sticking out cruelly de-curlered, and streaky mascara from crying, and reeking of booze. But he passed from my face fairly quickly and got to tasting all my nooks and crannies. It's not the kind of thing you'd like your granny to read, but I have to tell you he was feeding on me down there till I yelled and yelled in an ecstasy I'd forgotten I knew. Oh oh stop I'll come and I want you to screw me really inside me well you know my penchant for the old missionary position, I reckon it beats them all. Then he stopped in the heat of the moment, stood up, tall, leaned over me sprawled on his bed, and I'm popping all over and my head starts to spin and he's putting it in and I'm not protected, so I'm protesting and passing out at the same time.

"I'm using a durex" he whispers and even makes that sound sexy "but I don't like making love to a corpse, so make your mind up if you're going to stay conscious" slap slap. It really turned me off, so I snapped.

"And I don't like fucking headmasters either" as I kissed him slowly, licking his ear, then biting it for emphasis.

"Well Miss we really are a passionate pair" he's grinning again and I realise heavens above I'm in love in love. It always happens just like that, you know it from the first moments. I usually know it on sight, but that night it took me by surprise as he fucked the life out of me and the living back in, the loving and giving I'd been missing and yearning for and denying it, crying My freedom matters more 'cos you're not free in love you're in thrall, at least I am, or have been. This new scene could always be different of course. But since my foreign forays I've never let myself fall madly for anyone, and always stayed sadly on the sidelines emotionally, though it was pretty dicey with Heather I admit. But it's better not to. Better than being hurt again, and this man had that kind of power. Within an hour of our tired triste, I'd confessed my life story. Well a bit less. The whorey bits were censored. I didn't want him to get off on them like some men do. Like Toby, who's disgusted, but loves nothing more than a good session with me drunk, and piling on details, while he bristles sternly then leaves for the loo to pretend it's him.

I also wanted this man's respect. Well not genuflection or exaggerated stuff but I didn't want him thinking he'd picked up a bit of rough at a street party, hot stuff to be discarded with the empties. He's not got to regard me as available always, as I was I *was* any time's fine with me I must hide it or I'm open wide for exploitation. I'm open wide any way again today, fill me thrill me with heaven above you lovely lovely lover. I can't stop kissing him and missing him when he goes to the loo. It's half past two I see and this is the rest of my life this man, I already feel the threat of tomorrow when he might not want to see me again. Such dread and sorrow fills me suddenly. I start crying and he's lying there looking at me tenderly.

"Such pain such bottomless pain. It's the best thing you can do to cry. You're healing yourself little girl lost. You're finding yourself gradually. You're almost there. Relax. Unwind. I'm not going anywhere"

It's too good to be true, the father I never had who doesn't want me to be mother. I don't believe it can't believe it. A man who doesn't want mother would be so together and strong he wouldn't need me along at all would he, and where would I be then without him crawling at my feet for help and nourishment? I wouldn't have a function a lever for prising his passion and commitment and winding my twine all round him binding him to me for ever. I honestly never encountered the possibility before and it bewilders me.

"What's wrong?" he says in that husky tone.

"You're so strong" I moan "You don't need anybody"

"Oh dear dear" he says shaking his head and stroking my breast "The point is to *want* you." He starts sucking it and such unfulfillable longing assails me I can't bear it.

"You don't need anyone. You're autonomous and strong" I wail as my passion rises and I start stroking him bringing him closer bigger he's got to need me now. How dozy can you be? I really couldn't see what he was getting at. I wanted to lick his prick suck it dry. I tried to manoeuvre to do it but he was licking me now so lusciously lasciviously it seemed ungrateful to stop him, but I had to regain control somehow. It was now or never. But then I couldn't help it. I came all at once in great shuddering gasps, he was licking inside me sticking his tongue right in so I had an orgasm in my vagina too like you do when screwing, *which is what the anti-intercourse feminists miss.* You come in both places at once and it's paradise I say without a trace of irony. The only place to be is sensually sexually taken over transported. *But Madam what about YOU controlling the proceedings and really being a winner this time?* Shut up conscience, go away. No no. Don't torture me today. I need a break for God's sake how much can a

215

broken body take fatal mistake there are no limits to self-destruction . . .

I'd been distorted by drink and drugs so long and thwarted in all my relationships since those foreign jobs and slobs by my terror of being hurt again, rolling around and cavorting in dirt and dereliction for years, not facing my fears or realising taking risks is part of living. You do it again and again with more and more men till you're pig sick, but you have to go back this one last one prick may be the big one the one that moves boulders under shoulders and long legs pegging me to the ground. I've found bliss this time round. Taking the piss? Not a sound in that direction from me, I'm madly in love and you know how mirthless that can be. Still he asked my name and I knew the game was up. This was intimacy. "Charlie" I mumbled indistinctly. "Charlotte" he said. "No. Karl. As in Marx" I was fumbling for escape. "Ah yes. Obviously. You're a bit obvious altogether, Charlie"

Ah he likes the sly "mysterious" kind. We could all be crafty if occasion demands. I'll try my hand at Mata Hari. Wished I hadn't blurted out the story so far of my life, but I'd trusted him bloody hell as well as the lust and the love, which was wearing thin now he's getting it in about preferring subtle types swipe swipe he'd wiped me out stripped my tenuous bibulous confidence. I wanted to go home but I couldn't see straight or climb down the stairs. I frown at his lair a bit harder trying to focus. Why on earth did I drink so much when I started? It's time we parted though. He's snoring gently next to me now, and I never see how grand passion can survive the boring wide awake hours listening to a snorer, thinking of ways to kill him. No he won't do at all, and I fall asleep myself, soundlessly of course.

When I next negotiate consciousness, guilt hits me like a steel tipped sledge hammer wham bang boom you feckless loon you doomed old drunk who's lacking will and drive and spunk you're hardly alive to tell the tale. If only you'd stop yelling at me I want to wail to my super-ego which is the steel heel on the sledge hammer the slicing bit cleaving through my skull like a bull in a china shop no sensitivity at all for the paper thin walls dividing up my thought processes carefully reason from rhyme they're all beating time now madly together boom boom slice crunch boom and a lurking terror flashes darts through my nervous system heart and lungs my lungs are agony I puffed twenty cigarettes straight through them plenty plenty give me more more destruction devastation decadence the merry dance of death knows no half measures with me I do it all all until I pass out completely it seems and my dream of one day drinking in moderation is shown up for the sham flim flam wishful thinking it is.

I'm blinking hard at the light, fighting waves of panic and nausea. I must get out of here before he wakes up, sneering sardonic coldly platonic he's bound to be – me found sickly sad at his side, open wide to insulting rib crunching rejection. No I'm not staying there to hear it. I've fled his bed, bringing my fractured bits and pieces with me, wrapping them carefully in my poncho. Don't go don't go a voice is saying, but it's not his, it's my libido treacherous bitch wanting more of a good thing, even though most of me is dying and crying never again any more men or drink or cigs or gigs in streets with strangers who say they were mates of Ronnie Laing. There's danger in that you half-baked bat, forever impressed by names and fames and genius claims. Go home and have some tea, and I tell you I must be better – tea is so ordinary safe and healthy, a herbal tea not a hair of the dog session, which usually would sock me senseless for the day and tomorrow and the next day. Hey hey I'm truly recovered blood brother, I say to a tramp shuffling past. He's not impressed bless him "50 pee missus?"

My resentment softens for a minute when I see this lolling old bum, strolling along so familiar after the palm trees in there behind me – psychiatry abandoned to its fate. I hate you clever Jewish shrink for thinking I'm *obvious*. I remember that, the hurt of it, though I don't remember a lot more, except the wonderful wonderful whoring. Such memories I'm storing and you can't have them back, however you attack and defile me. You did it you loved me. "*Love?*" you say, "that was just sex display." But I say you loved me as well. I'm an expert. Can tell the difference. But we won't mince words. You know my nickname too. I'm not even spared the humiliation of Charlie, a man's name after all which is not something I aspire to be, no matter how hateful is woman's condition, no matter how refined and "normal" and healthy mine appears now. A spark of something black and dark and unpredictable will always remain. I've been too far to be the star of a smug family soap opera ugh ugh ugh but a bit more stability is desirable. I can't lose my knickers and marbles and fall rolling off the wagon in calamity because I see a suspect. I should rally and follow him, sniff the trail, a holy grail of redemption for those three I now see were locked together with me influencing each other's weaknesses and couldn't break out. For that you had to stake out a different territory, a new map of the world entirely, and most women can't do this. They're wooed, stilled instead, filled full of tranx and tanked to oblivion. I dread to think what would have become of us without the crash catharsis. An endless drawn out death for four. Like this lively old sod slithering along in front of me oh let there be more recovery like mine, only better more infallible no mire allowed at all. Yet my fall did me good somehow. It gave me blood lust for love and sex again. I remembered what men taste like feel like smell like their roughness toughness electricity and frisson of a man like that. As far from Toby – the wally and the feminist wimpy pimply nerdy New Men comparing washing powder and joining women in their cages instead of abolishing the cages altogether – as you can get.

I'm reflecting on men again must stop it. I try to hop on a bus on the Kilburn High Road but I've just missed a bunch travelling together for company, so I head for the tube. I need to go to Bloomsbury and wallow in academic ambience, wondering whether to resume it somehow, now I've caught up with a hundred worthy tomes from the library, catching up on all I'd missed in the past six years of my Fall, and all my fears and intuitions proved correct that it was a lot of reactionary nonsense in my absence this PoMo with its toleration of everything as valid discourse and abolishing of Enlightenment critique and universal values as terrorism in practice, ending up welding together crude populism and tortured élitist philosophy to justify its French lesson pretensions. They pretend to be scientists these days and even Lacan has a maths model for prick elevation. Kristeva is a woman and I hoped for the plot to thin, but lo, she's as turgid as the other French men as she reduces poetry *poetry* to maths too. Althusser had long ago murdered his wife and died and Nicos Poulantzas killed himself. I bet it didn't induce any psychological insights from their groupies.

These thronging thrusting students of today, so far away from the Sixties. I can't say I recognise them at all in Bloomsbury when I get there. It's all polished gleaming neat foreign students steaming along with briefcases *briefcases*. Who ever heard of a briefcase in my day? Far off mystical moment, where are you now in these scurrying effigies rushing along, worrying only about jobs and money in the push hour, and there are the uptight clipped yuppies in their power suits and clicking high heels and efficient men. So straight this society has become. They're automated. There's not a laid back meandering academic in sight in the whole of London. No hint of rebellion at all.

I head back to Kilburn in a hurry, back to the underclass in its squats and its bands and its de facto rebellions and refusals of every day life, its Lumps and dumps and Rastas and Rumanians and richness, its marginals marching along, its drifters dopers profound no hopers, its criminals and shady politicos, its Muslim women covered in black like great crows with timid eyes shuffling behind their men as symbols of a feudal foe and yet under there they are safe from marauders and blatant applauders of Page Three. Who can blame a culture that wants to protect its women from vultures, who want them to get yer tits out for the lads? These are new sad reflections for me, who used to see such religious signs in our streets as insulting oppression of women. Yet now confessing how fancy free I would be, wrapped up like that, hidden, never bidden to show my wares no stares no rape? Or does it invite rape incite it like forbidden fruits used to? And what happens in those holy families too? Who knows? – they have a glow of sanctity I envy anyway, though I'm not as unaware as you may imagine, of the glaring contradiction between my own tit fixation and a simultaneous horror at its celebration in my culture of origin, sin original no denying.

But this multiculti kitch is so rich, I'm twitching with sensory overload. An inner city exploding with outcasts of the world, exiles styles wiles and wide boys, wise guys and woozy gals and pimp pals awaiting, the pushing shoving shouting and bawling, the hating fighting and caterwauling, the teeming seething chaos and chorus so bleak and dark and satisfying – if you're in the mood. The Kilburn High Road. My mode today is shame and dereliction and gross self-blame, or I'd have gone the other way to West Hampstead. Since my street is tucked halfway between Kilburn and West Hampstead, I can choose my way daily according to my identity. It's Kilburn for slumming and West Hampstead for twee and posh and fancy nosh and health food freaks and stripped pine still in evidence. But today is the moment of a patchwork of guilt, and I'm fleeing myself still. Though it mercifully will wear off now I've walked all day and drunk only tea and water and tried to breathe deeply. I cough and splutter and spit resolve. I'll swim again, bliss without men, except for Rambo sharks slicing up and down the lane "GETOUTAFUCKINWAY-GRANDMA". Well I must say, have a good day too Tadpole. Still I get a surge of optimism. Except for him. Oh God why did I do it?

23

I did it because my new pattern of living hadn't finally taken hold as the solid gold it is for guarding me against panic. If I'd held on hard and done some exercise and run about frantically instead of quick grab the booze, I'd have gotten over it and kept my dignity with the rotten bastard across the road. Not losing self respect and loving him like that, reaching out pouring out my innards into an empty vessel. He's got to be an empty paltry puny person, he's too good looking to be otherwise. I'd learned my lesson and now madly rationalise my imminent rejection. Well I wasn't going to give him a chance to reject me. I'd never speak to him again, dismiss it all as drunken orgy. I fall into the arms of charming men all the time. Won't do it again with you though. Won't come to screw me on your day off, you scoffing sneery Jew, leering every time I see you so far. But you'll lose interest now, except for convenience. Couldn't be more convenient, could it? A willing woman watching from her window for you to float freely across when you want it, boss of the situation and all you survey. But hey hey I'm not playing and anyway he won't come near ever again. That's the greatest fear. I'm not even an easy lay. I'm disgusting a lusting loony drunken whore. Why would a shrink want more of nutters when his work ends for the day? He'll pray for a princess of stability, who never confesses anything. A catatonic beauty queen must be his dream.

But things *aren't* what they seem, and just as I'm scheming an exit to the shops over the back gardens, my doorbell rings and he's standing there with a rare old grin, and he wins again. These bloody men the handsome ones get away with murder, though ugly ones seem to as well lately. I must shut the door ferociously in his face. He just wants to use me. Disgrace of it. I refuse to grin back. I must attack, but don't know how to do it. I'm dumbstruck just looking at him.

"If you'd like to fuck again I'm available" he says, unassailable in his right to be in the world and in women in particular. And he's right, why not? Why would any woman not want him in her depths? I try not to sound affronted.

"Well I'm not"

"Oh"

"Not ever"

"Oh"

"No"

"I see"

"You don't"

"No I don't actually. I would have said we were very compatible in that respect. Perhaps I'm too direct. But so are you. I thought you would appreciate it"

"You were wrong"

"I was indeed. But you ranted on so vividly about repression and free expression I though you'd want me to come to the point"

"No"

"You'd prefer me to be coy"

"God forbid. A Coy Boy"

"Well then"

"Look I don't want to fuck you. At least I don't want to make love with you. I shouldn't have. I wouldn't have if I hadn't hit the bottle damn and blast and eternal shit. Sorry you got the wrong impression"

"You mean you're a nice girl really?" he twinkled. Bastard.

"I have some restraint until I know someone"

"How quaint. I thought your spontaneity was the best thing about you. One of them anyway" he actually did look thoughtful too. I wanted to fuck him like mad now this moment madly.

"No" sadly.

"The neighbours are fascinated. Do you always conduct sex chats on your doorstep, or can I come in? I want to talk to you. Really. Talk. Forget the other thing if you like"

But I don't want to *ever*. I'll *never* forget. Don't ever expect me to. You can't just dismiss it so casually. I let him pass me and wander into the flat, craning round to see all my nooks and crannies again, invading intruding taking over, these men these bloody amazing lovers who make you shed all your skins, letting them in, winning battering down your autonomy. I-want-you-to-want-more-of-me, they say, Long-for-me, and soon I do, shedding all my layers of self-protection when I screw with a man like you, praying you won't leave me alone with my phone silent, like I love it usually, before you came. I blame an inadequacy in women's rearing, no matter who they are. We're geared so deeply to abandoning direction or seek for perfection as soon as a man appears, with his priorities needs and fears. We care for them. To make them happy we'll do all it takes, and that means abandoning our sakes like snow flakes melting on contact with the ground, as we're pelted bombarded with snowballs so firm and round and sure of themselves, while we're retarded rewound by the over-whelming egos we've found, submerging ourselves soundlessly to a process without mercy, as they take our creativity away, and waylay the energy, using it for themselves.

No matter that some want us to succeed. They do. They plead, Send me a successful woman. But we bleed instead from the wound of loving them and our life force flows in their direction, going away from ourselves our obsessions and inspirations. I really reckon women can't be creative and have a relationship. At least not with a real man, a strong man. You could with one of these servile serfs some feminists collect, while he did the washing and hoovering and footnotes to your book and mixed your paint for your Art. Some boring old fart with no will or drive of his own. Or a toyboy who looked pretty and did the washing up. But these are relationships you can keep, with mediocrities and creeps. If you want exciting men who're alive and challenging the world, you can't emas-culate them, enslave them, herd them along with your bossy feminist hectoring, a bunch of nerds will emerge this way. You have to say Nobody does the housework, not everybody. Let's liberate us all from the galling enslaving housewifery trade, and witless parades of arguments respecting its value don't impress me at all. Get labour saving devices everywhere, children in childcare, and off we go hand-in-hand happy harmony end of slavery and sacrifice.

Though in a trice I recognise the flaw in my argument, which is to be alone and create, when the impulse for that creativity is standing right in front of me. Where would be Art without big hunks of humanity like this one, larger than life, and the confrontation the struggle to relate to them, date them, mate them, then hate them and start all over again with the same kind of men exactly. I always do. Yoohoo yoohoo another dynamic dramatic handsome bastard to balls it up, my life. For men get strength from relationships, but women don't. They just get drained and strained unutterably. Well I do, fancying types who expect the earth to revolve for them, though they make it move for you too. A frisson is missing with the others, not lovers just substitutes. Perhaps the only solution is separate living, and having short sharp shocks of exposure now and again, with long recovery periods in between, hanging on to autonomy like mad, so they can't get in right under the skin like they love to burrowing burrowing . . .

Furrows in his forehead and crinkly lines as he twinkles and grins, and then watches me guardedly, assessing maybe. A wonderful winning way, whatever it means. But this scene is not going to degenerate too quickly into me, sickly sentimental, agreeing with every whim as I look at him. Fucking him please is the only easy way out of that gaze, appraising assessing.

"What a mess you got yourself out of Lady. I admire it so much, your effort. You should write about it. Tell people. It would really help them to know. You look so healthy and fit, in spite of your freak out last night. You have a glow about you. I've watched you before. I know you. Full of energy and life. And a story like that. It's incredible. Write it. Do it"

I'm stunned, outmanoeuvred, outflanked. I hear my ridiculous self *thanking him*, for Chrissake. Thus spake

Zarathustra. What's up with you girl, taken in by flattery? What else had I told him?

"My God what *didn't* I tell you?"

"Well I know all about Chasms of Chaos"

"Oh dear" My pet theory of irrationality sweeping the world after Marxism.

". . . and why Marxism's inadequate, but why post-modernism's worse, and how all the fragmentation had abolished a need for emancipation because metanarrative and critique are excluded"

"Oh God"

". . . and how Enlightenment and Reason have become negative points of reference and collapsed under epistemological and moral Relativism"

"Oh NO"

". . . and how post-modernism – you kept calling it PoMo – is the revenge of the idiots the mediocre the petit bourgeoisie the . . ."

"Oh shut up" I'm jumping up and down with mortification. The *portentousness* of it, and all he wanted was a fuck. "I can't *bear* it"

"It's true though?"

"No. Well yes. But not that awful droning certainty. I mean I'm very confused about it all. I'm having a crisis with Marxism"

"You're a bit late. The rest of the world had theirs while you were out of it"

"But mine is intensely personal too. It was my life. I grew up with it and became a Marxist academic and then collapsed and now it's all so . . . *peculiar* they're all talking this dreadful post-structuralist Speak, and the books are written in impenetrable jargon, and I *know* it's shit, but I have nobody to talk to ever about it all. So I go round in circles and then it all comes pouring out on a poor victim like you . . . Except I never saw less of a victim in my life . . . I'm sorry"

"I can look after myself and switch off if I like, and basically you were right. Though I do think some of these

225

imperialist metanarratives needed breaking up, no? Do I need to say that to a feminist? You must *be* a feminist"

"Why?"

"Any intelligent woman has to be, it's so obvious"

"Do you know many then?"

"Both my ex-wives for a start. And my son says he's one"

"Oh" Oh Oh Oh. A harem of ex-wives.

"My second son though is very macho"

"Like dad?"

"Judge for yourself dear lady. But I wanted to encourage you to write about your experiences. Seriously. As a vital therapeutic project for you too, as well as getting it published. Especially this theory about purity"

"You're having me on"

"NO"

"I mean the way I did the opposite last night of everything I'd said – drinking and smoking"

"A set back. That happens in recovery. I'm convinced you won't go back though. It's all this strategy for a new life to replace the old that's so positive, against the vacuum of just giving up, which is why most people fail. You won't"

"Thankyou" I murmured, rueful, impressed by his gravitas suddenly, and humility towards me, sounding almost like respect. I couldn't believe it. Too dangerous by far.

"Anyway I'll go. Just think about it and DO it. 'Bye now. Take care"

Don't go DON'T GO. But he was gone, dashing across the road on his endless long legs, running his hand through his curls, never looking back, slammed his door before I had time to retreat. A life faced me of curtain twitching infatuation if I didn't take hold very firmly of me here in the middle of my world free unfurled and feeling self esteem rising inside me the first time I can remember.

I'm trying not to reflect much on the General Election and its imminence in case it doesn't happen the Great Labour Victory. It has to it has to it does it does and I feel dazed and glazed like the rest of the nation watching these beaming and gleaming New Labour folk installed in Government so different from the Old Labour of male might. But are they quite as bold and brassy as they seem, dream on dream on we need to hope for a while before the moping and betrayal sets in. I will not I will not be an ageing old fart cynic and ingrate. Yet surreptitiously I try the word Blatcherism for size already, how dreadful it is to be poised with a sneer like the bloody pundits of Newsnight. I will fight will fight the urge to think global imperialism has won the day and national governments will have no say in free glorious flight of capital. No protection of the nation state or welfare or public services will interfere. The mighty dollar rules from sea to shining sea and nothing in between will be allowed to resist. No New Labour. No, nothing . . .

And what will pass for the underclass in this new globe without horizons? It will grow and flow out of its ghettos and these wannabe communities will be brutalised hell-holes instead, with everyone scratching on the dole and hating the grating ceaseless lack of hope and scope of a life in the dark in the gutter, scuttling away from the loonies because the loonies are always worse than others. There can be no Care in a Community that doesn't exist.

I feel a turgid soliloquy coming on so I'll spare you, but must point out that the Blair government is in full swing with Religion and the Family and Middle Aged Men's Morality, so what oh what of the Loonies? What does this upright uptight phalanx of middle class family men know of Outsiders? Of underclass loony tunes? Of anything except easing the flow of Capital's glow and leaving the rest to the Lottery. It's such a problem when you want to free the world for Capital but want safe little Stepford communities too and can't see the contradiction. Oh hey diddle diddle that's the riddle in the middle of New Labour: they want bold new norms that worship gold while their social forms are old and sold and cold as the grave.

I've just finished my long article summarising my theory and practice of addiction, and added critical comments about the

Left's philistinism about mental illness. I summed up in the way the Marxists in the University I worked in had discarded me the minute my vulnerability showed. The way they always did, hating loonies as dysfunctional, and it began by observing the way they'd totally ignored Laing's death, which seemed to me symptomatic of their hatchet hack mentalities. Not an article or particle of his truth about madness and the family and sanity of all of us and it's incredible significance to that age of ours, the Sixties. They had treated him like an affliction an aberration to be lived down or patronised, these wise guys of psychiatry who wrote his obits, while the Left have ignored him completely all these seven years since he died. A self-defeating orgy of impotence in face of sensitivity and psychological suffering, about which they knew nothing and cared less. Rent-asunder human beings weren't bums on seats and votes at meetings. You plunder people who're healthy, use them. But blunder into nutters at your peril. Better the devils you know all slow and worthy, than any flashes of originality. That way doesn't pay, to listen to loons. They might piss on the programme. Anything's possible with them, and revolution's no solution comrade, no matter how jaded and faded we feel. And the same goes for this New Labour Government whose pious gits will flush the misfits down the drain again. Was it ever thus? They make a fuss about us because we disturb the view we're all askew it doesn't do. *You'll fit in and work for your bloody benefits and that will stop you drugging around, we've found the solution for pollution like you.* Expose the Sixties radical pretensions of this bunch of careerist wise guys, expose, expose, I'm flowing flowery and try to be terse and succinct in conclusion.

I seal it all up and then feel silly at so much exposure, so open and close it again to see how it reads, and pretend I'm the Editor opening it and reacting positively. It *is* dynamite and needs publishing. I send it to the *New Statesman*, and then swim a mile freestyle and fast, and feel that the dreaded past is under control at last, related to, made positive. And all because of the slob across the road who'd ignored me for months, and the more he avoided me the more I wanted to see him, nay longed to see him, with a physical urgency I had to control with furious swimming, slap slap take that, every stroke revoking dampening my feelings, every kick dismissing the prick who permeates my life more by his absence. No presence could compete. A total defeat of my will was imminent if he just beckoned. I reckon he knew this was the true way to slay a woman, devastate her and then leave her alone. I refused to glance out of the window and hated my phone, even though he didn't know the number and I was ex-directory through fear of the past catching up somehow. But now the only thing I wanted was for him to ring at any price, saying anything at all. But he didn't. They don't. He won't. Forget it. But then it did ring and it was the Editor of the *New Statesman*, a charming man, who says Please can we print it in the next issue. Thank God I'd put my phone number on the letter.

"I particularly like your critique of the Left and their attitude to mental illness" he says, and I wait, hesitate to jump in. I'm feeling too much. It's such a privilege to be taken seriously by the world again, after all I've seen and where I've been and

"You must have suffered a lot. It's a privilege to publish it now. Perhaps the Left can make amends"

"Never. Except by changing itself so dramatically that that . . ." I tail off, wishing I'd shut up, never said it.

" . . . That it wouldn't be the Left any more?" his voice seemed to be smiling, a kind man and sensitive too. Who are you? There *is* somebody out there listening.

"Well thanks again. It will be out two weeks tomorrow. No alterations. Three thousand words. Fascinating" and he's gone. I sit stunned and wondering why I said anything at all. Why I was so inadequate? Why am I . . . and catch myself in time, recognising the signs of rising excitement, tension, and time to meditate, get rid of the adrenalin before it starts festering and turning into that old negative excitement, that rise inside and drive towards drink it's linked with so strongly. The wrong way to celebrate for me in my life, ever, and I never said *never* before, but now I do EVER and NEVER and

NO. And hohoho, like a gift from God comes my reward for good behaviour, a saviour in scruffy old jeans and his hair curling round his collar.

"Just called to see if you're progressing"

"With what?"

"Your project"

"You're certain I'd do it. That I'd take your advice"

"Oh yes. It has to be done" and I didn't tell him. I just stood cool and confident at the door, wanting to molest him more and more, but not doing, realising we have to play these silly games. They're old as prehistoric rituals in hills and caves: pretend you don't want him and he'll come running, but if you're "obvious" and willing, you're his slave any day and he won't want it. Play the game play the game, and I had that other awful "obvious" to live down. It's a gamble this game. You can only play if they want you anyway. I remember Bridie's face as she said it years ago, and Jean had intervened sourly "and if you're beautiful as well". Well bloody hell I don't agree. We can all at any level play devils in the daisies, and beauty's in the eye of the beholder, though sadly I suspect it isn't. But anyway I'm standing here, fearless, erect, upright, a sight for the respectable of the street to admire and envy. Such a fine figure of womanhood, with a fair covering of mousy hair on my head too, and being such a good girl these days I puff up my confidence, 'cos this bugger won't. I look into his eyes without flinching, and see him thinking well well bloody hell she's really different and doesn't want to, or does she? They all do. Can't resist me.

"Well then" he says coyly *coyly*.

"Yes"

"Er"

"See you" I say, and make to shut the door, and as I do he looks away rebuffed.

"I er" I start, but catch him instantly stiffen huffily. So I stop again, withdraw, shut the door sighing.

Why oh why these neanderthal games? But who can blame me? I'm out to tame the lion this time and he's not taming me first, getting me meek and berserkly besotted by

230

his body and mind, a find of gargantuan proportions I admit. But I'm not NOT lousing it up by getting into spouse roles of you and me in harmony and 24 hours a day surveillance and the agony of jealousy when you look the other way, which you're bound to, and fuck around and stray away, saying monogamy is for fools and uglies. Like the last handsome lay I had, who also said in passing that feminism was revenge of the ugly sisters, so you can tell *his* wisdom level. But *you*, a handsome sophisticated devil of the London psychiatry circuit, and lots of desperate dirty opportunities with grateful recovered patients falling in love with you all over the place. No. I couldn't take it. Will have to fake indifference, my best defence so far. Though it's tricky with that wicked grin of yours.

And then the applause for my work comes loud and clapping, and he's the first, back slapping in jolly camaraderie. Which is not what I had in mind with him at all.

"It's a wonderful article, and look at the letters" he says a few weeks later, arriving rushing on his way from somewhere athletic, in a track suit and towel slung round his neck and his curls all damp from somebody's shower. My jealousy level is appalling. Why should he be using any other shower but his own? But I'm sure he is. The willing women of Hampstead would never let this one escape, though he's escaped two wives. Takes some contriving to be number three, even with a big house and bank balance that the divorcees get out of their marriages. Wives seem to make it pay I've discovered.

"It's really wonderful, and full of warmth and compassion and possibility"

I glow. I thought my proposals would sound extreme. But folks in a hole are glad to be extreme, their extremities got them where they are, so they can respond to the drama of it, bang bang now start and me imparting my details to encourage.

"So many say they want you to start an Addicts' Centre. Why don't you do it?" he says, glancing through the letters, betraying an interest in my fate which makes me hate the situation. It's hopeless. He wouldn't mind a casual affair. Like he has with many I bet, and I could be another name in his diary. But he doesn't know my manic flows of energy, which flood out, shouting, cascading over, at the idea of sharing him.

"You could get a grant from Camden Council. I could help you. Give you a reference. You need a start after so many years. A push. Why are you looking so miserable?"

It's because I want you, need you, all to myself. I can't go backwards to this deranged state of being your friend and nosy neighbour, a cosy crazy cold comfort I can't cope with. No hope for me at all.

"I'm not miserable. I'm delighted. You don't know me professionally though. Could you still give me a reference?"

"Nonsense. I know you very well I think" I blink and resent the impertinence.

"Well hardly"

"Oh nonsense. Enough to know you'd make a terrific Head of an Addiction Centre. Better than all the straight doctors in the world"

"We feminists don't believe in Heads and things" I tried lamely.

"Nonsense. This has to be your baby. You in control. It's your programme. Based on your life. The more I think about it I'm certain. Do it girl. Do it" he speaks to me like Head Boy to Head Prefect. Why's the passion turned to compassion? For my plight as the poor pathetic victim of circumstance, needing another chance, give her a break. I must take advantage though, and quell the rage that's rising, rising, choking me almost.

"Apply to Camden. Do it. You'd be surprised at your own power. Do it" and he's off, jogging down the street, a watery wintry sunshine making his curls glisten, his car glinting as he climbs in behind the dark tinted windows, hinting of mystery and promise . . . and bloody pretension. I shake myself out of this ruddy awful reverie that descends every time I see the bloke. Fancy a creep who peeps from smoked glass windows, making passes at lasses all the way, and laying them in the back seat in his country retreat somewhere. I dare say he's got one in there now, you can't see into his car at all. That shows how far he's into seduction. I scowl as the car crawls past me hooting tooting. I slam the door viciously, but I'm already working on his idea in my mind. It's brilliant, and these letters are so enthusiastic yet pathetic. They all say there's nowhere to go for us that understands.

"The fan mail's growing" he says the next day, with a pile of letters he's taken from the postman. I don't want to let him in, but he's insisting, waving a letter of recommendation he's written, which is so flattering yet formal. It sounds like any normal reference for a normal person of excellence. Yet nonsense in the context where I only know him carnally sexually, but no more it seems.

"A dream come true. Make it happen baby"

"I think you should stop infantilising me – Baby baby glug glug makes me a mug."

"Yes, but it's safe"

"Safe!"

"Yes. I can be professional and paternal because you're off limits, so it's safe"

"Why?" I can't help it.

"Why off limits? You know why. You're so confused and vulnerable. Till you sort out what to do with your life you'd depend on me utterly and hate yourself for it. So off limits"

"I love you" I say foolishly, stupidly. But it works, never fails, if they love you too of course. He holds me and I cry, wondering why I feel so betrayed by saying it, simply wishing I'd never ever laid myself so open. He'd dive in and take advantage immediately.

"Take it easy" he says, as my head hangs apologetically as though I've hurt him.

". . . I'm a very difficult person to love. But since you do, you'd better know things. I'm pathologically possessive, for a start. Not physically. I prefer separateness. Just sexually. I want less intensity not more. I don't want an intimate claustrophobic 24 hour a day thing. That's the end of love. I don't want to strangle or be strangled. Suffocated. I'm very busy

233

and happy doing what I do. I don't have time for a relationship that consumes me. But I do demand commitment. And absolute trust. I couldn't trust you now. You're still too vulnerable"

"You mean you're monogamous?" I fasten onto this bit like a leech, I'm screeching at him "*You're* monogamous? That's very funny. Oh that's very very funny." I collapse, shaking with laughter and tears. My ideal man. He's materialised after all these years, and he doesn't *trust* me not to lust after other men. Oh brother, how wrong can you be.

"I'm glad you're amused. But I'm very serious. As my ex-wives found to their cost. At my time of life, sex is a barometer for what's going on. All that Sixties compulsive promiscuity for women, trying to be as ballsy as men, made them very unhappy, mainly because they assumed men loved it too and copied them. Well, I, for one, found it all very empty. There's something necessarily exclusive about deep love and passion and devotion. Of course there is. Its very intensity makes it exclusive, and a plea for non-exclusivity means we're not talking about the same thing. There you have it. My speech of principle. Sorry" He actually looked bashful.

"Thankyou" I say, and he searches my face for clues and sarcasm. I try to look humble and sincere.

"But what about that performance with me"

He reddened and looked uncomfortable "Well we all freak out very occasionally . . . It was a throwback to the old days. For both of us" He takes my hand and I feel I'm blending into him, melting away.

"Be big and strong and brave for me and save me from myself, that's all I ask" I say ludicrously. But he nods and squeezes my hand and kisses me gently, bending down from his great height to raise my fingers to his lips. You must be thinking I've flipped entirely, but it's all true it's true. It happened like that, Mills and Boon.

"Do it, just do it" he says, and he's off again, slogging away on his health routine, jogging round the block and back before I've made tracks inside. I wave to Beatrix who's peeping from her window. She mimes a violin and bow and smiles knowingly. I'm glowing all over and it must show. I have a lover who wants me and only me monogamously. Well I don't have him yet, but I'll get him. I have to. This is IT.

24

Then things happened so fast, I could hardly keep up with my life and live it and push sleep in between. And that man struck a mean hard deal too, never coming near to woo or win me. I begin to feel frustrated, and sublimate it all into my project, which blasts off into orbit with me trailing hanging onto the stardust, wailing about control – which I've never regarded as valuable before. But he's right, this is my baby, and I must fight for it myself, nourishing and nurturing, and these vultures must stop trying to pinch it. Like the Ministry of Health with it's strictures and structures. But I'd better tell you first how I got so far as to be interfered with by the men in suits inspecting my premises, and giving me a certificate to say they'd been and seen, and all was well . . .

I had to sell myself and my art-of-addiction-cure from the start as a bold brave venture by an addict of old, setting herself up as adviser in a proposed Drop-In Centre at first for addicts and other mentally sick patients, thrown on the street from the mental homes closing at incredible speed. And I didn't heed warnings that I must *select* the first alkies or junkies. I wanted open house, but with rules of my own to be respected or you'd be ejected baby. No substances were admitted. If found, you were out. Except the prescribed pills that many shuffling melancholics fished out of their folds, wanting to be rid of them, like Ethel. I'd seen her pouring her pills down the grate many a time. She'd hated taking them, said they tasted of fuck smell. Well you can't argue with that. But I let them keep this kind of dope, and tried to replace reliance on them with some new hope in themselves. But it wasn't easy trying to please everyone those few first weeks when I opened. It was so cold. I was packed out before the decorating was finished, but before long I had them decorating too. A load of loonies to you, with paint brushes, slopping red paint on everything and spontaneous bits of graffiti in black and white. I wanted it bright and brash and clean and attractive. Seductive's the word really. I wanted them to want to come and have some fun. Not those dreary drab enclaves where Addict Centres are usually hidden away, ashamed. I wanted mine to be famous, a free house for homeless liberated souls. My goals were the total transformation of lives and roles, nothing less nothing else would do, and bless 'em they knew. My first hardened dropped out drop ins knew they had to muck in and help me make it work.

I'd applied to the Council ambitiously, with a tarted up and tactful CV, glossing over my ten years of indisposition as necessary condition of the job. Kind of field research participant-observer, and stressing how much I'd learned practically, to supplement my academic training. Well I didn't actually insist on *what* I was a doctor of, but didn't say it wasn't psychology. And my eminent friend from across the road turned out to be a living God indeed, whose word was the deed as far as getting grants for therapy projects, and he rustled up two other mates for me to meet and tell about my project, who also wrote avid references supporting me. So there I was, suddenly supported with cushions that floated me there and back through interviews and tests and discussions, and after a couple of weeks they summon me and say we've rushed it through in view of the dire need in Camden for a Centre like yours. And they give me this huge derelict building in Camden Town to renovate, it's an old swimming pool which they agree to do up with another grant they've dug up, so desperate is the plight of the mindless wanderers, and they set up five posts for me to employ two therapists and two alternative medical folk, and a PE teacher offers to advise part time. Then Dan, the Man from across the road I may have mentioned, lurks in and says Would you like me to take some therapy sessions for you and Exploratory Encounter Groups?

"You mean like Laing?!" I squeal with delight, but then get a pang of fright as he glowers at me

"You have to stop your romanticisation of Ronnie" he snaps, tap tapping his foot impatiently, "His therapy was not all perfect as he himself admitted later. And you have to stop this glorification of mental suffering and agonised psycho sessions. You cured yourself through crude behaviourism. You'd do well to remember that"

I was shocked, felt mocked and minimised.

"Are you saying psychotherapy has no place at my Centre?"

"It's OK if it helps people to unwind. But not as a substitute for *getting on* with the treatment, changing behaviour, diet, exercise, yoga, all the rest of your Method. Therapy's a part of it somewhere fitted in to a total programme. Not an end in itself any more"

I was annoyed to hear this from a shrink who earned his living by giving just such succour to formless lives.

"For these people that you see, their big problem is addiction. They can solve the other stuff later. Your clinic can only start the process. You're not the Tavi. You can't be, shouldn't be. That's ridiculous"

I felt he was limiting the scope for curing. I was megalomanic, thinking once I'd rid folk of the dope and rocketed their self esteem by the simple act of giving up, I could then, practically singlehanded, provide a safe space for them to explore why they had no self esteem in the first place. A dream, I know I wanted too much. But I still couldn't bear to be primly reprimanded by him. It hurt it hurt. I blurted it out too

"You hurt me by saying I'm ridiculous"

"Oh come ON" he shouted "Get ON with it. Forget these silly emotions between us. You have lives to save. I'll help you if you want, that's all"

THAT'S ALL. I die a million deaths, but slink off to my room, my office, in my new enterprise. So happy and excited. Who needs him anyway? I do, any day. But can't have him, so there. S'not fair that you can't have everything. No wings either, look at me, worn out and covered in paint, and waiting for the pain to go, the mood to swing t'other way. It will it will, I will it to. Boo hoo, he's horrid. It's a relief. Stops this stupid naive belief that a man could be different and sensitive and considerate and powerful too. They can't, power corrupts and so does charisma. Whoever heard of thoughtful charisma? No. I'd bought him, hook, line, and was finally sinking, by a single humiliating turn of phrase, which raised so much however. Like, never ever in daily life speak to me like a sad old nagging wife, as though feelings should be suspended till struggle ended and victory sighted. My white Knight had buggered up my vision of him completely, and in a sense I was glad. Though deflated, I'm happier with the commonsense knowledge that men are bad and dangerous to know. Even though this one seems not mad as well. Unusual in my experience. I refuse I refuse to put up with shit, and compromise a bit, on being hurt. I'd rather be alone any day. So hey ho, it's back to an unplugged phone, and days my own again, stop energy leaking into sneaking fantasies. Put it all into my new practice, the official term for my Centre – "a practice"

I feel very awed by the responsibility, and sometimes floored, when I see this sad little queue when I open. Most of them have been out all night on the streets. But there's no real retreat in here yet, it's still getting treatment from the builders. So they're drifting round, bewildered by all the shiny new plastic furniture, bright red chairs and tables and doors and window frames. It's a blaze of colour, or it will be when the buggers who volunteered get on with it. People tell me I should have an official launch party when the building's finished, but it's not a bloody book, and a boozy Do, or even Perrier one, would look pretty cruel to those outside, not here for a ride but a rocky struggle. They stand in huddles outside, wrapped up like bundles, like I was then, trundling along when the door's open, immune to stares of the builders on the pool.

"What is it, a school for crazies?" says one, the laziest. So I tick him off, the big loud prick, feeling full authority for the first time, but I *hate* authority all the same

"Shut up they're humans just like you"

"They're a bunch of alkies"

"And there but for the grace of God go you or I" I say

sanctimoniously, smugly ugly and eying the can of Special
Brew he hugs to his chest daily like an accessory. And here
comes a fan I seemed to have acquired on the Council. A lost
soul himself, the cost of politics writ large on his face, all
wired up and tired out.

"I'm glad to see you Stan. I need planning permission for
the house next door. Can you see a way to me getting it as a
residential extension of this place? I can't really cure them
unless they can stay here"

"I'll enquire" he says lugubriously "Can I see you tonight
and we'll talk about it over dinner"

"OK" I say, taking pity, and knowing I need to promote
the interests of my Home from home in the right ears. I'll
deal with the leers and the lechery, should it arise. But surprise
surprise it doesn't, and I'm puzzled as he's sitting guzzling
and slurping vindaloo opposite me. Then he burps and farts
and I want to depart in a hurry, but spy the love of my life
from my eye corner. He's looking furtive, but nods curtly, and
glances cursorily not curiously, just perfunctory passing glance
at my companion. While I'm gobstruck by his, and have to
close my mouth snap shut, I'm gaping at him so ostentatiously.
She's icy looking, blonde and beautiful, a bit overdone for
this slummy Tandoori, in black suit and stilettos and lots of
jangly jewellry. But not the type I would imagine for him at
all. I'd thought something Hampstead and fey and a bit ethereal. But this was straight from *Vogue*, with polished talons
poised to clutch him. I felt sick and rose to leave.

"I'll take you, wait a minute" says the Council prick of
the appalling table manners, with a final belch.

"Don't bother" I say, then feel my legs are wobbly and
what's more, I recognise my negative excitement feeling stealing over me, leading to his glass of lager, I'll be pleading with
him for it soon, or getting my own. No, better not roam off
alone tonight, anything's better than booze. I'll have to use
you, ugh ugh ugh I think, looking at him. But I'm not safe by
myself in this mood, all the old anxiety comes flooding back.
I have to attack these moments in therapy seriously. For everybody, this is the moment when you fall off the wagon, when

adrenalin flows rising rising inside you, a drink a drink will stop the next stage which is panic. The point would be to insert a block of de-sensitisation between the rising negative excitement and the panic. It's at this moment that an addict's wavering, and you're lost till you know there's an alternative to going back to it all, falling falling . . .

"Or rather, *do* bother" I change my tune and smile at him "I do want you to see the house next door to the Centre. Maybe we could go back there now. I've got the key from the Housing Department"

His eyes are rheumy and bleary, he's had six lagers and there's a hint of a leer there now. He probably needs booze to get him going like a lot of us, and he's got a long way to go to transform him into the great seducer. I take a sidelong glance at the big romance, and am almost reduced to tears as she's smiling at him so perfectly, with white gleaming wonderful teeth. I can't catch sight of his face, but he's got to respond to a beaming blonde like Catherine Deneuve. Oh despond and desperation.

"Isn't that the chap who's helping you? The psychiatrist?" says Stan loudly, so he turns round.

"Hi there"

"Hello" I'm icy.

"Come and meet Amelia"

"Hello Amelia" I'm frozen.

"Hi there, and who are you?" honeyed tones honeyed hair. I glare at her ferociously

"I'm just a colleague" I mumble. "This is Stan" and I attempt to leave, clumsily, gauchely, wishing I was dead, but he grabs my arm he's oozing charm all over the place I want to spit in his face hit him cause a riot. Then he says, knowing,

"Amelia was my first wife"

"Oh."

"And who are you?" the honey's warm and I see her twinkling too. She's on my side, a woman after all.

"Charlotte McCloud" I offer my hand while Stan stands there blowing smoke on their meal, deliberately, I feel.

"I'm discussing the house next to the Centre with Stan,

as a possible residential extension" I have to explain his presence now. And to think how I nearly . . .

"Great idea. I'll catch you later and we'll talk then" He grins at Stan, who picks his teeth, but doesn't look grief stricken like he should. Good good there's no problem getting rid. I hid my joy when Dan patted my hand

"About ten then Charlie"

"Cooooeeeee" Amelia says, but sweetly, still twinkling. She's truly a beauty, not snooty at all when she smiles "He's told me all about you. I wondered if this was you. Lovely to meet you. You're very brave. And lovely"

The lovely ones always go round telling everyone else how lovely they are. I suppose they can afford all the gush and generosity. But despite their charm I wasn't disarmed. They made me feel inadequate and terrible, damned in hell to be an uncouth uncultured working class turd from t'North, worth nowt in a bout between t'classes. I'd heard of chips on shoulders before but I was carrying huge boulders of remorse at my Being and background, worse than anything I'd known before. I usually have stores of compensations, ready to wipe the floor with the snobby gits. But this situation nearly destroyed me utterly visibly in front of them. Cunt of a beautiful bitch, and him as well. I fled from the door bled and bleeding from this open wound of inferiority at being a crude Yorkshire lass without any class in the awful sense. A socialist feeling like that. Oh God I needed to get pissed and plastered at once.

It didn't last very long though, this strong feeling of self-loathing. I had a lot of competition that night at being loathsome and low, he was belching and farting right next to me all the way home on the 31 bus. I'd lost interest in showing him the house but I still didn't want to be alone, and I didn't want to be in at 10 o'clock, waiting for the charm to ooze and slide through my front door. He could sod off for ever. I plodded glumly along in the slush where snow should have been, in my mean narrow North it would have been snow. Squelch squelch plod, listening to the belching, but suddenly quite humorous about it all. Who the hell wanted a tall handsome psychiatrist anyway? But the twist in the tale is that just at that moment I'd given up hope, the man himself decides he must have me at any price, and is moping around outside my door when I get there at half past twelve, having tramped all round the Heath with Flatulence. A merry dance I led him too, ducking and diving out of his reach all the way. Let's be friends, I say, to his dismay apparently. His seventh lager from the pub produced a torrent of declaration, ovation to my courage and defiance of fate. Which was why I was giggling a bit as I rounded the corner and saw my wounded soldier gripping his musket and hopping up and down.

He frowned mightily when he saw me and dismissed Stan with a wave of the hand "Thanks for bringing her" He hustles me in, protesting "You can't be rude to him like that"

"I can I can I've got a pain in my balls" He's undoing his trousers and pulls them down, feeling his balls gingerly "look at them. Can you see anything?" And so help me, I sit next to him on my couch and peer at his testicles, a bit hairy but no raving infection I can see. But his prick's waving very satisfactorily. I pretend not to notice, eyes glued underneath.

"Damn. Now I've got a bloody erection"

"Goody goody" I mutter under my breath. Bloody bastard heard though I bet. He grabs me and whispers help help softly in my ear, and what would you do with a big Jew you're in love with next to you half naked? Well I did do, but felt a bit nervous the first time without wine with him. I kept wondering whether the painful balls were hindering him and was concentrating too much on him altogether, so he came without me and I was only moderately aroused. It gave me a measure of composure and control, sadly lacking I thought, in my relations with him.

"Was it a ploy to get in?" I say when he's opened his eyes again, sighing, looking at me.

"No. I don't need ploys"

Big deal big boy. I'm obviously feeling resentful.

"I'm sorry you didn't come. I couldn't hold it. There's something wrong" he started peering at his balls again, lifting

his limp wet prick to one side with such reverence I had to
smile

"Is your technique so infallible?"

"BALLS" he says angrily, then grins and tickles my chin.
I now feel prickling sensations of passion all over and he
knows he knows he always knows. He pushes me backwards
on the couch and starts kissing my belly my thighs my centre
inside, I'm lying there in ecstasy for ten minutes delaying
holding on this is too good to rush and serves him right for
all that coldness. I get bolder and wrap my legs round his
neck and rub myself roughly against him burying his face
disgraceful disgusting I'm lusting and loathing him at the same
time and the hymn the rhythm's getting stronger. But he
draws back and stops he says he's coming again, laying on top,
come on come on then, I'd always rather have men inside me
any day. So there we are, a hopping heaving mass of orgasma,
raising the ceiling with such intensity of feeling I could scream.

"I love you" he says indistinctly and way above me in a
dream. I'm floating floating away.

"Hey you. I love you"

When they say it finally, it sounds so simple, all you've been
wanting in the world. I've been haunted that he didn't know
the words, and I'd never hear them anyway, and here He, the
great God, is improbably saying it to me, the loathsome Yorkshire prole of yesteryear. My fears are over. I'll love you forever
and ever and ever. I'll never be happier than this moment.
Certainly not the next moment, for he says

"You have to stop being so sentimental about those
nutters, and cure 'em simply" so strapping and philistine I
haven't heard such crap since my time with my simple Sheffield shrink, who used to wail "Think what you're doing. You,
with a Ph.D. I beg you" over and over. Well I'm discovering
things very rapidly about so-called mates of Ronnie Laing. *He*
sang a very different song did that one.

"Your own romanticisation of self-destructive genius
stopped you getting better all those years"

I was outraged. "Oh no sir." I jumped up furious "It was this little thing called FEAR that stopped me"

"Well yes. But a large dose of romantics justified yourself to yourself, courtesy of dear Ronnie"

Light dawned "You were *jealous* of Laing."

"Oh dear. You silly silly girl. Grow up. I'm trying to help you. For God's sake, I *love* you"

That gave him a patronising blank cheque to fuck me up and over I suppose. I closed my eyes in despair.

"It's staring you right in the face your problem as self-important tragic bitch"

"What the hell do you know about why women destroy themselves?"

"A lot. A lot"

"I bet a lot. You men externalised all your pain and throw it around in aggression, while we internalise, and you say romanticise, our tragic suffering. How dare you how DARE you"

"I dare I dare"

He reminded me of Hannah suddenly. What a pair they'd make, suave sophisticated rakes, and fakes the lot of 'em.

"FAKE" I shouted, inspired. "LIAR and CHEAT and CONMAN"

"Oh why so, lady?" He gripped my wrists and sounded nasty.

"You've had me on about Laing. I thought you believed in him. *I* did. I do" I was sobbing boohooHOO.

"Silly silly girl. I'm as concerned with suffering as he was, as you are. But I hate self-indulgence and the idiocy of some of Laing's stuff about the superior insight of the insane, and he didn't really think that in the end anyway. He was a wonderful humanist, we needed that, and he did want to stop pain, devoted his life to it. But to say that everybody's mad so profoundly insults the suffering of the ill and disturbed, it disgusts me. And so do gullible disciples who swallowed it all along with those charismatic eyeballs of his. And no. Never jealous, you little fool. I loved him"

"I see" but I didn't then or later. Just hating him when I

heard him saying one day "There's something wrong with his hardware" despairing about a schizophrenic who wrecked my Clinic regularly, slowly, and systematically, as though possessed by a meticulous demon. It hurt me so much, but I never fell into such dirty and mean categories as brain defects. He simply needed more therapy. But Dan implied he was hopeless, a genetic write-off. How was *he* a *mate* of . . .?? Now I'm just hurt by the fury of his avenging angel, turned on me in a tender moment, and he hasn't finished with his frosty lecture.

"While at some level it may be true that we're all mad and we're all on the same continuum, there's a clear distinction between neurosis and psychosis, and between survival and pain, as you're about to find out my dear in the big wide world of dealing with the disturbed. Welcome" he says grimly, and then dissolves into little boy lost, picking up his underclothes, scratching his painful ball. I have an awful thought, Perhaps it's not a flea but gonorrhoea or Aids. It might be Aids, and I've recovered to discover a worse death than drowning in sewer slime that was overdue last time round. There's not a sound as he inspects his testicle and I reflect on the wages of sin, just taking in my stupid irresponsibility, let alone pregnancy possible. What will I do? But a period's due tomorrow, so perhaps that's OK, but anyway an Aids threat isn't.

"I donated blood yesterday, in case you're worried about Aids by the way" he says ruefully wonderfully. I hug him and say Thank you sir for telling me my psychiatric mistakes. It'll take a long time to shed my naivety about existential psychiatry, naivety? But help me, I'm willing to grow all the time, and it's a sign of the climes that we both separate, tucked up in our beds to sleep sleep, not wrapped round each other like spoons like I did when young. But now this love can keep a street between our legs, as long as we both need our rest and peace and space and strength for tomorrow. Mild sorrow at parting but no broken hearts. It's the start of a new civilised closeness in separateness. We'll see how it goes. I dream about a tangle of toes though.

25

Now I know you think I digress too much with such sordid details of my personal life while the plot thins and you're losing track of the other thing. But I have to tell it my way and the personal is always so neglected that an overdose is OK to redress the balance, and what's coming will take your breath away, but I've got used to such incredible coincidences in my life that I feel by now it's destiny anyway.

So I'm sitting in my brand new spanking Clinic, with its waywards and wankers all displaying their worst sides today, and I'm playing Leonard Cohen defiantly on my personal radio. I need a flow of darkness and derision to relativise the healthy sterility all around for a moment, and also provoked I am by a remark of Dan's that I remind him of Suzanne with my Salvation Army cast-offs and long skirts and herbal teas on offer. Which is all OK, but I wonder as I listen to that bit about her being half crazy . . . "and that's why ya wanna be there" . . . and I stare into space for a bit, remembering that trace of irony he often has around his mouth when he looks at me. It's not imagination, it's a memory of all the men I've ever known in fact, who've loved me. They always had that faintly tolerant air for a . . . what? . . . a loony after all, no matter what I do, and how tall and respectable I reach, no matter who I teach, they all know they're all on to me the world can see there's something there . . . a little . . . well . . . not *odd* exactly, but uncanny and free, sez he, when I challenge him on it as patronising me. Nay nay, he sez, it's part of your immense charm, it's an ultimate untouchability, unpredictable as the wind you are, hypersensitivity overcharged, a larger than life living, and I want to live like that with you and share it – that vision – always, he says, and what can I say to that, but lie back and enjoy. Yet still . . . gravel-voiced suicide merchant Cohen grizzling away doesn't thrill me in quite the same way as he used to. I want it all ways I guess, the mixed blessing of an outsider's vision, yet fitting in somehow, sick of being alienated, always looking out looking in, never just being, ticking over complacently, though complacency's a disease.

I feel uneasy as I look up at the face in front of me, a premonition a warning. I switch off the radio and tear off the earphones. I can't bear to look at him, Santa Claus with his paw held out towards me.

"I have an appointment with Dr McCloud"

Ah me. Thomas Hardy knew nowt, life's ironies are *enormous*. I sit there, stupefied, gormless. He coughs nervously.

"I'm Charlotte McCloud."

"Oh God. I thought you might be. It *is* you isn't it?"

"Looks like it."

"Well. The game's up I guess then" he flops relieved. "Do what you will with me"

"What do you suggest?" drily. Well, he's a wily bird, this might be a ploy for sympathy. This sudden sagging relief isn't him at all. But this is him in a new incarnation, lying low till it all blows over, and sliding slowly into alcoholism and despair. A rare and likely story for one more human, but I'm dealing with a monster, wanting healing at *my* Centre. That's pushing tolerance too far, tying me to professional silence I suppose. I can't expose him as a lying murdering paedophile – no less, when he's a patient, can I? Bless his little cotton socks, standing there before me, imploring me. This conundrum's tying me up in knots. Perhaps it's all an elaborate plot. Nothing would surprise me with that lot of murderers.

"Well, you're a Clinic. Cure me" and, bloody fool me, I suddenly want to, more than any revenge. He's so sad and droopy. At least I have to help him admit things. Where else can he go without giving the whole show away and getting himself arrested? But he killed my friends. Did he though? I have to know. There's only one way.

"Today I have you down for a preliminary session of therapeutic assessment"

He looks agonised. I relent.

". . . that's pompous talk for a chat about what can we do for you."

"How much is it?"

"You pay what you can, according to income, if we accept you for therapy. I'm not a therapist. I'm assessing whether you can be accepted here at the Centre"

"You're in charge?" he marvels.

"Yes. I've come a long way babe, as they say" I say snottily, and regret it immediately. He shrivels even smaller.

"It just shows what can be done, eh?" I encourage him, almost slapping his back bloody hell. A long way from Leonard Cohen now aren't we

"Come this way" I sit him down in a comfy chair of bright red plastic with a yellow cushion which he cuddles absently.

"I don't know how you feel about telling your personal stuff to me, but you have to if you're going to come here. There are plenty of other Clinics and treatments. You could go anywhere, and therapists are bound to be discreet"

"Not when it's criminal"

"Oh it's up to their discretion" I say airily, not having a clue if it's true but it'll do in the circumstances, which are very strange even for me. I gaze at him with intense distaste. This is what it feels like to be in charge and gazing at them, the victims. As every him knows every day in every way with her. Wowee I don't like the feeling much. It's such a responsibility, this power. I don't want power. I stand up from the desk and settle on a smaller comfy chair in front of him, trying to look humble, biting my lip, trying to forget the screeching tyres, the blip in my mind, the block I cultivate when the flashbacks come.

"Well tell me" I say. "This is as informal as possible, but you don't mind if I jot down a few notes for my colleagues? They need to know a bit if they're accepting you for therapy"

"Well you know the background. And I admit it all. It's true what that journalist said. Everything, it's true. I've decided to tell you everything. It's eating me away this thing Oh God Oh God" he's shuddering and sobbing and I wait.

What a funny fate to deliver this one to my door. But again it's this destiny thing that keeps bothering me, hovering every time I ask why me? Why didn't I die like they did? I scribble a bit while he dribbles and sniffles.

"I feel terrible. Absolutely terrible. It's been living hell"

"Always? Or just since you were confronted by Hannah Lehmann?"

"Oh, *that's* her name . . ."

Folk always fasten on irrelevancies under stress.

" . . . You don't want to do it. You have to" he says, "I've always felt terrible about it, but couldn't stop. It's like a disease"

"We're talking child abuse here?"

He looks surprised. "Well of course. What else?"

"Well. I'm running an Addiction Centre here and you said when you applied that you had a drink and sleeping tablet problem"

"That as well, but they're minor"

"Never minor, Brian" I try his name to ease his manifest pain a bit. He's eaten up with it.

" . . . The cures become the problem and *they* take over"

"Yes yes but not with me. The real reason I came was to talk to somebody about the um *other* thing"

"Yet you came to an Addiction Centre for that?"

"Yes"

"Why? Was it to see me? Did you know who I was?" Was it a plot?

"I, er, heard your name mentioned in places I go to. Drinking places. They say you've saved one or two good people. I thought maybe it's her, maybe not. I'll go, and if it is, that's fate taking a hand"

"You specifically wanted to see me?"

"Well I thought if it's her, it's meant, and I must do it"

"You mean I'm sent to save you?!"

He twists his handkie in embarrassment, and sniffs, nodding.

"Summat like that tha knows lass" in a mock Yorkshire

accent to put me in hock by sentiment. But that's the last thing to work with me.

"Aye well lad" I join in grimacing. "It's all a bit mystical to me this stuff"

He answers gruff, his voice full of tears and such wracking misery it's devouring him. "Help me Charlotte *please*", and I suppose addiction to sex with kids is the worst addiction of all and I'm duty bound to respond.

"Tell me about it"

"I've tried to kill myself"

"Tell me"

"I wanted to die at the thought of the kids finding out, and Oh God and Jenny, and my constituents, and the Party and oh God God God . . ."

"Nothing's so bad it can't improve Brian" gently.

" . . . Oh God Charlotte, it's dreadful dreadful too dreadful to live with God forgive me, even he can't. Charlotte, you don't know how low I am. What filth. What a terrible terrible person . . ."

"Tell me"

" . . . It's always been the little girls. But I've never had anything to do with my own" He was looking at his feet in utter abject despair.

"Go on Brian" so gently he hardly knows I'm there.

"Well . . . at least . . . there was only the once, when I became aware" and he broke down completely, howling howling away. I wanted to hold him, but sat there listening, feeling like a voyeur. But I *had* to know. So I kept sitting still so still hardly daring to breathe, and waiting, and eventually it all came tumbling out. How he had to do something about his urges, men had to, so there. He went to these houses where Gavin Knutton had laid them on just for company. Just to hold his hand and tickle them a little and get them to hold him and rub him back and forth till it all oozed out and he called it ice-cream and especially when one of them would lick it clean like real ice-cream. He'd never buggered them, not one. He wasn't a child abuser he wasn't he wasn't. He just liked little girls to take their clothes off and play with his prick. He wouldn't do them any harm none at all not a bit. I felt sick and disgusted and tried not to show it, he trusted me now, and I had to know, and he went on and on into remorseless detail, a reverie of remembering which seemed to be calming him, and I wondered if he was getting off on it with me listening, his forehead glistening and his eyes popping out. He keeps mopping his forehead. I sit in dread for the next episode, feeling I'll explode. I'm in the wrong job. I just wanted to help people give up dope and give them hope, not sit here listening to sleaze from a diseased mind. He's finding it's turning him on I reckon. I see Dan beckoning me through the window. He knows I'm fearful of these encounters, and always lurks around somewhere, nonchalant, in case I need rescue. I say, Excuse me, and rush to the door, closing it, gasping for air.

"What the hell's going on in there?" he demands, angry, worried.

"It's that bloody bastard Brian Cheetham, the MP, the paedophile, for Chrissake"

"Whazzeee doing here?!" shades of Jean. I have to smile.

"God knows. He's confessing all now"

"What. Murder?"

"No. The other though. It's heavy going. I haven't raised murder yet"

"Oh. A detail"

"Look I can do without sarcasm"

He takes my hands and kisses them. I glance round, harassed in case anyone should see me, embarrassed in any case. Public displays always faze me.

"Fuck him. And come and do me later" he says, in a bad attempt at fun. I'm running out of enthusiasm for sex of any kind. I have to unwind though, and go back in. It's harrowing, but it *is* my job. Get back and give the slob a chance. "We'll talk later" says Hercules, and swans off on his own mission. I feel I have permission now to go back and be ruthless. Fuck him indeed. I speedily get to the point.

"Are you taking medication?" Could account for his sudden elation.

"Anti-depressants"

"Well I'd like you to tell me about the murders. Who planned it and when?"

"What?"

"The muscle"

"What murder?"

I sighed. Is he lying or what? He *must* be involved. I can't solve those murders on my own. You have to tell me. "The murders of my three friends in the car I was in with our Social Worker"

"You mean they're *dead*"

"Yes. Come on now. You must know"

"Killed?"

"Brian. Don't make me be a policeman. I'm not qualified to interrogate you. And nothing would please me less. Just confess and tell me who planned it. I need to know"

"I really don't know what you're talking about. I didn't know your friends were dead, but if they are I'm very sorry. But *with respect*, I don't for the life of me see what it has to do with me, or the things I'm telling you"

"Brian. It has everything to do with you"

"Whatever are you saying woman?" He looks outraged, indignant, pompous almost.

"Brian" I say slowly patiently "They were *murdered*"

"So? How do you know anyway? I never heard about it. Then, I haven't been reading or hearing. But it wasn't on the telly"

"Brian. They were murdered because they were uncovering the seedy sordid blackmail that Gavin Knutton had you by the balls in. My friend Jean was the mother of three of the children you were abusing. I should have been killed too. I knew it all. Do you understand that? I saw those photographs. I *saw* Santa Claus"

He looks at the floor, then back at me, incredulous.

"You mean . . . ?"

"I mean" I nod, "that the brakes were tampered with by somebody working for Gavin Knutton, and you I thought"

"NOT ME. NEVER. NOT EVER. EVER. EVER. AND

THAT"'S THE TRUTH!" he screamed and his look of absolute horror convinced me he hadn't known, he truly hadn't. This was for real. He was just a fiend and a pervert but not a murderer.

"I had no idea NO IDEA they were up to *murder*, for God's sake. Are you SURE about the brakes? What do the police say?"

"Oh Brian. It's all such a mess. Will you confess to the blackmail to them, and implicate Gavin Knutton at least, and expose the paedophile ring at Brampton Lodge? Will YOU help US?"

I'm beseeching him, reaching out, help us help me to help you, I can't overcome my revulsion right now but I can see a way how I could if you would if you were willing to help us nail the murderers . . .

"I can't" he says slowly the loathsome toad.

I sigh and wonder why I bothered. Then something strange comes over me, rearranging my vicious venom, smothering it right away, and the thought is clear and bright in my mind: If you can't help another human being who's wretched, you don't deserve to exist Charlotte my lass. So it comes to pass that I'm smiling at him, as surprised as he, and no wiser, but sort of mesmerised by my intuition or vision or mission. Whatever it is it has me by the throat.

"OK" I say, floating "Let's try to talk about the alcohol shall we? How much are you drinking?" and quite constructively, I work out a plan for every day for his diet and withdrawal and exercise, and recommend him for therapy with Dan in the afternoons. And all the while I'm filling with a sense of his Being, as a suffering soul whose only hope is here, he's decided, and we have to nourish his hope as healers, so he stops hiding away, and make him face the day again with some self respect.

"And we'll talk about your other problem some more if you like. I know a men's group of ex-offenders of child abuse who meet regularly. It helps"

"Oh I couldn't. Not a group"

"We'll see" I say, defiantly cheerful "and now I'm taking

254

a meditation class. Would you like to come? It's only simple relaxation. Don't be put off by the word"

"NO"

"You have to be open to new things here. In fact I insist"

"The first day?"

"Your life's passing. No time like the present" These clichés used to disgust me, but I tend to trust platitudes more and more these days. They've survived better than many a wit, though a bit of that too is required.

It's a dire situation this, and I feel pretty pissed off, all wired up and wary of it all. But we go to the hall where bodies are spread out on mats, waiting. I've had this group of eight for a month and only two disappeared. I put the scumbag at the back, inconspicuous, so he feels comfortable. But I misjudged him. Reluctant as he was to be there, if he had to be, he was going to get his share of attention. He marched with his mat to the front, under my nose, intimidating I suppose. A cunt in clover, I thought bitterly, as he lay grunting. Will he get away with it again? These bloody men get away with murder, do they? do they? I'm fretting away.

"Deep yogic breathing" I say, and show them how – abdomen out for inhalation, the opposite of the usual way.

"Now relax. Try to switch it off. All off completely. Imagine a golden room"

He's grumbling and chuntering instead.

"A golden room full of sunlight" I fight the urge to kick him, poor sod poor victim. I wonder where my beatific feeling has vanished to. I want to banish him to an unimaginable kind of purgatory where Melanie has been for years.

"Now your brain" I say, in my deepest hypnotic tones "Try to switch it off"

"Whatever for?!" he bellows, sitting up "This is absurd"

"Shhhhhhhh"

"What's absurd?"

"Well I've spent most of my life cultivating my mental functions and now you demand I switch them off"

"Yes" keep calm "To get in touch with your subconscious,

your feelings, your inner depths, in tranquillity and calm in a safe space"

"I've had enough of this piffle" he gets up.

"Try it Brian" I try to soothe.

The others are getting fed up.

"Not on your nelly" he says "I'll see you tomorrow"

"Oh Brian, this is so important" I plead.

"Don't need to lie around. Got to get on with it. Life's for living not lounging around"

"Brian. This Protestant Ethic stuff is so bad for you. You must learn to relax. It's part of the total treatment"

"It makes me need a drink just hanging around here, expected to turn into a vegetable"

He's disrupting the class, so I let him go, and we're all back to slow deep rhythmic breathing, when there's an enormous explosion. The building shakes. They all wake up in a hurry, and I know, I just know that my worries with Comrade Cheetham are over for ever, and I'm shattered and shaken but have to take charge. There's a large hole in my wall and water's pouring through, but I still hesitate to open the door. When I do, there are bits of his car and him splattered all over the road and blood everywhere. I stare in horror, though I'd had a split-second feeling this had happened before seeing it. I start panicking shaking shivering and I'm sick all over the road, reeling around reeling reeling, my head's spinning out of control can't take it in they've murdered him . . . but who?

26

The clients of my Centre are wonderful. Used to living in hell, they can cope with tragedy better than anybody safely adjusted to normality. They fend off press and police, and defend themselves and their existences before a nation shocked and gaping on telly. Britain's underbelly, raw and exposed and mocking the nation's smugness in its own living rooms. Dan's wonderful too. He's hugging me, shoo shooing everyone out of my way. My knees are knocking every time I see a TV camera.

"Take advantage. Publicise the Centre" he whispers, winking. But I'm thinking desperately of all the implications. Blowing people up is political murder isn't it? But does it have to be the IRA, are they the only ones blowing people up in Britain? And what about the Ceasefire? Is this a splinter group? Unless unless . . . I daren't confess my real suspicion to a soul. The whole thing's too big for me to take in, and Hannah's here amid the clamour, seeking sleaze, reeking glamour, and wreaking revenge on all her colleagues by being on the inside.

Revenge? I daren't think of it.

"I'm going to blow this story wide open. Don't talk to ANY other press, Charlie. PROMISE"

"I promise" with relief.

"He had no Irish connections though" she's insisting, in between twisting my arm about the relationship with Dan. I'm terrified he'll succumb to that charm too. I've shared a man with her before, and always this atmosphere of death's door seems to accompany it. I watch them together when I've introduced them, waiting, hating them both in advance for treachery, jealousy knows no bounds now I've found him. But he doesn't seem too impressed, bless him. A Jewish Princess he'd married first, and his thirst was quenched and drenched utterly by the type he says. But do I believe him? She's gorgeous and in pursuit, in between seducing half the press corps. She had more men that week than I'd seen in ages. At least five a day, like a Sixties Queen on stage. A prima donna holding court in a cheap hotel round the corner, dispatching them off to the Reference Library to dig the dirt on Knutton for her story. Then getting the glory all for herself when she's sucked it out of them, along with their sperm. She's running a woman's harem, and none of them seem to mind sharing her or their news with her. They form a queue in the ante-room before she'll see them, chatting to each other and smoking. Then strolling in "a quickie darling before you tell me" she says, in her lazy luscious voice to seal their loyalty, steal their stories, and saturate her sheets.

"Charlie darling. You must let me sleep with you. This place is rancid and hideous with sweat"

"I've no room" I plea.

"But we could cuddle up in your double bed, *you* know, girls together sharing secrets. You can even invite that nice psychiatrist too"

"NO Hannah. NO"

"Charlie don't be so . . ."

" . . . prissy?"

"Well . . . yes"

"NO NO and NO again Hannah"

"Oh Charlie what a bore" but she brings her story round anyway and I don't want to let her in. So she pushes her way past, and what can I say to an old friend? She kisses me on the mouth before I know it, then slowly starts to peel her clothes off.

"NO Hannah NO"

"What are you afraid of?"

"NO"

"A staid old maid afraid of getting laid . . . that's your poem. Toby told me you dedicated it to him. He never forgot it"

"Still NO"

"Come on Charlie" She advances, but I'm faster, and out

258

of the door with her story copy she's asked me to read, leaving her there. I can't cope with it, can't cope with any more at all. I run to the man in time honoured fashion, my passion aroused I discover. But not by this lover when he holds me, I'm thinking of her. Yet not for long. I'm still in the fold of the heteros whenever strong arms and thrusting pricks are available. Though aware of other charms if they're not quick enough off the mark. I lie in the dark afterwards, throbbing all over, clinging to him, sobbing my heart out, frightened fearful tears pouring. He's none too adoring either.

"Give it a rest Charlie. You've been crying for a week"

"I huh can't huh stop huh sorry"

He pats my bum patronising "Good little girls pull themselves together better"

"Piss off. This one's got a lot of crying to do. I suppressed it for years. It's all got to come out. Don't DARE shut me up. Sniff sniff sniff"

"Oh Gawd"

"You're a psychiatrist"

"But you're not a patient baby. Never. Now what's really going on? What's this?" He picks up Hannah's story, crumpled on the floor. "*Hannah Lehmann exclusive.* She's a very sexy dish our Hannah, isn't she?"

I want to kill him and the sobbing turns into a howl.

"But definitely not my type" he's laughing "I prefer scrawny mice with scraggy bodies and sagging tits don't I?"

This stops the sobs "Your Amelia didn't look scrawny or scraggy or sagging I must say sniff sniff"

"Oh but she is underneath the packaging. All women over 40 are saggy and scraggy aren't they love?"

"I loathe you"

"Amelia wants to talk to you actually. But she's scared stiff of women intellectuals. I told her you didn't bite but she's very nervous"

"Of me?" I'm incredulous, recalling how frightened I'd been of the upper class ice maiden.

"Oh yes. She's seen a lot and been around in the world. A real wise gel. An impoverished Viennese Jewish nob her mother was. Cut off by the family for an affair with the gardener. Amelia's the result. Her name's actually Hannah too. She changed it to not be Jewish. Like her nose job and her bleached hair. A self-hating Jew. Desperately insecure. She's got gloss. And real sophistication. But she's no intellectual. She's an intellectual snob though, by heck. Collects tame ones for her gallery. No women though so far"

"Just what I've got in my mind for my life"

"She was a lovely wife till she realised I wouldn't stay in her gallery and be fetishised"

My eyes are wide with amazement at the idea of her being frightened of me *me*, as harmless as a warm spring day surely? The phone rings.

"Yes, she's here. Charlie, it's Hannah. Wants to know if Charlie has read it yet, and can she come to bed with us?"

"What do YOU think?"

He laughs. "I never rise to bait like that. Be seeing you and take care"

"Don't DARE leave me" I yell, throwing a pillow, but he's gone, striding down the stairs, door banging, car starting. My heart gives a lurch. I know he's not church-going but down the pub in the hub and the heat which defeats me still. I daren't go in till I'm absolutely certain I'm over it for ever . . . though never say never, never say no, always and ever, that's how it goes . . .

Hannah's story flows, she's a good writer. It's feisty fearless stuff too:

"Is the Ceasefire over? Is this the work of the IRA? Why should a man with no Irish connections be blown up by an IRA bomb? Who else murders by bombs in Britain?"

It's all innuendoes, but reaching a crescendo of insinuation

" . . . friend of property developer Gavin Knutton, now known to be developing the site of what was an alcoholics' refuge, blown up outside another one run by the same person" She didn't mention I'd been an inmate of the first one. It was a sensation of a story, and she'd scribbled across the bottom:

260

Front Page, tomorrow's *Guardian*. I went home to congratulate her, but she'd left a lethal note: "Gone to pub." What would they get up to together? But I had to control this jealousy complex. I couldn't follow him around to see if he was sexing every attractive woman. It's just that he's bound to fall for her. I don't see how he couldn't, and then he would, wouldn't he? Wouldn't you? Wouldn't any man, offered it on a plate by a beautiful dame? Who can blame him? I do I do boohoo hoo . . .

"But we both fancy *you* Charlie" he protests later, as I bang on his door and he appears in his little vest, fed up with me, my obsessions, my fears and tears.

"Where is she?" I demand.

He stands there shaking his head, then scratching it, watching me, amused, "We'll have to get married if you go on like this " he says "and glue ourselves to each other night and day"

"No no" I say drawing away "No. Never. I've got to try. I've got to overcome this possessiveness. I just don't trust you. Or any man. Particularly a man like you"

"Ho hum" he says. "Are you coming or going? I'm cold"

I turn and race across the road, slamming my door, hating them, all the world, the lot of them. Then it's tossing and turning for hours, sweating, burning up with frenzied uncertainty. Eventually I fall asleep and it's nightmares of ghouls with great staring eyes in Santa Claus disguises, rows of them with arms waving from a crowd of kids in the background, like that Coke advert, and the door bell rings and I wake soaking and so irredeemably sad. I'm glad he's dead bloody hell I spit out loud, hit the nail on the head of that massive disturbance at the back of my mind. I can't forgive him for that kind of crime, I can't I won't. It's all mixed up and churning round. All the Santas had grey curls, not white, with white flashing inviting teeth and wreaths round their necks, saying By heck just like Dan does, merry men with claws all poised to pounce. I must take a grip on myself. I feel healthy enough, but terribly stressed, with a latent lurking anxiety that's focussing on anything passing. The bell rings again. It's Hero in a day-glo head-band going jogging, waving the *Guardian* at me.

"How's that for breakfast?" and he's off, long legs bare, hairy, handsome, he's so bloody handsome, and holding me to ransom like a teenager again over Elvis, I got stung I hum, feeling better for seeing him, wanting him, crazy for him, it's not fair him daring to care for me, cuddle me, muddling my categories. Bastards don't cuddle, they keep you at a cold distance. But he does. He keeps me in a trance of adoration and contemplation of his Wonder. I blunder bad tempered again round in my untidy flat, bloody men, and determine to swim first thing. Haven't done it for a week, feel a freak without it, discipline slipping, mustn't slip. Then I flip over Hannah's story. It's gripping and gory and accompanied by a history of the man – From city slum to MP in a generation, a self-made hand-grenade so dynamic was he, speeding up the Labour Party like a comet who knew its own value, wouldn't burn out like they do, he would turn out a new kind of survivor with a family providing stability security, anchoring the shooting star in roots. "Tha's got to 'ave roots lass" I recall him saying. Ugh ugh ugh, a puffed up thug, that's all he was to huge applause, 'cos they were all the same in the Party, a hearty back slapping bunch of macho yapping bully boys, boorish to the poor beaten women who wondered why they left their socialism at the meeting and never brought it home where it ought to be, feudalism ruled there supreme. It seems pathetic here seeing it in print, the mad sprint to reach the top, crawling and trampling. He sampled power early on, Head Boy at the Grammar School, and ruling with a rod of iron I bet. Then key selection by the local branch to be a candidate, a picture of him canvassing with Jenny and the kids, a lovely girl with a little curl right in the middle of ugh ugh ugh Santa Claws Big Paws all over innocents.

I scrunch up the article enraged, crunch crunch can't read. It's feeding my hatred and bringing back the pain. Those kids abandoned, motherless. I'm quite insane with anger now. This vain fat prick with a write up for a King. Ding Dong I was going to knock Humpty Dumpty down though, watch me. I'm hatching a plot in my looking glass, eyes blood shot with no sleep and weeping endlessly. Mascara on, cover up. Time for crying's done. On with vengeance. Get the bloody Sons of Gore, get 'em get 'em.

Before long, I plug the phone in, my refuge my solace my peace to unplug it, and it's ringing already.

"This former MP with his unblemished family respectability. So what's the dirt, Dr McCloud?"

"Who the hell is this?"

"A friend of a friend. Danny boy says you know something sordid."

"Go to hell. And take him with you"

I slam it down, staring at it in revulsion. These things are such a damn invasion of privacy. It rings again.

"Go to hell"

"Well well, sweet as ever. It's a salt-of-the-earth soldier got himself killed, according to that. What do *you* think?" It's Dan Dan the menagerie man. Not dealing with his zoo, but wasting time with a jealous fiend who's too nasty to tolerate.

"A journalist pal of yours says you told him I know something"

"No journalist friends. Don't be a fool. Love you. Speak to you later when you're better"

"Dan I'm scared"

"Of course you are"

"They killed him"

"Sure did"

"Do you think the blackmailers killed him?"

"Why would they?"

"In case he spilt everything"

"Could have. But they say it's an IRA type bomb"

"But they could know how to make one and try to blame the IRA"

"Possible. Listen lovey. Come and live with me till it's over. You're in danger"

"Shall I tell the police everything?"

"They're no bloody good. They've closed the case once"
He hates cops.

"They'll have to open it again"

"Why should they? No new evidence. They'll just say Shove it or prove it. I'm coming to get you, curlers and all" and he's gone again, my lifeline my sanity. Watch it girl. Don't get dependent on those silver curls. You've done so much alone, don't jeopardise it by wise guys trying to tame you. It has to be done alone, this gettingtogether. The phone rings again. It's Hannah all breathless.

"You'll never guess"

I feel myself go pale and lean on the wall for support. I'm caught in a mad hysterical merry-go-round of ghastliness grinding me into dust. I'm drifting away. Whatever will she say next?

"They've arrested Gerry, Bridie's brother, and his cell. Did you know he was IRA, bloody hell? Had a cell? They say they've been watching them for weeks even after the Cease-fire. They say they're certain. They're issuing a statement on the 10 o'clock news, but why the hell haven't the IRA claimed responsibility for Cheetham's death then? Are you listening Charlie?"

"But he couldn't have done it" Not half he couldn't. You don't mess with a blessed beloved twin sister of these misters. I'd known all the time it might happen.

"Don't be silly. Of course he did it. And all the time I've been stupid, thinking the Irish thing was a red herring. I'm off to write it up. This is the story of a lifetime"

"Wait, wait. These men are dedicated, Hannah. They don't go bumping off MP's who might have murdered their sisters. They're not allowed to. It's an army"

"Silly girl"

Same words as Dan. I wonder . . .

"We must defend him"

"Well you can Charlie, all you like. But he's as guilty as hell. You know it"

I do as well, but can't admit it. The enormity of the error

264

is striking terror into me. I'm freezing suddenly. The door bell's ringing. I say desperately into the phone

"But he didn't do it"

"Charlie he did"

"NO NO NO. Not him. I mean, Brian Cheetham didn't murder anyone"

"A hit man then. But *he* was responsible"

"Hannah he wasn't" I wail "he didn't know. He was horrified at murder. Don't you see Hannah? He's murdered the wrong man." My door bell's shrill, insistent.

"Oh God, yes I see"

What a quandary, what a God almighty hopeless mess. I let him in, worried looking I notice, worried about me? Can't be. He is. He cuddles me

"You're frozen. What's happened? You're in shock. Lie down" He wraps me in my duvet, and I can still hear Hannah shrieking from the phone. He replaces it firmly, his face grey as his hair. "You'd better beware baby. I'm taking care of you now"

I put up a final struggle, raise myself up on one arm, and say "Thankyou you're very kind. But I've got to find Gerry a lawyer" I try to climb out of bed. He stops me with such firm gentleness and tenderness, cooing

"No baby no baby, not now, not anything"

and I give in, lying gratefully in his arms, shivering shuddering

"I'm going to cry Dan"

"Be my guest" he says, nuzzling me warming me snuggling me. I'm like ice, a steel vice of sheer fright gripping me from head to toe. The phone's ringing again, but he won't let me go to answer it. He's rocking me to and fro. It's the most comforting thing anyone's ever done, I'm thawing and even having a bit of fun secretly before long. This man's really worried about me. He cares for me. Dare I believe such a man could love *me*, a worthless creature of infamy, a jelly who collapses in crises, churlishly believing you'll always want a nice Jewish girl really. But you're *here* with me, and you keep coming back for another fling. The phone's ringing ringing but I'm singing inside suddenly. Don't ever let these loners, these emancipated types on about autonomy like I used to be, ever tell you different. There is nothing, *nothing* in the whole world, like being loved, being held by a lover you love. Only heaven above could be better, and there you'd never have to get up, go away, separate for a second, and *I'm* the one who reckoned, only a year ago, that the price of involvement's too high, resolving to try to be emotionally independent. But it was denying gravity for me, you see. I just love men and intimacy. Now and again is how it can be. I'm discovering living without smothering the other one by every day every night flight from yourself and self confrontation.

"I'll come over later. Thanks so much. I'm better now. It was a shock. Leave me now"

He looks doubtful, but goes, and I'm in control, on the phone to Hannah again in seconds.

"Where are they holding him?"

"Paddington Green nick. I'll meet you there in half an hour"

I sneak out over the back wall like a schoolgirl, and run for the tube, and get there as Hannah's gliding from a taxi with a small dark woman carrying a huge briefcase bigger than her.

"This is Pauline Simmons, Gerry's Brief" she says "This is blessed sister Charlie, Pauline"

I nod as bright intelligent eyes scan me.

"You know my client well then?"

"Oh NO, just his sister. We were great friends" I bit my lip. The "great" is grating. In the end I'd almost hated her. Over Toby. Over a sterile fella. How daft it seemed.

Hannah beams at me merrily. "This story's growing all the time"

"You two stay here. I'll see you soon" says Pauline, clip clopping into the building on efficient low heels, and I'm standing, feeling cold and uneasy with Hannah, whose manner is too voyeurish and calculating for me, when Pauline rushes out again, to the sound of sirens filling the air for the second time in a week. I freak out again, scared stiff looking at her face, all ashen now, and police appear from everywhere, racing around, pushing us out of the way.

"They've found ... they've found" she's gasping for breath "two bodies" she rasps "and one is Gerry's"

27

I didn't collapse this time though. Just stood petrified, staring at her, and Hannah's in hysterics, shouting her head off "Tell me tell me. My God, where's a phone?"

They won't let her in the police station. She gallops off.

"Who's the other bloody body" I mutter, terrified. Pauline turns on me wide eyed:

"Why the officer in charge of him of course"

"You mean . . . you mean somebody *murdered* them"

"Of course"

"But it's a police station"

"And full of the IRA suspects. They still round them up in case the Ceasefire fails"

The IRA, the others, the Brothers. Had *they* done him in?

"This is bizarre" I announce, and Pauline nods numbly, reading a piece of paper. Fine time for reading, I think nastily, and flounce over to the phone box. But she pounces on me suddenly from behind.

"Listen. Listen to this. Listen. I have an invaluable contact in there. A source of deliberate leaks. He's deliberately leaked me Gerry's statement. Listen to this. Gerry admits murdering Brian Cheetham. He admits it. He says "It was a revenge killing of Justice for the murder of his sister Bridie and her two friends. They were murdered by Brian Cheetham to prevent them exposing him as a paedophile and as a crooked MP who was being framed and blackmailed by a Sheffield Property Developer, who ran the paedophile ring. Cheetham got the Council to grant him prime development sites"

"Oh God" I'm reeling again.

"Woweeeeeee" Hannah is right behind me listening intently taking furious notes she rushes off again immediately

"Be careful. He had no proof. These are only his allegations" shouts Pauline after her "Be careful how you put it"

"Weeeeee" waves Hannah, euphoric.

I'm filled with infinite sadness at poor dead Gerry who died in vain. I *must* regain some stability. I'm wobbly again, and wishing my prop were available. Oh God, will it ever stop, this horror this pain?

"He mentions you Charlie. He says you are witness to most of these events. He says you will back up his allegations. He says this will force the police to reopen the investigation into those crash deaths. He says it was prematurely closed because the police were in the pocket of Brian Cheetham and the Labour Council. It's a terrible responsibility he's leaving you Charlie"

I brighten at that. A Task in the frightening mêlée. Something concrete I can do about something. It's pandemonium outside the police station, police cars screeching up and down, loud hailers now "Please clear the street"

"I'm going back in" Pauline says, and I stare after her with a rising sense of mission. It's my turn to act with more vision than Gerry had. What a bad futile way to end your life, in a single act of violence. Nonsense. No recompense or improvement or comprehension possible. Just Bang you're dead, snuffed out, and confusion reigns on why you did it really. You must have been feeling pretty weird to throw away your life, no matter what the immediate rationalisations are. I've always thought the men of violence must be deeply psychotic, though I used to say that this doesn't invalidate their cause. But I've had pause for reflection since those heady unconvincing revolutionary days in '68, when we plotted ways to smash the state, the hate and distortion pouring out of men's gills, getting cheap thrills, pretending it was a righteous war. What bloody exercise in killing is righteous? The politics and the method are inseparable. You can't plant seeds of hope and love by brutal deeds of barbarism, and I know the foe seems invincible, but we can't be poisoned by using their methods – insolent mirrors of all we despise. We have to wise

269

up to being the alternative ourselves and seducing people by our attractiveness.

Which is why Dan's way smells for me. It pays too little heed to personal empathy. Well maybe he's brilliant at his job. But he can't be if he says to me Stuff your emotions there's work to do. I'm a pain in the bum with my tears I know, but it has to come out my fears and my doubts and confusion. Yet he doesn't want to know. Get on with it, he says, refuses to play therapist with me, can't expect him to for free. You see romance needs finance and I can't be client and lover too. But my kind of therapeutic relationships in my Centre, of empathetic understanding Client-centred therapy flood over, flow over, to relationships in general. Well I'm working on trying to make sure they do. Whereas he seems to switch off listening after the work-day's last appointment. His shrinking is nine to five, it's not a life. And this, I think, is shirking on personal growth.

I'm working on all these speculations, rather than think about Gerry. It's very clear I can't face the whole thing and have such emotional indigestion I can't take in what's happening. It's a kind of catatonic withdrawal, except my mind's working overtime, which it may well be too with catatonics. Just sulking existentially, says Dan. But I'm not sulking. That implies choice. I simply can't find a voice. I'm staring into space and can't speak. There's nothing to say, to communicate. I don't want to say *anything*. Even a little's enough to betray me, but not enough for them. There's an excruciating noise outside, with workmen drilling and filling in holes in my building. But their activity's shielding me, no-one would believe anyone's in here today. So I'm staying hidden in the innermost room, trying to sort my head out, and three of the regulars have found me and are sitting in the same room, frightened of the noise and the explosion wrecking their haven. They're clinging to me as driftwood, sanity, on a sea they feel is sinking them. Their dependence brings me out of my trance. I've been in it for hours. But these people are my responsibility, and it shakes me up. They're such valuable souls, vague, worried now, wondering how they'll survive if we shut the door.

I got to know yesterday that we have planning permission for the house next door. So, soon I can offer these three a home. I start to relax at the thought of them, brought in off the streets to a safe space to explore their pain, without plugs and drugs and bottling up, without pills and potions to trap their emotions in steel cages of addiction. They're still reeling and wobbly from withdrawal, but the diet and vitamin therapy they get here every day, and yoga and meditation and gentle exercise at first, is making a difference, and the two therapists are listening, and my group – when they all talk together – is a riot, with me being quiet, absent, almost silent host, as their voyages of discovery unfold. They're finding solidarity, similarity in each other, yet their own separateness preserved. But they do deserve a home, the good effects of food and rest can all be destroyed in the endless void of the streets of London. I get annoyed regularly with the Man from "Mind" in Camden, who is such a good soul, but he thinks I'm a megalomaniac trying to do too much with limited funds. You can't give them a total alternative life, just show them ways of self-help, he says, though he's full of praise for my optimism. But I know myself. If you don't give addicts a total break, they'll take the dope again as soon as the pain surfaces.

There are wonderful self-help groups around. They're listening grounds for supportive solace, and psychiatric survivors do need each other a bit of the day. But then, I say, They must get off their bums and get a high through exercise. Another way of living which gives them pleasure, to replace that other, that awful negative way. The talking's not enough. You need a strong tough code of disciplined play, enjoyable exercise. Get those endorphins working as a body's natural opiates, they create another way of living entirely, where pleasure is in your hands, at your body's disposal, when you know how to use it, and get mind and body harmonising in their total way that's so surprising if you've neglected your body for years, like addicts have. I want to save you from all those years I spent in the cold and the dark and the prostitu-

271

ting parks with no benches to lie on and shoulders to cry on at your peril. I'd wrenched away from the devil and saved the day only by a massive transformation of habits and routine, not by sitting and scheming and dreaming in a room only.

But the loneliness of mental pain needs breaking too, and that's all taking place in therapy groups. They're just not enough alone. We need group exercise and meditation and yoga and juice drinking too. So self esteem, that impossible dream for an addict, comes surging through at last. You can only break with past habits savagely, I say solemnly to Betty, whose ravaged face I glimpsed one day at Camden Tube sitting on steps like I used to, all wrapped in rags, a fabled bag lady of Camden Town labelled schizophrenic years ago and never knowing what it meant. As if anybody does. But she trudged around as though she'd found some truth of doom she says. How can anybody raise a struggle against a verdict like schizophrenic? she asks.

The first task in a therapeutic community like I want to build is to rid them of their labels, foils for convenience of the medical profession, and nothing to do with my experience or yours or hers or mine of you and you of all of us. I want to create a context for making sense of Betty's pain, for hearing it, far away from the leering peering menacing crowds of Camden Town who harass and confuse her and use her body in the same shoddy way I let them misuse mine.

Though *my* prime time on the skids was different. I had my heaven-sent sisters after all, and an obsessive compulsion to suicide somehow coexisted with a fairly manic and juvenile sense of humour which would always sneak in while I was humping the worst of them, carrying me through, and even in the midst of the terrors I could see the farcical view. But such a perspective is totally new to women like Betty who never had a giggle in her life. There's something obscene about trying to make a schizophrenic laugh, Dan says, not lavish with praise when I raise my theories. What's funny about being fucked over? Well I know I know, but without that Sheffield laughter we'd never have got through. GOT THROUGH, shrieks Dan, Look at you struggling, and where are they? Dan dat was murder. But he never heard my protests, switched off belligerently, saying Laughter's a sign of mental health, it's the cart before the horse, fool, meddling in schools of psychiatry I know nothing about. But still, I shout, that's a Leninist argument – you can't do anything unless you do everything – and *I'm* going to make my clients laugh during their cure, if possible. Well at least a winsome grin I'm managing with Betty, forgetting Gerry completely as I see her smile widening and wonderful.

"You're full of shit Charlie" Dan says later on when I've gone home, finally lying with my feet up, telling him he's a creep and I won't live with him. Certainly not. Nor sleep with him either I've decided "I have to live my life my way. And you're having a bad influence on my Centre. You're too conventional a psychiatrist. Not like Laing at all. He would never have said Shut up and get on with it, like you do to me"

"You're sure about that?"

"Yes"

"Well I lived with him for years, shared a house. He said that often"

"I don't believe it"

"Believe it babe"

"You talk like Charles bloody Bronson"

"Listen. Laing was straight with people. That's all I am with you. It's time you sorted your life out by doing something in the outside world. The howling phase is over. You're cured. You'd better get on with living"

"How do you know?"

"I know. I'm trained to know"

"Big deal"

He looked so gorgeous too with his wet curls glistening from the rain. But his disdain was palpable.

"Listen. I get countless ladies of leisure trying to come to me for expensive therapy as grotesque self-indulgence, when they're perfectly OK and their only problem is that they don't address the outside world. They never had to they have so much money. These are often women who could be creative too. But they don't do anything except be professional therapy patients, trailing from couch to expensive couch, baring their childhoods. You've been out of it so long too, for different reasons. It gets to be a bad habit, not facing the world. I'm trying to wean you gently back into it. That's all"

"I never heard anything so philistinish in my life. And what do you say to these women?"

"I tell them to go to hell"

"You refuse?"

"They're frauds kid, frauds"

"No. Just wretchedly unhappy. You should be helping them"

"You naive little fool. They're not even unhappy. Just bored stiff. They want an hour a day lying on my settee, fantasising about me jumping on them. Some take their clothes off. Several never wear knickers. They pricktease all day round the therapy circuit. Who the hell do you think keeps all these charlatans in business? It's not the bloody National Health Service, I can tell you"

Light is beginning to dawn about Dan. He's not the snarling snivelling man I'd got him for this morning.

"Is that why you do all this counselling for public agencies like "Mind" and Community Care? To escape? I always wondered why you're so hard up and live in this dump. I'd thought it's because your ex-wives screwed you for every penny"

He looked disgusted with me, as well he might. He trusted my judgment to love him anyway, and I betrayed him the first sign of lack of empathy. But could he be right about me?

"Yet the pathway to hell's paved with good intentions, in this case thinking you know what's best for somebody else"

"But I do. I do"

I'd heard that one before too, but it may be true. I spend too long languishing with grief about the wasted years instead of getting on with it. Fears will only vanish entirely when confidence grows, and that flows when you achieve goals you set yourself. I believe him, I do. Well I want to, and that will suffice for now.

"I just wish you weren't involved with all *that*" he says, with his worried look again. I ruffle his curls, and murmur

"It will all be OK" reassuringly. But he's not having any

"It won't you know. Unless they arrest these bastards. The police get worse" He goes off cursing and grumbling and unconvinced. I can stay here safely, but it's a choice I make to take responsibility at last. With *my* past, that's such a big thing, the biggest one of all.

The phone's ringing, never stops. I nearly drop it when I hear this one from Hannah, sounding so excited and overwound.

"The IRA's issued a statement that they did it for his acting 'unpolitically'. This does not break their Ceasefire. Did you hear me Charlie? The IRA killed their own man for unpolitical behaviour. Charlie this is a sensation. Charlie say something. It's too much. Can I quote you? The cops are going to act. They have to, on your murders. I mean, Charlie, are you there . . ."

My murders MY murders. Oh God it's getting ghastlier ghoulier. I say in a holy ethereal sort of way "I feel as if I'm floating above it, elevated, suspended. It's very distant. So the personal isn't political for wise guys. Hey ho hey. Surprise surprise . . ."

"Charlie this is no time to take off. I'll talk to you later" She rings off, indignant. I must do yoga, deep breathing. My chest is heaving and I'm leaving it all to them to solve. It's me, *my* life, but sit up suddenly. Bugger this dropping out. This is *my* fight *my* struggle, sent to me courtesy of Bridie and Natty and Jean, and I had to get in the limelight, hating it, yet Dan's right, my date with the world is nigh, and my high noon is coming soon, just around the corner I can tell. Might as well enjoy it. Stop hiding, pretending I'm not here, defending myself as usual, frightened of fear itself descending. What the hell cowardice is that? Where I'm at is the brink of incredible opportunity for justice and publicising the fate of all those kids like Melanie and dirty old men of power, who collude together, a mafia in operation. Well their final hour had come.

It took some doing, but I finally got through to the person in charge at Scotland Yard Serious Crimes Squad of the investigation over Gerry. We were going to come and see you, he says laconically. Well here I am, and I'm full of information.

"Fects we need fects" he says nasally. But he's arranged to take my statement, all of it, yards of it, and still says "Fects. Not one fect. It's all speculation."

"Rubbish" I say. "Cheetham dead. Gerry Donoghue's dead. Your policeman guarding him's dead. These are dead bodies. My three friends are dead. I've told you, six dead bodies and they're all connected in one big scandalous conspiracy"

"To do with the IRA"

"Not originally"

"To do with child abuse"

"In the beginning"

"It's so fantastic. And not a single fact"

"Bodies are facts" I scream, appalled.

"Don't yell at me Madam. You're telling me such a fantastic series of stories and it's all speculation that they're related. The only thread is you lady. *You* run right through it. Why is that?"

I'm exasperated and want a lawyer. He's taking advantage and making me look a fool.

"No lawyer necessary. You're not under arrest"

"No, but I'm not getting through to you"

"Listen lady. I'm investigating a straight assassination of one murdering piece of IRA scum by another. He's murdered an ex-MP It happens. Then this little lady and her journalist friend start yelling at me that the IRA scum did it for private reasons to do with his sister, who was murdered in her turn by the MP. Then you're all yelling that this MP is a child molester and his sister knew. And I'm supposed to re-open a case that South Yorkshire police closed weeks ago about brakes on a van which were inconclusive. And you keep mentioning this priest. Where the hell does *he* fit in?"

"He's probably the hit-man"

"*Whose* hit-man?"

"Gavin Knutton, the property developer in Sheffield who was blackmailing Brian Cheetham who was abusing children and we found out so he was sent to kill us and he failed and he followed us from then on then only me when I was the only one left and . . ." I remembered the orgasm in the hospital bed with all the dope going round and round randy as hell:

"and?"

I feel ashamed and look at the floor. A whore a whore a whore I've bin. A sinner no more though. Me and monogamy's made a pact. This cop thinks I'm enacting some elaborate fantasy.

"and he followed me to London and hospital and London again and set fire to my flat except it was the one next door and then . . ."

He's peering at me closely, not taking notes I notice.

" . . . well you know the rest and I know the connections sound tenuous without proof but they're true I swear" I hardly dare look at him for fear of rejection of all of it, but he's reflecting and speculating and the nasal sneer's all gone. Why the flush of devotion? Could a rushed promotion suddenly have wafted into focus, and hocus pocus turns into possibility . . .

"You're saying it's an elaborate chain . . ." He blows smoke in my face, which I resent, but he's scenting victory so I must be patient.

" . . . of cause and effect involving all these other actors as it goes along?"

"Steamrollering. Yes. Exactly" I beam at him.

"And you, dear lady, are pivotal"

"Er, yes"

"Dead centre every time"

"Yes I suppose"

"Well don't go anywhere"

"No"

277

"I'll be in touch"

"Yes" I rise to go, but he waves his hand.

"This priest"

"Yes?"

"He's the centre of your story"

"Yes"

"Yet we only have your word he even exists"

"Yes. I suppose you do. But he does, I assure you. He *does* alright." It's his hands convinced me, Officer. They're expert at fondling in the right female places. I fight hard to push it down. His face darkens frowning:

"But why a *priest*? I don't get it"

"Maybe that's his permanent persona. Easy access to everywhere. And people trust you"

"True. True. Well, I want details. Go next door and give a complete description. Anything you remember. Anything at all. Everything"

Like it took him three minutes to bring me to orgasm, a few smart tricks with sticky fingers, could teach you a few things I bet Chief Inspector.

I'm setting down the polite details in the next room when he rushes in excited "We've got him we've got him"

"How on earth?"

"South Yorkshire have nicked him. They've opened the case again officially, but one Inspector never stopped looking. He's not even a D.I. either. He knew the Irish girl who was killed. Wasn't happy with them closing it. I've just been on to him. He's been working with your journalist friend. Boy is she going to have a story"

"But what have they nicked him for?"

"He was chief suspect as soon as your Social Worker said the dead women mentioned a priest hanging around, connecting the threads"

Not the dead women at all, it had only been me. I'd raved at Toby on the phone just recently about my recurring cleric. So he'd taken me seriously after all. I must revise my vile judgments, my hasty dismissals, my intolerance, my . . .

"He's a known hit-man, dressed as a priest. They've suspected him for years. Never pinned anything on him, but they've got him now. He's broken down under interrogation"

"Never. He'd never do that" Those ice-cold eyes.

"Oh yes. Tears and everything. Said he didn't know they were messing about with kids. He'd never have taken the contract"

"You mean he's confessed to murder?"

"The lot. And he's naming names, and famous they are too some of 'em"

"My God this is fantastic. But why did he confess? They don't. He's a hardened case. I *know* he wouldn't confess"

"Well he did ducks. Said it's more important to do the kiddie porn market. Keeps crying about it. Some rum bugger. Can commit murder, but cries at kiddie sex. Can you believe it? He's full of regrets 'cos he helped 'em. Says child-abusers should be strung up"

"But why?" I had him sussed for the role of cold clinical operator and manipulator, totally in control. Crying in the nick just didn't fit. Had they *tortured* him? He still wouldn't cry though, not him.

"You never can tell what throws 'em. Mass murderers can go soft suddenly. Often about their Ma's. Look at the Krays, loved their mum. All have a weak spot. It's finding it. This was lucky. Turns out he was sexually abused himself as a kid"

28

The old cronies of fate are multiplying at such an alarming rate, and the danger here is that my fears and tremblings will paralyse action and they mustn't they mustn't. I have to earn the satisfaction of seeing this thing through, though there's not much left to be done until the trial. We've won through all the twistings and blisterings. I just wish those sisters could see this revenge plastered all over the *Guardian* in loud enraged headlines:

POLICE FORCED TO RE-OPEN MURDER CASE
SHEFFIELD CONFESSION BY M1 MURDER SUSPECT
WIDENS MP DEATH MYSTERY

Following the confession and death in custody of
IRA member Gerald Donoghue to the murder of former
Sheffield MP Brian Cheetham, and the implication of
the MP in the murder of his sister Bridget Donoghue
and 2 other women, South Yorkshire police were forced
to re-open the investigation into the murders.

An undisclosed confession by Andrew James Birks, 52, arrested on suspicion of murder of 3 women in a car on the M1 on Xmas Eve 1988 has led to the arrest in Sheffield of Gavin Knutton, 48, businessman, in connection with the crime. A further 13 members of the Sheffield City Council and 5 Social Workers from the Brampton Lodge Children's Home were detained for questioning in connection with separate allegations made during Knutton's interrogation.

On the same day Brampton Lodge Children's Home was closed down until further notice and the children transferred. A spokesperson from the Council denied any implication of its Councillors or Social Workers with the murder case.

A massive scandal linking the M1 murders with the recent "non-political" murder by an IRA member Gerald Donoghue of former Sheffield MP Brian Cheetham was hinted at yesterday by several sources close to the Council.

Underneath and still on the front page was a profile of me plus photograph. What an epitaph Hannah.

STILL CENTRE OF THE STORM

A key figure in these several overlapping murders is Dr Charlotte McCloud, Director of Camden's Drop-In Centre for Addiction in North London. She was a survivor, along with Social Worker Toby Dobson, of the van crash on the M1 which killed 3 of her friends Natalie Johnson 33, Jean Sykes 30, and Bridget Donoghue 26 – sister of IRA confessed murderer Gerald Donoghue who was himself murdered in Paddington Green Police Station when under arrest along with the police officer guarding him.

Dr McCloud, a former Sheffield University lecturer, was living in Sheffield before the crash, and working against the closure by the Council of a Women's Refuge on the Moor, Sheffield's prime shopping site. This site was later sold to Knutton Holdings PLC, the multi-million development company owned by Gavin Knutton, now under arrest on undisclosed charges of conspiracy.

Dr McCloud is a tireless supporter of the rights of women, addicts, and the mentally ill. Her own courageous cure from multiple addictions forms the Method of Cure at her Centre which she runs with her partner Dr Daniel Feldman, a former colleague of the late anti-psychiatrist R.D.Laing. The murdered ex-MP Brian Cheetham was a patient of the client-centred therapy practised at this Centre when he died. He was killed outside the Centre by a bomb planted in his car by the brother of Dr McCloud's late friend Bridget Donoghue.

Dr McCloud was unavailable for comment last night on the

convoluted drama surrounding her. A colleague confirmed that she was still working with clients at her Centre.

So that was it. Night and day. Never get away from them. Hounded, rounded up, pursued. They're glued to the windows and doors and telephone. I'm never on my own or away from the meejah for a minute. But I'm biting my lip and swallowing the flip send-up comments on the tip of my tongue and sweetly trying to prolong the ordeal to get as much appeal and publicity for my cause as possible. Applause is pouring in. The postmen deliver sacks of mail. Congratulating, enquiring, demanding, begging letters I answer, begetting more and more till I have to stop answering individual enquiries for places at the Clinic. And interviews. I'm interviewed and photographed and talked to and questioned night and day every day and I don't mind. I'm finding adrenalin from nowhere and my fears have disappeared overnight. This all feels right. This cause this cure are being promoted and I'll put up with anything for that, even the telly, which I've hated since '68 coverage distorted the women's aborted attempt to contribute. It suits me now to use them, and all the while refusing to say a word about the "Crimes" as they call what's happened collectively. I'm sworn to pre-trial secrecy by the cops and the lawyers, who say it will jeopardise the foolproof case against everybody if we leak anything now. But I've wanted to blow it wide open.

Instead, I tell and show how to cure addictions, which is what they pretend they want to know. I'm now a "personality" they say, whose views are news since my *Guardian* interview with Hannah when I talked about women and addiction and this common affliction of our times – that misery is medicalised and social problems individualised into being your own fault. I launch an assault on the tranquilliser manufacturers and the booze lobby and how we should have clinics to cure us all financed by taxes on them. Why should just the snobby few be treated in private clinics? We want Health Cure Centres for everyone to cure them first, so they can tackle the problems that made them mad. Well, you can imagine this kind of stuff is hardly guaranteed to puff up my personality into a meejah queen. But what *does* is the key witness business, the brave and lonely heroine who nearly bumped herself off with booze and drugs, and then was nearly bumped off by a gang of murderers, and now maybe bumped off any day by any number of random hit persons threatened by my intended disclosures at the trial. And all the while my beloved Daniel is lurking, protecting, in the background. A big furry spaniel, or Svengali? His silver curls all awry with worry. But he still strolls around in his sexy unhurried way when the jogging's over, saying Calm down baby, it's all under control. Yet I know it isn't at all. It's one gigantic frenetic haul. But a girl's gotta do what a girl's gotta do and who can blame me for exploiting fame when it's offered on a plate?

"You're a national heroine" says Hannah enviously. "We must do something with your hair and clothes. You're a mess Charlie, still a Sixties hippy"

"Leave her alone" Dan moans.

"All the men love the sweet innocents" sneers Hannah "but are they really afraid of sophistication?"

"Sophistication isn't in clothes" he snaps, and I'm secretly delighted they're fighting.

"No but they help. Oh they help. I'm going to transform you Charlie" and she presents me with a tight black dress and high heels and supervises the hairdresser to cut and shape and bleach. I stare down at my mousy fragments, so tenderly nurtured, on the floor, and feel like an amputee. It's opportunity knocking at my door but I feel my identity is being skinned alive in this drive for a new appearance, cropped and sleek and blonde, a freak for fashion. It isn't me. I see Dan looking shocked and hurt and weirdly angry.

"I'll kill that bitch. I warned her to leave you alone"

"But I thought she was right. I don't want to be a dowdy old feminist"

"You're elegant and beautiful, particularly when you can walk" He means Not like a stork, tripping in four inch heels with my bum sticking out six inches.

"And that bleached hair is atrocious" So much for my platinum trim. But he doesn't like longer tresses and messes with curlers, so what's a girl to do?

"OK, I'll go back the other way. Anything you say" It doesn't bother me, so I can afford to compromise on this one, and it does seem to matter to him.

"I hate to see that tramp manipulating you"

Oh Lord, last word in moralism. How will I ever tell him of the past transgressions if he's running round with categories like virgin-whore. I can't take any more of this.

"I'm my own person" I hiss over my shoulder "and what kind of emancipated man calls women tramps?"

"A spade's a spade" he says grumpily. Got the hump, they'd say in Yorkshire, far away Yorkshire, I'd love to see its hills today I realise abruptly. Out of my way, moralist psychiatrist, with your misogynist categories flapping flying in the wind, sapping our womanhood.

He sighs "It's so difficult with you Charlie. You choose to misinterpret me"

"There's no ambivalence about words like 'tramp' "

"She's a promiscuous bitch, who uses her body to promote her career. That makes her a tart prostitute tramp, whatever word you choose – we have to *use* words you know"

"Women have to use everything they've got to survive in this world"

"Bodies and sexuality are sacred. If women use them for gain, rather that expressing their emotions and sexuality, it disgusts me. I can't help it"

"Why can't they do both?"

"I can't help it"

"Well try" I say, despising him. "Men have so much else to exploit – their toys and weapons and power and entrenched positions. Women's bodies are the one thing of power they have while men still want them. They use them as they wish. You're just a priggish old Victorian at heart"

"No. I'm not. I need to respect women though. That's a very modern idea. And I can't do that when they sell themselves, when they use their bodies instrumentally and casually, yes casually. They undermine themselves"

"Arseholes" I say this to really offend him. It does. He's distended with fury. A curiously prim reaction for a man who's supposed to value personal freedom. But perhaps not freedom for women to dispose of themselves at will. What's really going on with me is still self-defence, and a lurid sense of my own history. He'd hate me if he knew about me screwing around for a drink. But then, he'd never been hounded by withdrawals. It's all very righteous, being principled, when you're not crawling around on the freezing ground, so desperate to ease your pain your purity is definitely not your main concern.

Mind you, Heather used to argue he was pure as driven snow, pickled purity you know, never compromised at all. That's why he left academia, to keep his principles intact. An act of dubious wisdom. His grubby life afterwards killed him. But he'd still say Better dead than compromise with the bastards. It's only hard being poor kid, he'd say. That's all, that's all. The world's full of sad old, failed old farts of '68, dreamers, romantics, couldn't scheme their way in a society that stinks. Why do you think the best and brightest and finest of that generation burn themselves out, he'd say. As though it was a privilege to lay down and sleep in the gutter and sneer at the creeps and careerists crawling their way up, while he supped and slurped his way to final catharsis in a dark gutter, dying of dignity.

Dan sighs again, before he huffs off pompously. Stuffy old fart. And he must be *old*, though we've never discussed it. I trust my wily intuition that it's a well-kept secret, my sage is at an age that it's delicate for ladies to ask, and I honestly don't want to know. But the generation clash sometimes does show. Nobody who lived through '68 as a militant could trot out prudish remarks about women's bodies being sacred. Where *were* you in '68 daddy? Screwing mummy for all you were worth in safe matrimony, while we were overturning the very concept of monogamy. Though maybe he's just less brutalised and sexist than we were in those days, the women too, though they knew inside it was tearing them to pieces, a time for boys with girls as toys, as every revolution has been. But it does seem that the same behaviour that in a university is liberated, becomes sullied and dirty once outside, in a petty and mean universe, rehearsing tired old words like whore and tramp and obscene, as though the Sixties had never been.

So it's no unalloyed joy this affair with Dan Dare, and there's also the little problem of his patients. I'm jealous of them too. They're too good to be true some of these women trip tapping up his path. I stare outraged some days, curtain twitching like Beatrix next door, who's convinced it's a whore house he runs anyway. The other way, you know, she says – he's a male one. Well you've got to be modern and imaginative, she twinkles at 85, with less wrinkles than I have. So when they stand at his door and he lets them in with that smile and his raggedy curls all beguiling and tousled, I'm frazzled by jealousy at that concentrated attention from my man they'll be getting, and what else besides. Though I hide it all from him. He'd be enraged at such poking in his life. But these well-preserved middle-aged matrons he patronises, really these deserving patients he says he selects and vets, they don't seem dying of angst to me, on their HRT and climbing out of Mercs and Porsches in this scruffy street, where the beat of Aff-Cab disco is perpetual and rowdy, and their cars in serious risk. But they tap tap briskly to the glorious man's consulting rooms, way up there on the top storey of his house. While underneath is his big brass bed, spouseless, and waiting for his whorey girl friend with a past . . .

I refuse to get paranoid about my past though. If he's really such a moralistic prick he'd better go anyway, and there is the question of his age. I can always console myself I ditched a dirty old man. Though I've always been a fan of maturity, they mustn't be *elderly* for Chrissake, and I reckon he must be over sixty, silver curls notwithstanding. I mean ole Ronnie Laing was 62, though his wife has a young child. But geriatric passion ain't for me quite yet, so we'll see how he behaves. I'll save the grandpa insult for a rainy day when he's telling me to Shove my pain and get on with it. Meanwhile my hairstyle will stay, though I must say it looks tarty rather than smart to me. Yet maybe there's a thin dividing line, and who am I to use words like tarty in a disapproving way after my speech today screeching at him for intolerance. But I do look as though I'm going to the party or the dance, decked out in my high heels and black dress, with blonde crop stuck on top. I tuck it under a black beret from a jumble sale.

There's a howling gale outside and I wish I was riding the Castleton bus out along the Hope Valley in hiking boots, and that doesn't tally with my roots rejection at all. Though on reflection, a nostalgia for grandeur of the Peaks is fine, doesn't undermine my steadfast loathing of Northern macho working class culture, and how it broke people like me, sapped the life out of women.

That's the buzz I'm getting from these letters. They're mainly from women, condemning the male political process they've always felt excluded from. No choices for women and their lives, except as wives and extensions of men and the family. I begin to see the depth of the political crisis all around. My programme on telly was a sounding board on a need for a new kind of politics of sensitivity, where outsiders and nutters and loonies and underdogs and women can all find a home and a way of articulating their views. Not refracting them always through prisms of hatred of usual politics, adversarial power flipping, ego tripping and male. I'd unleashed a long loud wail of discontent by that chat, and I sat back now and marvelled at the outpouring of grief finding a voice. Nobody had listened in the lifetime of these folk. I sat and soaked in their pleasure at my performance. Then I stood up and found a relevant kind of dancehall for my new tall tapping tapping heels. They'd offered me a slot for half an hour on Channel 4, a chat show. Hot shot I would be, bringing loonies onto the screen, and putting them in every suburban family for all to see, with tea and crumpets. Bump bump would go their safe assumptions of sanity. Could be you and me that, given enough flak. We'd see a victory for empathy at last.

But the past keeps catching up with me too. I get a call

from the Inspector who pursued the case in Sheffield. I knew her well, he says of Bridie. I know what he isn't saying, what he's hiding from his safe little family too, and he's praying I won't remember his face, hot and flushed under Wicker Arches, pressed against her breast, sucking screwing fucking my friend, disgraceful tut tut. But I do I do. Though I may be wrong about the actual screwing, I never witnessed that. In fact, I wonder if she ever actually did it. She hid her secrets from me, so really he'd no need to be scared. I wondered how he dared ring me up, in case I knew. But he had to say something to someone, and the funny thing is, his story had a ring of such authentic misery, I had to believe it.

"You see I loved her" he says, relieved to get it off his chest. "I had to tell you. She loved you. You were her best friend"

"I see" I say, not wanting to remember my savagery to Bridie in my demented private jealousy, hating her as I had in the end.

"Did she tell you about me?"

"Not really. She mentioned a policeman" and how we'd fallen about laughing about that one and its potential for real exploitation. But Bridie'd been horrified at any suggestion that she should take advantage, other than the necessary money for survival.

"Oh God" Yes Mr Plod. She had mentioned you, but your secret is safe with me. I'm into therapy for miscreants, not moralism. So don't worry don't worry.

"I'm sorry. You must feel bereaved"

He heaves a sigh of relief and says "But it's better now we've got them all. I want to say I did admire you on television"

"Really? I mean *really*?"

"Oh yes. Very much. I see what she meant about you. You're the best"

Oh Bridie. Rest in peace, and forgive me. As long as I live, I'll never be jealous again, I swear.

"But you really liked all that stuff about drop-outs and loonies and rejects giving us pause for reflection on ourselves?"

"Oh yes. Everybody can be down on their luck"

"Some are lifers down there though. What about them?"

"They have a point of view"

"Would you come and say this on my programme?"

"Oh NO I couldn't. I can't"

"Not for Bridie?"

"I'd lose my job"

A slob after all. Oder?

"At least . . . What would I have to say?"

"Just what you're saying now. That these people that the world treats as scum are as human as you and me and deserve a place, a point of view"

"Well . . ."

"*Please*"

"Is that all I'd have to say?"

"I promise"

"OK"

"OK!"

29

Of course I fucked him. I had to. As soon as he got off the train I knew my biggest turn on is men of power, and he was wearing his uniform, and all this scorn I'd been getting about whores, well, might as well if he thinks it anyway. I buy him a drink in the pub. Feels weird in a Kilburn pub with a copper, with those mocking Irish eyes all around. But I can't stop the shocking fantasy taking hold of me. I want to be underneath all that stiff uniform, with its gold braid and buttons sticking in me all over, and your big policeman prick plug plugging away. I must have it today. Whatever I say politically about abolishing power, my deepest instinctual layer must be so macho, beyond my control. A police patrol has always thrilled me a little, for the wrong reasons, filling me with blatant schemes for getting a big strong one inside me. While on another rational level I think, revulsion to power propulsion and authority. But take me up an alley anyway and undo that uniform. But leave it on. I must see it, as you're heaving away.

Actually I notice it's not gold braid at all as I'm getting laid. But there's lots of steel, cold as ice, and it's so bloody nice to be doing it illicitly, across the road from His Prissiness, on the floor in the kitchen, as crude and uncomfortable as I'm able to arrange it. He's pretty drunk now. I'd bought a bottle of whisky, thought about it all the way on the C11 bus from St Pancras. A new achievement it would be, coping with the presence of booze. Get used to it, and pubs. Be a nun in fun palaces to prove I can do it with dash and verve. So I filled him up a bit nervously, then flashed my tits in his face. I know they can never replace Bridie's, but a tit man's a tit man for all that, and within seconds I had him sucking away like a babe in arms. Oh the charms of a big blond policeman on the kitchen floor. But the door opens when he's coming, flood flooding inside me, my legs open wide, wrapped around him. I just get the sound of Dan's curse as the door slams. It couldn't be worse, wham wham, though I can't stop, I'm coming too. He's got through all reserves of rectitude. It's rude and raucous rapturous fucking. I stop looking over his shoulder, just surrender. It's splendour. It's never ending glee. Please please more more, and never give a man your door key . . .

I'm pleading with Dan to answer the door within minutes of pulling my party frock down. He looks shocked out of the bedroom window.

"Go away. We're finished"

No NO NO. I can't bear it. Don't do that to me.

"I can *explain*"

In vain, the age old story. He'll never listen again. I'm a whore I'm a whore and I proved it to a moralistic bore I happen to love. How could I do it? I blew it. I've done it again, cocked it up with men. As soon as it gets too close I give them a dose of bad behaviour, delivered with aplomb of an atom bomb, boom boom take *that* for caring for me. I swear it defeats me why I do, apart from the heat of the moment, which is very real. But you can't be perfect. I gave up so much, booze and tranx and cigs, but I can't forgo the touch when it teases. A massive release I feel from repression, depression, confession of commitment. I feel rebelling swelling as soon as they say they love me. It moves me to run run away as hard as hell from the roots, cloying clinging begging me to stay, begging me on a line of boring convention, and you and me the centre the still of the storm, till I want to be the rain and the hurricane and not the peaceful core at all.

It's turbulence in the soul or summat. A restlessness with comfort and conformity so deep in me that whenever something is "normal" and "safe" I chafe in agonies of suffocation, must be off, scoffing at your treasured normality. My pleasure's in exploring the precipice the high cliffs the treachery of chance, like romance in the gutter whose final shutter is death, so near, the frisson of fear keeps you alive a survivor on the edge. And now, though I've taken the pledge of sobriety and will never self-destruct with chemicals again, my new health has given me a peace a serenity a self esteem I never dreamt was possible – but it's not total. I'd always be rebel first last and always. A pact with the devil within me in your terms. A devil who pops out now and again and lies, legs apart, panting and breathing fire on a kitchen floor, with a dire dark force of evil in uniform – for Dan, who hates every last man and woman of them with a venom uncharacteristic in him.

But now I'm stuck with one pissed policeman, and my programme's due for filming in two hours. So it's into the shower with him, hot then cold, then gallons of water, then pep talk reminding him of his duty. Then buttoning up all my buttons again. It's a men's preference dress with buttons head to toe, and it's on with the show, and I feel wonderful, glowing with health and orgasm, though with spasms of terrible guilt about Dan creeping up on me stealthily. Serves him right, I keep saying to myself, and I'm almost convinced by the time we trip trop home again and flop into bed, and I get lots more of being the whore of the Law, and suddenly collapse with laughter at the thought of a great phallic truncheon for luncheon. The rhymes and the rhythm in time for dinner. By God he's a winner this lover, this lawman. I can quite see how Bridie was loyal to him, wouldn't exploit him. He's a dear if you can steer clear of what he does for a living, and I can't do that very well since I sell myself on No difference between personal and public. But I can't stop this orgy for anything. The phone keeps ringing and we can't stop. It's over and over, and I make him wear his uniform, his jacket at least. It's a feast it's a joy. We use ten packets of durex in a day, and then lie panting and wanting some more.

And the door's firmly locked and chained, though I never imagined Dan would have used the key he took one day off the hook in my kitchen. No business. He was asking for it, his discovery, barging in like that, this is my space. But God, I'm getting grief from my guilt. It's a good job the police and I are going together to Sheffield, then Leeds for the trial, while this passion lasts. It's better to go, and fast, from here. Steer clear of silver haired psychiatrists. In fact I'll have to move. Can't sit in a groove, loving him hopelessly from across the road. It's not my style. Bloody men, I'll shove them away.

It's another December today and I still haven't taken in all that public grief for Diana which was beyond belief. It fills me with weird relief because I was wondering if folk weren't much *nastier* after the Tories and here they were crying over an Outsider dying. Some Outsider, worshipped by the world, yet she defied the Monarchy itself. I'll tell you in stealth but nobody else that I slunk down to Kensington Palace too and planted a posy of pale pink roses and winked at her picture, thinking how we lost her just as she became our best Republican. Still, a vestige of reality remained because I restrained myself from identifying her as a sister under the skin – it's the skin that you have to consider. You could house all the homeless in London on that empty estate where she's buried, and she could still be allowed the island for herself since we deprived understand the special needs of Outsiders, we do we do, boohoohoo.

Anyway, hooray for today and the pouring rain, my favourite weather, lashing down on the train windows from a sky bleak and threatening. We don't speak much, quite shy, me and the happy policeman. He's taking a nap, and I search his face carefully for a trace of intelligence. But it isn't there, anywhere. I stare out at the landscape instead, dreading the cold dead leadbelly lump in my tummy, telling me I've made a crummy old choice here. I had a Man, and this is a Joke in front of me, with its mouth wide open, gaping an unspoken awe of sinnin' wimmin it reflects. He has to respect them in real life, his wife a pillar of police respectability. But at the secret policeman ball they'd all be whores like me and Bridie, flashing our tits and saucy bits for him to fondle and feel with greasy mits, our only appeal that we're forbidden hidden ladies you steal into in the darkness, dirty dealing in parks, under arches, where students were marching arm in arm defiant under your stern eye earlier in the day. Get them out of the way for the night, the black will fall and shroud your filthy pilfering fingers, lingering lunging longingly up cunt out front sucking. I'm cluck clucking in disapproval with my tongue.

He must have heard me. He wakes up, glaring, disgusted. You often are when the lusting's over and there's nothing left. You're all bereft. It's called triste, ducks, replacing trust, a must when you lay incompatibles, the terrible price of following vice and facing her when you've shot your lot and want it back. So attack her instead, all out. Start shouting at her as if she seduced you in the first place and you hadn't wanted it, wouldn't have murdered for it.

Speaking of which, this shitty trial is due to open in two days at Leeds Assizes. But we have to register with Sheffield police tomorrow for reasons to do with the child-abuse thing, and we're bringing much fuss and meejah attention to these Northern wastes, they're tasting blood. Even *I* got mentioned on the national news today, hey hey celebrity pay too – fancy being paid for being yourself. Makes such a change when I've spent my life being vilified for it. It's hot entertainment and a ravey way to start the day – hear loonies defending other ones. The Drugs Tzar was in the studio too as his views are hottest news. But he was all patronising with me and he's a big bold policeman and we know how noble they can be in their buttoned up uniforms. He's going to round up the pushers and dealers and inTone along with the Government about crime and addiction and unwise afflictions that will be eliminated so folk can lead decent lives again. The Stepford wives and their merry men can sit on the patio in dayglow suits and feel safe we must feel safe from the losers and refusers and abusers who want to steal and rape and pillage our village greens and wreck our precious communities woooo woooo our communities our sanctities our properties our Pride.

The laughing policeman is having hysterics suddenly at his tits and bums tabloid. I feel sad and glum. It's a bad scene, devoid of any redeeming features, like fondness or friendliness. We just lent each other our bits and pieces, and now it's over, finished done, and I feel the first time Dan's revulsion for sex on its own without love, emotion. Leaves you all lonely. Lonelier than before, when you know the score. At least all alone is so different. So lonely. I can be alone indefinitely, and it's solitude, without being lonely – which is servitude. You're at the mercy of anyone to fill the space. Any face will do, and I feel lonely now in his company, and used. Though I was a user too, an abuser almost, making him live out my silliest fantasies, be authority for me in your uniform and I'll be little girl being bullied, and then I'll rebel bloody hell. But this wasn't even rebellion. Just indifference, the worst attitude of all for another person. He's all pursed up and salaciously tut tutting at his smutty rag, the Sunday Slime, and I'm reading about myself in the *Sunday Times*, and there's a photograph of me laughing and happy and mousy tufts in a duffle coat, with Dan standing by me in sweater and jeans. We're the perfect alternative couple I think, and I'm blinking back tears. Don't be so bloody stupid, playing cupid to a man and being part of a couple was never on the cards. I worked so hard at my cure, don't go all demure and doting now the difficult bit is done. You've won without a man in tow, why have one now? Not even a lawn to mow, but seeds could be sown elsewhere . . .

And that's one I daren't confront either, having kids or not having them. It's almost too late. Any date with maternity just vanity, I've always argued, wanting to perpetuate your ego in others, and anyway the nuclear family is off limits. But isn't it a pity and a shame that I can't tame my hormones to agree with me and my rationality? They scream and wreak havoc every month a week before my period. I feel so broody and breedy, I'd have any weedy old man as dad, and Dan isn't weedy, he's wonderful. A cruel reflection now. But how can a woman who's always treated babies like rabies, as threat to career, now leer into prams and find these dear little darlings irresistible? A terrible admission I still can't come to terms with. So I won't. No, don't. You're doing enough for one day, all the way to Sheffield with a laughing policeman you've laid, winding you up, reminding you of Dan who you've betrayed and banished utterly. I'm muttering Damn damn damn, and he says Now now, in such a tone of admonishment it aston- ishes me, and secretly turns me on a bit. Oh shit shit shit this sexuality defeats me. But I end up meeting him in the loo nonetheless, I confess, and I do things to him there that I'd never dare with Dan. Like kneeling on the floor and licking him as he sits there, bum all bare, and feeling him coming and running all down my chin. Then putting it in all sad and saggy, and making him hard again, while the train rushes North North North. It was all worth it, the guilt, for I came like I've never come before, leaning there on the loo door, a whore a whore in all but name.

If you blame me for my wayward sexuality, are you sure I'm not just doing things you've always dreamt of, and I'm tempting you now? How easy it is this carnal pleasure, and addictive too, and I'm supposed to cure addictions. But this sex thing's an affliction I can't control. So don't enrol with my Centre if pricks are your problem. They're mine too, as is guilt, that guilt, it silts me up for days afterwards. But I still go back for more, the naughtier the better. Might as well get hung for a sheep as a . . . But then I weep, and flail around despairing at my one true love sailing off into the sunset, disgusted disgusted. He trusted me, and I'm fallible gullible insatiable it seems sometimes, for that nonsense called experience to run its course.

No wonder my relationships fail, I expect you're wailing. But I kept my nymphomania under tight wraps then, nobody knew, not even me. Which is why it's crap such a concept. Nymphomania is any woman who likes sex as much as men, and when she says so she's a nympho for life, a fantasy wife all the same they all dream of taming. He's doing it now, the policeman. We're seated again, and that smug look replaces the lust on his face, and I loathe him. That's the basis of fantastic sex for me, it must be, lust and loathing.

"I'll see you in Sheffield will I? We'll have to be careful" He looks greedy already. "I know a hotel near the station. Will that do?" Seedy and suitable.

"No. Hotels are out. It'll have to be, er, secret. In my car. We can drive somewhere. On the Moors if you like"

Oh I like I like I love it. You shove it old Son. That's back to Square One for me, though I'd do it for free this time, not even a drink required. He's done a good deal here, swapping me for Bridie. Doesn't pay, and no love in the way to complicate.

"I think I'll pass. I'll be very busy" And a better class of cop will be available to a shameless hussy like me who's famous. Can't you see, I expect posh hotels these days. But that's not why he's crazy for my body. It's only desirable in shoddy smutty circumstances, a dance with danger, a flavour of garlic to savour in his long hours of duty, looking snooty and severe and safe for the public to approach, and he looks reproachful now.

"You're not getting out of it? I thought we had an . . . agreement"

"Agreement?"

"Well, we share similar . . . er . . . tastes"

"Do we?"

"Oh yes indeed"

The same needs for ritual humiliation. But I'm determined to shed mine. I've fed them long enough. Life's getting tough now, no more bits of rough on the side in the gutters and galleys, huts and alleyways. I'm joining the mainstream, with a dream of fitting in well, the alternative mainstream, sitting pretty, me and my witty psychiatrist. Except he's gone. I'm alone, and couldn't fit in if I tried a million years. A tear trickles down. I'm not so fickle as it appears. I've tasted true emotional commitment and realise the waste of anything else. It makes me feel rueful and humble. I'm mumbling all sorts of savage asides that endless long ride to Sheffield. North North North pulling me back. Won't go. Counterattack. It's a black abandoned city, and I don't pity it a bit, as I stand in the rain with industrial ruin stretching for ever over the valley . . .

I'd be a shallow old stick if I didn't feel a prick of affection as I say goodbye to the cop. He's shopping for flowers at the station stall for the little wife though, so how can I summon any? And I refuse to be a hypocrite, big a lump of shit as the bugger who's running home, Missed you so, darling. And it never enters her sweet head he may have Aids to bring as her other present. These decent types and their private swipes at everything they stand for. A whoring policeman in the van when they're arresting the kerb crawlers, how does it feel, laughing policeman at the flower stall, so big and tall. Are you every man I know? I may be a bit unstable still, but I'm able to distil the difference between men and boys, and it's not just toys. The essence of a real man is maturity and ease with himself. The same as with women exactly, and it's nothing to do with noise or poise, this one looks graceful too as he strides off into the night. No, it's to do with inner peace and tranquillity and behaving in a way you identify with all the time, not plunging into reveries of guilt and despair and going lairy in acting out some childish fantasy. No matter how wild the sex can be, it lacks the comfort the tenderness the real intimacy that love can be, a love I've thrown away knowingly. There's no excuse. What's the use? I knew he'd leave me for ever, and that made me slaver and sweat and sex all the more. Like this perverse verse, it takes control. I just have a flow of prose all rosy and arranged, a bit purple perhaps, but at least it's prose. Crap and whoosh, it's disposed of, pushed out of the way, by a rush of this rhyming all the time, won't go any other way, a voice in my head says this way, no choice, do it do it. Just like that day when the cop came to stay, I had to woo him. Come on, I say, and lay on the floor, a fine display of tit showing, just knowing his propensity. How could he refuse? So it's a losing battle of reason with feelings so powerful, they send me reeling wrecking a real relationship, leaving me standing here on the station where I left for Oxford, returned to teach, and now come back to preach justice for the poor the insecure the low unlovely, and slowly but sure we'll get there.

I'm deposited in a posh hotel, courtesy of various lawyers, living in style and luxury I'm not accustomed to since I flipped and fell. I must say it leaves me pretty cold. There's none of that old hankering for 5-Stars and smooth bars and restaurants. I'm quite content with an average sandwich, tucked up in bed and watching the telly, well away from the meejah glare that's waiting baiting me to divulge things. But I'm not singing to

298

anyone, nor selling my exclusive story. An hour of glory on my dead friends would offend me deeply. I slip to sleep, sliding around on glossy sheets, alone alone. Bleep bleep goes the phone.

"Don't forget your story's mine" says Hannah, maddeningly. She's found me, though it's not difficult.

"Mine exclusively"

"You don't need me" I say sleepily. "You know it all. Night-night Hannah"

"I saw Dan"

I'm wide awake. Would he take revenge? With her? The "tramp"? Oh horrors and hurricanoes. I wait desperately. She knows. Sadistically, slowly, she drawls

"He's a . . . very interesting man . . . Why did you let him go?"

"Did he say I did?"

"Said You preferred policemen. What *did* he mean?"

"Where did you see him?"

"I visited"

Oh God.

"Why?"

She sighs, insinuating everything.

"You don't have any claims on me Hannah. Not now. Not ever. No story. Goodbye" Slam bam, fuck off Ma'am.

At the trial in Leeds, where they've transported me by car with two Briefs, I avoid her. I'm sitting upright, riveted to the story, the fights, the plots, the skill of the lawyers, my face feeling tight and clenched with tension. They mention me every three seconds – a key witness in a star trial, and all the while my heart is breaking. He's forsaken me for a tramp, ironies ironies. I'm quaking when I take the stand, and refuse to look at any of them – the priest, Gavin Knutton, the Labour Councillors, the Social Workers, Toby, the press, Hannah. The complicated mess unfolds, the description of the van brakes, the crash, a video of the smashed up vehicle, sickening slides, I want to hide away many times, but stay stay baby, this is your day to settle the score. I don't catch it all. Keep drifting away. Just snatches of slander.

"She's a whore. They all were."

"You're suggesting they deserved to die?"

"No, but you can't take the word of a tart for anything"

"Dr McCloud is a respected academic and clinician"

"Not then she wasn't. She was a tramp. A street slut. Anybody's for a gin. They were all drug addicts and drunks. How can you believe her?"

"You're suggesting she's deliberately deceiving the court?"

"Couldn't help it"

The trouble was, they were proving so many things at once I don't know how the jury followed it all. Normally there would be several trials all separate. But these events were so inextricably tied, they were all being tried together in one gigantic knot, and me testifying first to the child abuse. Then all these characters I'd never met, except perhaps on a dark wet night in the back of a car or in an alleyway, saying I was a drunk and a tart and an unreliable witness. Then Toby was wheeled out to say how great I was, to much applause from the gallery from a little group of women who kept getting into the packed Court. Then they called me again, and everyone assessing whether an academic whore can be relied on.

"You've no idea where you lost these photographs?"

"No. I dread to think of them floating around the town. It was criminally irresponsible of me"

"Irresponsible. Not criminal. And you're absolutely certain it was the late former MP Brian Cheetham as, er, Father Xmas?"

"Yes. And he admitted it to me later in my Centre"

"We have admissions of eight children from Brampton Lodge Children's Home that they were given presents to pose with Santa and it wasn't the first time. But you're also certain you saw Gavin Knutton at the home that day collecting the photographs?"

"Oh yes. He dropped them"

"You were disguised in the home?"

"Yes. I was researching for the mother of three of the children"

"Jean Sykes, who was killed in the crash?"

"Yes"

"Tell me. Do you often do this Miss Marples act?"

"Sometimes. When it's necessary"

Laughter and cheers from the women.

"Like a Scarlet Pimpernel?" The sarcasm oozed.

"Er?"

Louder cheers.

"And these photographs were pornographic, obscene evidence of paedophilia in your judgment?"

"Without doubt"

"Your detailed descriptions are circulating. Tell me, Dr McCloud. Are you a feminist?"

"Why?"

"Are you?"

"Yes, but I don't see . . ."

"And don't feminists see a paedophile behind every tree?"

"Objection!"

And so on and on and on. Then all over again for the first Kilburn encounter. Then the hospital and the night of the fire, and never looking at him, but remembering my wild desire for de-frocked frolicking when he sidled up to me in my street. I stare at my feet, in trainers again. Those indiscreet stilettos have gone for good, as have tarty black mini dresses that button up and down so you end up with a lycra band round the middle, and he's there too. Yoohoo yoohoo, how do you do, you laughing policeman. I don't know where to look without hooking into some pair of eyes devouring me remorselessly, coarsely, and some of them remembering. While I try to look blank, and thank the Lord I've lectured before. Otherwise it would be impossible, this spotlight, on stage, pinned down, a sinner for all to see, drowning in her own ecstasy she must have been, this story's too fantastic for words . . .

Yet when it's heard and proved and summarised they all look wise, as though it happens every day that dirty old men get their way with children and pay off other men to cover it up and kill off those who get in the way, mercilessly pursuing them until the one that got away turns up and says Gotcha at the top of her voice, a hoarse old voice after all it's been through – teaching Marx, and playing in parks with other dirty old men for money for drinks, a thinking heroine of the streets, you meet one every day to judge by the bleary weary way your expressions gel into putty and fudge and bland grey clay. I have to hand it to the English. They're so buttoned up you could scalp them alive and they'd only say I need a hat, never batting an eyelid, with a steel clamped grid fastened down so hard on emotion, they have to explode in wars of aggression so it can all come tumbling out, the aggression, shouting rumbling for years. We'll never get peace while this release of feelings is a structural necessity of Englishness. Imperialism deep in the soul and hearts of men men men . . .

Why are they nearly all men at this trial? Another bloody cover up, I suspected, imminent. Yet it all went well over the murders, where the priest was convicted of murder, gets Life; Gavin Knutton of blackmail and conspiracy to murder, gets 10 years. But then the catch comes, the hatch lifts, and the baby chickens come running out squawking. The 13 Labour Councillors are cleared of conspiracy and participation in the paedophile ring, as are the 4 Social Workers at Brampton Lodge. No evidence you see. Can't prove it. Kids confessions, keep talking about Santa, lots of Santas, phantom abusers they couldn't recognise. How I despise this system of justice. The men go free, all chivalry without. But someone's acting as Cover Up Guy in a high high place, whose total disgrace is one day nigh . . .

But I sigh. I've done enough. It got too tough in London in the end, the scandal pouring all over my head like boiling oil, burning burning. And though I spurned all the sneers and jibes and the smut of the gutter scribes, I nevertheless felt weak and battered and small as I ran through the hall at the back of the Court, out the window of a loo I'd reconnoitred, running running away for a Sheffield bus, to say goodbye goodbye for ever . . .

30

I don't know why I'm subjecting myself to this sadness but I want to lurk around in the Bus Station and tell any random spooks that justice has been done. Oh Natty and Bridie and Jean where are you now my real queens, it all looks mean and bleak without you to celebrate. This joy our joy we nailed the boys the men, we won, amen and you're dead and there's no joy or justice without your laughter in the teeth of pain. I'm cold to the core and old so old. Yet suddenly bold, it's snowing. It isn't hell afer all. I get a mellow glow inside, watching snowflakes slowly falling. It's snowing for me, gentle chunky flakes, a white mantle covering, healing the hateful dirt . . .

But what's this striding towards me, hunky handsome and awesome in this place, stands out a mile, Jewish, distinguished, wearing an awkward smile on a face in a million. Makes me go all silly again. I swear my love of men will fair be the death of me. Oh heavenly sight, the mighty warrior stoops to conquer, his pride in his pocket. Whoops, I'm slipping in the snow, and down I go, bump bump. Hello handsome hero. I look up at him and he's grinning, and then I remember Hannah.

"What the hell are you doing here? I thought you'd be busy with the Jewish Princess. This is *my* place. Is nowhere sacred?"

"Get up and shut up" He pulls me up and kisses me, full on my open aggressive mouth. I spit

"Don't give me your Aids and diseases"

He slaps me gently on the cheek, upon which I scream my head off, passers by looking interested. Two of them stop dead with open mouths of their own

"You tell 'er mate"

"Aye that's what she wants"

"Give 'er one for me 'an all"

I start bawling even more, and he bundles me into a taxi that's following him, kerb crawling, dawdling, fascinated by a stranger behaving like a mountain ranger, picking a deranged woman up in the street and shoving her into your taxi. He'd drag me by the hair if I had enough, poxy bastard. I dig my nails hard into his hand. He lets me go.

"Stop being so bloody silly Charlie"

"You get back to your Jewish whore. How the hell did you find me?"

"You told me the only place you had left here was the Bus Station where you Ladies spent so much time ... er ... hanging out. I knew you'd come here after the trial. So I got the first train when it was over, then a taxi at the Station. I didn't know it was only across the road. And here I am" he grins again. Bugger off and win somebody else. I'm a shiksa and a trickster and don't deserve the honour.

"I've decided to forgive you and try to sort you out instead. So I came to the trial to give you some support"

Some bloody support, a report from your tramp that she's visiting you.

"You came to be with her no doubt"

"Her who? What the hell's wrong with you – I thought you'd be pleased to see me"

"Hannah. Hannah. Hannah. That's who you're into, isn't it. She told me"

"What? What did she tell you?"

"That she visited you and ..."

"And?"

"And, well it's obvious"

"Little fool you are. It's not worth a response all this"

"Well aren't you?"

"NO"

"Never?"

"NO"

"You sure?"

"Yes yes. I ought to know"

"Never ever ever?"

305

"No"

"Not even a cuddle or two?"

"NO"

"Why not?"

"Shut up"

"WHY NOT?"

"I love *you*"

"No"

"Yes. I do. God help me"

"I'll show you what they did to this place" and I instruct the driver to the pit tip way up in the hills above the valley of the stations and their waiting rooms too familiar to bear. I glare balefully at the scenery, but he stares entranced at all the greenery and parks growing where the dark Satanic steel mills had been, open furnaces, fire and steam and industrial dreams of transforming the wretched life of man. But you're all wise to what happened here after *The Full Monty* aren't you, and I'm glad they told the fate of the lads so well. As you know though I'm more concerned with the lasses of the working classes and underclasses and those who pass too low for any class to want to know them at all.

He wants to stroll in this depressing hole so we troop out towards the pit tip, where the pit shaft's drooping a bit wayward and battered but still standing. The pit closed down years ago.

"God it's history writ large" he whistles.

"Yes. Coal and steel and it's all finished"

"Oh it's so sad Charlie. You must feel so sad to see all this finished, wound up"

It's hallowed ground to folk like him, I know that. But I spat on it in disgust.

"Sad? No. I'm glad. Those miners and steelworkers had terrible lives. It's awful on the dole, but a life of coal was so nasty and mean, and I find it obscene that you're sad it's over"

"But it's infinitely sad nevertheless. A dying culture"

"Do you hear me?"

"Yes dear. It's still sad though"

"You're atrocious. What's sad about awfulness coming to an end? Those pits were awful. Their history was even worse. Women and children bent double down those mines, crawling for 16 hours a day. A life lived in darkness. A history of troglodytes. And you're lamenting it, in your fine bourgeois way of seeing it as a quaint art form or something, an historic artifact for your dinner party discussions. These were real people who suffered and died young from emphysema and bronchitis and lungs full of coal dust, and you romanticise the bloody industry. It stinks"

"But miners were desperate to keep their jobs. Remember the strike"

"But they didn't used to be you know" I soften my tone a bit. I suppose it's not his fault he's so bloody middle class

" . . . Every miner used to swear when I was young that his son wouldn't follow him down the pit. Until the Tories and the dreaded Thatch. After that there was nothing else for the sons to do. Now there's nothing at all. But it was never better. There has to be something new. You can't go back to that. That was terrible"

I'm gazing at the Pennines beyond the pit-top, thinking of the men of violence on picket lines here, all over here, with lousy jobs but nothing else to do but fight for them, and no other way to do it except with their fists. And the other men of violence, who live and die by it, who know no other way to defend their country, their rights, except by fighting and violence and brute strength. The methods of the oppressor thrown back in his face. But lesser and weaker and therefore doomed, and no room ever for an alternative way. I still hear Gerry saying, lilting softly, "You have to use violence in self-defence against the violence of the state" and all that hate he'd held inside since childhood exploded with his bomb, and him playing avenging angel, entombed along with her, the womb reclaiming the two of them again, from the savage maiming holy father . . .

And those other holy fathers, the lot of them, free to go, after a show trial which incriminated all of them, but couldn't nail them finally. All hail to the sanctity of the holy fathers, back intact in their jobs, running the municipal show, and wielding that great male power club to shield child abusers in the name of happy families. Oh Labour patriarchs and happy families in the Socialist Republic of South Yorkshire. Our stark patriarchies linger still, they will they will till the dark dark ages are over and a new way of loving is part of our every day living politics, where the personal is as political as the currency crisis, and the kids and women don't get attacked for thrills of demented men. *We must get rid of patriarchy* I remark, and he stands still and stares deep into my eyes. I suppose you'd call it a penetrating look, and feel threatened if you didn't like penetration. But as it is I feel quite hypnotised, the wise guy psychoanalysing me on the spot. I wait breathlessly for the verdict.

"I've decided you need therapy Charlie"

"Oh yes?"

"Yes. Serious daily therapy"

"Oh yes?"

"Yes. You have so many unacknowledged problems. We have to sort you out. For it to work properly with us"

"Well we must have it working properly"

"Yes. I know an excellent person. A colleague. She's just right for you"

"A woman?"

"Yes. It must be a woman. There's so much sexual stuff you have to sort out. In fact it's essential"

"I see"

"Yes. And then we'll see about living arrangements"

"Oh yes?"

"Yes. This ridiculous jealousy has got to stop. Maybe the best way is a big house where we both have flats, yet could, er, sleep together, be sexually close at least, but still have space"

"Oh yes?"

"Yes. But you must have therapy first"

"But I was just feeling sorted out"

"Oh My God My God NO. You've got a lot of work to do on yourself young lady"

"But I'm not so young. And I really do feel sorted out. Particularly today. I sort of had a revelation. I think I'm healed"

"And all was revealed in the bus station" he says, dripping insight.

"Well yes. And don't be so sneery. It's up to me to know how I feel"

"Not entirely. You are very sexually disturbed for one thing"

"Oh yes?"

"Oh yes"

"How come? I feel that's the least of my problems"

"Oh NO. Oh NO"

"Why?"

"Oh NO dear me NO"

"For instance?"

"For instance you're so bloody inconsistent – railing against macho heroes in politics, yet sneering at wimps in your bed. Talking about *real* men. A feminist would eat you for supper"

"I know I know but it's how I *feel*. I'm bound to be full of contradictions, given my background"

"Come on Charlie the game's up. You use the concept of contradiction as an excuse for intellectual incoherence"

Do I? do I?

" . . . you need to confront a bit of logic in your life. Think things through. And see them through. You can't just *adore* Jewish 'cosmopolitan' intellectuals, without seeing the price that culture has paid historically for its internationalism. The over-compensation involved in never having your own nationhood to relax into. Or criticise. But at least relate to . . ."

And of course he's right. It's a culture founded on pain, as most intellectual and artistic achievement has to be, with Jews carrying a cosmic sense of outsidership that I can never dream of. I'm an amateur at it. A cocky bigoted amateur. As bad as the class I come from. As I was with poor old Toby. That arrogant awfulness. That bilge in the name of humour. That casual affront to people's deepest hypersensitivities, and Toby had been right. Who the hell am I to decide if they're entitled to their pain? Me, always bleating about my own precious sensitivities. It's preposterous. My petty knee jerk hostility to Zionism was as crude as the left wing bigots I'd learned it from. The oppressors themselves are so oppressed, and we have to remember it always. Defensive aggression's as old as history, and the simplest mystery of the human soul to solve. Look at me and my history, outpourings of gory hatred and lashings out, punctuating this story. I'm only sorry for them, but claim an integrity in the telling. The hate is real. It's how I feel about so many things in my past, needing so often wings, and fast, to get up and out and away. Yet if I'd stayed, with a bit of discernment I could have learned a lot about what a copout people like me are, who flee as soon as we can, looking back in anger but leaving them to it. An abstract bit of intellect in me recognises my self-loathing as the class loathing it is, the self disgust distrust as class disgust and distrust. So where do I go from here?

I'm going to grow, that's where I'm going. Growing growing slowly, but growing into my ideal person. A real person. Free of these vile imbecile prejudices, nasty shallow narrow as the day I emerged on a polluted grass verge of a Yorkshire slum, a lovely proud mum giving birth to a convoluted tale, but not entirely worthless I think. I blink back tears of remembered pain I caused to Toby, with unthinking contemptible so-called "fun". It would never be Yid or Frog or Kraut again I promise Toby, and I'll never call you humour-less bore or earnest whoremaster half-man again I promise *I promise*. I'm sorry so sorry. Political correctness will rule every utterance and censor every turdpile bit of bile from my vile and bigoted background. So sorry and chafing for inane laughing and jeering jokes at other folks' expense, no defence at all. Overtures of sorrowful repentance I'll make, not fake, if you're mistaking the rhyming for having you on, old son, and daughter. Sorry I am, but better sorry than safe, so stop this guilt and grief, what are you a Jew or something?

A cursed Northern English accent apparently disqualifies you even from "cosmopolitan" claims. Thee and me just cannot be sophisticated, can we? Oder?

God is answering me, and looking black about it

" . . . Cosmopolitan consciousness is composed of integrity in where you come from, and nursing it and mingling with other cultures and extending your own, not reviling it constantly like you do. Be glad you have a place you come from. Most Jews don't want romanticising, just like your despised working class. The only reason Jews seem so cosmopolitan is because they had no homeland until recently, and they became bits of everywhere they were condemned to wander . . ."

"But a fantastic virtue they made out of necessity? Imagine speaking twenty languages, like so many Jews do"

"Give me a break. They'd rather just have one and have a peaceful homeland. The need for roots is so profound in everyone"

"I just don't get it. I just don't have any need. I think rootlessness and restlessness and escape from localism is part of modernism, part of modernism's drive to escape tradition – the narrow the tight the hearth and home . . ." I say fervently.

He gets blacker and more formidable, incensed with the stupid cow. Oh where has cupid disappeared to? Not here at all, he's fierce and interrupts savagely.

"And the family above all. Wreck the family. That's it, isn't it? But this absolutism is so bloody crude. One reason the Jewish family is so strong is because other securities like the nation and state are so fragile, even in Israel. And it's the same with Black people. Many Black women find such security in their extended family because they're so oppressed in every other way, by racism and absent men. I see so many schizophrenic West Indian women who would be dead without their vast matriarchies"

" . . . Instead of just being mad?"

Wrath chases contempt across his face.

"The family's their refuge"

"Yuk"

"Charlotte. You can't just stalk around with some absolute condemnation of the 'family' in the abstract, like Ronnie did. Like anything else, it depends on the context"

He looks fearsome and forbidding. But he can't forbid thoughts, and I think relativism is seeping in everywhere, fuzzing the edges, confusing the issues, renouncing pledges. Does ambivalence really have to be the name of the contemporary game? Because really, I should be agreeing with him, with my hatred of dogma and certainty. It's just that a few things *are* certain and true in principle, and the family stinks in principle, as a haven for irrational authority where anything's possible, and abuse of power is probable, and you can't wobble away from that, no matter how jolly and happy are your individual nests. I detest the whole concept of a unit where people own each other, eat each other behind closed doors, and with impunity immunity from any rational interference.

Anyway, the economy is eroding the family faster than Ronnie Laing could ever have hoped for with the lady mums working and roaming now. They don't need to come home to some shit sitting there waiting to be waited on, why should they? We have to get millions of nurseries so everyone can go out and play, and then the family way is done, Laing's won, and patriarchs have had their day.

Because Laing was right. The family *is* absolutely wrong. And defending it *sometimes*, is the same song as me, when I used to justify violence of the oppressed against that of the state. But now I just hate it all, blanketly, absolutely. It's *never* justified. There *has* to be another way, a *different* way, to change, to convert people democratically, and Bugger violence, I hear myself say in my aggressive way. Oh dear, I'm all wrong again, he's disapproving. I always lose the argument with men . . .

And yet and yet, as the net is closing and I'm loving you whatever, am I also slowly losing identity, space, time, a rhythm a rhyme a beating time, will it ever be mine again? The time I mean, with a man around, a sounding board or the sound itself? The stealthy way they invade your space your mind, they find every nook and cranny and harry it out. A lot of the shit in my head wants clearing out, no doubt about it. But the dread I have about his shit instead planted

312

there, decanted there, when I need time, that precious time to stand and stare and work it out for me myself my reality, and He, He, He, all pervasive upsetting abrasive invasive like now.

"It's time you confronted these paradoxes as more than interesting contradictions. They're almost psychotic incongruities. Particularly sexually. All this power nonsense you're fixated on"

"How do you kn . . ?"

"I know. I know. You're sexually sick"

"Sick! What do you mean *please*? What have I done that's *sick*?" I'm starting to get worried, but needn't. It's only

"Fornicating on the floor with the fuzz is"

and getting a buzz out of it even worse oh cursed one

"Ah"

"Yes"

"You mean I need therapy because you're jealous."

"Charlie. You're ridiculous. You need therapy because . . . you need therapy"

"Because *you've* decided I need therapy?"

"Because you're not in control. You're not responsible"

"Oh but I am"

"NO"

"Oh yes. You just don't approve of what I take responsibility for"

"Don't be silly. You don't know what you're doing half the time"

"But I do Dan. I do. That's your trouble. You can't see that I do"

"You don't. Nonsense"

"Dan, I do"

"Nonsense darling. Now come on. I know what I'm talking about. I really do. Trust me. Together we'll make you better. I do love you. I want you to be completely healthy. And happy. With me. I promise it will be OK. You'll see it my way. You will"

"Oh Dan. Dan. Dan"

holy man holy father thou shalt not take my reality from me and reinterpret it give it back to me differently from my experience of it defining me anew from your point of view to glory your story history as usual me no mystery just accessory appendage bondage to God as always I'm fond of you lust for you sod it but I'll not be dominated nor mated again if that's the cost instant lost identity sacrifice of personality the price of a cuddle's too high I'm flying away and you're in my way tying me down with false promises premises of healing my blemishes making me perfect for you to enjoy a ploy for increasing your pleasure no measure of my needs how could you heed them how do you know me except through the filtering of your own monumental ego you've never listened to my flow just the bits that you think you know already about women so predictable but I'll not have a man speaking for me women don't need men to talk for them to parrot them to parody them in transposed fantasies of how they feel we can say it ourselves with bells on pealing and tinkling away the opposite way to your big boom bang clang clanging ones of doom and duty just snooty virgins and whores these bores are your categories fixed permanent separate but women want to be both a troll and a doll and droll as well as witty and easy and pretty and teasy and strong and long as a winter day that's not very long but relatively so we'll not be restricted by your dreary weary expectations of us we'll not have it not have it No.